I0822147

LEGEND

OTHER FICTION BY A.J. CALVIN

THE RELICS OF WAR
The Moon's Eye
The Talisman of Delucha
War of the Nameless

The Ballad of Alchemy and Steel

Serpentus

THE CAEIN LEGACY
Exile
Guardian
Harbinger
Legend

HUNTED

WRAITH AND THE REVOLUTION

LEGEND

THE CAEIN LEGACY
Book Four

A.J. CALVIN

This is a work of fiction. All of the characters and events portrayed within this book are fictitious, and any resemblance to living people or real events is purely coincidental.

LEGEND

ISBN 979-8-9908169-0-9

Absolutely no portion of this book, including its artwork, was generated using artificial intelligence.
Human authored registration # 6641735,
https://authorsguild.org/human

Cover illustration and design by Jamie Noble
(www.thenobleartist.com)

Map illustration by Dewi Hargreaves (www.dewihargreaves.com)

HUMAN AUTHORED

For my readers,

Those who have championed this series
from its inception to its inevitable conclusion:
You are the true legends.

Thank you

AUTHOR'S NOTE

It's always bittersweet to conclude a writing project, and I find ending a series to be even more difficult than a standalone novel. And since this series holds such a profound place in my heart, it was harder than I'd anticipated.

By the time I reached the final chapters of this book, I'd been working on the series as a whole for more years than I can count. It was both exhilarating and sad to see the end looming, when I'd immersed myself in Andrew's world for so long. I loved these characters and grew along with them, both as a writer and a person.

But as we're often reminded: All good things must come to an end sometime.

I rewrote the final chapters of Legend multiple times, trying to find the "perfect" ending. I'm not sure there is such a thing, but I liked this one, and I hope you do too. After all the strife and hardship I forced Andrew and his brothers to endure, I felt they deserved a reprieve at the end.

That's not to say they didn't reach the end of this tale without receiving a few scars along the way. None of them are the same men they were when this journey began.

And if you skipped past the dedication, you may want to look at it if you're reading this.

Because this one is for *you.*

Thank you and happy reading,
A.J. Calvin

AUTHOR'S NOTE

NOVANIA AND THE SOUTHLANDS

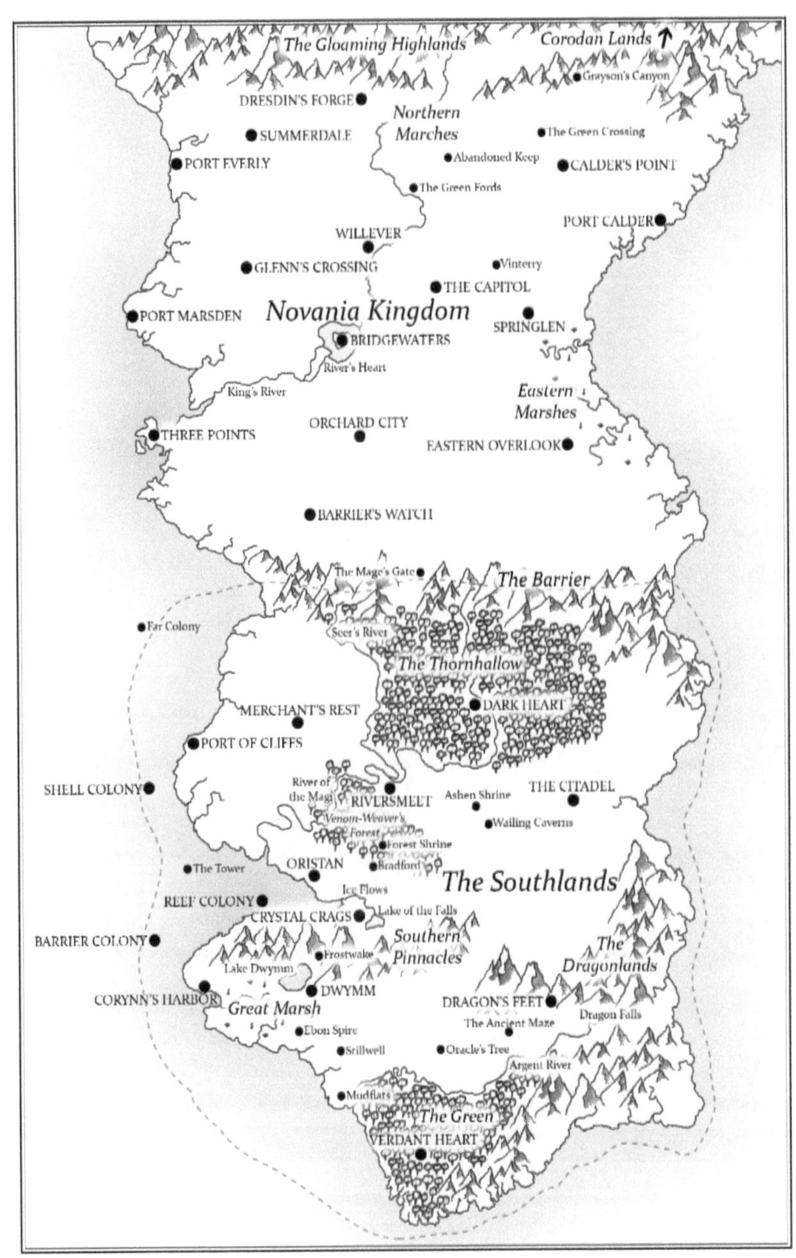

ONE

When I became aware of myself again, it was to the acrid scent of woodsmoke wafting toward me on a gentle breeze. I didn't immediately open my eyes; my head felt as though it had been stuffed with cotton, and I didn't know how long I'd been unconscious. The last memories I had before succumbing to the darkness were vague, fuzzy impressions that slipped away each time I tried to grasp them.

Every muscle ached, I was bruised in numerous places, and there was a sharp, searing agony shooting through both my hands and feet. When I attempted to shift into a more comfortable position, I realized I couldn't. I'd been bound tightly from head to tail, and the seemingly small movement intensified the pain in my extremities.

I grimaced, and my jaws were met with unyielding resistance. An iron muzzle had been fitted around them, allowing for only minimal movement.

I was a prisoner, then.

"I think he's waking, my lord," I heard someone say. The voice wasn't far from my location, but it sounded strange and distorted through the haze that clouded my mind.

Slowly, I forced my eyes open, but the lids remained heavy. It was early evening. A number of soldiers were gathered around a pair of campfires some distance ahead. They wore the crimson and ivory colors of the royal house, and upon seeing them, my elusive memories began to return in a disjointed torrent.

The battle at the abandoned keep. The king's new commander in his crimson cloak, ordering his men to charge despite the obvious folly of his plan. The trebuchets. I'd destroyed many of them, but not all.

One had struck a weakened point in the keep's outer wall, and a portion had collapsed. I'd spied Rynn, scrambling away from the precipice, her leg bent awkwardly beneath her. I'd been compelled to save her, determined that I would not lose her as I'd lost Vera—no matter the cost.

I'd understood that I was in range of the trebuchets, but I'd refused to let her fall. Foolishly, I'd believed that any trap the enemy had contrived would be no match for my strength, that I'd break free with ease.

I'd been so damned wrong.

The king's men had done their research and had been ready. I'd been blinded by confidence, by arrogance, a fatal flaw I'd cautioned other soldiers to avoid throughout my military career. Yet I'd followed that same damned path. I was a fool if ever there was one.

I was still in my dragon form but unable to shift. I could no longer detect the item that had pierced my wing when the net had enveloped me and decided it must have been removed. The continuous, throbbing pain that afflicted my extremities seemed to be the current cause of my inability to change forms, for when I attempted it, that strange, pulling sensation I'd felt when my wing had been pierced returned.

Peering from the corner of my eyes, I could just make out my scaly, taloned right hand strapped cruelly down with chains and the strangely flexible material the enemy had constructed their nets from. I was on a cart, and I could just make out the rim of a wheel beyond the end of my talons. Dark blood seeped from the center of my agonized hand. I stared, horrified, refusing to believe what my eyes perceived. A metal stake had been driven through the back of my hand.

The pain radiating from my other hand and both of my feet was identical. I didn't have to look to know that stakes had been driven through my flesh at each location. I understood now why I was unable to shift; impaled as I was, my body could not accommodate the transformation.

Holy hell. I was thoroughly trapped.

The sound of footsteps forced my eyes away from my injured hand, drawing them forward to take stock of the man striding toward me. He wasn't tall, but had a solid build and carried himself with an air of authority. His pale blue eyes held no warmth as he sneered at me from his pock-marked face. His head had been recently shaved, and a small nick was visible atop his scalp. He wore the crimson cloak of Colin's chosen commander.

His name floated to me through the fog that enveloped my brain: Robert Claybourne.

"You put up a mighty struggle back at the keep," he remarked. "Not that it has done you one whit of good." He kicked the side of the cart near one side of my jaws. "The king will be exceptionally pleased that I've managed to capture you, beast. He has grand plans for your return to the Capitol."

I clenched my teeth in frustration, but was uncertain if I'd be capable of making a reply with the muzzle cinched around my jaws.

"Why?" I managed through my teeth, my voice a low growl.

Claybourne threw his head back and laughed. "You were born and raised in this kingdom. You ought to know her laws by now. The king demands that you abide by them, just as the rest of us must." He smirked knowingly and spat on the ground. "He has declared he'll mete out your punishment himself. A fitting sentence given your duplicitous nature."

I was unsurprised by the news. I'd suspected Colin wanted the so-called glory of killing me himself, though in my current state, it would make for poor sport.

"Any further questions, beast?" Claybourne asked with a sneer.

I needed to know our present location, but I doubted Claybourne would be forthcoming. Once we began moving, I believed I could learn where we were; I'd traveled the Northern Reaches of Novania Kingdom many times throughout my life and was familiar with most of its locales.

I decided speaking wasn't worth the effort. Claybourne only seemed interested in goading me and inciting my ire, and it was better to save my strength than to waste my breath arguing with him. I'd need every ounce of stamina I possessed if I hoped to break free.

"No," I growled.

"Well, I hope you're comfortable with your new accommodations." He smirked and turned away, retreating toward the campfires, while I was left alone with my thoughts.

As the last vestiges of fog began to lift from my mind, I came to the unfortunate realization that whatever concoction Claybourne had used to knock me unconscious had also dulled my sense of pain. Within an hour of waking, both my hands and feet became excruciating. It required every shred of willpower I possessed not to cry out in agony. Even subtle movement shot bursts of blinding pain through my extremities.

I felt my wounds attempting to heal, only to be continuously disrupted by the presence of the stakes piercing my hide. I had experienced a greater agony only once before, when several of my dragon scales had been forcibly removed. But that pain had been *my* decision. This was a merciless hell without hope of respite.

Claybourne and most of his soldiers turned in for the night sometime later, leaving only a solitary guard to keep watch over their tiny camp. I watched as she patrolled the perimeter, wary of what she might do given the chance. With her leader asleep and no one else to bear witness, might she become bold enough to cause me further harm? I certainly didn't like the notion; I could scarcely tolerate my pain as it was. Fortunately, she gave me a wide berth at each pass, and her watch ended uneventfully.

Just after midnight, another soldier took over the watch. I recognized him immediately; he was the same man who had thrown the flasks toward me after I'd been captured. While he'd been under orders to do so, I didn't believe I could trust him any more than I could trust his commander. Anyone who followed Robert Claybourne was no ally of mine.

He appeared unconcerned by my presence and said nothing as he made his rounds. Each time I heard his footfalls draw near, I steeled myself, but he did nothing to further my misery.

I fell into a fitful sleep sometime before dawn, only to be awakened a short time later. Claybourne shouted curses while he began rousing his soldiers, preparing to break camp. It wasn't until the tents and gear were stowed that anyone bothered to pay me any heed.

Claybourne drew one of the men aside and pointed in my direction. "The king wants this creature alive when we reach the Capitol. It's your job to feed it."

Claybourne smirked as he spoke while the other man visibly paled at his words. I knew I appeared intimidating, and it was clear that Claybourne had given the man this task as a form of punishment. In my current state, I couldn't harm him even if I wanted to. I wasn't hungry and didn't trust Claybourne, but knew I must eat in order to regain my strength. Enduring the constant pain had sapped most of my energy.

"What's left in the porridge pot can go to the beast," Claybourne continued, smiling maliciously as he handed the man a key. "Don't stand there gaping like a blasted fool. Get to it! We depart soon, you lazy fucking lout."

The man nodded, eyes wide with terror as he turned away to disappear behind a cart of supplies. Claybourne stalked off to oversee other aspects of the departure, staring daggers at everyone in his path. Moments later, the soldier returned carrying a heavy cast-iron pot. He placed the pot at the end of the cart I was bound to and stared at me for several long moments. His hands shook as he fumbled with the key.

I sighed, weary of his hesitation and unnecessary fear. I didn't know whether his reaction stemmed from Claybourne's propaganda or from having witnessed what I was capable of during the recent battle, but I doubted there was anything I could say to ease his fears. Even if I'd wanted to lash out, I couldn't, bound as I was.

The man stepped onto the cart mere inches from my jaws. He forced the key into a lock holding the iron muzzle firmly in place as sweat dripped from his brow. He gazed at me, terror in his eyes, as he carefully removed the lock from its hasps.

The muzzle sprang open and I experienced a wave of relief. I hadn't realized how tightly the contraption pressed against my face. I worked my jaw from side to side, grateful to have even that limited movement granted to me. The man leapt backwards, startled by the motion, and scrambled off the cart.

"Considering that your commander has me strapped down to the point of immobility, you have nothing to fear from me," I said dryly.

His eyes grew wide as I spoke and he swallowed hard, but he didn't respond, nor did he finish the chore he'd been assigned. He stood gaping, his face drained of color.

Claybourne reappeared then, glowering like a storm cloud. "Norris, you lout, I'll have you flogged if you can't pick up the pace." He cuffed the man in the back of the head and sneered. "Get on with it, man. The damned beast can do little more than gnash its teeth."

I glared at Claybourne, tired of the constant barrage of insults he'd spewed at me since I'd awakened. "My name is Andrew," I growled.

Claybourne shrugged as if my words were of no consequence, then turned to spit. "The names of beasts have little meaning in the realm of men." He shoved Norris roughly. "Finish your task, or I'll have *you* fed to that creature as its next meal."

Claybourne stomped away while Norris nodded adamantly. He was visibly shaking and the color had not yet returned to his cheeks, but he stumbled forward. I pitied him, then wondered what compelled him to remain in the employ of a man like Robert Claybourne.

"I don't eat people," I said, unable to keep the irritation from my tone.

My words seemed to give him some measure of relief. He picked up the porridge pot and hefted it onto the cart. There was little left inside and it was likely cold, but I was grateful to receive anything at all. Based on how my time had played out as Claybourne's prisoner so far, I'd expected to be left hungry.

Norris unceremoniously dumped the meager contents of the pot into my mouth, then backed away once more. It was little more than a mouthful, but I would not complain. It would only provide Claybourne with a measure of satisfaction as he prolonged my torment, something I was unwilling to give him. As I swallowed, Claybourne reappeared behind Norris.

"Good, you've finished." He held out his hand. "Give me that damned key and help me secure its muzzle once more."

I growled low in my throat, weary of being referred to as "it."

Claybourne narrowed his eyes in momentary rage, then pulled himself onto the cart and launched a kick at the side of my jaw. The blow was solid, but I scarcely felt it. The pain was inconsequential when compared with the agony radiating from my limbs.

"I've no patience for your games, beast," he snarled even as he and Norris managed to close the muzzle around my jaws once more. Claybourne snapped the lock closed and leveled another kick in my direction before leaping to the ground. "You'll do well to mind your manners around me. Your life, such as it is, may well depend on what I see fit to tell the king."

I narrowed my eyes and clenched my jaw, though I managed to hold my tongue. Nothing I said would change my fate—Colin would have me executed when we arrived at the Capitol. My heart was heavy with the knowledge that my own brother had become so heartless and cruel.

Claybourne continued to glare for several seconds before wheeling away to address the soldiers under his command. Within a few minutes, a team of six horses was hitched to the front of the cart, and a different soldier was assigned the task of sitting mere inches from the end of my nose in order to guide the animals. She appeared less afraid of me than Norris had been.

With every rut the cart struck and each bump in the road, jagged shards of agony shot through my limbs. The stakes had been pounded into the bed of the cart, but even slight movement made them shift, reopening my wounds.

I clenched my jaw in an attempt to internalize my anguish. I refused to give Claybourne the satisfaction of learning the extent of my misery.

We made slow progress. The horses strained against their harnesses, managing little more than walking speed due to my weight.

We traveled through farmland, angling south and east along roads that were in a state of disrepair. Though a few curious onlookers stopped their work in the spring-greened fields to watch our passage, none ventured near the procession of soldiers leading the bound and suffering dragon to the Capitol. By the time Claybourne called a halt as dusk began to fall, my wounds were raw and bleeding, my pain so intense that my limbs trembled beneath the chains and straps that bound them. My jaw ached from being clenched against my anguish, and my skull thundered in time with my heartbeat.

When the cart mercifully came to a stop, the cessation of movement was a profound relief. It was only then that I realized the extent of my exhaustion, but it would be some time before I'd relax enough to sleep. Pain continued to lance through my arms and legs, though it was a mere shadow compared to what I'd endured while we'd traveled.

I observed Claybourne's soldiers as they set up camp, wondering how Thomas fared at the keep where the battle had recently taken place, and if Alexander had reached the designated rendezvous point at Willever Ferry. I didn't know if Claybourne had been informed of his army's defeat in the south, but he'd been unaware of it when he'd attacked Thomas' forces.

I replayed the final moments of the battle in my mind. Claybourne had known it was lost as he'd worked to apprehend me. He'd come to the Northern Marches specifically for my capture, and though I'd striven to avoid his damned nets, I'd been unable to escape in the end. My only solace was that Rynn had survived.

Ah, Rynn. I could envision her bright smile, the vibrancy of her blue eyes, the way her blond curls bobbed and swayed as she walked. Though I'd been in love before, she'd captivated my heart in a way that no other woman had. I hoped I'd one day be reunited with her, even if only to look upon her one final time.

Colin wouldn't hesitate to execute me when we reached the Capitol. He'd made the mistake of delaying similar plans with Alexander, giving me time to free him. I didn't believe Colin would make the same mistake twice. He was a heartless bastard, but he wasn't stupid.

With those thoughts, I fell into a fitful sleep, broken by dreams of battle and unending pain.

TWO

I was awakened roughly by a solid blow to the side of my face. Startled, I jerked aside. Both of my hands pulled against the stakes impaling them, and I roared from the sudden onslaught of pain even as I realized the source of my initial discomfort had come from Robert Claybourne. He stood near my head, hands on hips, sneering, his cold blue eyes filled with malice.

"So, the beast feels pain after all," he mused. "I was beginning to wonder how much it would take before you screamed. The king will no doubt be interested to learn of my findings."

Though I wished to reply with a scathing remark about Colin's unworthiness to rule, I knew it would only provoke Claybourne further. I teetered on the brink of endurance as it was, and I didn't want to further my misery. I merely glared at him in response.

"We'll be breaking camp soon," he said after a time. "I'll have Norris bring your feed as he did yesterday. It's a pity the little shit failed to wet himself. I'd hoped he would. He's a coward and deserves some humiliation, in my book." He turned to spit toward the ground below. "No matter. We'll reach the Green Fords this afternoon, and there will be plenty of time to watch *your* humiliation at the hands of the townsfolk. I rather look forward to seeing the spectacle."

When I made no response, he leapt from the cart and stomped toward the campsite. During our brief exchange, he'd revealed our location, and based on the pace the horses had maintained the previous day, I had a week before we reached the Capitol. A week to free myself—or prepare for my inevitable death.

The Green Fords was a river crossing that had grown into a bustling town. Whatever Claybourne had in store for me there would be painful and humiliating, but I would endure. I must.

The main route between the Green Fords and the Capitol would lead us to a point only three miles from Willever Ferry. If Alexander were there…

I pushed the thought firmly from my mind. It was folly to rely on hope that might not exist. I must find a means to escape my bonds without counting on outside assistance, and I had approximately one week to do so.

The day passed much as the previous one had. My injuries reopened with each jostle and bump of the cart, and beneath the pain, I began to feel the first true pangs of hunger. The meager rations Claybourne had allotted me weren't sufficient for one of his soldiers, let alone for sating the appetite of a wounded and miserable dragon.

We arrived at the outskirts of the Green Fords late that afternoon. Claybourne ordered his soldiers to make camp just outside the town, but our arrival didn't go unnoticed.

Curious onlookers soon appeared, and Claybourne was thrilled to oblige them with fabricated tales of my terrible misdeeds. Not a word he said was true, but I doubted his audience knew that. He relished the role of perverse showman, adding new supposed crimes to his list with each rendition of his story. Attempting to contradict the man would get me nowhere and would likely result in further torture later that night. I remained silent and miserable, and did my best to ignore the insults and jibes shouted in my direction.

As word of our arrival spread, the crowd grew larger and more boisterous. I was beginning to understand why such fanfare and revelry had taken place on the eve of Alexander's scheduled execution. Claybourne thrived on the attention he received and the renown he'd earn for capturing the last of the dragon-kind. The audience hung on his every word, eager to hear more tales of the terrible beast the mighty Robert Claybourne had captured. In his tales, he was the hero, the man protecting the realm from the horrors of magic and depraved creatures like the one pinned to his cart.

I closed my eyes and clenched my jaw as I battled my pain. I would not react to the taunts of the crowd. I was trapped in this hell, but wouldn't provoke an increase in my suffering.

Once night fell, Claybourne ordered his soldiers to disperse the crowd. He posted six to each watch during the night, far more than I believed necessary for the size of their camp. Was he concerned the townsfolk might return and cause trouble?

I secretly hoped some would. It might provide a chance to escape—if I could convince someone to assist in the removal of my shackles and the damned stakes that pierced my hide.

My hope was not realized. As the night drew on with no movement and nothing for the guards to concern themselves with, I knew I'd be at Claybourne's mercy another day. I slept but little.

I woke before dawn, avoiding a repeat of the brutal awakening I'd received the previous morning. The camp was quiet, but after a while, I heard the rhythmic sound of hoofbeats traveling in our direction. It was a single rider. After a few moments, I spied the man as he raced around a thick stand of trees. He wore the armor of the king's garrison and sported a broadsword across his back. As he noticed our camp, he urged his horse to a greater speed.

He reined in at the perimeter and dismounted. "I've an urgent message for the commander," he said to the nearest guard, who disappeared amongst the tents. He returned several minutes later with a surly Robert Claybourne in tow.

"Out with it, man," Claybourne growled impatiently.

"The king sends word that your army in the south has been defeated," the messenger replied with a frown. "While he understands the reason for your detour to the Northern Marches, His Majesty is sorely displeased with your lack of progress so far."

Claybourne's shoulders tensed as he braced himself. "I had every confidence that the men I left behind would be victorious. They've failed me, and they've failed their king," he snarled.

"The king has requested an audience with you once you've reached the Capitol." The messenger paused to survey the camp, his expression impassive. "Is this meager company all that remains of your forces, Commander?"

Claybourne hesitated. "No," he lied, "the rest will follow me to the Capitol in the coming days."

The messenger crossed his arms and looked down at Claybourne with a contemptuous glare. "While it is not my place to doubt your words, I will return to the Capitol ahead of you and inform His Majesty that you have at least managed to complete one of your tasks." His gaze drifted to my location. "I believe he'll be pleased with that bit of news despite your other shortcomings."

"I assure you, the rest of my army will follow," Claybourne growled, incensed that he'd been contradicted by the messenger. "Include that in your damned report, or you'll—"

"Or I'll what, Robert?" the man demanded, cutting him off. "I don't answer to you. I answer only to His Majesty, our king, Colin Marsden. You may be the commander of his army, but I command the castle's garrison and the king's personal guard. As such, I outrank you."

Claybourne glowered for several seconds, then spat to one side. "Very well. Tell the king what you will. I'll be back in the Capitol in less than a week's time."

"He'll be awaiting you," the man replied before turning toward his horse.

Claybourne grumbled something to himself, then turned on his heel to begin shouting at the soldiers under his command. "Break camp! We've wasted too damned much time already!"

I'd found the exchange between the two men illuminating. They clearly didn't like one another, and Claybourne resented the presence of someone who outranked him. I hadn't recognized the messenger, but that was unsurprising. In my previous life as the former king's commander, I'd also been in charge of the castle's garrison. That Colin had split the role and had given the garrison's leader rank over Claybourne might prove useful information if I managed to break free.

The tone of Colin's message indicated a measure of disapproval with Claybourne, and I found it interesting that he'd been compelled to lie about the whereabouts of his army. They would not be following in his wake as he'd reported; he'd taken severe losses during the battle with Thomas, and I doubted that any survivors would return to follow him.

The atrocities I'd witnessed him commit against his own people had been a source of disgust and outrage. If any of his army had surrendered, Thomas would have offered them the choice to defect or return to their homes. Those seeking to rejoin Claybourne should have overtaken us by now, but there were no new faces in his camp. It seemed Claybourne had few friends and commanded little loyalty once the soldiers were beyond his immediate reach.

As the first rays of dawn broke over the eastern horizon, we resumed the trek towards the Capitol. The only route through the Green Fords was the main road through town, which would lead to a shallow river crossing beyond.

After the previous afternoon, I was uncertain what awaited me within the town and braced myself for a potential onslaught. In my current state, I could do nothing to defend myself, and struggling would only deplete my energy further. I was weak from hunger and the constant pain in my limbs, and lacked the willpower to engage in even verbal combat.

Several residents paused in their morning routines to study us as we passed into the town's outskirts. A boy of about ten shouted somewhere ahead, then raced toward the town center. I had no doubt he planned to gather as many residents as he was able to watch our passage. Claybourne had made me a spectacle.

Claybourne motioned to his soldiers. "Keep an eye on the commoners. They've had a taste of the beast's misfortune and seek to add to it. If not for my orders, I'd let them, but the king wants this brute alive." He spat on the ground to further his point.

A milling throng became visible as we rounded a bend in the road and began making our way through the marketplace. Though it was still early, most of the population of the Green Fords had crammed themselves into the space, elbowing and jostling one another for better views. When the crowd took note of me, a cacophony of shouts and cheers rang through the market; insults mixed with exclamations of surprise and shouts of outrage.

The current driver of my cart turned to glance over his shoulder. "The commander certainly didn't help matters by putting you on display yesterday," he whispered. I sensed he feared to speak any louder, lest Claybourne overhear the exchange. "For what it's worth, I believe what he's done to you is wrong, but we all fear for our own skins around the man."

"Hmm." I didn't want to risk a reply, but I wanted to let him know I'd heard his words. The sound was nearly drowned out by the angry mob encroaching on our path.

Something soft and pulpy hit my left flank, and sticky liquid began to run down my side from the point of impact. I couldn't turn my head to look at what had been thrown from amidst the crowd, though based on the feel, it was likely a piece of fruit. Soon more projectiles were thrown, though I couldn't determine if I was the primary target or if the king's soldiers were. Our whole procession was subject to the barrage.

Claybourne snarled as a soft apple hit him squarely in the chest. Without warning, he drew his sword and slashed at the nearest townsperson. The young woman's eyes widened in shock as his blade cut through her woolen dress and ripped across her abdomen. He wrenched the weapon free, then spat as she fell to the ground. Several others knelt to assist her, but she was bleeding profusely. I doubted she'd last more than a few minutes.

A hush fell over the crowd as they took in the scene.

"I'll have the lot of you damned commoners thrown in the dungeons!" Claybourne bellowed, seething. "Be gone, all of you, before I make good on my threat!"

Stunned, the townspeople began to disperse. I'd been hit during the onslaught numerous times, and though none of the missiles had caused any harm, I was coated with rubbish from head to tail and helpless to remedy the situation.

I released a despairing sigh. I was weary, hurt, and humiliated. Even Colin could not have devised a worse fate if he'd set his mind to it.

From one of the windows above the street, a woman's voice carried over the marketplace. "Release the dragon!" she cried, her tone impassioned.

A new wave of people poured from within the surrounding buildings, charging toward the cart. They were armed, brandishing swords, axes, knives, and one man held a pitchfork. Claybourne laughed mirthlessly as they approached, signaling to the soldiers. There was an equal number of townspeople and soldiers, but none of the commoners wore armor, and it was unlikely they'd ever trained for combat. Within seconds, it was apparent they were outmatched, and Claybourne was a merciless foe.

I struggled feebly against my bonds, but only succeeded in tearing open the wounds in my hands anew. The bolts of pain that shot through my arms were blinding in their intensity. I was forced to cease all movement immediately, incapacitated by the agony.

I watched helplessly as two dozen townspeople were cut down while Claybourne shouted curses and insults. The fight was over in a matter of minutes.

Claybourne turned to survey the damage, seemingly satisfied that none of his soldiers had been seriously injured. He pointed to several, indicating he wished to speak with them.

"Find that woman," he growled. "Find the bitch who shouted from the window. I want her hanged for treason!" When the three blinked at him, uncomprehending, his face became almost purple with rage. "Do as I've ordered, or you will join her!"

The soldiers scrambled to obey, angling away from the devastation on their appointed errand. Claybourne turned to glower at the rest of his soldiers, his pale eyes alighting on mine after a time. "I suppose you hoped they would succeed, didn't you, beast?" he snarled.

I held his gaze but kept my expression carefully neutral. Nothing I said would help my situation. Claybourne was more volatile than I'd anticipated, and it wouldn't do me any good to incite his ire further.

My limbs throbbed, and I grew weaker by the hour. I was no longer certain of my ability to withstand any further torture he might inflict.

After a moment, he made a sound of frustration and spun around. He shouted further orders, and within a few moments, we'd resumed our slow progress through the streets. The slain townspeople were left where they lay, bleeding on the dusty cobblestones, while their sightless eyes stared in horror at the cloudless spring sky.

I grunted in pain as the cart hit a rough patch in the road. My foolish attempt at breaking free had left me bleeding and raw, and what little healing my body had managed during the night had been rapidly undone. The cart driver glanced over his shoulder, compassion in his dark eyes.

"I truly wish there was something I could do," he whispered, his words scarcely audible over the creaking of the cart's wheels.

Silently, I thanked him for his empathy despite his reluctance to act on it. Claybourne would likely have him killed if he knew.

There were no further entanglements with the locals as we made our way through town to the river crossing beyond. The crossing was little more than a shallow place in the river bracketed on either side by the road, the water only knee-deep for most of the soldiers.

Claybourne ordered a break once we reached the other side. He pointed to several of his people, then jerked his chin in my direction. "Clean the filth off that beast. He smelled foul enough before he was coated in grime, and I'm in no mood to tolerate the stench." He shifted his gaze to meet mine, his lips upturned in a smirk. "Don't think I'm growing soft, beast. If you so much as twitch while they're bathing you, I'll put you in such agony you won't stop howling until the king takes your fucking head."

I averted my eyes and said nothing. I'd been right to assume Colin wanted me dead and hoped to do the deed himself. But at least I wouldn't remain covered in rotten fruit and refuse any longer.

Once his soldiers had finished rinsing the grime from my scales, we moved on. I kept silent despite the ache that had grown in my jaws from clenching my teeth against the pain.

We made camp that evening three miles south of the Green Fords. I trembled from the agony the trek had inflicted on my wounded extremities, no longer capable of controlling my response to the continued pain. I didn't believe I could tolerate much more of Claybourne's prolonged torture. I'd never been so helpless and it was not in my nature to give up, yet I began to doubt that I'd survive the journey to the Capitol.

I was losing my strength, and with it, my hope.

THREE

A piercing cry broke the stillness of the early morning air as we set out from the camp the next day. I recognized it as the cry of a raptor but didn't bother to open my eyes to investigate. I'd been awakened roughly by Claybourne as he'd kicked at my muzzled jaws only moments before, and the jolt had torn open my wounds yet again. In my weakened state, I lacked the willpower to entertain curiosity, so I ignored the bird. The cry issued again, closer this time, but I continued to ignore it.

What good was seeking the source of the cry, when locating it would only remind me I was no longer free? Unlike the bird, my wings were useless, bound tightly to my agonized body as they were.

"What sort of bird is that?" One of the nearby soldiers asked. "I've never seen its like before."

"It's a hawk, you dolt," another answered. "They're always flying around this area. It's good hunting for them. Plenty of rabbits."

"That's no hawk," the first replied. "It's too large."

"Cal's right," a third said, this one a woman. "I'm from this part of the kingdom. I've never seen a bird like that. It looks like…an eagle, perhaps."

At her words, my eyes snapped open and I peered skyward, seeking the source of the shrill cries. I dared to hope the bird would be one I recognized, that it would be the eagle bonded to Alexander. Unable to turn my head, I had a limited view of the sky, and I was unable to locate the bird they'd spoken of.

"Ah, it's gone," the second man said, disappointed. "I would have liked to have a better look at it. I'm certain it was a hawk."

"And you're a fool to think so," the woman countered. "That was no hawk."

"Enough chatter!" Claybourne shouted from the head of the column. He was surlier than usual and everyone seemed to sense it. The conversation died as quickly as it had arisen.

Dismayed and cursing myself for a fool, I closed my eyes once more. Even if Alexander had reached the ferry at Willever, I didn't know if he'd learned of my capture. Communication had been difficult between Thomas and Alexander due to distance, and it was folly to hope he was aware of my present situation.

It was almost midday when Claybourne called a halt to the march, and I was provided with a brief respite from the rhythmic jostling of the cart. I lay with my eyes closed for some time, too weary to open them, and merely listened to the sounds of the soldiers as they talked amongst themselves and shared a cold meal. Some were eager to return to the Capitol, while others seemed to dread it. From their snatches of conversation, I gleaned the city had been starkly changed during Colin's brief reign, and not for the better.

Another piercing cry broke the air, and this time I opened my eyes immediately. The bird flew high in the sky, spiraling overhead. It sported at least a six-foot wingspan and was slate gray in color, but I detected a slight reddish hue in the raptor's tail feathers.

My heart stuttered to life with renewed hope. There was no doubt this was a gray eagle and could very well be Galewing himself.

"Look at that," Cal muttered. "The bird came back."

"It's definitely not a hawk," the woman stated. "What draws it here, I wonder?"

Seconds later, one of the supply carts erupted in flames, seemingly of its own accord. The soldiers nearest to it cried out in alarm and backed away, surprise and fear evident in their expressions.

Claybourne stormed towards them, his face like a thundercloud. "What have you louts done?" he demanded angrily. "We need every scrap of those supplies! Get that fucking fire out!"

As he turned away, a curtain of flames erupted only a few feet in front of him, blocking his intended path. His eyes widened in momentary surprise, then narrowed into furious slits as he understood.

"Mages," he hissed. "I should have known."

He bellowed the command to draw arms and brandished his sword.

At that moment, a cloud of dust filled the air, bringing with it the distinct scent of tilled earth. Claybourne had been correct; there were magi nearby. I grinned within the muzzle, certain the magi would succeed where the people of the Green Fords had failed. Claybourne's people were unused to combating magic.

I sensed movement on my periphery, but it was far too rapid for my eyes to follow. Several of the soldiers standing near my side cried out in shock, then went silent as the unmistakable sound of bodies falling heavily to the ground replaced their shouts. The odor of spilled blood filled my nostrils. At least one of them had been wounded, if not killed outright.

The cloud of dust coalesced around several of the other soldiers, effectively penning them in. They could not penetrate the curtain of fine sand that had enveloped them, though they tried. One woman struck the cloud repeatedly, terror in her eyes when it failed to dissipate.

Claybourne bellowed insults, enraged that they were incapable of following his commands. Again, I detected rapid movement nearby, but this time, the blur of motion stopped a few feet ahead of the cart.

Profound relief washed over me and I recognized Alexander's countenance. He'd allowed his hair to grow long while we'd been apart, and it was pulled back into a short blond ponytail. He grasped an ordinary sword in his left hand, and held the red-tinged cursed blade I recognized from his trials in his right. He wore his black dragon scale armor, though he'd foregone the helm. He glanced over his shoulder and nodded to me once, deep sorrow in his green eyes.

"Alex—" I managed through the muzzle.

He shook his head imperceptibly and turned his attention to Robert Claybourne. I knew we'd have time enough to speak once the battle was over and I was freed.

And I no longer harbored any doubts that I'd be freed. Alexander's presence ensured it.

Another gout of flame gushed skywards, blocking a trio of soldiers from joining their commander. Claybourne was cut off from his soldiers and had but one option left remaining to him. He must face Alexander—and my brother was furious.

Alexander adjusted his grip on both weapons and braced himself, while Claybourne squared his shoulders and began to charge. I watched with growing wonder as Alexander stood his ground, moving rapidly at the last moment to evade Claybourne's initial strike. He stopped a dozen paces away from Claybourne and now faced in my direction.

Claybourne spun around, nearly losing his balance as his swing failed to meet with resistance, then glowered at my younger half-brother menacingly.

"I've no time for tricks," he growled. "Face me, coward!"

Alexander's gaze flicked past Claybourne to meet mine for a moment, and I was certain I knew what he planned.

"You're no match for me," Alexander replied with a smirk. "But if you insist…" He shrugged, implying he was not responsible for the outcome should Claybourne choose to charge him a second time.

The driver of the cart rose slowly and turned toward me. His expression was troubled, and it was clear he was uncertain of what he should do next. As Claybourne began to stalk toward Alexander, the driver appeared to make a decision.

"It's time to make right some wrongs," he said in a low tone, drawing a knife from his belt.

I stared at him, abruptly terrified of the only man other than Claybourne who had deigned to speak with me during my tortured captivity. As he stepped swiftly toward me, I squeezed my eyes shut in an attempt to protect them from the strike I was certain would come.

A moment later, one of the bands holding my head down slackened and gave way. Stunned, I opened my eyes to find him sawing through a second band with his knife where it met the bed of the cart. When he noted my expression, a faint smile crossed his rugged features.

"I told you once before this wasn't right," he said before continuing with his task.

I turned my focus back to the scene unfolding between Alexander and Robert Claybourne. As Claybourne came within striking distance of Alexander, he swung his sword in a deadly arc of steel, only to have the blow parried swiftly by the sword Alexander held in his left hand. Alexander shoved him away with little effort, but my brother's strength far surpassed that of an ordinary man. Claybourne stumbled backwards but immediately recovered.

Another strike by Claybourne was parried by Alexander, this time by both of his blades. He shoved the commander back with even more force, and Claybourne faltered, losing his balance. He landed heavily on his backside mere inches from the wall of fire that continued to blaze along one side of the battlefield.

The driver of the cart cut through the last of the straps holding my head in place.

"Allow me to assist," I heard a familiar voice say.

Now that my head had been freed, I turned slightly to seek the source of the words. From the corner of my eye, I made out the distinctive red hair and friendly smile of one of the Roche twins. Whether it was Nevin or Niall who stood alongside the driver, I couldn't tell.

"Don't use magic," I warned him through the muzzle.

He didn't know of my sensitivity to magic, that an errant flame would wound me more thoroughly than anything Claybourne had inflicted. It was a secret even Alexander was not privy to.

He looked at me strangely for a moment, then nodded. "As you wish." He drew a short dagger from his belt and began to saw at my bonds as well. "We may need your brother's help with the chains. A dagger won't be of much use with those."

At the mention of Alexander, I turned toward the battle once more. Claybourne had regained his footing and was shouting curses at Alexander. Alexander's expression was grim and becoming darker by the second.

Finally, Alexander said, "I believe I've heard enough."

He charged toward Claybourne in a blur of motion that was difficult to follow. In the instant before he made contact, I saw both of his blades rise up in preparation to strike, but Claybourne had no time to react. Alexander struck him in the temple with the hilt of his ordinary sword, and Claybourne collapsed in a heap, unconscious.

Alexander closed his eyes for several seconds, his chest heaving. He turned to the remaining soldiers, those penned in by the dust cloud or blocked by the wall of fire.

"I offer you the chance to return to your homes," he called, "or you may surrender to me. The choice is yours."

With his words, the fire winked out of existence, and moments later, the cloud likewise dissipated. Alexander continued to hold his weapons at the ready, prepared for another attack. Most of the king's soldiers appeared stunned, unable to comprehend the events that had just transpired.

I couldn't blame them for their shock. It was the first time I'd witnessed Alexander's newfound abilities in action. Though he'd mentioned he could make himself faster and stronger, I'd never understood the full extent of what his magic made him capable of. He hadn't been boasting when he'd said Claybourne was no match for him. I doubted anyone was.

I overheard the two men working on my bonds talking quietly somewhere behind my head.

"I'm Niall Roche," the twin said.

"Wes," the driver replied. "Wesley Carrick, but Wes will suffice."

"Well met. It's nice to find someone with empathy amongst the king's soldiers."

Wes chuckled, but I could not make out his response.

Galewing released another piercing cry overhead. Four other magi slowly emerged from the trees bordering the western side of the road and came to stand alongside Alexander as he awaited the decisions of Claybourne's soldiers. I didn't recognize any of them, but that was unsurprising. According to the numbers Thomas had received from Alexander, he'd recruited several hundred magi, and I'd only met a scant handful during my travels in the Southlands. Even though I could not see their Marks, each possessed an ageless quality to their features, distinguishing them as something more than mere humans.

"What do you plan to do with the commander?" one of the men asked, finally finding his voice.

Alexander smirked. "He can run back to Colin with his tail between his legs for all I care. Knowing my brother as I do, he won't be lenient. Claybourne will be punished for what he has done, one way or another." He shook his head, then glanced briefly over his shoulder to meet my eyes before turning to address the king's soldiers once more. "Truly, Claybourne deserves death for what he's done to Andrew, but I've spilled enough blood for one day. Let Colin decide his sorry fate."

Alexander looked down at Claybourne's unconscious form. He shook his head, his expression one of disgust mixed with disappointment. When he looked up again, he said, "You've heard my offer. If you choose to surrender, we'll treat you fairly. I need to tend to my brother."

As Alexander turned away from the soldiers, several began to move forward tentatively, placing their weapons on the ground in an act of surrender. A few chose to walk away, leaving their commander lying in the road behind them. One woman cast several hateful glances toward Claybourne even as she lay down her sword. Moments later, she sprang to her feet and rushed toward him, kicking him savagely several times before the others pulled her away.

Alexander stopped a few paces from the cart, his eyes moist with unshed tears. He studied me for a moment, then shook his head again before wiping at his eyes.

"Holy hell, Andrew, I'm so glad you're alive."

Niall and Wes continued to cut my bonds. They'd made it halfway down the length of my spine, but the chains remained. My arms were free, with the exception of the stakes driven through my hands, as were my head and neck. To have elicited such an emotional reaction from my brother, I must have looked even worse than I realized.

Alexander dropped his gaze to study the ground for a moment. "When Galewing saw you this morning, your eyes were closed and you were unmoving. I'd feared…" His words caught in his throat, and he shook his head, stubbornly refusing to weep.

"Alex…" I managed through the muzzle, which caused him to look up sharply.

"Where is the key to that vile contraption?" he demanded.

"Claybourne keeps it," I said.

He frowned and shot a glower in the commander's direction. "I'm just as likely to kill that bastard as I am to leave him be if I go near him again." He tensed his shoulders, but after a moment, mastered his anger. He turned to face me once more. "There is another way. Lay still, brother. I'll break the damned lock."

I obliged him, and he drew his ordinary sword from its scabbard. He turned the hilt end toward the lock, then struck it once, powerfully, causing it to shatter. The muzzle sprang open, and with a sigh of relief, I lifted my head to allow Alexander to clear it away. It fell with a clang on the ground below.

"Alex," Niall called from somewhere behind, "do something about these chains, will you? They're fastened to the cart in such a way that we're unable to release them."

Alexander's eyes met my own, and he reached over to place one hand along the side of my jaw. "We're getting you out of here, brother. Give us a few minutes."

I nodded gratefully. I owed my continued existence to Alexander and the five magi who had accompanied him. "Thank you," I said as he turned away.

He chuckled, though the sound was strained. "I suppose we're even," he replied as he made his way to the end of the nearest chain. "Colin has attempted to execute both of us now."

I watched as several of Claybourne's soldiers began to bind their commander's wrists and ankles with a length of rope. They dragged him toward the supply cart that had not been blasted apart by Niall's fire magic and left him propped against its side.

I'd suffered extensively at Claybourne's hands, but I understood why Alexander had decided against taking his life. Too many of Novania's people had already been killed during Colin's brief reign—Alexander didn't want to add more to the tally.

As the remainder of my bonds were severed, I relaxed somewhat, giving my sore muscles a brief respite. Alexander came to the front of the cart once more, a frown creasing his face.

"Andrew, I'm not certain how to best remove the stakes. I suppose I could ask Iva to pull them out with her air magic—"

"No," I replied emphatically.

Alexander raised an eyebrow, alarmed by my response. I knew I'd be forced to tell him what I'd learned in the days before Rynn and I had departed the Southlands, but now was not the time. I could not be certain if the soldiers nearby would prove trustworthy, and I could not risk news of my greatest weakness making its way back to Colin or one of his cronies.

"Why, brother?" Alexander asked, baffled.

"No magic," I said again. "I'll explain later."

He sighed. "Very well. I suppose I'll have to work them free myself." He frowned as another thought crossed his mind. "Tell me one thing, Andrew. Why did you not simply change forms to escape all of this? Surely, you could have—"

"I can't, Alex," I replied. "The stakes… I don't know how Claybourne learned of this, because I didn't even know it myself. I can't shift while something is…*lodged* in my body. It's also why I couldn't escape that damned net. There was something attached to it, and it caught in my wing. Believe me, shifting was one of the first things I tried once I realized I could not break free of the net. But I couldn't."

Alexander's expression was troubled. "This is vile news, brother. It means Colin or one of his people have been seeking ways to subvert your natural abilities. What else have they learned, I wonder?"

"Claybourne said he'd researched my kind." I had no further answers for him. After a moment, he simply shook his head and sighed.

He climbed onto the cart, moving toward my left hand. He studied the metal stake for a time, then glanced toward me, fear and compassion warring in his eyes.

"I can pull these out, but I may have to enhance my strength to do so."

I nodded. "I trust you."

Alexander's magic was perhaps the only variety other than a healer's that couldn't harm me. He didn't know that, but I'd tell him when we discussed our situation later.

He frowned. "This is going to hurt, brother."

"I know."

The metallic scent of spilled blood permeated the air, and I realized belatedly it was the result of Alexander's magic. I braced myself as much as I was able, though when he pulled the stake, removing it in one swift motion, I was unprepared for the blinding sheet of pain that coursed through my body.

Unable to stop myself, I roared in agony. Black spots swam across my vision, and it took me several seconds to realize Alexander had moved and was now standing in front of me.

"I'll wait until you're ready for the next one," he said, his expression pained.

The sound had startled the others standing in the road ahead, and I noted with some surprise that one of the women was silently weeping. I drew several deep breaths and waited for the spots to clear from my vision. Already, the pain in my left hand was beginning to subside.

"I think it's best if you pull the rest of them out in rapid succession," I said after a time. "Don't prolong this. I've been in constant pain for days…"

His expression revealed the depth of his concern. "If you feel it's the best path, then I'll do it." He paused and blinked away unshed tears. "Hearing you just now… It brought to mind that day in the Oracle's tower. I'd hoped to never hear you in such agony again."

I nodded once, understanding his concern. "Hurry, Alex. *Please.*"

He made his way toward my other hand and steeled himself. The result was much the same, but beneath the pain, I felt a profound sense of relief. Alexander moved on to the remaining two stakes, removing them despite my screams. I blacked out for several seconds as the last was pulled free, but the sensation of being trapped was gone. I could shift if I wanted, and my wounds would finally be granted time to heal.

When I regained consciousness, Alexander knelt beside my head. His face was pale and his expression was drawn. He forced a smile when my eyes opened.

"Tell us when you're ready to move on from here, brother," he said. "Rest as long as you need."

I sat up carefully, fearful of placing too much weight on my damaged extremities. "I want to be away from this place, away from *him.*"

I nodded toward where Claybourne was propped against the supply cart. It seemed he'd awakened as well. He shot murderous looks at those around him and snarled orders at the remaining soldiers. They ignored him as they collected what belongings they planned to take with them.

"Alex," I said after a moment, "I don't believe I can walk."

"Can you fly, brother?" he asked.

I stretched my wings experimentally. They seemed intact, but were bruised from the chains that had bound me. "I think so."

He nodded, then turned to the others. "Niall, Siorus!"

He paused to allow the pair to walk toward us. Siorus was a tall man with broad shoulders and a build reminiscent of a blacksmith. He had short dark hair and striking hazel eyes. Though Niall was tall, Siorus towered over him. Despite his size, he had a friendly, amiable face, and offered a smile in greeting.

"I need you to go with Andrew," Alexander said. "He can fly to our camp. I'll send Galewing along as a guide. But…" he hesitated and glanced toward me, uncertain if he should go on. When I nodded, he said, "He's going to require your help once there. He can't walk. Lydia will need to tend him."

"Of course," Niall said, unable to hide his excitement at the prospect of flight.

"I'll shift forms once I land," I said, "but I'm afraid I won't be able to put weight on my feet. I'm sorry."

"Oh, hell, Andrew," Alexander said, exasperated, "you have nothing to apologize for. This was not your doing! Besides, I'm well aware of what you did for Rynn and how you ended up here. No one faults you, brother."

I nodded and took some encouragement from his words. He'd been in contact with Thomas, after all.

I lay down while the two magi climbed atop my back, finding seats between my stiff black spines. I craned my neck to peer at them, ensuring they were settled before I attempted to fly.

"We'll talk once we've both returned to camp," Alexander said. "Follow Galewing."

As he stepped away, I rose carefully, balancing on my knees and elbows. It wasn't an ideal position to take off from, but I didn't believe I could stand without incurring further injury. I pushed off from the cart, beating my aching wings powerfully to gain elevation. After a few moments, we soared above the treetops while Galewing led us toward Alexander's camp with a piercing cry.

After the torture and humiliation of the past few days, I felt a strange sort of peace as I glided freely through the skies, free once more. While I typically enjoyed my time in the air, I was too exhausted and battered to truly appreciate it now, but the peace was welcome. I simply wanted to find the camp, rest, and eat a decent meal.

I followed the gray eagle's lead and hoped we didn't have far to go.

FOUR

Alexander's camp was bordered on one side by the river, and sprawled through much of the wooded area that lay between the ferry crossing and the city of Willever. I was at once both surprised and thrilled by the number of people Alexander had rallied to his cause—hundreds of tents had been erected, far more than I'd imagined possible. I spied the ageless faces of magi, green-skinned Merael, and countless humans in the crowds below.

Once Thomas joined us, our numbers would swell even further, and with the defeat of Claybourne's armies, I truly believed we had a chance of ousting Colin from his throne. Despite my fatigue and the pain in my limbs, I was overjoyed by the scene as we soared above it. Alexander had promised an army, and he'd delivered.

"Aim for the grassy area just ahead," Niall called over the wind. "We've used it as a practice field, but no one is there at present."

"It's near the healers' tents as well," Siorus added.

As we began the descent, I said, "My landing may prove difficult. Hold on."

I wasn't certain how to manage the landing with both hands and feet wounded as they were. I was likely to stumble and fall as soon as I touched down.

"Do as you require, Andrew," Siorus replied. "We'll manage."

As my feet struck the ground, a blinding pain shot through them and arced along my legs. I crashed forward ungracefully and tucked my arms in to avoid further injury to my hands. I lay still with my eyes closed for several moments, breathing heavily as I grappled with renewed waves of agony. I was aware as the two men slid along my side to the ground, but the sensation was muddled by the pain.

When I finally opened my eyes, Niall knelt a few paces away, his blue eyes filled with concern.

"I'm going to shift," I told him through gritted teeth. "I know I can't walk—"

"We know, Andrew," he replied. "It's why Alex sent us with you. We'll help you to the healers' tents."

Siorus nodded silently in agreement as he moved to stand alongside the other mage.

Galewing released a cry overhead. Glancing skyward, I noted he'd circled the camp and was returning in the direction we'd come from. No doubt he planned to rejoin Alexander.

I nodded, and shifted into my human form. The transition usually left me feeling diminished, but this time, it came as a relief. The inherent freedom of being able to shift between my two forms once more brought a weary smile to my face.

Only a few hours ago, I'd believed I was well and truly stuck, that I'd perish on that damned cart given another few days. I would be forever grateful to Alexander and the magi who had accompanied him during his mission to rescue me.

Siorus gripped me beneath my arms, while Niall took hold of my ankles. I was unclothed, but I was so damned thankful to be alive and amongst allies once more that I didn't care.

The two carried me with some effort to the nearest tent, but before we reached it, Lydia intercepted us, clearly expecting our arrival. I managed an exhausted grin as she approached. She returned it with a tremulous smile, unable to hide her concern.

She'd changed little since I'd last spoken with her, perhaps five months past, though it was evident she was now with child. Her long brown hair was pulled back into a thick braid that reached nearly to her knees, though a few stray tendrils had come loose to frame her face. She brushed one aside and turned to face the two magi.

"I have a mat ready for him in our main tent. Come."

She turned away and motioned for them to follow. Siorus adjusted his grip on my shoulders and Niall nodded.

"I was thrilled when Alex said Galewing had located you this morning," Lydia said over her shoulder, her voice thick with emotion, "then devastated when he said he feared you were already dead."

I looked down for a moment, but didn't respond. I'd share the details of my captivity after Alexander had returned and we had time to speak privately. I didn't want to admit in front of the others that I'd nearly given up on any hope of rescue.

"Well," she said after a few moments, "I'm certainly happy you're alive. Rynn would have been heartbroken."

At the mention of Rynn, I looked up eagerly. "Do you know how she fares?"

We entered the tent, and Lydia indicated the mat she'd mentioned. Several neatly folded blankets had been placed next to it, as well as a number of bandages and a basin filled with clean water. I was laid upon the mat, and Lydia placed a blanket over my torso. I glanced around the space and noted it was empty; I seemed to be her only patient at present.

She smiled gently. "Rynn's leg was broken in the battle, but based on what Alex has told me, you already know that. Your brothers have been in contact daily since our arrival here." She glanced at the others. "Thank you both. I can take over."

Niall nodded to me once before departing. "My brother and I will return to pay you a visit later. There is much we'd like to speak with you about."

Lydia turned a sharp-eyed gaze on him. "Andrew will have no visitors until I can assess his condition further. Depending on the severity, I may not allow it for several days."

She turned toward me and knelt to take one of my hands gingerly in her own, a pained expression creasing her fair features. A hole ran through my palm the size of a large coin.

I grimaced at the sight. My body had begun to heal the wound and it was no longer bleeding, but I knew it would be some time before I made a full recovery. Before I'd shifted, I'd been cognizant that the scales covering the area had been severely damaged. Injuries that involved dragon scale took much longer to heal than others I'd incurred over the course of my life, and even with a healer's aid, it might take weeks. But the scales had been intact, not removed; perhaps there was a chance I'd recover sooner.

"Oh, Andrew, it pains me to see you in such a state," she said after a time. "After all you have done for your brothers, I would have been devastated if we lost you. And Alex…" She shook her head, blinking away tears.

"Lydia," I said gently, "I'm here thanks to Alex. That's what matters."

She wiped her eyes. "Yes, you're right." She turned my hand over in hers, shaking her head sadly. "Even with your natural healing ability, these wounds aren't going to mend swiftly. Belora and I will do what we can, but you may not be able to walk for a while."

"I know."

She moved the blanket away from my feet and studied those wounds for a time. "It seems your hands are worse off, but only by a small margin. The bones have been demolished, and the tissue is raw." She glanced at me then. "Was your dragon scale injured?"

"Yes. I know this will be a slow recovery."

"What I don't understand is why any of this was necessary," she replied. "You were a prisoner. Wasn't that enough? What he did was extreme. And appalling."

I averted my gaze. "It prevented me from shifting. I wasn't aware I'd be affected in that manner, and it concerns me that Colin learned of it before I did. What else does he know of my nature that I still don't know myself?"

She didn't answer.

Lydia spent the next hour channeling her healing magic. She spoke sparingly while she worked, gently tending to each wound while the green, herbal scent of her magic permeated the air. She cleaned the wounds and began to bandage them deftly, yet with tenderness and compassion.

As she wrapped my hands, I sighed. I'd be almost helpless until I healed.

Alexander appeared in the opening of the tent as Lydia finished with my hands. He held a tin cup, and the aroma of roasted meat and vegetables wafted toward me. My stomach grumbled in response—I could use a good meal or three. He remained where he was until Lydia moved on to begin wrapping my feet, then strode across the tent to sit at my side.

Lydia glanced at him and offered a knowing smile. "Thank you, Alex. He'll need to eat. It will bolster the healing process."

Alexander returned her smile. "I'd like to think I've learned a thing or two about this over the past few months," he replied. He helped me take hold of the cup in my bandaged hands. "It's stew. I thought it would be easier for you to manage than something that required the use of a knife."

"I'm just happy to have anything at all," I replied gratefully.

Alexander studied me silently, his expression pensive, while I swallowed a few mouthfuls of stew. "Andrew," he said slowly, "I know you went through hell during this past week, but—"

"What?" I spluttered, nearly choking. "A week? I can only recall the past three days."

"Yes, brother, it has been a week since you were captured."

He looked down at his hands, uncertain of what to say next. I took a few more bites of stew. It was difficult to manage the cup in my bandaged hands, but I was ravenous and determined to eat my fill.

"Did Claybourne say anything regarding why he'd taken you alive? I understand Colin ordered it, but did he share any details?" Alexander's green eyes were fixed intently on my own.

I considered the sparse conversations I'd overheard during my captivity, but nothing stood out in my mind. "I assume Colin wanted to kill me himself. To answer your question, no, I didn't hear anything specific. Claybourne was more interested in insults than information."

"From what I've learned of him, I'm not surprised. And you're likely right. Colin would have been thrilled to play the role of executioner." Alexander frowned and looked away, his expression troubled.

"Alex, what is it?" It was clear he wasn't telling me everything.

"Tom and I have been writing almost daily since you were captured," he replied. "I know Claybourne offered a trade of sorts before the battle. He'd allow Thomas and all of his forces to go free in exchange for you."

I nodded. "He did. We thought he was lying, and as you know, surrender isn't in my nature."

Alexander cracked a grin. "No, it isn't, brother." He paused to study me, then became serious once more. "We've been trying to puzzle it out. Why has Colin suddenly changed his tactics? Until now, he wanted you dead, and now he's seeking you alive. What is he playing at? I don't like it."

I shrugged uncomfortably and set my empty cup down. "I don't know. One thing is very clear, however. If you hadn't arrived today, I don't believe I'd have lasted much longer. Claybourne is without mercy and enjoys inflicting pain." I paused and looked away as I gathered my thoughts. "I was hoping you'd finish him off when you had the chance. After what I've seen him do to his own soldiers, the bastard deserves death twice over."

Alexander shook his head. "My abilities allow me to make a massacre of any battlefield if I don't restrain myself. I'm glad we defeated Colin's army in the south, but I'm not proud of what I'm capable of. I've shed far too much blood already, brother. Claybourne may deserve it, but I believe Colin will mete out that punishment. He won't tolerate his commander daring to return empty-handed."

I arched an eyebrow. "Do you believe Claybourne will follow us here?"

"No." Alexander chuckled. "We made certain he won't be moving anywhere for some time. He'll be forced to wait until some charitable soul feels compelled to free him from his bonds. Besides, Iva and Janos worked their magic and it would have been nearly impossible for Claybourne to determine which direction we traveled."

"He was awake when I departed," I reminded him. I didn't have to tell him I was a rather conspicuous target while in my dragon form.

"If he attempts to attack us here, it will be the last mistake he makes," Alexander growled. "I won't hold back a second time."

I studied him for a moment but made no reply.

He sighed heavily, a sound filled with despair. "I'm beginning to understand how difficult this is. Even without summoning my power, there have been times when I've been too forceful with someone or something, and I didn't mean to be. How have you managed it, brother?"

I looked down and laughed softly. "I've had my whole life to become accustomed to unusual strength. You've had but a few months. Give it time, brother." When he rolled his eyes in exasperation, I laughed again. "When I was a child, our mother told me that I must remember *everything and everyone* I encountered was far more fragile than I am, that I must *always* be vigilant in my dealings with others. I don't know if that advice will help you, but it helped me."

"If Mother were still alive, none of this would be happening," he said somberly after a moment. "She was the only person in the world who could persuade Colin into seeing reason."

"Your father believed I'd be able to do so," I replied. "It seems I've failed him there."

The king had believed Colin was simply a nuisance that could be tamed, and at the time, I'd believed him. How wrong we both had been.

"Alex," Lydia said gently as she rose to her feet, "I think it best if Andrew is allowed time to rest. You can speak with him again later."

Alexander nodded and collected the empty cup before standing. "I must write Tom, in any case."

"Alex," I said before he could make his exit, "I'd like to send a note to Rynn."

Though there had been much on my mind, Rynn had remained near the forefront of my thoughts. I desperately hoped my last actions during the battle had been enough to keep her safe. I would not stand idle if Rynn was in danger, and I'd protect her at any cost. My current wounded state was a testament to that, but I would not have acted differently, even knowing the outcome.

Alexander smiled knowingly, but it was Lydia who answered. "Rest first," she ordered. Her expression was understanding, yet firm. "I'll make certain Bryson is prepared to send your message once you wake." She turned to face Alexander, hands on hips, though she wore a playful smile. "Go, husband, before I chase you away myself. Your brother needs his rest and you're nothing but a distraction."

Alexander grinned mischievously. "We'll talk later," he promised. "Perhaps when my dear wife is feeling less protective of her charge."

Lydia took a few steps toward him, her arm raised. He laughed again, then ducked out of the tent. She shook her head, amusement sparkling in her eyes as she turned to me once more.

"Alex will always find the humor in any situation, if it's to be found," I said with a tired smile.

"Yes. For that, I truly am grateful. Joy seems to be a precious commodity in these northern lands, yet he somehow finds the means to spread it." Her smile faltered, and she looked down at her hands. "I hope you can make things right for the people here. Some of what we've seen while traveling…" She shook her head as though to clear it, then offered me a wry smile. "It seems I've become just as chatty as my husband. You need to rest. I'll leave you for now, but I'll be nearby should you need anything."

FIVE

"Please, Alex? I promise—"

I awoke to the sound of pleading outside the tent. The voice was one I recognized, but could not immediately place as I tried to shake off the last vestiges of sleep. The light filtering through the canvas was dim, and I sensed that evening had fallen outside while I'd slumbered.

"Andrew is asleep," Alexander replied patiently.

The other speaker made a sound of frustration. "Will you tell me when he wakes? *Please?*"

I grinned as I recognized the voice—Emmarie. I'd promised to write her when we left the Southlands, but given how difficult it had been to send communications to Alexander, I'd been left with only a few brief words passed to her via my brother. I was thrilled to hear her voice, elated that she was well.

And despite Lydia's earlier orders, I wanted to see her. I'd slept enough for one afternoon.

"Emma!" I bellowed, hoping she'd hear my call through the tent's heavy walls.

Outside, Alexander sighed in exasperation. "Lydia will give me hell for this. She even drove *me* away earlier."

Emmarie laughed as she pushed open the tent flap and strode inside. "Lydia went to fetch supper, as I recall," she said with a smirk. "If we make our visit quick, she'll never know we were here."

Alexander chuckled and shook his head. "You've never experienced the wrath of Lydia Marsden. It's terrifying, Emma."

Emmarie ignored him, her dark eyes alight as they met mine. She raced across the tent to fall on her knees at my side, her small green hands reaching forward tentatively. I offered her a bandaged hand, and she accepted it gingerly.

"Andrew, I am so happy to see you again!"

I smiled. "It's good to see you as well." I glanced at Alexander, who lingered at the entrance, his arms crossed. "I'm also glad you managed to talk your way past my guard. I certainly didn't hire him."

While she laughed, Alexander rolled his eyes. "And a poor guard I've been too," he replied. "Lydia said you were not to have any visitors, no matter who they were. She'll have my hide for this, brother."

I smirked. "No doubt you'll enjoy that."

"Oh, hell, Andrew!" Even in the dimming light, the flush creeping across Alexander's features was unmistakable.

I snickered, then focused my attention on Emmarie. She hadn't come to listen to our banter, and I didn't want to waste her limited time. No doubt Lydia would chase them both outside when she returned.

"How have you been, Emma?" I asked.

She shrugged. "Well enough, I suppose. I've been teaching my people some of the combat skills I've learned from you. Did you know we have a whole division of Merael in the camp?"

"I heard something about it from Tom," I replied. "I'll admit, I was surprised."

"As was I!" She grinned, then tossed several dark locks of hair over her shoulder with her free hand. "But my people's mages were sent the Oracle's summons too. By the time we reached the Thornhallow, they were waiting for us—and my uncle was with them." She shook her head, her eyes wide with wonder. "He apologized! I never believed he would. And what's more, I'm no longer an exile."

"That's great news!" I leaned forward to offer her a gentle embrace, careful to avoid pressure against my injured hands.

"He's here," she continued excitedly. "There's one other Tree-speaker as well. Most of us have never watched them work, but *everyone* saw what they were capable of during the battle! Those soldiers didn't know what to do when the trees uprooted themselves and began to fight alongside us. It was incredible. I wish you could have been there!"

I grinned, genuinely happy to be speaking with her after months apart. "I've no doubt I'll see them at some point. And what of you, Emma? Were you part of the battle?"

She clenched her jaw in momentary anger and cast a glare at Alexander. "No, I was forced to remain behind to assist the healers. Alex wouldn't allow it, even though there were other Merael fighters younger than me on the field."

"Emma, you can't stay angry with me forever," Alexander complained from the entrance. "You weren't ready, and I—"

"You underestimate me," she replied haughtily before turning back to me. "I convinced several murders of crows to fight for us. It was all I could do from afar."

I didn't fault my brother for attempting to protect the girl. She was only an adolescent, after all. While I acknowledged she'd become skilled enough with a blade to defend herself, the enthusiasm she possessed when excited could very well prove fatal on the battlefield. I didn't share my concerns, but was secretly pleased Alexander had kept her away from the fight.

"I'm glad you came," I said in an attempt to change the subject. "I've often wondered how you fared, and it's good to see you're well."

She studied me carefully for a moment, her dark eyes shiny with emotion. "Galewing told me how he found you."

"I'll recover," I promised. "I always do."

She nodded, though she appeared unconvinced. "I hope so."

"*ALEXANDER!*" Lydia shouted from outside, fury in her tone.

"Shit. I'm caught." Alexander offered me a guilt-ridden grin, then ducked outside to face the healer's wrath.

Emmarie smirked, her eyes alight with mischief. "I should be going. It seems I've landed Alex in Lydia's bad graces."

I chuckled. "Alex will survive. Thank you for coming."

She grinned, then rose and scampered toward the exit. "I'll come back when I can, Andrew."

A moment later, Lydia entered, her face flushed. She carried a bundle of fresh bandages in one arm and a pitcher of water in the other, then placed them on the floor beside my mat.

"I told your brother to let you rest. No visitors, I said!" She knelt down and began to unbind my left hand, shaking her head all the while. "He listens as well as a stone at times. What am I to do with him?"

"It wasn't a bother," I replied, hoping to placate her. "I'm glad to see Emmarie is well."

Lydia frowned. "And you defend him, enable him. I suppose the better question is: What am I to do with *you?*" She placed the soiled bandage aside and began to examine the wound gently. "Your bones have already knitted back together. I'm astounded by how rapidly you heal. Had this been anyone else, I'd be spending several more hours pouring magic into the wound to achieve even half this."

"Well," I said awkwardly, "I'm not exactly normal, am I?"

"And in this case, it's a very good thing." She reached for a clean bandage, then worked in silence for several moments, her expression troubled. Finally, she said, "Alex mentioned something earlier that worries me."

I frowned. Alexander could have mentioned any number of items to Lydia that might give her cause for concern.

"What did he say?"

"That you insisted no magic be used to free you."

"Yes." I glanced toward the door. "Is Alex outside?"

She paused in her work and rocked back on her heels to study me. "I assume you'd like him here for this discussion." When I nodded, she called to him, then resumed her work.

Alexander entered a heartbeat later, concern in his green eyes.

"Sit down," Lydia said. "There's a matter we must discuss."

His eyebrows rose and he glanced in my direction questioningly.

I laughed. "You're not in any trouble. At least, not as far as I'm aware."

"Ah, good." He grinned and strode toward us, then seated himself near the end of my mat. "What's this about, then?"

"When you and the others freed me, I told you not to use magic."

"Ah, that." He scratched at the back of his neck and flicked a glance at Lydia.

"Yes, that," she replied with a frown. "I'd like to know why he was so adamant."

"Something happened before we left the Citadel, something that I feared to share with you in case Colin learned of it somehow. I wanted to tell you, but we thought it best to keep it a secret."

Alexander's previous good humor fled, and he crossed his arms. "We? As in you and Rynn?"

"Alex…" I looked away, frustrated that he'd immediately taken offense.

"Alex, let him speak," Lydia interrupted without looking at my brother.

"Rynn was there, yes. As were Lileen and Emma," I said evenly. "On the advice of Caelmarion, we chose not to speak of what happened that day."

Alexander gazed at me steadily in the growing darkness, his expression unreadable. "It was the day we were married, wasn't it, brother? When you returned to the tower, you looked like hell."

I nodded, relieved his frustration was fading. "By that time, I was feeling much better. I had a close call."

He said nothing, merely continued to stare at me, his eyes devoid of emotion. I looked down as guilt twisted in my gut. I loathed keeping secrets from him.

"As I recall," Lydia said, pausing to give me a stern glance, "you had healed significantly by the time you arrived. There was nothing left for me to mend, though I advised you to avoid a recurrence of whatever you'd done to inflict such harm."

I forced a dry chuckle. "You did. I discovered my greatest weakness that morning. It's magic."

Lydia froze, her eyes wide. "Should I have—?"

I shook my head. "A healer's touch doesn't harm me, but nearly any other mage poses a threat. My body is intolerant of magic, even varieties that are seemingly innocuous, like Lileen's." I paused to look at her earnestly. "Caelmarion assured me you can do nothing to hurt me, Lydia."

Alexander narrowed his eyes. "What happened, brother?"

I shared my story—my father's request to speak with Rynn, Lileen's idea of using me as a conduit between them, and the resulting violent illness that had overtaken me. I told them of my father's horror once he understood what had occurred, and described Caelmarion's blistering rage.

"Holy hell," Alexander swore as I finished speaking. "No wonder you were so insistent. But you allowed me to use my power to free you! What were you thinking, brother?"

"I said *nearly* any other mage poses a threat," I repeated. "I asked Caelmarion specifically about you. He believed that since your power is internalized, you aren't capable of causing me harm. But I had to be free of those stakes, Alex. It was a risk I needed to take."

Alexander swore and rose to his feet. He began pacing the length of the tent while Lydia replaced the bandages on my feet.

"And if I had accidentally killed you, brother? What then?" he demanded.

"You didn't, and you won't," I replied stubbornly.

"What if I had, Andrew?" he asked again, desperation in his eyes. "I would have been forced to tell Rynn what happened. And Thomas… Without you, I don't know if we can storm the Capitol! Damn it, Andrew, we *need* you!" He looked away with a shake of his head, frustrated, hurt, and terrified.

"And you'll have me," I replied evenly. "There's no use dwelling on it. Besides, now you know my greatest weakness. Even Tom doesn't know, and I'd rather keep it that way."

Alexander raked a hand through his hair in exasperation, pulling several strands loose from their binding. "It's a wonder it's still a secret at all. Emmarie will chatter to anyone who will listen."

"And yet, she didn't tell you," I countered.

Alexander snorted. "Alright, fine. I was being a bit unfair. She idolizes you, brother, and she'd do anything you asked of her." He paused midstride to fix me with a furious gaze. "I'd never forgive myself if something had happened to you because of me. You should have told us sooner!"

I sighed. "I know, and I'm sorry."

"Alex, we know *now*," Lydia said softly. "That's what matters."

He growled several curses, then sat down heavily, refusing to meet my gaze.

I squeezed my eyes shut, willing my aggravation with Alexander to disappear. When I opened them, he continued to sulk. I suppressed a sigh.

"Did you write to Tom?" I asked, hoping a change of topics would put him in a better mood.

"Yes, and I mentioned to Bryson that you wanted to send a note to Rynn, but…" He glanced pointedly at Lydia, who was now binding my right hand.

I laughed. "Might I send her a message tonight?"

"Tom's response indicated that they should arrive here sometime tomorrow," Lydia replied before Alexander could respond. "You should rest, Andrew. No doubt she'll find her way here as soon as she's able."

I closed my eyes momentarily while a smile crossed my face. Even if I wasn't allowed to write her tonight, I'd see her tomorrow. My reckless gamble had saved her life, and though I'd paid in blood for my act, I wouldn't change the outcome for all the gold in the kingdom. She was alive. Nothing else mattered.

Lydia rocked back on her heels and placed her hands on her hips. "I need to apply further healing magic to your wounds, and I doubt you want Alexander to pen a note for you. It's best you wait to speak with her until tomorrow."

Alexander feigned outrage. "What do you mean by that? I'd be a perfect gentleman when writing to Rynn."

I snorted. "I know you better than that, brother. Your wife is right—it's best I leave the writing to someone else."

"You forgot to mention you need to *rest*, Andrew," Lydia cut in with a pointed look in my direction.

"Is there any chance I might have something to eat first?" I asked.

"Of course," she replied, then motioned to Alexander. "Your brother can fetch something, since he doesn't seem to have anything better to do than loiter in your tent."

Alexander snickered and headed toward the door. "I can take a hint, dear Lydia. I hope you don't mind stew again, brother. It'll be easier to manage."

With Alexander's departure, Lydia sat back to study me carefully in the gloom. "While Alex may not understand why you chose to keep your vulnerability a secret, I do. I'll speak with him later. He'll come around."

I smiled, grateful she understood. "Thank you."

She patted my shoulder gently, then rose to her feet. "While you can see well enough in the darkness, I require light in order to continue. There are candles in the next tent. I'll only be a few moments."

I nodded and watched her depart. I was disappointed Lydia wouldn't allow me to send a message to Rynn, but I was elated that Thomas' forces would be joining Alexander's by the end of the next day. Rynn would come, even if half the camp stood in her way. I knew she would not be deterred.

When Lydia returned with a lit candle, she placed it carefully in the corner of the tent nearest my pallet, then paused to scrutinize me for a moment. "What were you thinking of before I returned?"

I smiled and looked down at my bandaged hands. "Rynn."

"Ah, that explains the longing expression." She laughed softly. "You'll see her again tomorrow. Tom mentioned several times that if her leg hadn't been broken, she would have gone after you herself… I don't believe Robert Claybourne would have survived that encounter. She's grown rather protective of you, just as you are of her, it seems."

"That morning, before the battle resumed, I—"

I stopped as Alexander burst into the tent, carrying a tin of stew in each hand. "I've managed to secure an extra helping for you, brother." He flashed a grin at Lydia. "You've allowed him to eat, but you didn't say he couldn't have extra."

She shook her head, amused. "You may help Andrew with his supper while I work some magic on his wounds."

Alexander laughed. "Of course. What were we talking about?"

I glanced at Lydia with a shake of my head. What I'd been planning to tell her wasn't something I wanted to share with my brother present, and I was in no mood for jibes regarding my love life. No doubt he'd hear of it once I was reunited with Rynn.

"Only that Tom will be here tomorrow," Lydia replied. She closed her eyes as the herbal scent of her magic began to permeate the space.

"Ah, yes." Alexander grinned as he helped me to take hold of the first cup. "It's been far too long since we were last together. I look forward to seeing him again."

SIX

Unable to walk and left alone after Lydia's latest round of ministrations, I stared at the canvas ceiling of the tent and imagined patterns from the pinpricks of light above. I'd never been one to enjoy idle time, and being forced to sit while my body healed was mind-numbing. I would have given almost anything for a deck of cards and a friendly face to pass the time.

I listened to the sounds of the camp beyond the tent's walls. Footfalls accompanied the passage of people going about their assigned duties, snatches of muted conversation carried through the air—never near enough for me to make out what was said—and the occasional clack and clang issued from the direction of the nearby practice field. The camp went about its business while I languished in silence, alone.

I was still staring at the ceiling when soft footsteps approached outside as it neared mid-morning. I shifted my gaze to the entrance, hoping for someone to appear and alleviate my boredom. A moment later, Emmarie ducked inside bearing a tray laden with fruit, bread, scrambled eggs, and two mugs of steaming liquid. I grinned.

"Alex asked that I bring you something to eat. He's preparing for your brother's arrival, and Lydia doesn't know he sent me." Emmarie placed the tray carefully across my lap and sat down nearby. "Lydia had someone posted outside. I needed to wait until he left."

I laughed. "I'm glad you've come. I can't *do* anything, and I could use the company, no matter what Lydia might say. She's likely to return any time, you know."

Emmarie shrugged. “I won’t be here when she does. I have much to do this morning, but I couldn’t say no to seeing you again.” She looked down at my bandaged hands sadly. “How long will it take before you’re well enough to spar? I’ve been trying my best to teach the Merael how to fight as you taught me, but…” She sighed. “I could use your expertise. And Alex is *always* busy now.”

I forced a smile. “It will be a few more days. I’ll help you when I can—if my brothers don’t have other plans.” I shrugged. “For the first time in my life, my two youngest brothers are giving the orders. It’s strange.”

“Lydia says the same about Alex all the time. Your brother is strange.” She grinned mischievously, then glanced toward the exit. “I’ll come back, but I’d best go for now. Alex has everyone in an uproar. He wants everything to be just so before Thomas arrives. I’ve never seen him like this.”

“Tom will become king if we defeat Colin,” I replied. “It’s only natural for Alex to feel this meeting of forces ought to be something worth remembering later. He’ll calm down eventually. He always does.”

“Until then, he’s going to be nearly impossible to deal with. You can tell Lydia I said as much too.” She smirked knowingly. “Speaking of Lydia, I should leave before she returns.”

After her departure, I began the awkward and inelegant process of eating without use of my fingers. My thumbs were bound to my bandaged hands to prevent me from moving them too far or too frequently. It was necessary for my hands to heal properly, but it made grasping a nearly insurmountable task. I was forced to use both hands to manipulate any item, and eating proved a messy affair. I was glad Emmarie was busy and had been forced to leave—having an audience during my helplessness would have been humiliating.

Lydia returned sometime later with another healer in tow. I nodded to Belora in greeting, pleased to see she’d joined Alexander’s army. It had been months since we’d last spoken, and she’d tended my wounds then as well. She paused just inside the entrance, hands on her ample hips as she studied my condition. Lydia moved past her to collect the empty breakfast tray and move it aside.

Belora shook her head, her expression unreadable, then strode toward me. "I didn't expect to be tending you again, Lord Dragon," she said with an air of mild disapproval. "I suppose I should be thankful it's no fault of your own this time."

Lydia disappeared outside, then returned carrying an armload of blankets. She began to spread them at intervals throughout the tent, while Belora knelt and began to unbind my left hand.

"Thomas has a number of wounded with him," Lydia said over her shoulder. "We've been preparing the other tent for their arrival, but I'm afraid you'll no longer be alone in this one, Andrew."

"May I ask you something?" I watched her as she went about her work, efficient and precise with her movements.

She glanced at me, one eyebrow raised in question. "Of course."

"I know that Rynn's leg will need attention. Can she—"

Lydia cut me off with a merry laugh. "I'll make certain we reserve a space for her next to yours. I doubt we'd keep her away from you if we tried."

I grinned, relieved by her response. "I know it's only been a few days, but… I've missed her."

Belora made a sound of disapproval. "Alexander told us you'd been captive for a week."

I looked down. "I know. I was unconscious for several days after my capture. Claybourne had a substance… It rendered me unconscious on the battlefield. I don't remember anything until I woke bound and chained to his cart."

Belora paused, a troubled glint in her eyes. "And how does one knock a dragon unconscious? Are there other wounds buried beneath the surface that I need to search for?"

I shrugged helplessly. I didn't relish the notion of retelling my captivity, though I suspected Alexander had shared most of what he'd uncovered with his wife. Claybourne had been cruel when I was awake, but I knew little of what he may have done otherwise.

And his actions had been sanctioned by Colin. Damn him on his cursed throne. I'd make certain he paid for every horror he'd inflicted one day.

"I don't believe so," I said to Belora. "I don't sense any other injuries, but I don't know what Claybourne did while I was incapacitated."

She grunted and reached for a clean bandage. "From the stories we've heard, it's likely he did any number of things." She paused to cross her arms. "Tell me everything you remember. And I won't take no for an answer."

I shrugged wearily and described my final moments during the battle at the keep. My determination to save Rynn at the expense of my freedom, Claybourne's specially-designed nets, and what I recalled of the substance he'd used to render me unconscious. I glanced at Lydia, concerned she'd react adversely when I began to speak of the circumstances of my captivity. She stared at the floor, her eyes moist, but I knew she'd heard the story before. Belora remained stoic, though I detected rage in the depths of her eyes.

"Knowing what I do of your physiology, I doubt we'll find any damage remaining from that chemical," Belora said after a moment. "I'll inspect you for internal injuries while I work today. Your hands and feet will be useless for some time yet, but no doubt Lydia has mentioned that to you."

When I nodded, she said, "Good. I expect you to behave yourself in the interim. You are to stay off your feet until one of us tells you otherwise, and limit activity with your hands. If you undo all the work she's done—and in her present condition no less—you *will* answer to me."

I chuckled, recalling a time months ago when she'd uttered a similar threat. I'd been wounded then too, but not as severely. Belora's no-nonsense attitude and outwardly gruff demeanor hadn't changed over time, despite the Oracle's dire visions and the war. It was encouraging to know some people would remain steadfast and unchanging in the face of adversity.

Lydia finished laying out blankets and walked toward us. "I can take over from here if you'd like, Belora."

Belora looked up sharply. "Absolutely not. You need to rest while you can, girl. I won't let you overextend yourself with a child on the way." She shook her head and muttered under her breath.

Lydia sat down at my side. "I haven't even reached the halfway mark with this child, Bel. I'm perfectly capable of working alongside you for a while yet."

"And I won't risk your child's health when I don't need assistance," Belora retorted. "Sit and chat if you like, but you'll do nothing further."

Lydia rolled her eyes, though she smiled fondly. She seemed to enjoy the attention, and I had no doubt she was pleased to be speaking of her child.

"I'm happy for you and Alex," I said. "We were thrilled to hear the news."

Lydia laughed as a fine blush rose in her cheeks. "Thank you. I only wish Rynn hadn't waited so long to read my message! The longer she delayed her response, the more I worried that you were displeased or disappointed. I know the timing wasn't ideal, given everything else."

I grinned. "On the contrary, Rynn was concerned when she received your message. Since we'd only received letters from Alex until that point, we feared something had happened. I'm damned glad it was good news—we've had too little of it lately."

"I sent that before you finally came together, didn't I?" When I nodded, she smiled knowingly. "While Alex was still on his pilgrimage, she and I spoke often. She enjoyed your company, and as time wore on, she realized she was in love. We both knew you were still grieving, yet she couldn't stop her feelings. I'm certain even *you* noticed when she began to seek your time more and more. And watching you together seemed so…*right*, for lack of a better term."

"Is that why Alex kept insinuating that I needed to move on?" I asked pointedly.

She blushed and looked away. "I may have put him up to it."

I snickered. "I suspected as much."

"She's a true friend," Lydia continued, "and I wanted to see her happy. Her life hasn't been easy, given her condition. You are the only person she can interact with normally, and I know that was a factor…"

I shrugged. "The reason why it happened doesn't matter. It took me far longer to come around than she would have liked, and I'm aware of that. But as you said, I was still grieving. Losing Vera was devastating, and there are still days I mourn her loss. But Rynn understands that, and she's done more to help me overcome that than anyone."

Lydia beamed. "You love her. I can see it in your eyes every time you speak of her."

I nodded. There was no use in denying my feelings.

"She's likely to storm in here and rage at you once she arrives," Lydia said after a few moments. "She's called you a damned fool—and several other colorful names—in her letters. I know she appreciates what you did, but it *was* reckless."

"I have no doubt she's angry." I averted my gaze to stare at my bandaged hands. "I couldn't risk losing her too. I'm not certain she understood that, but Colin already murdered Vera. I couldn't go through that pain a second time."

"I'll try to talk sense into her before she makes it this far," Lydia promised, her expression compassionate. "I believe she'll understand."

I began to doze before the healers departed and didn't wake again until late in the afternoon. I was roused by voices outside—and it took me only moments to recognize the speakers.

"Please allow me to look at your leg first," Lydia said in a pleading tone.

"No." Rynn's voice was firm, though I detected a trace of irritation in her response. "You can look at my leg once I've seen him, but not before. My leg will mend whether I wait ten minutes or not."

There was a pause, then the sound of measured, yet uneven footsteps approaching. Lydia sighed in exasperation, the exhalation followed by her own rapid footfalls.

"Very well, but he was asleep when I last looked in on him. He needs to rest. He's been through…too much." Lydia's voice cracked with emotion as she spoke the final words.

"Then I'll sit at his side until he's awake," Rynn replied, undeterred.

I chuckled, amused at the exchange and overjoyed by the sound of Rynn's voice. "I can hear you," I called.

Rynn laughed. A moment later, the flap enclosing the tent was drawn aside. Lydia held it in place while Rynn hobbled her way toward me with the aid of a makeshift crutch constructed of several stout branches. Her left leg was bound to a rough splint, and it seemed she could not put much weight on the injured limb. She grinned, her vibrant blue eyes locked on mine.

Lydia frowned and shook her head, her arms crossed. A moment later, she rolled her eyes and departed without a word. I knew she'd return, but I was secretly pleased she'd given us a few moments alone.

Rynn remained standing as she studied me for several moments. Finally, she shook her head and her smile faltered. "Damn it, Andrew, I hope you never do anything so stupid and reckless again. When Tom's scouts couldn't locate your trail, I'd feared…" She blinked rapidly in an attempt to stave off tears.

"Rynn—" I began, but she cut me off with a nervous laugh.

"Jonas said you likely saved my life," she managed, "but you risked your own to do so. You shouldn't have done that. You should have let me fall."

I sighed and looked down at my bandaged hands as Rynn awkwardly sat down at my side. She took my left hand between both of her own, gingerly, as though she feared she'd injure me further. I sensed the frigid temperature of her skin even through the layers of bandages, but she would do no harm. Slowly, I looked up to meet her eyes and was surprised to find her smiling.

"Rynn," I said again, "I didn't want to imagine my life without you. I couldn't lose you. To me, you were worth the risk, and I'd do it again."

"Hmm." She looked away, tears spilling from her eyes only to freeze on her cheeks moments later. Abruptly, she pulled her hands away and swiveled, then threw a well-aimed punch into my shoulder. The strike wasn't powerful enough to cause any damage, but I hadn't expected the reaction. I gaped at her, stunned, then looped my arm around her and began to laugh.

She stared at me, her expression filled with anguish, her eyes fierce. "Never put me through an ordeal like that again!" She leaned into my embrace and managed a shaky laugh, despite her tears.

"I don't plan to," I replied gently. "I truly believed I'd break free from the net. I didn't plan to be captured, but I had to take the risk. I won't lose you. I *can't*."

She was silent for a time. Finally, she said, "I suppose I understand. Had our roles been reversed, I would have done the same." She sighed and leaned further into my one-armed embrace. "I didn't know falling in love would be so painful. And of all the men on this damned world, I had to fall for a skin-changer who does nothing but further complicate my life."

"I never meant to be a complication."

She laughed. "I can't imagine it any other way now that I know you."

I bent my head toward her, intending to plant a kiss atop her forehead. She turned, intuiting my plan, and reached up to touch the side of my face, meeting my lips with her own. I was relieved beyond words that she'd survived the remainder of the battle, overjoyed she was once again sitting at my side, thankful we were together again. I lost myself in the moment, poring a dozen emotions and more into the kiss. I'd done the right thing, and I'd do it again if it meant spending even one minute longer with her.

We parted, breathless, and gazed at one another for some time. She beamed, her expression as brilliant as sunlight sparkling on water.

"I love you, Rynn Gwyllias."

She leaned against my shoulder, seemingly content. "And I love you still, Andrew Caein." She shifted slightly to find a more comfortable position, then grimaced in sudden pain.

"Rynn?"

"It's just my leg," she replied dismissively. "It will heal, given time. Now that we're here and I've had a few moments with you, I'll allow Lydia to tend it. But I had to see you first. I had to make certain you were well. Alex wrote to us yesterday, and when Tom told me how he'd found you…" She shook her head. "If I ever see Robert Claybourne again, he will not walk away unscathed. Alex should have killed him. He doesn't deserve to live."

"Alex had his reasons," I replied, though I agreed with her sentiment. "I wasn't in any position to argue. I was weak and wounded, half-starved…"

"I know. Alex thought you were dead when Galewing found you."

"I wasn't, but I was in sorry shape." I lifted my right hand and turned it toward her. "Lydia said the bones have already healed. In a few days, I'll be back on my feet."

Rynn snorted. "I know how quickly you heal, but I doubt Lydia will allow you to wander off so soon." She looked down, then frowned at the blanket covering my legs. "Did they not give you any clothing?"

"The blankets have sufficed so far. There aren't many people my size, and there was likely nothing to be spared." I shrugged. "My things were in the trunk along with yours. I assumed when Tom finally reached us, I could have it brought to me."

She nodded. "When Lydia returns, I'll ask her to have someone fetch it. I left it with Tom. He wanted to make certain no one tried to make off with your armor. One of the Novanians already tried once."

"What?" I asked before I could stop myself. "Who would do that?"

"One of the men who surrendered after Claybourne fled the battlefield. I caught him going through the trunk a few nights ago, and I put a stop to his thieving. Tom was furious and sent him away once his hands were bandaged properly."

I arched an eyebrow. "What did you do?"

She laughed hollowly. "I reacted instinctively, nothing more. He was so self-assured in what he was doing that he didn't hear me behind him. I pulled his hands away without thinking. His frostbite will heal eventually." She shrugged. "What matters is he's gone and your things are safe. I'd hate to see that armor fall into someone else's hands, and your father would have been livid if I'd let it happen."

I nodded, unsettled by her tale. Had he simply wanted the armor for himself, or had he planned to take it to Colin? If Colin managed to acquire dragon scale, I feared what he'd do—or what else he might learn about my nature.

I smiled at Rynn and pushed my dark thoughts aside. "I'm glad you're here."

She smirked. "I should be the one saying that to *you*. I don't care how much you or your brothers object, but when the next battle ensues, I am *not* leaving your side. I will *not* go through this agony again."

Before I could reply, Lydia ducked inside. "Belora will be along soon," she said. "There are several more people who require our attention, and the other tent is at capacity. I'm afraid you won't have your privacy any longer."

I shrugged. "That's fine. I have all I need right here." I smiled at Rynn, eliciting a blush from her.

Lydia nodded, then shifted her gaze to meet Rynn's. She placed her hands on her hips, her expression stern. "Will you allow me to look at your leg now?"

Rynn's leg had been broken in two places; once in the thigh, and once in the shin just below her knee. Though she'd splinted her leg under Claire's guidance, the breaks had not been properly aligned.

Lydia rocked back on her heels with a sigh. "We must reset your leg, but there is only one person who can do so, and I don't like the prospect." She fixed me in a steely gaze. "I know the bones in your hands have mended, but I don't know if this process will tear open the remaining wounds. I don't like to ask this of you, but no one else can help her."

Rynn glanced at me, her expression unreadable, but said nothing.

"I'm willing to try," I said. "You'll need to tell me what to do."

Lydia guided my hands while Rynn braced herself. Rynn grimaced with each adjustment, but she didn't vocalize her pain. Instead, she clenched her jaw and gripped the edge of my blankets in her icy fists, her eyes squeezed shut throughout the process. Though I knew it was necessary for her leg to heal properly, it tore at my heart to know I was the source of her present discomfort.

Once finished, Lydia allowed Rynn to bind her leg to the splint once more. As she did, the herbal scent of Lydia's magic began to permeate the space, and Rynn began to visibly relax. Lydia knelt at her side, her hands splayed above Rynn's leg as she worked, but she deftly avoided physical contact.

Rynn leaned into my side. "I've never required a healer's services before," she said softly. "It's incredible. The pain is nearly gone."

Without looking up, Lydia said, "What I do simply promotes your body's own healing response. You'll heal faster than you would have otherwise, but it *will* take time. You need to stay off your feet as much as possible until Belora or I tell you otherwise."

"And how long will that be?" Rynn pressed.

Lydia looked at her sharply. "It will take as long as it must."

Rynn rolled her eyes and sighed dramatically. "I suppose it could be worse. At least I have Andrew to keep me company while I'm forced to sit here." She flashed a grin, and her next words were accompanied by a teasing smirk. "I'll bet Lydia allows me to walk away before she allows you to, even with your natural healing, Lord Dragon."

I laughed despite her use of the unnecessary formality. "I'm not certain it's wise to bet against you this time."

Lydia's eyebrows lifted in surprise, but she made no reply as she continued to channel her magic. Rynn noted her expression and tilted her head to one side, studying the other woman with mild amusement.

"Do you think I'm wrong, dear Lydia?" she asked, teasing.

"No, but I wonder about Andrew's lack of reaction to your use of 'Lord Dragon.' Alex said you dislike the title." She glanced at me briefly, clearly perplexed.

"I, ah…" I shrugged, uncertain of what to say.

I recalled the conversation that she referred to. Alexander and I had been talking privately, and he'd called me "Lord Dragon" in jest. While Rynn's use of the term had also been part of a jest, I felt differently now than I had previously. I'd become more comfortable in my dragon form during the long winter months spent in the highlands, and perhaps I was finally coming to terms with what I was.

Or perhaps it was merely my feelings toward Rynn that overshadowed any adverse reaction I might have had to the moniker. I didn't know.

Rynn frowned in thought. "What's wrong with using your rightful title, Andrew? You *are* dragon-kind, and in the Southlands, we know it's only proper to address you as such, at least upon our first meeting." She tilted her head to one side. "As I recall, I didn't know what you were when we met. It wasn't something you were very forthcoming about either."

I nodded as I considered her words and all that had happened over the past two years. I couldn't deny that I'd been changed by my experiences, and I sincerely hoped those changes were for the better. I was no longer forced to withhold my true nature, and with that freedom had come countless opportunities to explore what I was capable of. Though I still had much to learn, I'd also gained more than I'd ever imagined possible.

I was dragon-kind, and I'd begun to embrace my heritage.

"I was unused to people accepting me as I am when Alex and I had that conversation," I replied. "Things are different now. I no longer have any reason to hide."

SEVEN

"I should have come by yesterday, but there were a hundred items to see to and as many people who needed to speak with me." Thomas sat near my feet, his face haggard despite the determination in his eyes.

I laughed. "You've become the leader of the revolution, brother. I wasn't expecting to see you even this early."

He heaved a sigh. "It's hardly early, Andrew. Half the morning's gone, and I've already met with a dozen people. It doesn't matter. Their needs can wait. I wanted to see you."

I shrugged. "I'm not going anywhere until the healers deem me mended. And I understand the toll leading an army can take. I've been there, Tom. I don't fault you for the delay."

"Nevertheless, I'm sorry. I would have accompanied Rynn when she came if I'd been able."

I glanced at Rynn, who sat nestled against my side. "I've been apprised of the news."

"When he hasn't been snoring in my ear," Rynn added with a smirk. "But we understand, Tom. Relax."

"I'll relax when this is over and done. After Alex sent word of how he found you, I believe more strongly than ever before that Colin must be stopped," Thomas replied, his tone impassioned. "Robert Claybourne may be a vile man, but Colin placed him in his position. Colin is the driving force behind the darkness that has descended upon Novania."

I nodded my agreement. "I didn't learn why Colin changed his directive and wanted me taken to the Capitol alive. Claybourne wasn't forthcoming, and I wasn't in any position to argue with him."

"Alex told me why Claybourne staked you to the cart," Thomas said quietly after a moment, his expression troubled. "Andrew, if we'd known—"

"I didn't know myself," I replied, cutting him off. There was no sense in allowing my youngest brother to wallow in frustration over a point none of us could have foreseen. "I'm still learning about certain aspects of what I am. The idea that I could be forced to remain in one form never crossed my mind until I was unable to shift."

"While we were traveling here, I did a bit of research." Thomas paused to stroke his beard thoughtfully. "I believe I mentioned once before that I salvaged a few books from Vinterry."

I nodded. "You did. It's fortunate not everything was destroyed or taken by Colin's lackeys. Vera's library was unique."

He peered at me sharply. "Colin's people took items from her library?"

"Claybourne alluded to as much, and based on what he put me through, I'm inclined to believe him." I shrugged. "What did you learn?"

"There is very little regarding skin-changers, I'm afraid," he said.

"Have you met Nevin and Niall yet?" Rynn asked. When Thomas shook his head, she said, "Ask Alex or one of the other mages to introduce you. They're historians. Their primary area of interest is magi and Mark inheritance, but they *do* know quite a bit about dragons. As I recall, they spent countless hours bombarding Andrew with questions during our time in the Frostwake."

I eyed her curiously. It was true I'd spent a considerable amount of time with the twins, and they'd shared several pieces of information about my nature that I'd been unaware of previously. I hadn't realized Rynn had been paying attention to those conversations—or that she'd taken such an interest in me immediately after our first meeting.

She returned my glance with a knowing smirk. "You're a difficult man to ignore. It became almost impossible when I realized what you were and that I couldn't harm you. Don't act so surprised."

Thomas chuckled at the exchange. "I'll ask Alex to introduce me. We must learn all we can while we have the opportunity to do so. I fear Colin won't delay much longer, and we'll be facing him on the battlefield sooner rather than later." He looked down, his expression pained.

I nodded, and we fell silent for a time. Our situation was difficult, made more so by the prospect of warring against family. Despite the rumors we'd heard of his camps and the numerous executions he'd sanctioned, Colin *was* my half-brother. It pained me to consider his fate if we succeeded in ousting him from the throne, but I doubted he'd react as we did; I wasn't certain he was capable of feeling guilt or remorse.

If Colin was victorious in the end, all of our lives would be forfeit. Alexander would be killed for bearing the Mark, I'd be condemned as dragon-kind, Thomas would be executed for inciting the rebellion, and all those who followed us would be likewise doomed. Colin had ended the lives of others for far lesser crimes.

To correct the mistakes of our brother, we had no choice but to continue our fight. Even if we managed to avoid execution, we'd face certain exile, and the Southlands wouldn't always be the haven it presently was. The Oracle had foreseen the Barrier's failure, and without it, the Southlands would be in danger with Colin in power. He'd march his army in pursuit if we fled, and he'd kill everyone he deemed a threat, no matter their involvement in the war.

I understood it was particularly difficult for Thomas to pursue our present course. He'd been closer to Colin than I had ever been, and the fact remained the tyrant king *was* family.

"We're in this together, and we'll get through it," I said after a time.

He managed a weary smile. "That we are, and I certainly hope so."

Belora entered and glanced in our direction with a disapproving scowl. "I'd advise you to keep your conversations short. I know you dislike it, but you require more rest in order to heal." She turned toward a nearby soldier with one arm in a sling, but said over her shoulder, "Your brother may be king, and you may be dragon-kind, but *I* am in charge of your welfare."

I chuckled while Thomas rose to leave.

"I'm certain we'll have time to speak later," Thomas said. "It's good you're with us once more. We're going to need you in the next fight, Andrew."

We spent the next several days mired in a similar routine. One of the healers would tend my wounds in the morning, then take a few moments to assess Rynn's progress. They'd go about other business for a few hours, only to return after midday to change my bandages and remark on my progress. Meals were often brought by the healers' assistants, and we were allowed visitors on occasion. One of the healers would return again in the evening before we turned in for the night.

By the end of the fourth day, the damaged tissue in my feet had completely knitted together, but the skin remained raw and would for some time. My hands were slower to heal, but they were mending better than I'd anticipated. I was no longer in constant pain, but neither healer would allow me to attempt walking yet. I protested, but was summarily ignored.

"You know," Rynn said as Belora departed the fourth evening, "I may have been wrong. They'll allow you to leave before me." She'd been restless most of the day, but now appeared morose. Instinctively, I drew my arm around her in an effort to buoy her spirits.

"I have my doubts," I replied. "Besides, we may as well enjoy this reprieve while it lasts. Colin will strike again, and soon. Our location isn't a secret, and we're not far from the Capitol. When he does, we'll both need to be prepared."

Rynn nodded, her expression becoming grim. "I will not let you out of my sight. After what happened at the keep… I'll go where you go, and I don't care what your brothers have to say about it."

"And if I must fly?" I asked.

"I've overcome my aversion to flying, Andrew," she replied firmly. "If their plans require you to be airborne, then I shall fly with you. I will *not* lose you to that damned monster."

I wasn't certain if the monster she referred to was Colin or his appointed commander. The term aptly described both men.

Regardless, I was heartened by her response and relieved that she'd be near no matter my appointed tasks. Her magic would prove invaluable in battle, and if I found myself trapped a second time, I had no doubt she'd do her damnedest to free me. I'd been wrong to insist she remain at the rear when the keep was besieged, and I wouldn't make the same mistake again.

I marveled at her determination. I didn't know how I'd become so fortunate to have met this incredible woman, but I was glad fate had determined our paths should cross. No matter the outcome of this war, at the end of it, I knew we'd remain together. I loved her more with every passing day.

"Alex won't like it," I said slowly, "but if you want to fight at my side, I won't object. I don't know if you'll be safe, given what Claybourne is capable of, but I'll stand by your decision."

Rynn frowned and crossed her arms, her eyes narrowed. "Perhaps *you* will be safer with *me*. Have you considered that?"

I smiled despite her obvious frustration. "I have. You're a powerful woman, and I wouldn't dare cross you."

She snorted and rolled her eyes. "What good is such power if it alienates me from nearly everyone I meet?" She sighed and leaned against me, seeming to deflate. "At least I have you."

"And you always will," I promised.

She looked up sharply. "Have you considered the future? *Our* future? You said once that you'll follow me wherever I choose to go once this fight with your brother is done. Have you given any thought to what else might be in store for us?"

I'd ask for her hand in marriage, but unlike Alexander, I was determined to wait until our business with Colin was concluded. It didn't seem right to ask it of her now when so much remained uncertain. Given my recent captivity and the suffering I'd endured at Claybourne's hands, I didn't want to leave her a widow should I find myself at the mercy of Colin's whims a second time. She deserved better than what I could offer at present.

"I have," I said guardedly.

She held my gaze for several moments, her expression unreadable. Finally, she looked down with a disappointed sigh. "You aren't ready to say more. I suppose I should have expected that from you."

"I'll tell you when I'm prepared to do so, but this isn't the right time."

"What should happen if the right time never comes, Andrew?" she demanded.

Her question was valid, but I was undeterred. I frowned stubbornly for a moment and glanced around the tent. Some of the others were listening keenly to our conversation, unable to hide their interest. I glowered at them before returning my attention to Rynn.

"It will come, but not now. Not tonight."

She crossed her arms, unable to hide her frustration any longer. She scooted away and shrugged out of my embrace, her expression wounded. "I once told you that I'd wait as long as it took for your stubborn ass to come around, but after you were captured, I'm not certain I can wait any longer. I have been nothing but patient with you, and I need more than your meager assurances. Damn it, Andrew, I love you, but I can't wait forever."

Her eyes had become shiny with emotion, but she didn't weep. She stared at me for several long moments while I grappled with what to say next. I loved her, and I certainly didn't want to lose her, but this had come too suddenly for my liking. Adding to my discomfort was our unwanted audience, who seemed to be drinking up every word of the deteriorating conversation. I scowled in their direction again, but only one woman had the decency to avert her gaze.

I sighed, moving to run my hand through my hair before I realized I couldn't. I dropped my hand to my side and hung my head, defeated.

What else could I say to make her understand? I didn't want her to be angry or bitter, but she didn't seem to realize I was trying to do right by her. Of all the women who had been a part of my life, Rynn was the one I cherished the most, and I'd never forgive myself if this matter drove a wedge between us.

I had to say something, but what would she accept?

When I raised my head once more, I shot a glare at the nearest listener, hoping he'd take my hint and turn away. Instead, he merely flashed a grin and continued to watch us.

Damn him, I needed privacy, and he wasn't keen on allowing it.

I suppressed a groan, understanding what I must do. She'd pushed me, forcing me to divulge my plans when I wasn't prepared to do so. Despite my frustration, I'd tell her. I was backed into a corner and could see no other way out.

I'd hoped to surprise her when the time came. I'd planned to take her somewhere private, perhaps a place no one else could hope to follow, then ask her to be my wife. I didn't doubt she'd say yes, but I'd hoped to go about it differently. A makeshift infirmary with unwanted listeners was no place to make a proposal.

I shifted my gaze to my hands and wouldn't meet her eye. This wasn't how I'd envisioned this moment, and I was as disappointed as I was angry.

"Andrew?" she asked in a wary tone.

I looked up and steeled myself. "I'm going to tell you something that I truly wish could have waited for a better time. Perhaps a time when we were without an audience."

I shot another pointed look at the eavesdropper. This time, he had the decency to turn away.

She watched me silently, her expression impassive. Her arms remained crossed, and a deep hurt shone in her eyes. If I could have done so, I would have kicked myself for my failures. It pained me to see her so upset and know that I was the cause.

"I want to marry you one day, but I'd like to have the opportunity to ask you properly. And in this tent on this night is not the right place nor the right time."

I frowned and looked away, sullen. She'd forced my hand and it rankled.

She shuffled toward me, but I didn't immediately look up. Only when she took one of my bandaged hands in her own did I risk a glance in her direction. Her expression had softened and she no longer appeared wounded, merely thoughtful. She held my gaze for several moments before she broke her long silence.

"I'm sorry. I should not have pressed the issue." She risked a tremulous smile, her eyes never leaving mine. "Did you truly mean what you said just now?"

I nodded. "I did. Know that when the time *is* right, I will ask you properly."

Behind her, the eavesdropper turned to flash a grin in my direction, shattering my illusion of privacy. I chose to ignore him and focused on Rynn alone.

The tentative smile she'd worn transformed into an elated grin. "I will hold you to that promise, you know."

"I know."

"I suppose this means I must finally tell my brothers." She laughed softly. "I'm not certain how they'll react to the news that you aren't fully human, though they seemed to like you well enough."

"I know you miss your family." I drew my arm around her once more, and this time, she didn't shrug away. "When this is over, would you like to return to Dwymm?"

Surprised, she tilted her head to one side. "Yes, but I wasn't certain you'd want to. I thought you'd rather remain near your father. We could go to the Citadel."

I shrugged. "I have many lifetimes in which I can spend time with my father. I have but one that I can spend with you. I wouldn't mind visiting him from time to time, but we may go wherever suits us best."

She looked away, her expression contemplative. "I often forget that you'll likely outlive everyone here, but I'll never forget your reaction when you learned it. That day seems so long ago, doesn't it?"

I laughed as I recalled the day I'd learned of my longevity. I'd been wholly unprepared for the news that as a skin-changer, I shared the same incomprehensible lifespan as a full-blooded dragon. That day at the Frostwake had only been seven months ago, but it seemed a lifetime.

"It was the day I first shook your hand," I replied. "You hadn't made contact with anyone in eleven years."

She flashed a mischievous grin. "And here I am, holding your hand in mine. Or as much of it as I'm able to, given the bandages." She leaned into my shoulder, a content smile on her lips. "I'm glad we've had this talk, Andrew. I look forward to building a future with you, no matter what it brings."

EIGHT

Early the next morning, Belora returned according to her usual routine. I focused on Rynn as the healer went about her business, accustomed to the process as Belora began unwinding the bandage encasing my right hand.

"Claire and Elanor are making more banners," Rynn said. "I'm not certain how many gowns your former wife took with her when she fled the Capitol, but she continues to discover more cloth in the proper colors."

I chuckled, familiar enough with Claire's habits to surmise she'd packed at least one trunk's worth. "Thomas continues to use the dragon standard, then?" I asked.

Rynn rolled her eyes. "Of course. And after your captivity, his banner holds even greater meaning for most of us."

Belora peeled the remainder of the bandage away and gasped, drawing my attention. I turned toward her, startled, and hoped I'd done nothing to incur further injury. She held my hand in hers, eyes wide, while she examined it closely. The wound was gone, my flesh whole, as if an iron stake had never been driven through it. Not even a scar remained to mark my ordeal.

"It took you far longer to heal when you donated scales for Alexander's armor," Belora said after a moment, her usually gruff tone softened by wonder. "I assumed this injury would take just as long, but it seems I was mistaken."

I shrugged uncomfortably. "As far as I'm aware, the scales weren't forcibly removed during my captivity. They were damaged, but perhaps the circumstances are different. I don't know."

She leveled a stern glare in my direction. "It appears that way. I'll look at the rest of your injuries before I make a final decision, and perhaps I'll ask Lydia to look at you as well, but you may walk away much sooner than we anticipated."

Rynn laughed softly. "I wish I healed as rapidly as you. If Lydia has her way, I'll be relegated to this tent for the rest of the war."

"You are not dragon-kind," Belora replied matter-of-factly as she began to unwind the bandage on my right foot. "Your leg is broken in two places, and as with all mere humans, it takes time to properly heal."

Rynn huffed. "There is no harm in wishing it were otherwise, is there? I didn't make this journey to sit about and do nothing. I want to do my part."

Belora paused in her work to glower at Rynn. "You'll have your chance to fight again *after* you're healed. I'll not have you leaving here only to undo all the effort that Lydia and I have put into mending your leg." As the bandage fell away, Belora shook her head. "This wound has closed and healed itself, just as the other has. You are damned remarkable, Lord Dragon."

She pressed her thumb against the bottom of my foot, gauging my reaction. There was no pain, only the pressure she applied. My foot felt whole, just as my hand did.

"How does that feel?"

"It feels *normal*," I replied with a grin.

"I have no doubt the others will appear the same." She began to remove the bandage on my left foot, an expression of bewilderment on her broad features. "I want you to remain where you are until Lydia can see your progress for herself. She has spent far more time in your company than I have, and I'll defer to her judgment. But to my eye, you appear well enough."

I chuckled, certain that Lydia would allow me to walk away. I was looking forward to assisting my half-brothers with the next step in their plans; I'd idled long enough.

Rynn sighed, dejected. I understood she wanted to make good on her promise to me, but she'd have ample opportunity once she was well enough to walk. I wrapped my right arm around her shoulders and leaned toward her.

"I'll return as often as I can," I promised.

She managed a faint smile in return. "I know you will. I just hoped I'd be well sooner than this. When we first arrived and I saw the state of your wounds, I believed it would be weeks before you'd be allowed to walk. It's a bit sobering to realize just how different you truly are."

I looked down, uncertain how to respond. She'd known since we'd met that I wasn't fully human, and we'd shared countless conversations detailing some of my unusual attributes. Her words unsettled me. This was the woman I planned to marry, and it seemed she had doubts, now that she'd had time to consider what I truly was.

"Rynn, I—"

She laughed softly. "I didn't mean to sound as though it's a bad thing, Andrew. You have a wondrous ability, and I'm…envious. To watch it firsthand reminds me that you aren't what you currently appear to be." She sighed and shook her head. "I fear what my brothers will say when they learn the truth. I've already done so much to strain my relationship with Petyr. You know he didn't approve of my choice to become a mage, and now I've fallen in love with the one man in all the world who isn't truly a man at all."

"Petyr seemed to have accepted your path when we were together in Dwymm," I replied.

She shrugged. "He had eleven years to come to that conclusion. He and Syllas thought highly of you, especially after your interactions with Petyr's children. Perhaps I'm overthinking this." She sighed. When she spoke again, her tone was glum. "I'll ask Bryson to send a message today. I may as well tell them and be done with it—I've certainly put it off long enough. I hope they accept my decision."

"If memory serves, the people of Dwymm have long held the dragon-kind in high regard," Belora interjected in her usual no-nonsense tone. "You should have nothing to fear. I'll speak with Bryson once I'm done here."

Rynn blinked in surprise and managed a nod.

"Thank you," I said as Belora moved to unbandage my left hand.

"As I suspected." She shook her head and rose to her feet. "Your recovery is impressive. I'll speak with Lydia. No doubt she'll be here soon. Then I'll talk to the Feige boy."

After Belora was gone, I asked Rynn the question that had been plaguing my thoughts. "Do you truly believe your brothers won't accept me?"

She shrugged, clearly miserable. "I don't know. Once my condition made it apparent that I'd never have a normal relationship, my family stopped making inquiries regarding marriage. But you're different. I can be myself around you. I can touch you, interact—all without fear. My brothers know at least that much about you." She paused to brush a stray blond ringlet from her eyes. "When I left Dwymm to pursue my future, I never once believed I'd be forced into isolation. Syllas understands how difficult my life has been since I became a mage. I believe *he* will accept my choice. But Petyr… Petyr refused to acknowledge my decision as valid for years. Will he react as adversely to this one?"

"Petyr seemed reasonable to me," I replied, hoping to buoy her spirits.

In truth, I didn't know how Petyr would react. We'd spoken only a handful of times, but he'd mentioned in passing he was grateful there was someone Rynn could turn to when she needed a friend. I wanted to believe he'd accept our union, but as an eldest child, I also knew he'd likely be mistrustful of my intentions when it came to his sister. I was protective of my own younger siblings, after all.

She sighed. "I don't know if I can swallow another blatant rejection as I did when I chose the path of the mage. I was never given the opportunity to speak with my father, to apologize for leaving as I did. I hoped one day I could make him understand that I was meant for something greater than fishing on the lake, but I returned home too late. And Petyr always sided with him."

Her voice grew strained as she spoke, and when she stopped, she hung her head in defeat. I drew her into my embrace, offering what comfort I could. I touched the side of her face, gently brushing away the first tears freezing to her skin.

"No matter what happens, I'll be here for you."

She nodded. "I know, and that's part of the reason I fell in love with you." She lifted her hand to place it over mine, leaning her face into my palm. "I have missed your touch, dragon-man." She giggled, a mischievous smile playing upon her lips as she used the Corodans' term.

I grinned and leaned down to kiss her, oblivious to the others nearby.

A moment later, someone cleared their throat in an attempt to garner our attention. I sat back reluctantly, while Rynn blushed crimson and stammered an apology. Lydia stood near my feet, smiling knowingly, her eyes gleaming as she studied us for a time.

"Well," she said slowly, "I didn't mean to interrupt, but I have others to look in on after I'm finished with you." She smirked at Rynn. "No doubt you're hoping I'll order him to stay a bit longer."

Rynn's blush deepened. "I know he's needed elsewhere."

Lydia laughed and knelt down to inspect my feet. Her hands were cool as she pressed against the areas where the wounds had been. "Do you feel pain, Andrew?"

"No. I feel fine."

She nodded, then rose briefly to walk around my mat. "Let me see your hands."

I relinquished my casual embrace of Rynn to comply. She pressed her thumbs against the backs of my hands before turning them over to press against the palms. She studied them for a time, then sat back on her heels and released them.

"You've healed completely," she said with a smile. "Alex set up a tent for you near the center of the camp yesterday. I mentioned last night that you'd be well enough to resume your usual duties within the week." She crossed her arms. "You've made a liar out of me. You're well enough *today*."

I chuckled. It was typical of Alexander to act on his excitement without consulting anyone, though in this instance, I was grateful. I'd only need to move the trunk containing my belongings to the new tent, though I'd sorely miss the hours spent with Rynn.

"This means I'm free to go?" I asked.

She nodded. "Yes. I'll fetch your boots and ask Alex to carry your trunk. While you appear healed, I'd like you to mind yourself for another day or two. No doubt Thomas needs a break from Alex as it is, and this will give my husband something worthwhile to do, if only for a short time." She smiled fondly despite her words.

"You'd best visit me when you can," Rynn said as Lydia began to rummage through the trunk, seeking my boots.

"I will," I replied. "It won't be long before you're back on your feet as well."

Rynn snorted, and Lydia said, "We'll see."

Lydia dropped my worn leather boots at my side as she moved toward Rynn. "I'd like to see how your leg is mending before I take my leave."

I entered the command tent erected at the center of camp two hours later with Alexander at my side. Thomas, Jonas Everly, Rizzt-tok, Everett Crossley, and a Merael woman I didn't recognize huddled around an oblong table, poring over a map of the region. They didn't look up at our arrival and continued to discuss strategy for several moments.

I didn't remark on the delay. After days confined to the healers' tent, my mood was buoyant. The mere prospect of walking through camp, of standing at my brother's side, was enough to sustain my good cheer.

Thomas looked up after several moments, then his face broke into a relieved grin. Without a word, he darted away from the table and drew me into a rough embrace. "Andrew, it's so damned good to see you on your feet!"

"You as well, Tom." I grinned.

"Andrew, this is Shyala," Alexander said, gesturing to the Merael. "She's an elder and a Tree-speaker. At the behest of her people, she has been placed in charge of their forces and speaks on their behalf."

Like most of her people, Shyala stood no taller than shoulder-height when compared to my brothers. Her green skin was several shades darker than Emmarie's, and she bore a distinctive black diamond-pattern tattoo on the left side of her neck. Her black hair was streaked with white, marking her age, and it was bound in a tight bun. She studied me warily as I approached the table, her hazel eyes unreadable.

I didn't know how she'd react to my presence since I'd masqueraded as a full-blooded dragon when I'd last visited the Thornhallow.

I dipped my head deferentially. “It’s an honor, my lady.”

Her eyes remained sharply focused on mine for several seconds. “Emmarie has spoken very highly of you, Lord Dragon. I wasn’t certain I should believe the girl’s tales of your heroism and your kindness, given your unnatural origins. Our dealings with your kind have always been few.” She lifted her chin and arched one eyebrow critically. “Over the past few months, I have come to know Alexander well enough. While he has a tendency to exaggerate certain details, he is trustworthy.”

“What?” Alexander spluttered.

Thomas and I shared a laugh. The elder’s words were on par with our brother’s nature.

“I won’t repeat myself,” Shyala replied with a knowing smile. “I have spoken with the other elders who accompanied the magi north. We’ve made the decision to acknowledge your status as dragon-kind, though many of our people will remain wary of you. Your existence as a thing half human and half dragon is not of your own doing. Your parents are to blame for the result of their aberrant union, and we should not discredit you for their shortcomings. We will work alongside you as necessary, but don’t expect all of my people to become as friendly as Emmarie.”

I nodded. “I understand. Thank you for offering me this chance to prove I am not a person to be feared.”

Her words conveyed more than I’d hoped for. To learn the Merael had chosen to acknowledge me as an ally was a relief and a blessing.

Alexander smirked. “I suppose when it comes to your allies, you aren’t a source of terror, but to Colin’s people…” He shrugged and laughed, leaving the thought unfinished.

I frowned and hoped his words hadn’t unraveled the rapport I’d been attempting to build with the Merael elder. “Alex—”

“Your brother means no ill-will,” Shyala cut in, much to my surprise. “I have grown rather accustomed to his unusual jests, but his words are true. The dragon-kind possess unrivaled power. It is inevitable that other people fear you, knowing what you may be capable of.”

“We were about to discuss that very item,” Thomas stated, returning to his place along the table. “I was hoping you’d enlighten us as to what happened at the keep, Andrew. Alex relayed some of what you told him, but I'd like to hear the tale from you."

"We all would," Jonas agreed, while Everett nodded his assent.

"We hoped your recovery would be smooth," Thomas added. "I wanted to ask for the details sooner, but I was cautioned against it. Lydia said you were on the brink of collapse when you arrived, and she was astonished that you managed to fly once you'd been freed. But clearly, you've healed—and more swiftly than any of us believed possible."

I drew a breath and began to tell them the story of my capture by Robert Claybourne. I left out nothing; even a seemingly insignificant detail might bring insight into the workings of Colin's mind. Claybourne had admitted to researching dragons and skin-changers before he'd ordered me rendered unconscious, but I didn't know the extent of his knowledge.

I shared what I'd experienced upon waking, strapped and staked to the cart, unable to shift forms, my mind in a haze from the chemical fumes Claybourne had employed to keep me insensate. I relayed the conversations I could recall and spoke of the massacre Claybourne had committed against the townspeople of the Green Fords.

"By the time Galewing found me, I'd given up hope," I said. "If I'd remained trapped for even one more day, I don't think I would have survived. I'm fortunate—and forever grateful—that Alex arrived when he did."

Contemplative silence permeated the space as the others pondered my words. Rizzt-tok tilted her triangular head to one side, then the other, all the while watching me with her enormous compound eyes. Though her insectile face relayed no emotion, I knew she conversed with the Corodan hive. Perhaps the hive, with its collective memory spanning generations, could provide further insight.

"I don't know if your experience brings us any closer to understanding the king's mind," Jonas said, breaking the silence. "But I know your actions at the keep saved Rynn's life."

"I can't believe Claybourne executed the townsfolk at the Green Fords." Everett crossed his arms and scowled. "I knew the man was a blasted lunatic, and his actions during the battle proved he bears no love for his own soldiers, but to slaughter people simply for a minor act of defiance…" He shook his head in stunned disbelief.

"It has become the king's favored method of managing unrest," Jonas replied. "Those who don't agree are swiftly and permanently silenced. Claybourne carries out the king's will, like it or not." He began to pace, made restless by the conversation. "You have missed much during your sojourn in the highlands, my friend."

Thomas snorted. "Sojourn? I feared my people wouldn't survive the winter. Thanks to the Corodan, we managed well enough, but—"

"Tom," Alexander cut in, his expression uncharacteristically grim, "Galewing has seen something."

I narrowed my eyes and studied Alexander. He closed his eyes and an array of emotions flitted across his features. When he opened them, he fixed his gaze on Thomas. "A group of soldiers marches toward us from the south. I recognized the armor as that of the king's garrison."

"How long will it take before they reach us?" Jonas asked, his gray eyes boring into Alexander's with intensity.

"We have until tomorrow, perhaps," Alexander stated. "I estimate there are two hundred soldiers. The man at their head is not Robert Claybourne. I didn't recognize him, though he wears the crimson cloak of the commander." He glanced toward me. "You mentioned there was someone who spoke directly to Claybourne, perhaps a week ago. Tell me of him."

"I didn't learn his name," I replied, "but he pulled rank on Claybourne. He claimed he was the leader of the king's personal guard and had been sent to assess Claybourne's progress. I don't believe they care for one another."

"This must be the same man," Jonas said. "It can't be a coincidence. No doubt word of your rescue has reached the Capitol by now."

"Do they know we're here?" I asked.

Willever Ferry had long been a staging point for the various branches of the king's army, a place to rendezvous. It was possible they were traveling to our location for that purpose alone.

"I don't know," Alexander replied. "I can see as Galewing does, but unless he flies closely enough to overhear their conversation, I can't learn anything more. I don't want to risk his discovery unless it's imperative."

"If more of the king's men are headed here, they'll be in for a surprise," Jonas said, his tone grim. "We outnumber them significantly. We can shore up our defenses today and be prepared to face them by tomorrow."

"I'll help you," Everett offered.

Jonas nodded in silent agreement.

"I'll inform the other magi," Alexander said with a wicked grin. "We can make certain the king's soldiers won't be troublesome."

"The hive is prepared," Rizzt-tok added in her buzzing voice.

Outside the tent, rapid footsteps approached as someone sprinted toward the entrance. I turned toward them, while the others continued their discussion.

"Andrew, what is it?" Thomas asked, cutting Jonas off in mid-sentence.

"Someone's coming," I replied.

A heartbeat later one of the scouts pushed hurriedly through the tent flap, breathing heavily. I recognized Hulda immediately, and was glad to see she'd survived the battle at the keep.

"My lords," she said, panting for air, "a force approaches from the north. I fear Duke Winston has betrayed us."

NINE

Thomas' face had become a thundercloud, a veritable mask of fury. "Elias assured me he'd help us and was no friend to Colin." His voice was a low growl. "He claimed Colin was a damned menace!"

I'd rarely witnessed Thomas' temper turn so swiftly and was stunned by his vehemence.

I recalled the conversations with Duke Winston during our brief stay outside Dresdin's Forge. He'd been amenable to meeting with Thomas and had provided both encouragement and support as we set our plan to draw Colin's attention in motion. He'd even gone to some lengths to protect Claire's identity in the report describing the attempt on Thomas' life, which had ended in the subsequent death of the would-be assassin.

I believed Duke Winston was sincere in his desire to see Colin removed from the throne and didn't think he'd betrayed our trust as Hulda suggested. Elias Winston was our cousin, was well aware of what had transpired between my mother and father years ago, and I trusted him.

"Tom," I said evenly, "let us hear what Hulda has to say before we jump to conclusions. I don't believe our cousin has turned on us. There's something else at work here."

Thomas glowered at me before turning his gaze on Hulda. "Very well. What have you learned?"

By this time, Hulda had managed to catch her breath. "There's a band of perhaps one hundred soldiers marching toward our location from the north," she repeated. "They sport the green and gold of house Winston, with its brown bear motif. If we hadn't stopped in

Dresdin's Forge weeks ago, I wouldn't have recognized the design. They are Duke Winston's people."

"Allow me to meet with the duke," I said as a plan began to form in my mind. I still didn't believe our cousin had sent soldiers to waylay us and was convinced he remained an ally.

"No!" Alexander shouted, as Thomas replied, "Absolutely not, Andrew. You've only just healed from your last entanglement with Colin's forces."

"I don't believe Elias has betrayed us," I repeated stubbornly. "Given his reception in Dresdin's Forge, I think he'll be willing to talk."

Ignoring me for the moment, Thomas returned his attention to Hulda. "How long do we have before Winston's people reach our location?"

"They'll arrive before nightfall," she replied.

"We have the fortifications and the people to defend both positions," Jonas stated before anyone else could chime in. "We must see to our defenses now, for if Duke Winston truly does plan to strike, we have little time in which to prepare. I'll focus on the northern front. Ev, please take the south. Alex, prepare the magi. Split them between the north and south perimeters. Shyala, I would like your people focused along the northern perimeter. There are more trees in that direction. Rizzt-tok, the hive is needed in both locations."

"And what of me?" I asked as the others began to disperse.

Jonas chuckled and motioned for me to follow as he made his way outside. Once we were out of earshot of my brothers, he said, "I understand your line of thinking, Andrew. I'm inclined to agree, based on what I've learned of your interactions with Duke Winston. Thomas doesn't trust him as you do, but I can't blame him. He's more vulnerable than you or Alex. But I also understand your brothers don't want to see you come to harm again so soon."

I snorted. "I'm well enough, and I wasn't insinuating that I'd fly out to meet the duke alone. I want to do my part, Jonas."

"Good. I'd like to see you put your plan into action." He gestured toward the tent that Alexander had set up for me earlier in the day. "Strap on your armor, and meet me at the southern perimeter. I'll make certain you come away from this encounter unscathed, and if we're lucky, your brothers will be none the wiser."

A half-hour later, I was armed and armored, surrounded by two dozen soldiers at the camp's northern perimeter. They were part of Jonas Everly's garrison, remaining loyal to their duke long after he'd been stripped of his title and lands for his defiance of the king. I didn't know any of them personally, but I trusted Jonas and was glad to have them with me as I went to meet my cousin.

If I was wrong in my assessment of Elias, we'd inevitably be drawn into a fight. Jonas' soldiers were seasoned veterans who could hold their own in battle, and they were aware of the risk we were taking as I marched to confront the wily duke. I held onto my conviction that Elias was innocent, but prepared for the possibility that I'd erred in my judgment of his character.

Before we embarked, Jonas handed me a white standard. "Stay near the center of my people. If we're wrong, you must return unharmed, and my people can protect you. Thomas will have my head if you're injured again, and Alexander will likely skewer me on the spot. Do us both a favor and stay safe."

I chuckled. "I'll do my best, Jonas."

Even if Duke Winston wasn't here on an errand of betrayal, I'd receive an earful from both brothers once they learned of my errand. And if Alexander's temper was riled, I wouldn't hear the end of it for days.

He nodded. "Luck be with you, my friend."

We marched north from the camp. The landscape was flat and grassy, broken by stands of trees in the early stages of reawakening from their winter hibernation. To the west, the docks of Willever's ferry were visible, standing on the shore at the nexus of two rivers. The city lay beyond the water, its buildings shrouded in haze from the distance. The verdant landscape was broken by occasional farms to the east. The day was warm and the air slightly humid, but the weather was pleasant enough.

It took the better part of an hour before Duke Winston's people became visible ahead. I raised the white standard as we approached. Within moments, I recognized the duke, so like Alexander in appearance. He called a halt even as we continued to march forward. Our group of twenty-five was outnumbered four-to-one, and I desperately hoped I had not misjudged my cousin during our recent meeting in Dresdin's Forge.

Duke Winston signaled to several of his soldiers, and together they began to move toward us. The bulk of his army remained behind, and I knew then he was amenable to negotiation. I motioned for a halt as we neared the range of the duke's archers, taking another gamble with the cousin I scarcely knew.

As he had in Dresdin's Forge, Elias Winston recognized me beneath my helm—though my black dragon scale armor was admittedly distinct. He grinned and turned to motion for his people to stand down. "Andrew! I'd hoped to find you here."

I lifted an eyebrow. "Is that so?" I asked, uncertainty clawing at my belly once more.

He laughed and gestured to his soldiers. "I received word several days ago that you and Thomas had defeated the king's army. I'd been preparing for that eventuality. I put my garrison on standby and marched to meet you once I was certain of the battle's outcome. As I told your brother in Dresdin's Forge, I want to see him on the throne in place of the tyrant. I've come to lend my aid, now that I know my family will remain safe."

I returned his smile, allowing myself to relax. "When Thomas heard you were nearby, he was less than happy about the news. He feared you were here at the king's behest."

He frowned in confusion. "I've had no communication from the king in months. He didn't even bother to reply to the message I wrote on Thomas' behalf. I wasn't certain he received it until I heard of your victory. I knew then that he had."

I nodded, relieved. "The warning of your approach came on the heels of news that soldiers from the castle's garrison are nearing our location as well. We couldn't be certain of your intent, and truthfully, Tom didn't want me to engage you as I did." I didn't mention the reason for my brother's reticence; Elias would learn the details soon enough.

"The garrison is marching here?" The duke's expression was dismayed as he looked away. "That means I most likely received a summons to rendezvous here, but it would have arrived after my departure. If the king's messenger found me gone, it will only be a short time before word reaches your arrogant half-brother that I'm not in Dresdin's Forge. It won't take him long to piece together what I've done." He drew a breath and steeled himself. "No matter. I have cast my lot with Thomas. My people are here to support his claim to the throne."

"Thomas will be pleased to hear it," I replied. "If you'll have your people follow us, we'll lead you to the camp."

As we began our trek back, I glanced toward the duke, who had taken up position at my side. "Do your people know of our unusual allies?"

He nodded. "I've told them of the Corodan. And about you, of course."

"Alexander's people are here," I said slowly, gauging his reaction. "He is changed, Elias, as all mages are. You'll recognize him, and his personality is much the same, but it will be evident that he's different than the Alexander of your memories. There are a large number of other magi with him, and many Merael as well."

"Ah," the duke said thoughtfully, "I understand your meaning. I informed my people that Alex would be joining you, though I didn't know he'd already done so. As you'll recall, the king's soldiers weren't kind to the people of Dresdin's Forge when they scoured the area looking for Marks. Most of my soldiers lost family or friends during the inspections. I don't believe they'll pose trouble for the magi, though we should monitor their interactions for a time."

I nodded. "Alex will no doubt be waiting for my return. I'll leave the business of magi to him."

I carefully omitted the fact that Alexander would likely berate me the instant we came into view. But my gamble had paid off, and Elias Winston had come as an ally—my brothers had no reason to be upset.

"I don't know of the Merael," the duke mused after a moment. "Tell me of them."

While I described what I knew of the Merael people, we drew nearer to the camp. The duke listened attentively, and when I mentioned the Merael were particularly wary of me, his eyebrows rose with surprise.

"The very people who are capable of speaking to the trees and wild creatures fear you because of your own unusual nature?" he asked, incredulous. "To me, *their* gifts seem strange and worth fearing far more than your own."

"Those gifts are rare amongst their kind," I replied. "Most of the Merael you'll encounter have neither, but they've come to lend their support to the magi nevertheless."

"You didn't answer me, Andrew."

I sighed and shrugged noncommittally. "I've spent most of my damned life terrified of discovery. That Tom and Alex accept me as I am, and that most of the people from the Southlands hold the dragon-kind in high regard brings me much consolation. That a small number of people fear me is to be expected, I suppose. Even amongst my father's people, skin-changers were rare, and based on what I've learned from my father, I was the first in several generations. I'm the only one he ever encountered, and I've estimated his age at more than three centuries."

He stared at me for several seconds, a spark of curiosity burning deep within his green eyes. "You speak as though you've met your father. We were told for nearly four decades that they fled this world, abandoning its people to fend for themselves because we humans were too cruel."

I nodded. "They left just as we were told, Elias. My father and two others were responsible for opening the gateway, but powerful magic doesn't come without cost. They were petrified during the process. They're aware of their surroundings, and with the assistance of a mage, I've spoken with them."

He nodded thoughtfully. "That explains why he refused to take your mother with him when he departed Dresdin's Forge. He knew what his fate would be, that he would have no future with her."

"He told me once he would have taken her, had he known she was with child." I shook my head, wondering how different my life might have been had my mother left Dresdin's Forge with my father. "If he'd done so, I wouldn't have grown up on this world."

"Do you regret your fate, Andrew?"

I snorted. "No, and you aren't the first to ask me. I'm glad I've had the opportunity to grow up with my brothers, despite Colin's recent downward spiral. I'm grateful I was given the opportunity to meet my father and speak with him. He *knew* me, Elias, even before I changed forms." I smiled at the memory. "Apparently, I look just as much like him when in my dragon form as I look like my mother right now."

"Carra was smitten," he said wistfully. "Her father—my uncle, the former Duke Winston—was furious that she'd taken such interest in a mere merchant. Now that I know the truth, I understand why she was so heartbroken when he departed. There was another merchant with him, if I recall that time correctly. I was but a boy, then. My memory may be faulty."

I nodded. "That would have been Caelmarion Zorai, though I don't recall what name he gave while posing as a merchant. Like my father, he was trapped in stone when the gateway was opened. I've spoken with him on occasion too."

"Ah, yes, Cael Masterson. It isn't so different from Caelmarion." Elias flashed a grin. "Your father went by the name of Zayne Blackwell, though Carra called him by another name sometimes. It was something along the lines of Cane or Con. It was a strange name, one that stood out in my memory."

"Caein," I said. "My father's name is Zayneldarion Caein. I've taken the Caein name as my own."

Elias studied me for a time, his expression unreadable. "Andrew Caein does have a better ring to it than Andrew Marsden ever did. I wondered what you might do when the governor's council stripped you of your former name."

"I went without for a time," I admitted. "It wasn't until after I met my father that I took the Caein name. Vera learned of the two dragons who had traveled to Dresdin's Forge and shared her findings with me, but I was never certain which was my father until the Oracle mistook me for Zayneldarion. I knew then."

Elias frowned. "Your mother never told you of him?"

I shrugged. "She once mentioned I looked like him when in my dragon form, but she said little else. She was bitter about his departure, even when she lay dying. I'd hoped she would tell me more, but she refused. I didn't even know his name until Vera discovered it in one of her late husband's books."

He laughed. "Old Lord Sandson had a penchant for illegal books? I'm not surprised. The old man did as he wished, no matter what the laws stated."

"Tom loved Vinterry's library. There were a number of books containing information about dragons. During the summer when he and Alex came to visit, Tom spent hours there. We had to remind him to eat, he was so enthralled." I shook my head, amused. "Those were better times. Happier times."

"It may take a while, but we'll see days like them again," Elias replied. "Tyrants like Colin make a mess of things, but in the end, they always fall. Life carries on, and eventually what was broken is mended, what was destroyed regrows. I believe peace will return to Novania if we fight against the oppression your brother is responsible for. From the looks of it, you've made a good start." He gestured ahead, indicating the camp as it came into view, half-hidden behind stands of trees.

There was movement near the northern perimeter. As we drew nearer, I spied Jonas and several soldiers shading their eyes from the afternoon sun as they watched our approach. Not far behind them was the unmistakable figure of Alexander in his dragon scale armor. His arms were crossed and he scowled in my direction, clearly furious. Jonas and his men stood just beyond the wooden palisade that had been erected around the camp, while Alexander glowered from a gap in the line. I signaled to Jonas that all was well, hoping to mollify Alexander before we arrived.

"Ah, damn," I muttered. "Alex is going to give me hell for going out to meet your party as I did."

"He does appear displeased," Elias agreed with a laugh. "I'm certain you've survived worse in your time."

"You don't know the half of what I'm in for today," I replied cryptically.

Jonas strode toward us when we were a few paces from the camp's perimeter fortifications. "Thomas will be expecting you, Duke Winston," he stated, his steely eyes assessing the other man carefully. "I've sent word ahead of your arrival."

"Thank you." Elias gestured toward his soldiers, clustered behind us. "I'd like to see my people settled before I meet with him, if that is acceptable."

Jonas nodded warily. "Of course. Several of my own garrison are ready to assist." His eyes shifted to meet mine. "Alexander wants to speak with you."

"No doubt." I glanced beyond Jonas to the gap in the palisade where Alexander continued to fume. "I'll speak with him now. We'll talk again later, cousin," I said to Elias as I strode toward my furious half-brother.

I hadn't even reached Alexander's position when he launched into a tirade. "Damn it, Andrew, you've only just recovered from your last ordeal, and you go and defy us both! We have enough to deal with as it is, given that Colin's people will be within sight of this camp tomorrow. We don't need you laid up with injury again, you reckless damned bastard. For the love of all that is holy, why did you get it in your damned fool head to do this, exposing yourself to who-knows-what? Holy hell, you can be the most stubborn, the most difficult…Argh!"

He'd grown red in the face as he shouted. Having expended much of his rage, he stomped away and stood with his back toward me for several seconds. I knew from experience not to approach him—he was likely to strike me if I came within arm's reach.

Before his pilgrimage, I would have risked the move; my superior strength would have given me a marked advantage over any physical assault he attempted. Now that he'd changed and was still learning the limits of his newfound power, I decided it was best to leave him be. It wouldn't do for our old antics to be the source of an injury. I may have deserved a pummeling for my insubordination, but it would leave him wracked with guilt afterward, and I didn't want to fight.

I remained where I was and studied his back until he was ready to speak.

When Alexander finally turned around, he stared at me in silence for a time. The fury that had colored his cheeks during his outburst had faded and he appeared exhausted.

"I expected you to storm toward me as you typically do," he said after a moment. "I understand why you didn't. I… I may have done something I would have come to regret."

I nodded. "I know, brother."

He sighed wearily. "You should not have gone to meet Elias on your own. What if he had attacked?"

"He didn't, and I suspected that he wouldn't have done so. Tom allowed his emotions to get the best of him, but given the news you received from Galewing, I understand. I trust Elias." I crossed my arms and frowned. "I should remind Tom of what was said in Dresdin's Forge. Elias bears no love for Colin, and the only reason he didn't join us sooner was out of concern for his family. Once he learned we'd won the battle against Claybourne, he moved out immediately to join us. He said he hasn't received any word from Colin in months, and I believe him."

Alexander nodded. "You've made your point, brother. You were right about Elias and proved we had no grounds for worry. But if he *had* been hostile, we would have been without your aid tomorrow when we'll likely need it. Not to mention that Lydia would have flayed me alive," he added with a wry grin.

I laughed. "She's good for you, Alex."

"Yes, she is. For what it's worth, I'm glad we were wrong about Elias. Of the little family we have remaining from mother's side, I've always liked him the best."

I avoided the center of the camp for the remainder of the day, busying myself with various tasks from Jonas in preparation for the arrival of the king's men. I spotted Alexander on occasion, as well as some of the others who had been present when news of Duke Winston's approach had reached us, but I saw nothing of Thomas.

As evening descended, I made my way toward the healers' tents with the hope of visiting Rynn. The day had been filled with activity, and after having spent nearly a week idling in recovery, the sudden flurry of tasks had left me fatigued. I'd see Rynn, find a meal, then turn in for the night. I had no intention of speaking with my brothers.

Thomas had other plans.

I was waylaid as I strode through the last of the soldiers' tents and neared the area where the healers were set up. Thomas stormed toward me with a scowl on his face, his blue eyes hard and unyielding. Seldom had I witnessed Thomas angry, and this was the second time in one day. I halted as I noted his approach and raked one hand through my hair.

"I'm aware of what you did, Andrew," he said by way of greeting. "I'm not pleased."

"I assume you've spoken with Alex?" I asked. I was weary and didn't want to prolong the conversation, nor did I want to relive a repeat performance of Alexander's tirade.

"Yes. You're damned stubborn, though I'll admit I'm glad I was wrong about Elias." He sighed with a shake of his head, seeming to deflate. As his fury drained away, he appeared deeply exhausted. "I can't keep up the pretense of being angry with you. You gave us an opportunity to truly focus our defenses where they needed to be, rather than spreading ourselves unnecessarily thin. I still have much to learn when it comes to leadership—and even more regarding military affairs."

"I'll remind you once more—your father had a number of advisors and the governor's council to help him with various matters of state. You'll never be forced to make a decision on your own unless you choose to do so."

He forced a tired smile. "Yes, and I thank you for that as well. I wasn't angry with you for meeting with Elias. Someone needed to do it. I just wish you would have allowed another to go in your stead. By your own account, we nearly lost you to Claybourne's torture. I don't want to think about life without my eldest brother in it. Alex has always looked up to you, and though I didn't know you well before this winter, I've come to respect you. I consider you more than just a brother, Andrew. You're a great friend. Please don't put yourself at risk like that again."

I nodded as I belatedly understood the source of Thomas' frustration and Alexander's rage. Perhaps I'd acted rashly, but I would not apologize for the outcome. I'd done what was needed when it was required, just as I always had.

"I suppose you came to see Rynn," Thomas said after a moment. When I nodded again, he said, "I won't keep you. We'll speak later, perhaps tomorrow, if circumstance allows."

"Take care, Tom," I said as he began to walk away.

He paused briefly to glance over his shoulder, smiling in spite of his obvious fatigue. He hadn't been sleeping enough, and the burden of leadership weighed heavily on him. I wished there was more I could do for him, if only he'd give me the chance.

I resumed my trek and entered the healer's tent without invitation. Rynn was propped against a pillow, her eyes fixed on the canvas ceiling above until I seated myself at her side.

She turned toward me with a grin. "I'm glad you found time to visit. I've heard rumors you were busy."

I grimaced. "I met with Duke Winston."

She smirked. "I know. Lydia said your brothers were furious, but it seemed everything worked out well enough."

"They were, and it did." I shifted slightly and drew my arm around her. "I'm certain you've also heard the king's men are moving toward our location."

Her smile faltered as she nodded. "And I'm relegated *here*, where I'm less than useless."

"You'll be on your feet again soon enough," I assured her.

She sighed. "Not soon enough for my liking. Lydia said it may be weeks. I can't sit here for *weeks*, Andrew."

"If I could share my healing ability with you, I would," I replied. "But let the healers determine what's best, Rynn. Tomorrow won't be the only battle."

She rolled her eyes. "I'm not eager for battle. I just want to do my part, and I can't while I'm stuck here."

We chatted for some time. Before I left, I promised her I'd return when I was able. She drew me toward her and we kissed passionately. When our lips parted, I gazed at her, yearning for more—but now wasn't the time, nor was it the place. There was little privacy in the confines of the healers' tents, and the same smug bastard who had shamelessly stared at us a few nights ago was still there, grinning like the damned fool he was.

I gazed at her longingly, transfixed by the vibrancy of her blue eyes. "I wish I didn't have to leave. But I must."

"I know," she replied with a smile. "Be safe, dragon-man."

As I rose to leave, Lydia entered the tent in a flurry and nearly collided with me. I blinked and stepped aside, narrowly avoiding her.

"Andrew, I apologize," she said breathlessly. "I'd hoped to find you here. Have you seen Alex?"

"It's been a few hours," I replied, "but he's likely with Tom or one of the others planning our strategy for tomorrow."

She nodded briskly, though her expression was troubled. "If you see him, will you ask him to meet me here? I've a number of people to tend to, but something has come up, and I must speak with him."

"I'll tell him," I promised. "Is everything well?"

She laughed nervously. "Perhaps, but I need to speak with Alex first. Please tell him it's important."

I nodded. "Of course."

She managed a smile then. "Thank you." She turned toward Rynn, and I was left with the task of locating my brother.

I found Alexander at the heart of the camp, standing in the open doorway of Thomas' tent, deep in conversation with Elias. The two were thoroughly engrossed in their discussion and didn't heed my approach. I stopped a few paces away, hoping to catch their attention without interrupting.

"...and then he told me *I* was changing," Alexander said with a laugh. "I told him the irony of that statement wasn't lost on me, given that *he* is the expert on change."

Elias chuckled and looked up, noting my presence. "It seems your expert has arrived, cousin."

"I didn't mean to disrupt your story, brother," I said dryly. "I know how you love telling tales about me."

He snorted. "Elias hasn't heard half of them yet. We could go on for hours, you know."

"Truly, Alex was sharing more of his own tales than he was of yours," Elias said. "I wanted to learn more of the magi."

Alexander grinned. "Since you were present during my trials, it was impossible to leave you out of the story, Andrew. Now, what brings you here, brother?"

"Lydia," I replied. "She's busy, but she said she wanted to speak with you. She wouldn't tell me anything more."

"Then I should go." To Elias, he said, "We'll talk later, cousin. I've many more tales to share of our adventures in the Southlands."

Elias chuckled as Alexander departed. "He seems remarkably well, considering everything you've been through." He paused to fix me with a concerned expression. "He told me what Claybourne did to you."

"I've recovered," I replied briskly. I didn't need more sympathy—I'd heard my fill over the past week.

He nodded. "Yes, I can see that. Thomas said you heal rapidly, but I still find it difficult to believe you were rescued less than a week ago." He shrugged, allowing the matter to drop. "Where can one find a decent meal in this camp? I haven't eaten since before I arrived."

I motioned for him to follow. We walked between several tents before arriving at an open area not far away, where several campfires burned. A number of people stood near the fires, some cooking, others awaiting their portions while they engaged in casual conversation. The aroma of roasting meat wafted through the air, and my stomach rumbled loudly in anticipation.

Elias laughed. "It seems I'm not the only one in need of a meal."

"It's my last order of business for the day," I replied as we joined the queue.

"While I was speaking with Alex, he told me much about the magi, but also many things about you. He mentioned you seem to have gained a penchant for flying." A wistful smile played across his lips. "Tell me—what is it like to soar amongst the clouds?"

With a laugh, I began to describe the sensations as best I could. Alexander wasn't wrong; I had developed a love for flight. The rush of the air across my scales, the exhilaration of a steep dive toward the earth, the ease with which my wings caught the air to keep me aloft, the spectacular view of the ground, so far below as I sailed through the sky—all were moments I'd come to cherish. Fortune had played its hand against me, and much of my time in the air had been borne of necessity rather than pleasure. Perhaps one day that would change.

Elias gazed skyward as I finished speaking. "To have such freedom must be incredible. To be denied it, a travesty. It's no wonder your father's people quit this world when they did." He shook his head. "We must do something to bring about change. You should not succumb to the same oppression they endured."

"I've never considered it in those terms." I sighed, melancholy.

If I survived to see the end of this war, I'd ask my father what his feelings were on the matter of the dragons' departure and their reasons behind it. It wasn't a topic we'd discussed during my brief visits to the Stone Grove. When I encountered the spirit of Davereth in the Dragonlands, he'd expressed disapproval when I'd informed him the dragons had fled. I'd left my encounter with Davereth with the belief that not all dragons had agreed on the exodus, but in the end, the only dragons who remained were those responsible for opening the gateway.

As the only member of the dragon-kind not currently petrified, I was utterly alone in representing our specific plight. I believed Thomas would keep his promise regarding the elimination of the old laws should we succeed in ousting Colin from the throne, and that knowledge gave me a measure of comfort. If we failed in our mission, there was a good chance I would not survive my final encounter with Colin, and the legacy of the dragon-kind would come to a bloody and brutal end.

"I believe Thomas will make things right," Elias said in an effort to lift my spirits. "We simply must place him in a position to do so. And we will."

TEN

The southern perimeter of the camp was heavily fortified as we awaited the arrival of the king's garrison. The mood amongst the soldiers and magi that morning was one of cautious optimism mingled with the tension always present before the onset of a battle.

We had the advantage of superior numbers, and my brothers believed the king's soldiers were unaware of our presence. The Corodan dug trenches a short distance from the ramshackle wooden palisade, further bolstering our defensive position, while several magi had prepared various traps farther afield. A number of trees had been coaxed toward a new location that better facilitated our needs, thanks to the Merael Tree-speakers.

To witness Novanians working alongside magi, Merael, and Corodan was an event that hadn't occurred since ancient times. I was proud of Thomas and Alexander for their determination and charisma—to facilitate this gathering of forces was remarkable. No matter what lay ahead, I knew my two half-brothers would share a bright future.

I paced the southern perimeter as the morning dragged on, unable to remain still. Jonas had not given me an assignment, deferring to Alexander's overprotective eye on the matter. My brother hadn't sought me out, busy as he was with the positioning of the magi. I was restless and tense in anticipation of the battle to come. The sensation was familiar, but left with nothing to occupy my time, the wait became intolerable.

It was nearing midday by the time Alexander appeared. He wore his black dragon scale armor, the helm cradled in the crook of his arm, and a pair of swords were scabbarded at his waist. One was of standard craftsmanship, while the other was his cursed blade. In all my years of campaigning with him, he'd never carried more than one weapon into battle, but the physical changes he'd undergone at the conclusion of his trial had granted him the strength and confidence to wield both simultaneously. I recalled his confrontation with Claybourne when he'd utilized both weapons skillfully—and seemingly with ease.

He flashed a grin. "I'm glad I finally located you. I should have known you'd be pacing like a caged animal in anticipation of the fight."

I grunted noncommittally and crossed my arms. "Jonas said you'd seek me out eventually."

"Well, yes." He scratched at the back of his neck and made a face. "Tom and I were discussing the strategy early this morning, and I thought it best if we stayed together. Like old times."

I lifted my eyebrows, certain there was more to this placement than he'd admitted. "No, Alex, it's not like 'old times.' Tom wants to make certain I won't get captured again, and with your newfound abilities, you thought you'd be equipped for the task."

Alexander laughed uncomfortably and stared at his boots. "Today will be little more than a skirmish. We can't risk losing you, and you've only just recovered."

"I'd like to remind you that I have far more experience in battle than you, brother," I replied evenly. I wasn't angry. No, I understood his concerns well enough. "I'll be fine, though I'll admit I'm curious to see your mage-warrior skills in action."

He brightened when he realized I wasn't upset by their decision. "I suppose you were a bit preoccupied when we raided Claybourne's position." He motioned for me to follow him, and we began to walk toward the center of the camp's southern fortifications. "Based on what Galewing has shown me, the king's garrison should be heading directly toward that point." He indicated an area near the center of the palisade where Thomas' dragon standard hung above our forces, rippling gently in the breeze.

"And knowing you as I do, you plan to be in the thick of it."

He grinned. "I do. Most of our soldiers will be focused there as well. I've asked the mages to strike from the sides, but from a distance." He glanced at me, his green eyes concerned. "I've asked them not to strike near our location. We should be distinguishable enough from the rest with the dragon scale we both wear."

I nodded. "I hadn't factored in the magi. I should thank you for warning them away from me."

He clapped his hand against my shoulder with a laugh. "What sort of brother would I be if I allowed my own people to inadvertently cause you harm?" He eyed me for a moment, mischief in his glance. "Perhaps it's best you don't answer that."

I laughed good-naturedly at his insinuation; I'd never compare Alexander to Colin, and he knew it.

As we approached the palisade, we were greeted by Jonas and Elias. Jonas' gray eyes were unreadable, but Elias grinned much as Alexander had moments before.

"We've received a report from our scouts," Elias said.

Jonas frowned momentarily at the other duke. "The king's soldiers should be visible beyond the trees within minutes. The fight is nearly upon us."

"We'll move into position," Alexander replied.

He led me to a place just beyond the palisade, where a number of our soldiers formed ranks in anticipation of the skirmish. He stopped near the center of the line, pausing to flash a grin in my direction before donning his helm.

"I've been looking forward to this day, brother," he said. "It's the day when you no longer have to act as my protector, and I have the chance to show you what I'm truly capable of." He laughed wickedly. "Try to keep up."

I chuckled and pulled on my own helm. I recalled how swiftly he moved when he utilized his magic; he'd become a veritable blur of motion at times during his brief fight with Claybourne. I would never keep pace with him while he was in that state, and he knew it.

"If I can trust you to refrain from using your magic, perhaps I'll manage," I shot back with a smirk. "I wasn't completely unaware of how you handled Claybourne."

Alexander's jovial mood soured at the mention of Robert Claybourne. "I held back. I wanted to kill the bastard for what he'd done to you, but I didn't want to be labeled as merciless. I will not be compared to Colin."

I nodded but made no reply.

The next few minutes were spent in tense anticipation. When the first of the king's soldiers appeared, cresting a gentle rise in the lightly forested landscape, my hand instinctively reached for my sword. They pressed forward for a short time, then someone called the alarm as they recognized Thomas' banner. Behind us, Jonas began to call orders to the archers and magi.

As the king's soldiers hurriedly assumed a battle formation, the trees near their location began to rustle with far more energy than the breeze wafting through them could have produced. I glanced questioningly at Alexander, but his green-eyed gaze was focused on the enemy and he didn't notice. I wondered if I was witnessing the work of the Tree-speakers or if one of the mages was responsible.

The enemy began to march forward, and Jonas shouted for the archers and magi stationed behind the palisade to begin the attack.

The movement within the trees intensified. I watched, transfixed, as one of the trees bent nearly double and swung its heavy branches directly into a pair of soldiers. Cries of surprise erupted from the king's soldiers, but the man at their head ordered them to press on. More trees joined the assault, bending and swaying in unnatural patterns to strike with their boughs. The king's soldiers scrambled and cursed as they skirted the trees. Arrows began whistling between them. A few soldiers fell, but most avoided the missiles.

"Holy hell," I whispered, astonished.

Alexander laughed. "Our Merael friends may not be magi, but they certainly have impressive talents."

I detected a hint of pride in his tone. He was pleased with the outcome of his dealings with the Oracle and the peoples of the Southlands and had taken his role as their leader in stride. Without Alexander's prompting, it was likely none of them would have traveled north from the Mage's Gate, and our hope of defeating Colin would be far more precarious than it was.

"I'm certainly glad they're on our side," I replied after a moment. "Shit. I didn't know trees could bend like that."

Alexander grinned. "You haven't seen anything yet."

The king's people continued to advance, but gave a wide berth to the trees where they could. As the first ranks reached a point midway between the crest of the hill and the palisade, the ground erupted into a flurry of motion as dozens of Corodan poured from a concealed trench. I glimpsed Rizzt-tok in the center of the melee as she slashed and stabbed with her serrated forelegs.

Jonas called for the ground troops to engage and ordered the archers to hold their fire.

Alexander cast a sideways glance in my direction, his eyes mischievous within his black helm. "Are you ready, brother?"

Without waiting for a reply, he pressed forward with the other soldiers and unsheathed both swords. I drew my own weapon and kept pace with him easily enough—for the moment. I hadn't yet detected the metallic, blood-drenched odor that accompanied his magic, but as we drew near the epicenter of the battle, I realized it would be difficult to smell it. The stench of blood would accompany the wounded and uninjured alike.

Near the edges of the fighting, blasts of fire began to erupt, no doubt the work of one or both of the Roche twins. A bank of thick fog formed near the rear of the enemy lines, blocking their escape and concealing anyone who might be present on the other side. Small rocks and pebbles rained down amongst the enemies on the fringes while the trees continued their unnatural assault.

My attention was drawn from the array of magical attacks as we came upon the ranks of soldiers engaged with the Corodan. Their leader stood in the midst of the fray, issuing orders to his people calmly.

With his helm lowered, I was uncertain if he was the same man who had spoken to Robert Claybourne outside the Green Fords, but it wasn't Claybourne who led this group. This man was cool under pressure, calculating, and far more efficient. His soldiers formed a semi-circle, holding their own against our assault, while simultaneously protecting their commander. These men had faced Corodan before and had prepared accordingly.

Seconds later, I was engulfed in the battle. The clash of steel, the cries of soldiers from both sides, and the buzzing hum the Corodan produced while fighting melded to become a roar in my ears. One of the king's soldiers cut through the abdomen of the nearest Corodan. The giant insect produced an ominous clicking sound as it fell forward, ichor spilling from its wound to paint the grass in a blue-gray sheen. Alexander and I moved forward to fill the gap, swords at the ready.

I was no stranger to battle, but I'd rarely been forced to turn my blade against my own people. The necessity of what I was about to do wasn't lost on me, but it filled me with a deep regret all the same. The fate of Novania should never have come to this bitter struggle that pitted us against our brother, fighting for our right to exist.

The man who had slain the Corodan faced me, and I caught a flicker of recognition in his eyes. He frowned grimly and braced himself even as I swung my blade toward him. He deflected the blow with his shield, but the force of the impact caused him to stagger backward. Alexander was engaged with a pair of soldiers, parrying their attacks with apparent ease.

"Stop holding back, Andrew," he growled. "We're not on the practice field any longer!"

I'd never utilized my full strength against a human being, and I was terrified to do so. I feared the carnage I was capable of, the destruction I'd leave in my wake. When it came to sheer power, I had a distinct advantage over everyone present on the field, with the exception of Alexander. But to utilize it could very well change the fundamental perception I had of myself. I harbored the potential for devastation, the potential to become a monster.

The man I faced steadied himself, his keen gaze locked on mine as he waited for my next strike. I feinted left. He lifted his shield across his body in an attempt to block the anticipated blow, but the action exposed his side. I turned my blade in a maneuver borne from years of practice and struck. I didn't use my full strength, but my blade pierced his armor as though it were constructed of little more than parchment. I wrenched it free as he stumbled and fell.

At the same moment, Alexander dispatched one of his adversaries while simultaneously inflicting a superficial wound on the other. He focused his full attention on the remaining soldier, engaging both of his swords in the fight. I didn't believe he'd channeled his magic yet, but his opponent could scarcely keep up with the dual assault.

Another pair of enemies pushed forward to fill in the hole left by their fallen comrades. I heard their leader some distance away, shouting for his people to hold the line and to focus their attacks on the "black-armored fiends."

Alexander and I were in for a deadlier fight than we'd bargained for. I braced myself and faced the next wave.

I parried a blow from one soldier while blocking the other's attack with my left forearm. The dragon scale armor withstood the strike, and I shoved the attacker backwards with as much strength as I could muster. She was lifted off her feet to fall amongst the ranks of soldiers to her rear. She appeared dazed but unhurt. I shifted my attention to her companion.

I shoved him backward with my blade, which forced him to disengage his axe to maintain his balance. He narrowed his eyes and charged forward silently. At the last moment, he swung his axe in an underhanded fashion, planning to strike my left side while I adjusted my stance. I'd anticipated that his second strike would be a mirror of his first, a costly mistake that would have been dire had I not been clad in dragon scale.

The axe struck my side with a thud. I expected to feel the bite of his blade as it buried itself in my flesh, but the black armor refused to yield. I'd sport a bruise for a time, but my armor—and my side—were unscathed.

Stunned, the man stepped back, his eyes wide. What should have been a near-fatal blow had failed to make a scratch. I smirked in response.

I had a fraction of a second to react. I darted forward, thrusting my blade toward his abdomen with tremendous force. He blocked the blow with his shield, but when my sword met the wooden disc, it cracked, then shattered. He took another step backwards and breathed heavily while shaking the remnants of the broken shield free of his arm. He shook his head and brandished his axe, prepared for another attack.

A glimmer of movement at the periphery of my vision drew my eye. I lifted my sword just enough to parry the intended blow from a new opponent. I shoved my assailant away, but he nimbly maintained his footing and charged toward me again. The axe-wielding man did the same.

I could not block both blows. I stood my ground, facing the man with the axe, while hoping my armor would withstand yet another strike to the same side.

The axe-wielding soldier reached me first, and I arced my sword toward his head, forcing him onto the defensive. There was a flicker of motion on my left, and I braced myself for an attack that failed to come. Startled, I glanced away to find Alexander had seemingly materialized in the space. Both of his swords had found their mark, piercing the attacker's abdomen and left shoulder. The axe-wielding adversary shoved me forcefully while I was momentarily distracted.

Alexander glanced over his shoulder, his expression fierce. "Damn it, Andrew, we've no time for games. Stop holding back. Colin won't hesitate to kill us, given the chance."

With a grunt, he wrenched his swords free, then pivoted swiftly to face the next set of attackers. He moved in a blur, the scent of blood in his wake, no longer assuming the pretense of an ordinary soldier. His next strikes came so rapidly, the enemy wasn't left with an opportunity to react. They fell before him, even as he turned toward his next intended target.

I refocused my attention on the man with the axe as he charged forward once more. I clenched my jaw in frustration. My brother was right, yet I wished for all the world it was otherwise. These people didn't deserve to be killed due to the folly of their king, but if I refrained from holding myself back any longer, many of them wouldn't survive the day. Alexander seemed to have accepted this inevitability, but I remained conflicted. Each life I ended would weigh heavily on my soul.

Colin was the true villain, not those who had been duped into fighting for his cause, but what choice did I have?

As our blades collided once more, I stared down my assailant. "Why do you persist in this attack?" I growled, hoping his answer would put an end to my dilemma.

He narrowed his eyes and shoved at my blade. I didn't backpedal, nor did I yield. I loomed over him, daring him with my eyes to provide an answer.

"The king has decreed that all unnatural folk must be destroyed."

I frowned, disappointed but unsurprised by his response. Perhaps Alexander was right and the time for civility was long past.

I shoved him backwards hard enough to make him stumble. I bore down on him, unrelenting. I swung my sword in a deadly, sideways arc before he recovered his balance, and paused only briefly to glower at him as he fell. My sword sliced through armor, flesh, bone… And my assailant fell, cleaved nearly in two.

I turned to face the next attackers. I couldn't afford to allow myself time to dwell on what I'd done. Blood dripped from my blade, gore spattered my armor, and I'd only just begun.

The fight continued well into the afternoon. Only after the king's soldiers had been nearly decimated did their commander issue the order to lay down their arms in surrender. What had begun as a force of perhaps two hundred had been reduced to a few dozen. They'd been unable to compete with the combined force of magi, Merael, human soldiers, and Corodan.

After my encounter with the axe-wielding soldier, I'd torn through the enemies with scarcely a thought. I'd become numb, yet incensed that Colin had persuaded his followers that what I was and what Alexander had become was unnatural. We were responsible for countless enemy dead.

I knew then that I'd never call Novania home again. The people would never forgive what I'd done, no matter the reason behind it. When the war was over, I'd depart south just as I'd discussed with Rynn. There was no place for me here any longer.

While Alexander and several others detained those who had surrendered, I turned away from the scene, my heart heavy. I'd long known that there would be no reasoning with Colin, but I'd nurtured the hope he'd give up the throne willingly before our conflict devolved into senseless bloodshed.

Instead, he'd sent an army south to face Alexander and one north to face Thomas. When both fronts had been defeated, he continued to order more soldiers to our location, regardless of our growing numbers, effectively wasting hundreds of innocent lives. Was Colin mad with power, unwilling to accept that he could not defeat us? Or was there something more driving his senseless behavior?

I found myself near the center of camp before I realized I'd walked so far. I sought my tent to remove my armor and don fresh clothing. I'd clean my gear the next day; I was weary and wanted nothing more than to sit at Rynn's side. I needed time to process the events of the day, the fragments of battle that I could recall, the knowledge I'd ended dozens of lives with relative ease. Maybe Colin was right in that respect—I *was* unnatural.

I stacked the blood-spattered armor in a pile near the door of my tent and leaned my sword next to it, making a mental note to thank my father for allowing me to use the armor he'd commissioned so long ago. I would have sustained severe injuries if I'd been wearing anything else.

After changing into clean garments, I felt marginally more human and less monster than when I'd quit the field. Battle was inevitably exhausting, but this was the first time in my many campaigns that I was heartsick over the result. Victory was ours, but I'd slain far too many Novanians to be pleased with the outcome. And it would never become easier.

Even after the rumors I'd heard of Colin's treachery against the kingdom and the pain I'd endured at Robert Claybourne's hands, I wondered if my actions were truly any better than theirs. They'd killed countless others, but now, so had I.

The battle at the keep had not left me as morose as I was now, and I'd dispatched my share of the king's soldiers during the first day of fighting. Some had been killed while I defended Jonathan Horace's position, but most had been slain after I'd flown him back to the keep. I'd known he wouldn't live to see the day's end. Rage and grief had spurred my actions then, and I recalled only brief scraps from that fateful afternoon.

I was uncertain why I felt as I did now. Today's battle had been pitched in much the same manner as its predecessor, yet my perception was markedly different.

As I entered the healers' tent and was greeted by one of Rynn's bright smiles, much of my melancholy melted away. I returned her smile and strode toward her, carefully avoiding the pallets of the injured who had arrived throughout the day.

I sat at her side and drew one arm around her. We didn't speak, and she seemed to sense I wasn't in the mood for conversation. I only wanted to spend the evening with her and allow myself a few hours to forget the grueling events of the day.

ELEVEN

The next few days passed uneventfully. There were no further signs that Colin had sent more troops towards our location, and the handful of Novanian soldiers that had surrendered were sent on their way. Most hoped to return to their families, though a few declared they'd return to their post in the Capitol, determined to continue their service to the "rightful king." Thomas didn't stop them, but he confiscated their weapons before they were allowed to depart. Those weapons were later distributed to our forces.

We'd lost a fair number of our people during the fighting, but hadn't suffered as severely as the king's soldiers. Several casualties were Corodan warriors, but Rizzt-tok assured us the hive remained steadfast in its desire to aid our cause. Most of the others were human, though two mages had been struck down as well. The Roche twins were kept busy each evening; they'd been tasked with lighting funeral pyres, while Lydia, Belora, and their growing number of assistants toiled amongst the wounded.

On the third morning after the battle, I was speaking with Jonas near my tent at the camp's heart when motion drew my attention. Rynn hobbled toward us clutching her satchel of belongings with a tentative smile on her lips.

I grinned and abruptly abandoned the conversation with Jonas mid-sentence. I strode toward her and gathered her into my arms. Damn, it was good to see her walking once more.

We kissed, heedless of who might witness the act. After a moment, she broke away with a soft laugh.

"I didn't mean to interrupt your conversation," she said, "though Jonas doesn't seem upset by your departure."

I chuckled. "We weren't discussing anything particularly important. It was small talk." I slipped my arm around her waist and led her toward my tent. "I doubt you want to carry your things about all day. Our trunk is within."

She smiled, then ducked inside while I returned to Jonas' location several paces away. Amusement twinkled in his steel-gray eyes.

"I'm glad she's recovered," he said, his eyes fixed on the tent. "Her skills are an asset to your brother's cause, and she doesn't seem the type to enjoy sitting idle."

I laughed. "She isn't."

Rynn emerged from the tent moments later and walked toward us. I watched her carefully; she favored her left leg, and I suspected it would be weeks before she was completely healed.

She arched an eyebrow as she stopped at my side. "I know what you're thinking, Andrew, and I'll not be dissuaded. I've done enough sitting during the past weeks to last a lifetime."

"I wasn't suggesting—" I began, but she cut me off with a laugh.

"Sometimes you are entirely too predictable." She laughed again, then turned to face Jonas. "I've been meaning to ask you this for a while. Has your arm healed properly?"

He nodded. "Yes. Alexander's wife saw to it after we arrived. She knew immediately what the cause of the injury was, even so many days later."

"Lydia is a good friend," she replied. "I'm glad there was no lasting damage. I would never have forgiven myself."

It took me a moment to realize what they were speaking of before memory crashed through me. While I'd been holding the crumbling section of the keep's wall to provide Rynn with time to drag herself to safety, Jonas had come from the other direction. He'd wrapped his cloak around his arm numerous times before reaching out to her, but it seemed the act hadn't been enough to protect him from a case of frostbite.

"I'd forgotten," I said after a moment. "I never properly thanked you for what you did that day."

"You had far more pressing matters to contend with," he replied with a shrug.

Footsteps approached from behind. I turned to find Alexander making his way toward our small group. He wasn't wearing his armor, but his sword belt was buckled around his waist, one weapon sheathed at each hip. He nodded to us, then to Jonas.

"Tom sent me to fetch the lot of you. He wants to discuss our next move." Alexander's expression was unreadable, but I detected a note of satisfaction in his tone.

As we began to walk toward Thomas' command tent, I glanced at Alexander. "You're in a good mood this morning."

He laughed. "Knowing that we're about to take the fight to Colin will do that."

I frowned. I'd known we'd eventually plan a direct strike against Colin's forces, but I hadn't been aware Thomas was prepared to act so soon. Alexander wouldn't elaborate any further, forcing me to wait until Thomas' group of chosen advisors and associates had been gathered.

We met around the oval table inside the command tent, awaiting the arrival of Shyala and Elias. Rynn leaned into my side, and I glanced at her in concern. She appeared uncomfortable, placing most of her weight on her right leg.

"Are you alright?" I whispered, unable to mask my worry.

She nodded, but stubbornly refused to acknowledge her pain. "Yes, just don't make any sudden movements. I'm using you for balance."

I drew my arm around her waist and held her steady. "You'll tell me if you need to sit down, won't you?"

Her laugh was mischievous. "Of course not." She shook her head, and her tone became serious even as she continued to smile. "I'm fine, Andrew."

"Hmm."

There was little she could say that would persuade me to place my concerns elsewhere. Her welfare would always be my priority, regardless of how loudly she protested—but I loved her independent spirit.

Several minutes passed before the last of Thomas' advisors arrived. Rynn and I remained standing at one side to allow those with more substantial roles to take up the central positions. I had no doubt that both Thomas and Alexander would have plans for me when it came to the next battle, but I was no longer in a role of leadership. The change suited me well enough—it gave me the opportunity to spend my free time as I wished, something I'd seldom been granted during my previous campaigns.

Thomas began by spreading a map across the table. It was exquisitely detailed, depicting the entirety of Novania, from the Gloaming Highlands in the north to the Mage's Gate and the Barrier in the south. The eastern and western borders ended at the sea. On the eastern side, where there had been extra space, the cartographer had drawn a stylized monster sporting a dozen tentacles. The map was not only detailed, but beautifully illustrated—it must have cost a small fortune to procure.

Thomas pointed to a location near the center of the map, where a stone castle was depicted. "I intend to make for the Capitol," he stated. "It's time we bring this fight to Colin's doorstep."

Predictably, Everett urged caution. "The Capitol will be heavily defended. As you know, it has been the seat of the monarchy for generations, and if Colin is within those walls, he'll have plenty of defenders."

Alexander laughed. "You're forgetting that we grew up in that city, Uncle. We know it well. Besides, Andrew used to head the garrison. He knows more about the city's defenses than anyone here."

I frowned at my brother, incredulous. "I can't claim knowledge of everything, Alex. I know what the Capitol's defenses *used to be* when your father sat on the throne. Rumor states Colin has been making changes."

"Nevertheless, it's the best start we have," Alexander replied, undeterred.

"We're in no position to move on the Capitol yet," Jonas said thoughtfully after a moment. "I wouldn't recommend trying to storm the city outright. If half of the tales regarding the king are true, he'll have few friends amongst the common folk, and we may be able to use that to our advantage."

"What are you thinking, Jonas?" Thomas asked.

"Perhaps we send a few chosen scouts to the city first, ones we can trust implicitly, who have the skills and know-how to avoid detection by the garrison," he replied. "The common people might provide information, and we can learn something of the king's arsenal as well. I'd like to take stock of the atmosphere in the Capitol before we march on it."

A brief flicker of disappointment flashed across Thomas' features, but he quelled the emotion as quickly as it had appeared. "That's wise."

Everett didn't fail to pick up on his mood. "We must do this right, my lord," he said evenly. "Even a seemingly insignificant mistake could upend all we've worked so hard to build. If we fail, there will be no recovery."

"I'm well aware of the stakes," Thomas replied wearily, pausing to run one hand through his hair. "My proposal comes now that we've defeated the bulk of Colin's army. Alex had success in the south, as we did in the north. And the battle earlier this week—"

I knew I must step in to say something. While he wasn't wrong about our victories, he was mistaken when it came to the true numbers of soldiers the king had at his disposal. I'd commanded those legions for more than a decade before I'd resigned my post, and I knew better than anyone present what we were truly facing.

If I knew Colin, he wouldn't have deployed his entire army to pursue us initially. He'd have sent only enough to feel confident in a swift victory. Our diversion in the north had forced Claybourne to split his men, and we'd taken full advantage of it on both fronts. But Colin had more resources at his disposal, and if we followed Thomas' plan and moved toward the Capitol now, it could prove a fatal mistake.

"Tom," I interrupted, "the army sent toward the Mage's Gate was impressive, but it wasn't half of what Novania can muster. I glimpsed that army when I traveled north toward the highlands. Your uncle is right—we must make our next move carefully."

"But the Northern Marches are on our side—"

Jonas chuckled and shook his head with amusement, while Everett reached out to place a hand on Thomas' shoulder.

"We understand your desire to move forward," Everett said gently, "but we have not yet witnessed the true might of the Novanian army.

Our location is no longer a secret. While I agree that we should move before long, I must urge you toward caution."

"I stand with Jonas in this matter," I stated. "We should send scouts into the city before we make a show of force. We need more information."

Alexander glowered at his boots, unable to hide his disappointment. "I say we move on the Capitol," he replied stubbornly. "Take Colin unaware and unprepared. One swift strike and all of this will be over. I stand with Tom."

"Ultimately, the decision will lie with him," I conceded, "but it would be foolish to attempt a strike on Colin's stronghold without gathering more information."

Thomas appeared troubled and slowly looked at each of us in turn. "I don't believe I can make a decision yet," he said after a few moments. "I thought our plan was solid, but it seems I was thinking rashly. Does anyone else have further insight to share? I've gathered you here because I trust your judgment and value your advice."

Alexander scowled, and I immediately understood most of Thomas' earlier words had been borne of Alexander's plans. They bore the hallmarks typical of Alexander—charging head-long into the fray without forethought, trusting in his skill alone to see him safely through.

How many times over the years had I been forced to fight my way to my brother's location in order to save him from a reckless ploy? With his newfound magical abilities, Alexander had only grown more brazen, and I feared he overestimated himself. I hoped Thomas would see reason where Alexander would not, that he'd avoid leading us to certain disaster.

"Speaking as one who is unfamiliar with these lands, I wouldn't be willing to risk my people in a brash gamble," Shyala said. "The Merael have long remained outside the realm of such conflicts, but we agreed to follow Alexander north when the Oracle foresaw the Barrier's destruction. This threat must be dealt with, but I won't see my people slaughtered foolishly because you choose to act without considering the consequences."

She stared directly at Alexander as she spoke, and I sensed her words had some effect. We needed all the allies we'd gathered if we were to succeed, and she'd made it clear we'd lose the support of the Merael if Alexander continued to push forward with his scheme. He looked down as she finished speaking and nodded thoughtfully, resignation in his eyes.

"I agree," Rynn said and pushed away from my side. She winced as she placed her left foot on the ground, but continued, determined to speak her mind. "You may have been placed in your role by the Oracle, but you're unfamiliar with the people of the south. Novania is strange to many of us, and we trust you to lead us through it safely. I know casualties are inevitable in any conflict, but minimizing them would be wise. I believe I speak for all of us when I say we'd like to see our homes again when this is over."

There were murmured assents from the group as she stepped back. She leaned into me to take the weight off her injured leg, but her eyes remained fixed on Alexander. I smiled at her, proud she'd spoken for the magi when Alexander's brash attitude would have prevented their concerns from being heard.

When I looked away from Rynn, I noted with some concern that Alexander appeared despondent. He'd never taken criticism well, and this was no exception. I hoped he'd allow me to speak with him once the council had concluded.

Rizzt-tok spoke next, her buzzing voice reverberating through the tent. "The hive supports the dragon-brother. We fight as he commands."

Thomas glanced uncertainly in my direction at her words. Clearly, he was as surprised at her use of the name as I was. It wasn't unusual for the Corodan to refer to people by their associated characteristics rather than their given names, but this was the first I'd overheard them refer to him as "dragon-brother."

Thomas shifted his gaze to meet our cousin's. "And what of you, Elias?"

"Perhaps I see much of myself in your brother," he replied with a wistful smile. "I should very much like to take this fight to the king, but I can also see the wisdom in a more cautious approach. I'm no battlefield tactician and can't advise you on the best path forward. I'll defer to your judgment. It's your place to command."

Thomas sighed with a shake of his head. "I feared you'd say something like that. I need time to think this over. I'll call everyone together again once I've made a decision." He glanced toward me, then toward Alexander. "I'd like a few moments to speak with my brothers privately."

Rynn stood up straight and carefully moved away from me. "I'll be outside," she promised before limping toward the exit with the others.

Once the tent had cleared, I felt compelled to say something to Alexander, who still appeared downcast. "Alex, I—"

"No, I needed to hear what was said," he replied with a wry chuckle, cutting me off. "Lydia reminds me often enough that I shouldn't be so reckless."

"We both needed the reminder," Thomas said, always willing to share the blame when it came to Alexander.

Alexander ran a hand through his hair, pulling much of it loose from its binding. The long strands fell around his face, and he shook his head in irritation. "I should have put more thought into my proposal. I've had other matters on my mind of late and I was seeking a distraction."

I narrowed my eyes and recalled the evening several nights past when Lydia had asked me to send Alexander to her. "Alex, has something happened?"

He looked at me sheepishly. "Yes, and no."

"You can't leave it at that," Thomas said with a laugh.

"Ah, well…" Alexander visibly reddened. He drew a deep breath before continuing. "Lydia received word from the Oracle. It seems her vision about my son wasn't in regards to the child she was carrying. The Oracle bore a daughter."

I didn't know how to respond to Alexander's news. His brief tryst with the Oracle had been a continual source of shame and frustration for him, and he'd been bitter about the incident for months. He'd never elaborated on the details of what the Oracle may have seen regarding his son; perhaps he hadn't known himself.

Thomas spared me from further uncertainty by asking the question that had been foremost in my mind. "Shall we congratulate you, brother?"

Alexander laughed, but appeared uncomfortable. "No. Since the child was a girl, I'll never be allowed to see her until she's grown. That's according to the Oracle's rules, and perhaps not even then. She'll become the next Oracle, and I'll only be graced with her presence when she sees fit to humor her…father." He grimaced and looked away. "Damn, it feels strange to say that. When we were growing up, I'd always believed you'd be the first to sire children, Andrew. I know now it could never have been, but back then… Well, things were different, and we both had secrets to keep."

I nodded as I considered his words. "This wouldn't be the first time the Oracle has been mistaken with the interpretation of one of her visions. If the Oracle's child was a daughter, does that mean the child she saw in her vision is Lydia's?"

"It appears so." He smiled then, his previous discomfort giving way to genuine delight. "Given another four months or so, I'll have a son."

"What more did the Oracle see?" Thomas asked pointedly. "While I may have disregarded her 'visions' as mere mysticism a few months ago, I now understand there's a measure of truth behind them. The vision you relayed to us regarding an assassin proved true enough. Based on your previous words, there is more to this vision than your son."

"The Oracle believes he'll bear a Mark mirroring my own." Alexander's tone was grave.

It took me a moment to understand the full import of his words. Alexander's Mark was much larger and more powerful than any of the other magi that had accompanied him from the south. His ability was also unique; he was the first mage-warrior to complete the trials in several centuries. From what we'd learned during his pilgrimage, a mage with his ability wasn't only rare, but also more susceptible to the madness that threatened all would-be magi before they had gained control of their abilities. There was also the matter of the cursed blade he carried.

"Do you mean he'll be a mage-warrior?" I asked.

He nodded, his expression solemn. "If the Oracle's vision is true, yes. Knowing what awaits him in the trial chambers one day fills me with dread. I've never spoken of what I endured, and I still don't want to. It was terrible…and very personal." He paused to study us in turn. "Lydia was thrilled with the news, and chided me for my 'lackluster' response. She's content in knowing that I'll one day pass my blade on to our child. She has become less fearful of it since hearing the news."

Thomas stared between us, confusion written across his features. "I'm afraid I don't understand."

"Ah, hell." Alexander drew the cursed blade from its scabbard and laid it carefully across the map spread across the table.

The dark metal of the blade gleamed reddish in the filtered light, and its hilt was carved from an unfamiliar black wood. Curious, Thomas bent toward the weapon and reached out to touch it. Alexander knocked his hands away, horror clear in his gaze. Thomas blinked and stepped backward in surprise.

"It isn't safe for you to handle," Alexander explained. "I should have said that before I brought it out. There's a reason why the magi call these blades 'cursed.' They'll break the minds of anyone who touches them without the proper magical attunement. Historically, only mage-warriors could wield these, but carrying one comes with a cost."

He glanced toward me briefly, and I nodded in encouragement. Thomas needed to hear the story of this blade and how Alexander came to be its master.

"What have you done, Alex?" Thomas asked, his blue eyes narrowed in concern.

"*I* haven't done anything," Alexander replied with a nervous laugh. "I went into my trial near the edge of the Dragonlands and emerged with this blade. While inside, I encountered the spirit of one of my predecessors. The spirit had been unable to rest, to find peace for centuries, because she was bound to this weapon. She could only achieve her desired rest by passing the blade to another—and there have been very few mage-warriors in the history of our world. I was the first she'd encountered since her death. I pitied her, Tom, and accepted the blade as my own."

"Are you saying that you're also bound to this weapon?" Thomas asked, his eyes wide.

Alexander nodded. "I am. And I will share the same fate as the spirit if I'm unable to pass it on to another before my end days come."

"Why did you do it?" Thomas asked. "To be trapped for centuries, perhaps even longer, on this earth seems…unthinkable, unbearable."

I frowned and looked down. Thomas' words had struck a chord, one which I had struggled against since that long-ago day at the Frostwake. There were moments when I wished I could stop the world simply to rail against my fate. I would outlive both of my brothers if I didn't fall in battle, and I'd likely outlive their descendants as well.

And I didn't relish the notion.

"It was compassion, I suppose," I heard Alexander say, and a moment later, his hand gripped my shoulder. When I looked up to meet his eyes, he said, "Andrew, he didn't mean anything by it."

I nodded. I knew he was right, and Thomas hadn't meant any harm.

"If your son is born Marked as the Oracle believes, then one day he'll inherit your sword," I said in an attempt to shift their focus away from me.

Alexander studied me carefully for a moment, then nodded. "Yes."

"What is the purpose of your weapon?" Thomas demanded. "If it requires such sacrifice to wield, it must be something more than an ordinary sword."

"It's far from ordinary, Tom," he replied with a mischievous grin. "With this blade, my abilities are enhanced even further. It's the reason I can move so swiftly and why I can strike with such deadly force. It also seems to be the source of my hubris of late." He sighed and picked up the blade to sheathe it. "I must remember there are others relying on us, that there is more at stake than our family. I can't allow my own successes to cloud my judgment, and our uncle was right to advise caution."

Thomas nodded decisively. "Then it's settled. We'll follow Jonas' plan."

TWELVE

My night had been plagued by disturbing dreams of the recent battles and I was unable to return to sleep. I lay awake for a while, then rose, dressed, and exited the tent. I took my sword as a precaution. Rynn would rest more peacefully without my agitation to disturb her slumber.

The only remedy for my unease was physical activity. I found myself walking toward the palisade at the camp's perimeter, where I'd patrol for a time. Even if there was no movement beyond our barricade, the self-appointed task would ease my tension.

It took the better part of an hour to circle the camp once. By that time, the thin clouds over the eastern horizon had begun to take on color as the sun approached the horizon. As I began my second circuit, I heard Alexander's voice, calling over the cool morning air. I stopped and turned to face my brother as he covered the remaining distance between us.

"I've been trying to find you for twenty minutes," he complained. "Rynn said you'd gone, but she didn't know where. I should have known you'd be traipsing about. It's your habit when you don't sleep properly."

I shrugged. "What did you need?"

"Tom wanted to speak with you," he replied with a frown. "He wouldn't tell me the reason, but I know he was speaking with Jonas and our cousin late last night. I hope this doesn't have anything to do with the scouting party."

I nodded, though I wished I knew why I'd been summoned at this early hour. As we began threading our way through the awakening camp, I said, "I don't know what Tom needs from me that I haven't already relayed to him or one of the others. I doubt this concerns the scouting party."

Alexander appeared unconvinced, but he made no reply. As we neared the center of camp, the aroma of fresh bread wafted toward us, and I realized I was ravenous. I paused for a moment outside of Thomas' tent, torn between my desire for breakfast and the need to speak with my brother.

Seeming to read my mind, Alexander laughed. "Go speak with Tom. I'll be back with some of that bread for you, brother."

I nodded my thanks before entering the command tent. Thomas was inside, pacing the length of the table, while Elias stood across from him, studying the map spread across its surface. Both looked up as I entered, and Elias smiled in greeting, Thomas appeared troubled. It seemed he had also failed to get enough sleep during the night; his eyes were ringed by dark circles, his hair was mussed, and his clothing was rumpled.

"Tom, what's this about?" I asked as I stopped alongside Elias.

Thomas frowned in our cousin's direction. "You tell him."

"I have an idea," Elias explained, unable to keep the excitement from his tone. "I came up with this yesterday while talking with some of my people, and Jonas thinks it may work. But I'll require your help."

"And it looks as though my brother is disinclined to agree," I replied, noting that Thomas' frown had transitioned to a glower.

Thomas crossed his arms. "I told him he could run the idea past you, and that you'd have the final say in it. What I don't like is the idea of placing you in danger again so soon."

I sighed. "You and Alex can't keep fretting over me like this."

He scowled in my direction. "I *saw* what Claybourne did to you when you were captured, and Alex *saw* what he'd done to you after he fled the battlefield. You may not want to admit it, but we both know you nearly died. I won't lose you to this war as I've lost so many others!"

Thomas had kept his composure through many of our ordeals, but in this moment, alone with family, his brave façade crumbled. He wiped briskly at his eyes and shook his head, dismayed. "Andrew, you are more than merely my brother. If we lose you, the dragon-kind are lost as well. I can't allow that to happen."

I sighed and ran one hand through my hair. "When you phrase it that way…"

It was strange to think of myself in those terms. I believed one day the curse that had befallen my father and the others would be broken. Since meeting my father, I'd ceased to think of myself as being alone, as the last of my kind, even if I was at present. But I conceded that Thomas had a valid point.

"Do you finally understand my concern, cousin?" Thomas demanded, his furious gaze on Elias.

"Of course I do," Elias replied, calm in the face of Thomas' ire. "As you said, Andrew will have the final word. If he doesn't want to partake in this venture, then I'll pursue it no further."

While Thomas continued to scowl, I said, "Let's hear it."

I wanted to learn of Elias' proposed plan, even if Thomas remained staunchly against my participation in the scheme.

Elias flashed a grin and pointed to a location on the map due south of Willever. "Bridgewaters was given to Duke Ellington after Duke Crossley fled to the highlands, and it's now the stronghold of Robert Claybourne since Ellington earned the king's disfavor. Based on what Jonas and Ev have shared, it's well within your abilities to fly there in a single night. Now, I don't believe for one moment that Claybourne has returned to Bridgewaters. I'm willing to wager all I have that he ran back to the Capitol with his tail between his legs after the trouncing Alexander gave to him."

I narrowed my eyes thoughtfully. "Go on."

"With Claybourne effectively out of the picture, the defense of the city will have been left in the hands of the Bridgewaters garrison," Elias said. "If I know Ellington's methods—which I do—he would have allowed the man in charge under Ev's rule to remain in place. Given what we also know of Claybourne, it's unlikely he'd have named someone else as well. The city garrison was operating well enough as it was, and Claybourne has been busy with his own errands for the king. I doubt he's had time to name someone new to the post. Which brings me to my main point."

Green eyes alight with excitement, Elias continued with animated flair. "I want Claybourne to think we're retaliating against him for his poor treatment of you. And by 'we,' I mean you, Andrew." He chuckled. "My plan is simple, and it doesn't involve you attacking anything—unless, of course, you choose to. That will be up to your discretion. If you travel to Bridgewaters and fly about for a time looking menacing—maybe roar a bit here and there—word will get back to Claybourne. It's a diversion I'm asking for, nothing more. If we draw Claybourne's attention toward Bridgewaters, it'll give our scouts more freedom to operate within the Capitol." He flashed another grin. "I ran it by Jonas, and he seems to think my plan has some merit. What do you say?"

It was difficult not to be infected by his enthusiasm. A diversion would provide a greater measure of safety for our scouts, but the tactic wasn't without risk. There were a number of unknowns within Elias' proposal, not the least of which was the present location of Robert Claybourne. While it was likely he'd returned to the Capitol, it was equally likely that he'd gone to Bridgewaters after reporting to the king. If he was in Bridgewaters, our diversion would be for naught, and I'd be in greater danger than we anticipated. For all his brutishness, Claybourne possessed a cunning mind.

"How much time are you willing to give me to think this over?" I asked.

I wanted to hear Jonas' take on the idea, and I also needed to speak with Rynn. I wasn't going to leave her behind again. Nearly losing her once had been trial enough, and I doubted she'd remain in camp even if I asked. She'd undoubtedly want to be part of the action.

Elias' smile faltered, but he remained optimistic. "The scouts are leaving this morning, perhaps even as we speak. It will take them three days to reach the Capitol. It would be best to have your answer by noon tomorrow. That way, we'd have a few hours to prepare should you choose to undertake this mission."

Thomas shook his head, clearly exasperated. "I should have known you'd consider this. If you agree, I implore you not to go alone."

"Don't worry," I replied, "I'll make certain to take at least one accomplice along for the ride if I go through with it. But first, I'd like to speak with a few people." I turned toward Elias. "I'll find you once I've made a decision."

"I've been itching to do something, *anything,* for days," Rynn said after I told her of Elias' plan. "My leg is much better than it was even yesterday, and I'm ready for some action. I'm with you, if you go through with this."

I grinned. I'd known she wouldn't pass up the chance of adventure, even if it involved flying. "I knew you wouldn't disappoint."

She laughed. "And it's Claybourne's stronghold, you said?" she asked with a smirk. "I don't know if I can sit idly by while you fly circles above the city. I may have to vandalize a few buildings from afar to keep myself from growing bored. And if I happen to see him... Well, I can make no promises as to what his fate will be." Her tone was grim.

"I have yet to speak with Jonas," I said after a moment. "Elias claims they've spoken of his plan, but I want to hear what he has to say regardless."

"Then let's speak with him," she replied brightly, then asked, "Does Alex know about this?"

I chuckled. I'd met Alexander moments after exiting the command tent. He'd brought the promised bread, along with a pair of soft but palatable apples. I'd informed him of our cousin's plan while we ate, and he'd merely shaken his head in amusement. He wasn't opposed to the idea as Thomas had been, but he forced me to promise I wouldn't attempt anything reckless. When I relayed our conversation to Rynn, she laughed.

"That's when you should have told Alex I'd be along for the ride," she replied. "I'll make certain you behave yourself, dragon or not."

I snorted. "You've spent entirely too much time with Belora."

She grinned in response but said nothing more.

It took a while to locate Jonas in the bustling camp. When we finally tracked him down, he was outside the eastern palisade, overseeing the construction of what would become siege equipment. Human and Merael soldiers worked in small groups, building ladders and what I assumed were mobile towers, while Corodan felled trees in the distance.

The former duke looked up at our approach and proceeded to study me for several moments before speaking. His steel-gray eyes were unreadable, his expression betraying nothing of his thoughts. Even after securing something of a friendship with him, there were times when I was completely uncertain of what he might say or do. This was one such time.

He nodded a brief greeting to Rynn, then turned to address me. "I didn't believe Thomas would send you in this direction. As you can see, I've all the help I need right now."

"Tom didn't send us," Rynn replied before I could answer.

"I spoke with Elias and my brother earlier," I added.

Jonas nodded his understanding. "Your cousin's plan carries risks, but if it works, it could buy us additional time to prepare for the next assault. I have no doubt more of the king's men will march this way before we move on the Capitol. Any diversion would help, but sending *you* may prove even more effective."

I crossed my arms. "Tom doesn't want me to go through with it."

"And Elias has no formal training in military matters," Jonas continued. "Which brings you to me."

"I agree that the tactic may be useful, but I wanted to hear your thoughts before I committed myself. I haven't been apprised of all the goings-on of late, and Tom has named you his commander, Jonas. I respect your opinion."

He smiled wryly. "I would never have imagined you'd utter those words, even six months ago. It's strange how quickly circumstances change."

Rynn rolled her eyes and snorted in exasperation. "You're no longer adversaries, yes. In fact, I'd even go so far as to say that you've become friends of a sort. That being said, let's move on to the real business, shall we?"

I arched my eyebrows in surprise at her outburst, while Jonas tipped his head back and laughed. Rynn folded her arms across her chest and stared firmly at us in turn, daring one of us to contradict her words.

"I suppose we *were* skirting the topic," Jonas replied, still laughing. "Ah, but good humor seems to be in short supply these days. Thank you, Lady Rynn, for your blunt reminder that I'm no longer dealing with royalty. We are, indeed, friends."

"I was never royalty, Jonas," I scoffed.

"No," he agreed with a shake of his head. "It's a pity, but there is no use dwelling on it. We've a tyrant to overthrow." He paused to glance over his shoulder at one of the work groups. "If you create a diversion, it will buy us time. Weeks, perhaps. We still have much to do before we march on the Capitol, and as I mentioned before, I suspect we'll have our share of skirmishes before that time comes. Thomas made it very clear to your cousin that the final decision would be yours to make."

"Tom reiterated that earlier," I replied. "If I decide to do this, I won't be going alone. I'd like at least one other person to accompany me."

"You mean besides me," Rynn replied. "I'm going."

Jonas frowned in concern. "Are you certain that's wise?" he asked. "Your leg is—"

"My leg is fine," she said firmly. "There is nothing and no one that will prevent me from joining Andrew on this mission. And there is no one on this earth who can claim to have spent as much time in the air with him as I have. I know what to expect and how to handle myself when he must perform certain…unpleasant aerial acrobatics. Besides, you'll want someone capable of causing damage from afar along for the ride, and I can provide that as well."

He glanced at me, seeking reassurance, before he nodded. "Very well. I can hardly argue against the points you've made, but I wish you'd remain here, where you'll be better protected."

Rynn bristled at his words. While I knew he hadn't meant to cause offense, he'd forgotten she wasn't Novanian and was unused to being treated as delicately as the noblewomen we were accustomed to.

"I do not need protection," she seethed, her eyes narrowed. "I'm more capable than most of your men, and more deadly when I choose to be."

Jonas held up his hands in a gesture of surrender. "I misspoke, Lady Rynn, and for that, I'm truly sorry. I certainly wouldn't want to be on the receiving end of your wrath, but I'm concerned about your injury. Have you spoken with Lydia?"

Rynn sighed heavily and looked away, her arms crossed. She made no reply.

"We haven't," I said. "But if she can't accompany me, then I'm afraid I won't undertake this mission."

I didn't want to part from Rynn a second time, and it was clear she would not be left behind. We'd embark on the journey together, or not at all.

With a nod, Jonas said, "I understand. While you speak with Lydia, I'll talk with a few others. I'd like to send at least one person with you as a precaution."

"Lydia won't like this," Rynn said as we turned to leave. "Thank you for siding with me, Andrew. That means more than you know."

"As I recall, I asked you to come along, didn't I?"

"Not exactly, but the implication was there," she replied with a faint smile. "These people treat women as though we're fragile, like we might break at the slightest gust of wind. How do they stand it? I know there are a few, like Hulda, who choose to take up arms and fight, but they are rare. Claire has told me it is expected—*expected*—of Novanian women to do all they can to remain beautiful for as long as they're able. To do so, they remain ensconced within their homes, covered in silks and perfumes and powders… *Ugh!*"

I laughed, enjoying her reaction. I'd never ask her to change. "It has been that way for as long as anyone can remember. They know no other way of life."

She groaned. "That's no excuse. There is a whole world out there waiting to be explored, and they sit by the wayside and paint their faces? And for what? A few brief moments of fame?"

I shrugged. "I don't know."

I drew my arm around her as we walked, once again thrilled that I'd met this opinionated, passionate, strong-willed woman who would allow nothing to stand in her way.

"Well," she said after a moment, "I hope I wasn't too harsh with Jonas. I know he didn't mean any harm, but sometimes I can't tolerate it."

"You shouldn't have to," I replied. "Perhaps more good will come of this war than we'd anticipated. Showing the Novanians there are other paths through life than those they've always followed is just as important as removing my worthless half-brother from the throne."

She smiled and looked down at the ground as we walked. "I hadn't thought of it in those terms before, but perhaps there's more we southerners can accomplish than simply fulfilling the Oracle's summons."

"I was hoping to bring about acceptance," I replied. "For Alex and the magi, if nothing else."

"You know," she said, "since Alex joined us, those men who used to harass me have all but disappeared. Your brother commands respect amongst the Novanians and the magi both. Perhaps he truly is as important as the Oracle's visions implied. And I don't mean on the battlefield, though if the tales I've heard are true, he's terrifying."

"That he is." I laughed uneasily. "Alex has been known throughout the kingdom since his birth. He's a prince, after all, just as Tom is. That he's also Marked and has now become a mage seems to have impressed people on both sides. He was well-liked before Colin attempted to execute him, and it seems that hasn't changed."

"Your brother does have a certain roguish charm. It's no wonder Lydia fell for him." She sighed. "She isn't going to like our plan, but I believe I can convince her I'm well enough to fly."

"I certainly hope you are," I replied with a grin. "I'm rather looking forward to causing a bit of mischief for Robert Claybourne."

THIRTEEN

I stood in a clearing near the southern palisade, surrounded by my two brothers, Rynn, Lydia, Elias, Jonas, Hulda, and a number of curious onlookers the following afternoon. Once I'd agreed to Elias' plan, word spread through camp that I was undertaking a secret mission, and before my planned departure I'd be shifting into my dragon form.

I wanted to change and be done with little fanfare. I disliked an audience at the best of times, but the grassy space was packed. Only the eldest of the magi had encountered dragons before their abrupt departure, and those occasions had been rare. But even those who had met dragons previously seemed compelled to attend my farewell. As the first skin-changer in more than two centuries, I was a novelty, much to my chagrin.

As more people arrived to witness my transformation, Jonas ordered a dozen of his soldiers to keep the crowd at bay. I glowered at them, arms crossed in what I hoped was an obvious display of irritation. If anyone in the crowd realized they were the source of my displeasure, none of them acknowledged it. And more gathered with every passing minute.

"Don't they have anything better to do?" I groused, not expecting an answer.

"Oh, Andrew, not everyone has had the privilege of seeing a dragon in the flesh," Lydia replied gently. "Let them have their moment of wonder, and once their curiosity is sated, they'll leave you be."

"I damned well hope so." I shot another glare at the crowd, to little effect.

Jonas shook his head in disbelief. "Perhaps it's fortunate you're going on this diversion now, and we're not forced to deal with this throng at the onset of a battle."

He beckoned to Hulda, who strode forward to better hear what he had to say over the clamor of the crowd. She held a finely crafted bow in her left hand and a quiver of arrows was slung over her shoulder.

"I've chosen you to accompany Andrew and Rynn because you've flown with him on scouting missions in the past," Jonas said. "I wanted someone capable of adapting quickly, but who also understands the nuances this flight might entail."

Hulda nodded, then turned to flash a knowing smile in my direction. "Flight upon a dragon's back is not as easy as it might appear. I'm ready, as is my bow."

Thomas stepped toward me hesitantly, then drew me into a rough one-armed embrace. "You'd best come back from this fallacy, Andrew," he said so softly that I doubted anyone had overheard.

"I will, Tom. Trust me."

He nodded glumly. "Alex and I will be here. And if plans should change—"

"—You'll send us a message through Bryson," I finished for him.

It was at least the fourth time since noon he'd uttered the reminder, but I didn't fault him. Thomas had a dozen issues on his mind between the day-to-day operations of the camp, preparations for the next battle, and his bid for the throne. It was little wonder he'd forgotten the previous three instances of our conversation.

He glanced at the crowd, unable to mask his concern. "Be safe, Andrew. We'll need you at the Capitol when that time comes."

"That we will!" Alexander added with a grin. "Give Claybourne hell. And cause some chaos for me while you're at it, brother."

I chuckled. "I'll do my best, Alex."

I glanced at those nearby, each present to see us off for their own reasons. Thomas and Alexander were there as my brothers, Jonas as Thomas' appointed commander, Lydia had come for Rynn, and Elias was there simply as extended family. Everett had been inundated with supply requests since the last skirmish and had opted to remain in camp—but he had wished us luck earlier in the day.

The sun was beginning to dip toward the western horizon; its golden rays cast long shadows through the crowd. I could not put off the spectacle so many had been waiting for any longer. It was time.

I frowned at the throng. "I suppose I should change," I said to Alexander, who grinned in response.

"I can take your things," Thomas offered. "Alex moved your trunk into my tent. I won't allow anyone to make off with your armor while you're away, and Uncle Crossley is there now."

I nodded my thanks. Thomas always worried over the smallest of details, but in this case, I was grateful. Few knew the true cost of acquiring dragon scale, and fewer still had the ability to work it properly. My armor was invaluable, made even more so by the knowledge it had come from my father.

I walked several dozen paces away from the group while keeping a wary eye on the crowd. They obeyed the soldiers' commands to keep their distance; I wouldn't need to worry about inadvertently injuring anyone when I shifted.

I frowned again and wished I didn't have an audience present as I began to undress. Privacy was a luxury I'd been given little of since I'd returned from my captivity, but today its lack rankled more than usual. I tossed my belongings to Thomas and scowled at the onlookers a final time before I shifted.

I closed my eyes briefly and reveled in the sensation of power that always came with the transition. The crowd fell silent for a heartbeat, then erupted into excited chatter moments after their initial awe had passed. When I opened my eyes, Rynn and Hulda had moved to stand a few paces away. Hulda brandished her bow, her eyes alight with anticipation, while Rynn shouldered a pack containing a week's worth of rations for the two women. I planned to hunt when necessary.

Rynn wore a knowing smile, and her blue eyes sparkled in the fading sunlight. "For all your grumbling, you certainly seem to be enjoying the moment," she teased.

"A bit more privacy would have been nice," I replied, but my spirits had already lifted considerably with the transition and the promise of imminent flight. I longed to leap into the air, to feel the rush of wind across my scales, to leave my cares behind, if only for a few hours.

Lydia moved to stand beside Rynn and gazed at me, a curious expression on her fair features. "Andrew," she said slowly, "you sound…different."

Confused, I shook my head. "You've known for some time my voice becomes deeper when I shift. What do you mean by 'different?'"

She tilted her head as she considered my question, then brightened. "That's what it is! You've overcome that infernal hissing."

I threw my head back and laughed. "Ah, that. It has been months since we solved that little problem."

I grinned at Rynn. I'd become so accustomed to adjusting the position of my jaw when speaking that I no longer had to remind myself to do it. The long hours spent scouting during the winter had done much to improve my communication skills and it had done wonders for my self-confidence, as well.

Lydia gave Rynn an appraising smile. "Well, it seems my dear friend is an even better match for you than I'd imagined."

Rynn flushed crimson at her words and hung her head, then muttered something even I couldn't hear. Whatever she said caused Lydia to laugh uncontrollably for a time.

When she recovered, Lydia fixed me with a pointed stare. "Take care of yourselves. I expect all three of you to return in one piece. Don't do anything reckless, Andrew." She turned to face Rynn. "I have no doubt you'll keep him in line. Be safe."

Rynn nodded and reached toward Lydia, but stopped herself just before making contact with the other woman's arm. She sighed and dropped her hand to her side. "It seems the more time I spend with him, the less vigilant I am around others… I must go."

Rynn turned away from Lydia, a deep sadness in her eyes, one borne from years of isolation. Wordlessly, she clambered up to perch directly between my wings. Moments later, Hulda joined her, but seated herself farther back along my spine.

I rose to my feet in anticipation of our flight. Those gathered nearby approached to say their final farewells. Thomas' expression was forlorn, while Alexander flashed another mischievous grin. Elias nodded to me silently, keeping his thoughts to himself, and Lydia waved, her eyes fixed on Rynn. Jonas remained stoic.

"Do not engage Claybourne in a battle," Jonas said, not for the first time that day. "You are there as a diversion—nothing more."

I nodded. "We'll see you again in a week."

"Or sooner if you face resistance." His gray eyes were steely. "We need you hale, Andrew. Don't do anything stupid."

Alexander snickered. "What he means is you need to behave yourself, brother."

I rolled my eyes. "I'll do my best."

I peered over my shoulder to ensure Rynn and Hulda were secure, then leapt into the sky. I stretched my wings wide and allowed the wind to catch them, reveling in the faint warmth the afternoon sun provided as it struck my black scales. I circled above the camp once before turning south, and as I passed over the crowd, I noted with some satisfaction that many gaped skyward, following our progress while waving and calling their goodbyes. I pumped my wings a few times to gain elevation once the encampment began to fade into the distance.

"You're never one to disappoint, are you, my lord?" Hulda called over the wind.

I chuckled while Rynn snorted. "He claims to dislike the attention, but I think we can both see through that ruse easily enough."

"Indeed," Hulda replied with a laugh. "I can't say I blame him. If I were a dragon, I'd flaunt my scaly ass too."

Rynn broke into peals of laughter at the scout's comment. If I'd been human, I would have flushed with embarrassment.

"I can hear everything you say," I replied over my shoulder, which caused them to laugh even harder.

"I thought I'd be miserable for most of this flight," Rynn managed after a moment, "but this is proving fun. Even if our diversion doesn't go according to plan, at least we can say we succeeded in poking fun at our dragon. It takes my mind away from the fact that the ground is so far below."

She reflexively tightened her grip on my spines as she spoke, and a pang of regret shot through my core. I had known she'd travel with me if I asked—and most likely would have even if I hadn't—despite her fear of heights, but that knowledge failed to temper my guilt.

I suppressed a sigh and peered over my shoulder to ensure she was well. Her eyes were closed, but her expression was serene. It appeared as if she enjoyed the sensation of the wind rushing past her, but I could feel how tightly her hands gripped my spine. She'd never admit the depths of her fear with Hulda present, but she seemed to be handling this flight well enough.

We flew through the evening and into the night, stopping only once in the early hours of the morning. I spied a few deer bedded down in a meadow, and knew it may be my only opportunity to hunt before we reached Bridgewaters. After warning the women of my intention, I went into a steep dive, arrowing toward the unsuspecting creatures at an incredible speed. The deer didn't realize they were in danger until I was upon them. I killed one but allowed the others to bound away through the tall grass and into a stand of trees.

Hulda and Rynn slid to the ground before I began to eat. Rynn was pale and her hands trembled, but she didn't complain. Hulda was energized and elated.

"I'd no idea you could fly so fast!" she exclaimed. "I must say, I'm mightily impressed, my lord."

Rynn unshouldered her pack and dug through its contents. "We should eat as well," she said. "We've been given some bread, some mildly questionable apples, dried meat… Do you have a preference?"

"I'll try my luck with an apple," Hulda replied. "Ah, but I'm glad spring is finally here again. We'll have fresher fruit soon enough."

After we'd eaten, Hulda extracted a map from within one of her pockets and carefully unfolded the creased paper. She peered at it for a time, then said, "We should be nearing Bridgewaters within an hour, two at most. You'll see the King's Fork river first. If we follow that south and west, we'll come to the lake and the city itself."

"I haven't sighted the river yet," I replied. In the darkness, I'd be the first to see it as it snaked its way across the landscape.

"Perhaps when we find the river, we can take a few hours to rest," Rynn suggested. "We can fly over the city in the daylight—as I've no doubt was planned. The more townsfolk who see you, the better."

We couldn't risk stopping along the riverbank itself; the King's Fork was one of the busiest waterways in all of Novania, providing a link between the Capitol, Bridgewaters, and the southeastern coastal city of Three Points beyond. The river typically teemed with merchant vessels, fishing boats, and the occasional personal barge belonging to nobility. I'd traveled to Bridgewaters on occasion myself, and recalled there were several major roads that intersected at the city, one of which I'd spied while airborne. Our resting place must be far enough from the road to remain undetected, but as we neared the city, it would become more difficult to find a suitable area.

"If you need to rest, perhaps this is the best place to do so," I replied. "I don't know if we'll encounter a safer area along the remainder of our route."

"You mistake my meaning," Rynn countered, placing her hands on her hips. "I don't need to rest, but I think perhaps you should. I made a point of sleeping through the early afternoon while you were off with Alexander. If it becomes necessary, I'll sleep while we're airborne."

"I could use a nap myself," Hulda replied. "We can cover the remaining distance fast enough once we're in the air again."

"That's settled," Rynn said with a terse nod. "I'll keep watch while you two sleep."

I frowned, though I could see arguing would serve no purpose. Her mind was set.

"Very well, but promise you'll wake me at the first sign of trouble."

Her smile was enigmatic. "Like you, I'll not make a promise I can't keep." She crossed her arms and tossed her head, wordlessly challenging me to contradict her. "Sleep, Andrew. I have a feeling you'll need it."

FOURTEEN

I felt the warmth of the morning sunlight striking my scales before I opened my eyes, and immediately knew I'd slept far longer than I'd intended. What had begun as a mere nap had turned into several hours. I snapped my eyes open to survey the clearing. Rynn and Hulda weren't far away, talking softly, their backs toward me. One glance toward the sky showed it wasn't merely morning, it was almost noon. I sat up and stretched languidly.

The women heard my movements and turned. Both looked amused.

"I knew you needed to sleep," Rynn said, a playful smile on her lips, "but I didn't realize you'd spend half the day napping."

"I never meant—" I began, but was cut off by their laughter.

"It's best this way," Hulda replied. "We know you're rested and ready to take on whatever Claybourne's stronghold may throw our way."

"Once you're ready, we'll be off," Rynn added with a smirk.

I dug my claws into the ground and stretched again, arching my back and flexing my wings as I did so. I'd slept more deeply than I'd expected to, and it was proving difficult to clear the slumber-induced fog from my brain. After a moment, I yawned expansively.

Rynn made a face, disgusted by something she'd seen. "You've still got blood in your teeth, Andrew… And I'm not sure what else. If you're looking to appear more fearsome while we circle Bridgewaters, that will certainly help."

"It's not exactly easy for a dragon to clean his teeth," I replied, feigning hurt.

She laughed. "Let's go, since you seem to be coherent now. I'm eager to cause a bit of mayhem for Robert Claybourne after all the trouble he's caused us."

"As am I," Hulda agreed as she gathered her bow and quiver. "Duke Horace was a good man. Claybourne will answer for his death if I have any say in the matter."

A few minutes later, we were soaring above the trees once more. A paved road threaded through the trees some distance away to the west, and a merchant's caravan could be seen traveling south along the path. I could not distinguish individual people from our present distance, but I had no doubt if one were to peer in our direction, they'd see me. I didn't blend in against the daytime sky as well as I did the night.

After another half-hour, the King's Fork became visible, a silver ribbon winding through the landscape, bordered on both sides by thick stands of trees. As I'd expected, the river was choked with merchant vessels and smaller craft, becoming even more crowded as we neared the lake encircling Bridgewaters.

Our course ran parallel to the river, and I gradually drew nearer to its banks as the lake came into view. When my shadow fell across the rivercraft, panicked shouts issued from the decks below. I glanced toward the water and noted with grim satisfaction we'd been spotted. I banked toward the river to coast low over a merchant vessel and released a deafening roar. The crew scattered and erupted into a chorus of surprised curses and terrified screams.

I laughed as I regained altitude and turned toward the lake. Elias had asked that I sow chaos, and I'd oblige him. Scaring Claybourne's subordinates was strangely satisfying.

A rocky island rested at the heart of the vast lake. The city of Bridgewaters sprawled across it; buildings crowded one another and overshadowed the cobblestone streets, leaving little space for gardens or green spaces. Two massive bridges spanned the water, running between the island and the shores to the north and southwest. They connected the city to the main thoroughfares leading elsewhere in the kingdom, with Bridgewaters acting as its nexus. A stout stone wall ringed the island, broken only by a gate at the end of each bridge and another near the eastern docks. Boats of every size plied the placid, sunlit waters, while an array of birds wheeled overhead.

An elegant manor house sat at the highest point of the island, encircled by a low stone wall, the residence of the current duke. I had fond memories of the place; we'd traveled to Bridgewaters nearly every summer when I was a child at the former king's behest. His younger sister had been married to Everett Crossley, and they'd remained close even after the kingship and her marriage had forced them to part ways. Everett had maintained the manor's grounds throughout his tenure, and the house itself had been kept in immaculate condition. Likewise, he'd made certain the residents of the city were adequately cared for, and the city had prospered for the entirety of his tenure.

Even from a distance, it was clear the manor and the city had suffered since Everett had fled with Thomas. The manor's grounds were overgrown, and piles of crumbling autumnal leaves littered the space. The city appeared subdued, an air of gloom shrouding its once teeming streets, and I noted with despair that a number of buildings had been boarded and shuttered. There was no sign of the city's garrison, nor any evidence of Claybourne's war machines. It was meager comfort, but I wondered why he'd left the city undefended in his absence.

The decision made little sense, and the implications left me uneasy. Was the seemingly benign appearance of Bridgewaters simply a ploy to lure us into a false sense of security, only for the devious bastard to spring his trap when we least expected it? He'd outsmarted me once already, and I feared he'd do it again.

As we neared, the city's state of disrepair became more evident. The manor house's gardens and the vacant state of many buildings were only the first things I'd noted. The once populous streets were markedly empty, the once thriving market a mere shadow of the one I'd visited countless times in my youth. What had been a beautiful city was now little more than a grimy and dilapidated domicile. Was Bridgewaters' present state the work of the late Duke Ellington or Robert Claybourne?

I growled low in my throat, unable to contain my fury and disappointment. "Everett will be beside himself when he learns the state of this city. Damn."

"We're too far away for me to make out any details," Hulda called.

"Allow me to fix that." I wheeled over the water and arced directly toward the island city.

I banked and began to circle, then slowly descended toward the rooftops. Startled cries and panicked shouts erupted below as the scant townsfolk took notice of the dragon in their midst. Sullen and bitter at the state of Bridgewaters, I released a powerful roar. A woman's scream pierced the air, while Rynn broke into gleeful laughter.

"I say we head toward that gate, my lord," Hulda said. "If there are any defenders left in this city, they'll be there."

There was a decided lack of soldiers amongst the townspeople milling in the dingy streets below. The gate she indicated spanned the near end of the northern bridge and could be closed from within if the city were threatened. The gate was flanked on either side by defensive towers.

As we neared the gate, a handful of soldiers appeared in the broad, open windows encircling the towers. Orders were shouted from within, but the soldiers were more interested in gaping and pointing at us than in pressing an attack.

Hulda shifted her weight subtly between my spines. As I soared above the gate, the distinct twang of her bowstring was heard. A moment later, the voice shouting orders fell silent.

"I thought we were only taking a look at what might be at the gates!" Rynn shouted. "If I'd known we'd be attacking—"

Hulda laughed grimly. "That man had it coming. I lost to him in last year's archery competition only because he bribed one of the judges to falsely disqualify me. I told him afterwards my arrow would find its way into his sorry backside one day. A shame he turned at the last moment and I caught him in the gut instead."

"I'm glad you're on our side," Rynn replied with a nervous laugh.

I banked over the lake and turned to pass directly above the bridge as we circled back toward the city. The defenders must have made the decision to close the gates; the fortified wooden doors were slowly swinging shut.

I snickered. The gate was no barrier to one who could fly above the city's walls.

"Make a pass near the manor house, my lord," Hulda called. "I'd like to call on the new duke. Let's see if he's home."

I nodded and adjusted my course to fly directly above the duke's abode. The iron gate in the low wall was closed and I spied no movement within the house. The grounds had a decidedly empty feel to them, and I suspected Robert Claybourne was not within. It seemed the manor's staff had either left since his departure, or had been dismissed after he'd come into possession of the place based on the state of the lawns and garden. On a whim, I decided to land and touched down in the manor's front garden.

"He isn't here," I said, "but perhaps if word gets back to him that I've taken his residence as my own…" I shrugged, leaving the thought unfinished, while the two women slid toward the ground.

"That bit of wall won't keep the people out for long," Hulda replied. "It looks like the gate is locked, but that's a mere formality. I could scale the wall easily enough—and the garrison could do the same if they wanted to."

I peered toward the city and noted with amusement that a number of townspeople were gathering in the street not far away. Some pointed in our direction, while others spoke animatedly to their neighbors. I glanced at Rynn, grinning wickedly as an idea formed.

"Andrew, I know that look," she said with a laugh. "What are you—?"

I turned to face the onlookers and roared before she could finish the question. The noise sent the townspeople into a frenzy. Behind me, Hulda laughed. Rynn shook her head in amusement as she strode to my side.

"Let them believe I've come to claim the manor house," I said. "If word reaches Claybourne, he'll come running. That's my hope, anyway."

"It could work," Hulda replied. "From here, we can see most of the city, and it will be simple enough to flee, should circumstance require it. I feel a bit exposed, however. If we can see the town, the town can also see us."

"Then stay close," Rynn said with a shrug. "We'll know if trouble is making its way toward us, and if it becomes prudent to leave, we'll have ample time to do so."

I surveyed the growing throng. The working-class citizens of Bridgewaters were interspersed with the more richly-dressed merchant class and a few who seemed to have come directly from the docks based on their attire. I didn't see anyone bearing weapons, nor the armor indicative of the city garrison. Our arrival was being met with little more than curiosity at present.

Rynn turned on her heel abruptly to peer up at me, mischief in her eyes. "I believe Alex explicitly ordered you to cause 'chaos' on his behalf, Andrew. So far, you've done little but fly about and roar. While impressive, it's a bit lacking in effect."

I chuckled. "Did you have something in mind?"

"Why not put that brute strength of yours to use?" Hulda suggested, while Rynn merely shrugged. "I wager you can break through that wall easily enough or tear the gate from its hinges. Rynn is right—you should do something more than perch atop the island like an oversized vulture."

Rynn snorted a laugh. "Oversized, indeed."

I rolled my eyes. "Hmm."

I didn't want to cause too much damage to the manor house for Everett's sake. I hoped he'd return one day, restored to his former title and status. The wall would serve to make Hulda's suggestion a reality, demonstrating to the townspeople what I was capable of without leaving untoward destruction in my wake.

I leapt across the leaf-strewn lawn, leaving Rynn and Hulda behind where they'd be out of harm's way should the growing throng of curious onlookers become hostile. I made my way to the iron gate and glared at the crowd beyond the wall, hoping my expression was sufficiently fearsome. Though I didn't plan to injure any innocents, I needed to make my reason for appearing above Bridgewaters known.

I grasped the gate and wrested it from its hinges with another roar. I tossed it aside, allowing it to sail above the crowd, where it clattered into the side of a brick building beyond. Some of the stonework crumbled and the gate bent almost double as it crashed into the wall. Several of the onlookers scattered amongst startled cries and curses.

I peered through the hole where the gate had recently hung, noting more townspeople were walking toward the manor house. Beyond them, a half dozen of the city's garrison sprinted toward my location, shouting for the city folk to move aside. Some obeyed the command, but most were too preoccupied with gaping at the dragon in their midst to pay them any heed.

I glanced over my shoulder toward the rooftop as a plan formed in my mind. Hulda had climbed onto the roof and positioned herself near the edge, her bow at the ready. Rynn stood a few paces away from her, seemingly unarmed, but she wouldn't hesitate to channel her ice magic if it came to a fight. I nodded, reassured, then turned to face the crowd once more.

"Where is Claybourne?" I shouted, injecting as much rage as I could muster into my tone.

My outburst was met with stunned silence. It seemed that despite Claybourne's rude and malicious attitude, the people of Bridgewaters were unwilling to speak with me. I growled low in my throat and slammed my fist into the wall. The stone barrier gave way, nearly disintegrating from the force of the blow.

"Where is Claybourne?" I repeated.

This time, my words were met with a babble of terrified voices. Many onlookers decided it was time to take their leave of the situation before it escalated further. People began to run in several different directions, away from the dragon who had decided to storm their duke's residence. Determined to incite as much panic as I could, I roared again as they fled. The city guards were overrun by the terrified civilians and were forced to stop along one side of the nearest street to allow the people to pass before continuing on their way.

I smashed into the wall again for good measure, and a few more people scattered. One man shouted a string of curses in my direction. I fixed him with a heated glare and growled a warning, satisfied as his face drained of color. A moment later, he ducked inside the nearest building and disappeared from my sight.

The crowd had thinned considerably, and the small band of soldiers from the garrison were finally nearing my location. I turned my attention to them, leaning over the wall so they fell beneath my shadow.

Most of the soldiers were visibly nervous; their faces were pale, and a sheen of sweat covered their brows. The woman at their head stood her ground and planted her hands on her hips while she scowled up at me. Unlike most of her subordinates, she showed no outward signs of fear.

"Why have you come here, dragon?" she demanded, her strident voice carrying over the noise of those fleeing the scene.

I lowered my head toward her so my jaws were only inches from her head when I spoke. I'd prove to Hulda and Rynn just how intimidating I could become.

I growled for a moment, then said, "I want Claybourne's head."

She clenched her jaw for a moment, a brief flash of uncertainty in her dark eyes, but she held her position and didn't flinch. "The duke isn't here."

I'd suspected it, but in an effort to continue my furious charade, I lashed my tail savagely against another section of wall, causing it to crumble. "Summon him," I ordered her. "If he isn't in the city, draw him here. We have unfinished business."

"What could Lord Claybourne have possibly done to anger a dragon?" one of the guardsmen behind her asked, his voice quavering.

"Dan, you dolt," the man beside him replied in a low whisper, "this is no ordinary dragon. I'd wager it's the same beast from the tourney field last summer."

I clenched my jaw and narrowed my eyes as a sudden bolt of rage coursed through me. Claybourne had called me a beast too many times during my captivity, and my wounds remained raw. I stepped over the wall, looming over the pair.

"I am no beast." The words came out in an angry snarl. "I came here for Claybourne alone, but call me 'beast' again, and I won't hesitate to rip you in two."

"Stand down, both of you," the woman ordered, her voice firm. "I'll not have any bloodshed on my watch."

I stepped back, fixing her with another glare as I awaited her next words.

"I'll send a messenger to Lord Claybourne," she said evenly, holding my gaze in her own. "I'll inform him of your presence here. Do you have any other demands, dragon?"

I admired her courage. None of her underlings remained as steadfast and unmoved by my threats as she was.

"I'll be taking up residence for another few days," I replied. "Tell your people to stay clear. I will defend myself and those with me if provoked."

"There is one more item, Marie," Hulda called.

I peered over my shoulder to find her walking toward us. Rynn remained on the rooftop.

"Hulda Macton, I'd thought I'd seen the last of you," the leader of the soldiers replied, breaking into a ready smile. "You accompany the dragon, then?"

Hulda nodded tersely. "Your duke is responsible for some terrible wrongs, Marie, but that is a story for another time. We'll require standard rations—food and water—for the other lady and myself. My scaly friend has a larger appetite, I'm afraid."

Marie appeared thoughtful for a moment, then nodded, seemingly resigned. "We'll accommodate your wishes until the duke returns." She met my gaze warily. "I'd rather appease him than risk someone being killed because we've made him angry."

She turned to face the soldiers with her, then ordered one to prepare our message for Claybourne and the others to fulfill Hulda's request for provisions. When several of them gaped at her, she swore profusely. "Do as I've ordered, you damned louts! Go!"

Marie turned to us once more, her arms crossed and a knowing smirk on her face. "I heard your Duke Horace went north, and I'd assumed you'd gone with him. Now you show up here—with a dragon of all things! Hulda, what have you tangled yourself in this time?"

Hulda laughed and motioned for the other woman to follow her as she strode toward the manor house. She stopped beneath the sparse shade of an unkempt tree and leaned against its trunk for support as she began to tell Marie her tale. I knew much of it already and decided to allow the two their privacy. I lumbered back to Rynn, who had seated herself on the edge of the rooftop with her legs dangling over the precipice.

"I'm glad Hulda prodded you into action," she said. "I think that little display was exactly what these people needed to see. I almost hope Claybourne returns before we're forced to leave. I'd like to see you tear him apart as you threatened to do to that poor guard."

I chuckled darkly. "That was the only bit of my temper that wasn't merely for show. Claybourne used the same term while I was his captive. He refused to call me by name."

She reached out to place an icy hand along the side of my jaw, her gaze compassionate. "Andrew—" she began, but stopped short with a delighted laugh.

As had happened only a few times during my life, her touch elicited an inadvertent reaction. A rumble issued from the depths of my chest, a sound Vera had once likened to a cat's purr. From what little I understood, it only occurred when I was content—and in contact with someone I loved.

"You mentioned this happens sometimes," she said after a moment, her vibrant blue eyes dancing in the afternoon sunlight. "I've been waiting for it, hoping I'd experience this for myself one day." When she smiled, her expression was filled with a profound longing. "Andrew, you said only Vera had ever evoked this response in you… I don't know what to say."

I smiled and closed my eyes briefly as I leaned toward her hand. "You don't have to say anything."

She laughed uncertainly. When I opened my eyes, silent tears were freezing on her cheeks.

"Damn it, Andrew, I've never been so happy in all my life." She brushed at her cheeks roughly with the heels of her hands. "You'd best live through this war to fulfill your promise. I don't want to return to the lonely life I led before meeting you."

FIFTEEN

We spent the next four days waiting for word on Claybourne's movements. I made a show of aggression each time one of the townsfolk wandered too near the battered wall surrounding the manor house to ensure none of the curious bothered Rynn or Hulda. It took little effort on my part to appear intimidating, and most of the townspeople gave the area a wide berth.

Marie was true to her word and provided the promised supplies each day. She often drove the cartload of goods herself; the remainder of the garrison, sparse in number as they were, feared I'd make good on my threats. As long as they didn't refer to me as a creature or beast, they had nothing to fear—but they didn't know that, and I was content to keep it that way.

On the morning of the fourth day, Marie arrived with her cart and a missive from the duke. She smirked at us as she unfurled it, then paused for effect while Hulda unloaded the goods.

"The message I sent to the duke claimed a surly black dragon had taken up residence in his manor house and was causing an inordinate amount of mischief in his fair city," Marie said. "I may have embellished a bit, but you asked that I get his attention. And I have, though his response isn't what you'd hoped."

I narrowed my eyes. "What does that bastard have to say?"

"He says he can't leave to deal with the 'situation' himself." Marie glared at the message. "He claims to be on an important errand for His Majesty, though I have my doubts. After hearing Hulda's stories—which contradict what he's told the garrison here—I'm hesitant to believe anything coming from the duke's mouth. Or his pen, as the case may be."

I sighed, unable to mask my disappointment. "He isn't coming. Will he send anyone in his stead?"

Marie laughed bitterly. "No. He told the garrison—what is left of it, anyway—that we are equipped to 'deal' with the problem. There are less than two dozen of us. If you had a mind to bring about our destruction, you'd certainly succeed. We don't have the numbers or the equipment to 'deal' with an enraged dragon."

I hung my head. It seemed our plan to divert Claybourne's attention had failed.

"If he isn't coming, then we have little reason to linger," Hulda replied. "I'd hoped the sorry bastard would show his face. I'd like to put an arrow between his eyes."

"Not if I end him first," Rynn said fiercely. "I won't give him an opportunity to repeat what he did to Andrew at the keep. He will *not* live to see his next breath if he tries."

Marie lifted an eyebrow. Hulda had mentioned our relationship during their long conversations, but she had omitted the fact that Rynn was a mage. "And how would you go about protecting a dragon as decidedly ferocious as this one?"

Rynn's smile was grim. "By any means necessary."

"As you say," Marie said with a shrug. "I can invent some tale about how the garrison chased you lot away if you plan to leave. It will help my people save face when the duke returns."

"Our time here was nearly at an end regardless," Hulda replied. "We were only to spend a week here at most, no matter if the duke arrived or not."

"Take what provisions you require from today's load. It has been a pleasure seeing you again, Hulda." She smiled wistfully, then shook her head. "I'd best return to the gate."

Hulda nodded as she returned Marie's smile. I glanced between the two, certain there was more to their past than either had disclosed.

Once Marie was gone, Rynn began stowing as many provisions as she could in her pack while I tore into the day's portion of meat. I'd eaten well during our stay in Bridgewaters, courtesy of the local butchers and Marie's influence over them, and I consumed every morsel. If I could avoid hunting during our flight back to Willever, I'd do so for Rynn's sake. By the time I was finished, Rynn and Hulda were packed.

"Can you fly after that feast, my lord?" Hulda asked with a smirk.

I grinned. "Of course."

We departed not long after. I gained altitude swiftly—the novelty of scaring the townspeople had worn off and I no longer had any desire to swoop low simply to intimidate them. A thick blanket of clouds covered the sky not far above my preferred altitude, and after a short time, a fine mist began to fall. If I wanted to, I could rise above the cloud layer and into the sunlight above, but I feared Rynn's reaction.

I glanced over my shoulder. Rynn perched between my wings, clutching the stiff black spine in front of her with a firm grip. Hulda huddled in her cloak, clearly miserable from the damp and the chill air.

"Would you like some sunlight?" I asked.

Hulda nodded, but Rynn stared at me, uncomprehending. "Andrew, what are you thinking?" She gestured toward the ceiling of clouds hovering only a few handspans above her head. "The rain isn't going anywhere for a while."

"I can fly through the cloud layer to the sky above."

Her hands gripped my spine even more fiercely. "I don't know. The ground is so far below as it is. Not being able to see it..."

"I won't let you fall," I replied. "But if you'd rather remain where we are, I won't adjust my course."

I faced forward once more, but felt her shift slightly. I glanced back to find she'd turned to look at Hulda.

Rynn sighed with a shake of her head. "This mist and cold don't affect me as they do Hulda. I must face my fear, just as I've done previously. I trust you." She drew a shaky breath, then said, "Let's go."

I nodded and pumped my wings a few times to gain elevation. The clouds were cool against my scales as we flew through them, but they obscured my vision for several long seconds. I realized I could easily become disoriented if I was distracted, so I focused intently on our ascent.

We broke free of the cloud layer moments later and were met with an incredible sight. The clouds blanketed the sky beneath us, appearing both soft and far more substantial than they truly were. A pristine expanse of blue sky opened above. The midmorning sun shone brilliantly, illuminating peaks and valleys within the clouds that would have been invisible in the dark. Bulbous columns of cloud towered high into the air at intervals. Some distance away, a flock of birds moved in a vee formation as they squawked and called to one another.

Rynn gasped and her hands relaxed their grip. "It's beautiful," she murmured.

I glanced over my shoulder, grinning as I watched her gaze in wonder at our new surroundings.

"It was worth the trip," Hulda agreed with a nod. "I also appreciate that it's dry."

Rynn suddenly cried out in surprise. I glanced over my shoulder to see her frantically trying to snatch a sheet of parchment from the air in front of her. After a moment, she secured the sheet in her hands, grasping it tightly to prevent it from being ripped away by the rush of wind.

"Would you like me to land?" I asked. "No doubt that's from Tom or Alex."

She trembled; she'd been forced to release her grip on my spines in order to secure the message, and the experience had clearly left her shaken. After a moment, she drew a breath and said, "Yes, that's for the best. I'm afraid I'll lose the letter if I open it while we're still in the sky."

I began to descend. It was still raining when we emerged beneath the cloud layer, but the air was marginally warmer than it had been earlier in the day. Hulda shifted in her seat and grumbled inaudibly, no doubt remarking on the miserable weather.

I took a few moments to gather my bearings. An expanse of forest stretched below, and in the far distance, I could just make out the road running between Bridgewaters and the Capitol. We had strayed only slightly off course during our foray above the storm. I located a suitable location to land, and moments later, we were on the ground once more.

Rynn slid down my side before she unfolded the crumpled sheet of parchment. "We must tell your brothers to avoid sending messages while you're in the air. I don't enjoy relinquishing my grip when we're hundreds of feet above the ground."

I shrugged. "There was no way they could have known we were flying today."

She frowned in my direction before beginning to read. "It's from Lydia," she said after a moment, her expression morphing into one of concern. "Andrew, we need to return to Willever straightaway. She says they're holding up so far, but Claybourne is there with another sizeable force. He hasn't engaged our people yet, but Alex is certain he will before the day is out."

"Take a moment if you need to stretch," I replied. "We should be there by late afternoon, I believe."

"I'll tell Lydia that." She spun to face Hulda. "You wouldn't happen to have something to write with, would you? I wasn't certain if you'd brought any of your cartography implements along."

Hulda grinned. "I never leave home without them. Just a moment."

While Rynn dashed off a reply to Lydia, I resisted the urge to pace across the small clearing. The knowledge that Claybourne was preparing to strike against my brothers left me restless, and I had a score to settle with the man besides. At least now we knew why he couldn't be bothered to defend Bridgewaters.

"Did Lydia mention anything else?" I asked, my thoughts drifting to my previous capture. I hoped Claybourne hadn't rebuilt his damned trebuchets.

Rynn looked at me sharply, her gaze unreadable. "No. I've told you everything."

I nodded, disappointed even though I'd expected the answer. I turned away to peer into the trees as I grappled with the early stages of fear. I could hope he'd arrived without newly crafted war machines to plague my aerial assaults, but he'd proven cunning in the past, and if I'd been in his position, I would have done everything in my power to acquire replacements. But building them properly required time, and I wasn't certain he'd been granted enough of it. I hated unknowns.

"I hope it's safe to fly into camp," I muttered.

"You'll not have a repeat performance of what happened at the keep," Rynn said. "I'll see to that."

I turned to look at her over my shoulder, startled that she'd overheard. I silently cursed my inability to speak softly as a dragon, while she offered me a knowing smile.

"We'll keep you safe, Andrew," she said, then paused to complete her message. The crumpled bit of parchment disappeared from view a moment later. She handed the quill to Hulda, then strode toward me, hands on hips. "If Claybourne has acquired new trebuchets, we'll destroy them. You would never have been captured if it hadn't been for me, and this time, I'll be at your side. I won't lose you a second time."

"Rynn—" I began, but was cut off when she shook her head adamantly.

"Don't argue. I'll have it no other way." Her tone was unyielding.

I frowned. She would not be dissuaded, even if it placed her in significant danger, and I'd learned it was pointless to object. We'd spoken of this previously; I'd hoped when we were faced with the prospect of another battle, she'd see reason and remain on the ground. As a dragon, I was the most conspicuous target present on the battlefield.

"Fine. If you're both ready, we'll leave."

Rynn smirked but made no reply before she clambered up my side to her chosen perch. Hulda followed moments later.

"I hope we won't be too late," Hulda called as she settled herself between my spines. "I've a score to settle with that infernal asshole."

I wondered if this battle could have been prevented if Alexander had killed him after their duel, rather than allowing the bastard to walk free. If I was given the opportunity to face him, Robert Claybourne would not survive to return to the Capitol a second time.

As we rose toward the clouds, I decided to remain below them for the remainder of our journey. I couldn't risk straying off course, and I needed to see what unfolded on the ground as we neared my brothers' camp. The light drizzle did little to faze me, but Hulda would become cold and damp after a time, and even Rynn would be affected. She could use her magic to prevent the rain from freezing to her skin, but I doubted it was energy she was willing to expend.

Several hours passed before the camp became visible. It was a veritable hive of activity as my brothers and their supporters defended the camp against an onslaught of the king's soldiers. The mismatched colors and standards of Thomas' followers clashed with the crimson and ivory of Colin's. Screams and shouts echoed through the air, muted somewhat by the rain. I scanned the enemy ranks as we approached, but found no sign of Claybourne's war machines.

"That bastard wasted no time, did he?" Hulda called as I flew low over the camp.

I scarcely heard her words as I searched the northern palisade for signs of Thomas, Jonas, or Everett. Alexander was no doubt somewhere in the fray, wreaking his unique brand of havoc on the ranks of Novanians. I spied Everett first; he called orders to a group of soldiers, gesturing emphatically as he did so.

There was a small area not far from him that I believed was large enough to accommodate my landing, and I adjusted my course. Hulda slid down my scaly side as soon as we touched down and strode purposefully toward the palisade without another word. She'd seek Jonas for orders and join the defenders.

The scent of wintergreen swirled momentarily through the air before Rynn abandoned her perch. She slid to the ground seconds later and shook her head, smiling sheepishly.

"I had to de-ice myself before speaking with anyone. Most of Tom's people already believe I'm odd, and that would have been…awkward."

I tilted my head and smiled. "You have nothing to fear from them."

"That wasn't my point," she replied as Everett jogged toward us.

"You received Lydia's message?" he asked. When I nodded, he continued. "Claybourne arrived midmorning. He learned we were here from one of the soldiers we allowed to go free after our last skirmish. Thomas tried to negotiate with him, but Claybourne is out for blood. He knows there are magi amongst our number—" he paused a moment to glance at Rynn meaningfully— "and claimed it's his 'righteous duty' to exterminate them." He raked a hand through his dark hair and wouldn't meet her gaze.

"How do we fare?" I asked.

"As well as can be expected. Claybourne may have anticipated the magi and the Corodan, but he wasn't prepared for the Merael. Your friend Emmarie convinced a family of bears to fight alongside her. She went with Alexander and a number of others toward Claybourne's location." A shadow fell across his face momentarily. "Your brother may be skilled, but he's reckless. Thomas believes he's determined to kill Claybourne, as he should have done when he found you."

I frowned, a low growl emanating from the depths of my throat. "Inform Tom that we've arrived. I'm going to find Alex, then I'm going to destroy Colin's men. I'm done holding onto the hope that my damned brother will see reason."

"Andrew, wait," Everett cautioned. "Take a moment to speak with Jonas—"

He was interrupted as a loud crack reverberated through the air. At first, I believed it was from a clap of thunder, but there had been no evidence of lightning from the storm as we'd traveled. I turned to survey our surroundings, but could not determine where the sound had come from. As I faced Everett once more, his eyes were wide.

"What was that?" Rynn asked with a frown.

Everett shook his head. "I don't know."

"Whatever it was can't bode well for us," I replied. "Tell Jonas I'm here, but I can't wait any longer. I'll find Alex and the others, and if fortune favors me this afternoon, the Novanians will regret coming here."

SIXTEEN

Rynn gazed at me steadily as Everett turned away. Her vibrant blue eyes were unreadable, her expression grim. "Are you certain it's safe to face him again?"

I growled, impatient and unwilling to submit to an interrogation. Now that I'd made the decision to deal with Robert Claybourne personally, I would not be dissuaded.

"I'm going after that bastard. Are you with me?"

She studied me silently for a moment, then nodded slowly. "I told you I wouldn't be left behind. Let's go."

Once she'd clambered up to her usual perch, I leapt skyward to soar low over the camp. The field beyond the palisade was occupied primarily by the Corodan, who slashed and skewered our enemies with their serrated forelimbs. A small group of Merael were in their midst, Shyala and Tylmar amongst them. The Tree-speakers were bending the nearby forest to their collective will; the trees thrashed and swayed erratically, their branches cracking and snapping as they struck armor and shields.

East of the Corodan was the bulk of Thomas' army, engaged with more of the king's men. Occasional gouts of flame erupted amongst the enemy ranks, marking the presence of the Roche twins somewhere in the fray.

The deafening crack that had interrupted our earlier conversation echoed across the rain-soaked field once more. I watched as the earth split open beneath the feet of a dozen Novanians. Soldiers screamed as they tumbled into the abyss before the ground closed around them, swallowing them whole. I gaped at the spectacle, unable to comprehend what I'd just witnessed.

"That would be Siorus' doing. Damn," Rynn said, her tone a mixture of horror and awe. "He told me he wouldn't resort to using that tactic unless he had no other option." She paused and I felt her grip intensify. "I know you're seeking Claybourne, but can we assist the mages at Siorus' location? I think they need us."

I hesitated, torn between the pleading in her voice and my desire to see Claybourne's life ended. If I refused her, she would never forgive me, and that was an outcome I couldn't accept. And we'd need the magi's assistance when we finally made our move on the Capitol.

Reluctantly, I nodded. "I hope they know to avoid me."

Rynn huffed. "We have more control over our powers than you realize, Andrew. And we aren't keen on targeting allies. You'll be fine."

I banked toward Siorus' presumed location, though I didn't immediately spot him within the muddled confusion of the battlefield. There was no clear space to land; instead, I aimed for Claybourne's soldiers. As I descended, several shouted a warning, but it was too late for some to escape. I tore through two men with my talons while lashing three more with a vicious blow from my tail.

Others stumbled back frantically, but I was in no temper for mercy. I pursued them relentlessly, rendering countless Novanians dead or unconscious in my rampage. I roared a challenge as several more scrambled to retreat.

Rynn remained perched between my wings while I slashed at our attackers. The scent of wintergreen wafted through the air as she channeled her magic, but I paid her little heed. I trusted her.

Our soldiers pressed the assault and charged along with my advance. I didn't know if their situation had been as dire as Rynn had initially believed, but I'd given them confidence and provided an opportunity to rally.

We cornered the enemy into a stand of trees, where they abruptly halted, fearful of their proximity to the leafy boughs. Penned between our line and the forest, desperation shone in their eyes as they debated their next moves. Given what I'd witnessed of the Tree-speakers' ability, I didn't fault them for their hesitation. Our line didn't press them further, but neither did we retreat.

I growled menacingly, prepared to continue my assault if they dared move any nearer. It was as much an act as it was a true threat—my rage was for Claybourne and Colin, and many of these soldiers were merely following orders. My fight wasn't truly with them.

A moment later, Siorus appeared from within the throng and stopped at my side. He glanced at me and nodded once, then focused his attention on the trapped Novanians.

"You may lay your weapons down in surrender," he called, his voice carrying over the din of the surrounding battle. "If you continue the fight, I'll open the earth again, and you'll be forever lost to its depths. I implore you to make your decision swiftly, as I've run out of patience."

Rynn shifted slightly on my back. "Do you truly intend to kill them?" she hissed, her voice a bare whisper.

Siorus shook his head subtly for her benefit, but his gaze remained fixed on the faces of the Novanians. In a low tone, he said, "If they don't surrender, what choice do I have? I acted out of desperation earlier. We were surrounded, and if you hadn't arrived when you did, it's likely many of us would have perished." He glanced at me. "We owe you our lives, Lord Dragon."

The Novanians began to lay down their arms. Our soldiers swarmed them and collected the weapons, while others grasped wrists and led them away. Thomas would be pleased we'd captured some rather than killed everyone. Siorus' threat had quelled their desire to fight.

"I need to find Alex," I said as the newest batch of prisoners were led away. "Duke Crossley mentioned he left seeking Claybourne."

Siorus nodded. "He took soldiers and a number of Merael with him. I was left in charge of the magi. We were to remain at the rear of Jonas' formation where we'd be 'safer,' as he put it. Our line was breached, and we were surrounded. Alex pushed ahead some time before that, but I don't know his current location."

"I'll find him from the air. Get your people back to the palisade. We can't afford to lose any more to the Novanians."

"Of course." He bowed low. "I meant what I said earlier. We owe you our lives. You will forever have my thanks."

"I'd do it again. Now go."

When I leapt into the air, Rynn patted my side affectionately. "Thank you, Andrew." Her words were nearly lost to the wind, but I heard them clearly enough.

I smiled. "You're welcome."

I scanned the battlefield, searching for signs of Alexander. I studied the lines of each formation as our people clashed with Claybourne's. An occasional burst of fire or blast of wind ripped through the enemy ranks, but most of our mages had followed my command and were retreating to safety. The fighting was broken between stands of forest, making it difficult to see every movement and group from above. My vision was further impaired when the Tree-speakers coaxed the forest into another frenzied attack.

I glanced over my shoulder at Rynn. "I can't find Alex."

Rynn grasped the spine in front of her as she leaned forward in her seat to peer at the landscape. "If I see him, you'll be the first to know," she called. "Fly lower, near the treetops. We may see more from there."

I suppressed a groan. Though we hadn't spied any evidence of Claybourne's war machines or the specialized nets he'd employed at the keep, I feared recapture. Rynn remained confident that she could free me, but a tumble from the sky might be deadly for her. I was loath to risk her safety, uncertain if I would manage to arrest her fall if I became entangled.

I shook my head stubbornly.

She made a sound of frustration. "If you want to find your brother, we need to fly lower. We have no other choice."

"I don't like it," I growled.

"Trust me, Andrew."

I clenched my jaw. I wanted to argue, wanted to reiterate the reason behind my reluctance. But she knew. We'd been over it more than once, and wasting time and energy on a pointless debate placed Alexander at greater risk. I hadn't come so damned far only to watch my brother fall to one of Claybourne's schemes.

As we neared one end of the battlefield, I veered in preparation to make a second pass over the fighting. I descended as I did so and fervently hoped we wouldn't regret the decision. It would have been a simple matter to hide a trebuchet within a stand of trees and push it forward once it was needed. I prayed Claybourne hadn't managed to acquire new war machines.

We coasted a few feet above the treetops while the noise of the battle below swelled to a deafening cacophony. The Corodan were advancing, taking far fewer casualties than their Novanian counterparts. Rizzt-tok fought some distance down the line, her formidable bulk easily recognizable amongst the hive's warriors. Interspersed between the Corodan were human soldiers and Merael.

"Andrew, there!" Rynn called after a few moments.

I glanced over my shoulder to see where she pointed. Dread gripped my heart as I noted she'd located Alexander—and he was surrounded. He and several others were well beyond the Novanian lines, clearly making for Claybourne's camp in the distance. They made slow, yet bloody progress toward their goal, even though they'd been cut off from behind.

Beyond, Claybourne's stout figure paced along the length of a hastily constructed earthen wall near his camp. Dozens of archers flanked his position.

I didn't know if Alexander was aware of the archers, but Galewing circled above. The eagle would have spied Claybourne and his guards, even if my brother hadn't.

As I watched, Alexander charged, a blur of black scale and flashing blades. Two Novanians fell to his twin swords, while a third bashed him from behind with a shield.

I growled in frustration. "He's going to get himself killed."

I banked again and dove toward the Novanians blocking Alexander's path. Arrows could not penetrate my hide, and I'd shield my brother and those with him should Claybourne order his archers to fire. It was simply a matter of reaching his location in time.

I pushed myself faster, beating my wings, then arrowing toward Alexander's location. Rynn's icy grip tightened on my spines in response. As we neared, I studied the devastation Alexander had left in his wake; dozens of broken bodies lay bleeding on the spring grass, most unmoving.

Emmarie appeared behind Alexander, accompanied by four enormous brown bears. They'd left their own mark on the scene; several Novanians sported gaping claw marks across their faces and torsos. The bears roared ferociously while Emmarie stood her ground between them, a sword gripped in both hands. All of the bears were wounded but continued to fight, undeterred. Three other Merael were in the group, but I recognized none of them.

I groaned as I continued to survey the scene. Elias was in the midst of the fray, accompanied by a half dozen of his people from Dresdin's Forge. He appeared unhurt, but I knew he wasn't a skilled swordsman and could prove a liability. I hoped he'd continue to keep pace with Alexander and the others for his own safety. He possessed many physical similarities to my brother, but Elias Winston was not a young man and didn't have Alexander's magically enhanced battle prowess.

Claybourne's voice carried over the field as I prepared to land. "*Fire!*"

I dove to the ground, covering the remainder of the distance in seconds. I roared and batted several Novanian soldiers away, then lashed my tail in warning. A heartbeat later, dozens of arrows struck my flank, though each fell harmlessly aside, unable to pierce my scales.

Rynn slid to the ground on my protected side. I glanced at her briefly to ensure she was unharmed. She jogged toward Alexander. He was spattered with gore from helm to heel.

"Claybourne is just ahead," she said breathlessly.

He said something in reply, but I didn't hear his words. I turned my focus on the advancing Novanians. Claybourne's figure stormed toward me at their head, stopping just behind the earthen wall protecting his temporary camp.

The sight of him set my blood on fire. He would not survive my wrath this day.

I roared a challenge and dug my claws into the ground, then spread my wings in a gesture meant to threaten and intimidate. The bastard's time on this earth was over and done. I'd see to it.

"Holy hell," Alexander swore from behind. I ignored him as Claybourne began to speak.

"The king will reward me for taking your head, beast," he bellowed before he turned to spit. "I've a hundred good men I can call in an instant. We'll take you down. Your little display doesn't frighten me."

I bristled at his taunt. "Call them! They'll fall, just as you damned well will."

Alexander swore profusely. Within moments, he was at my side, a sword gripped in each hand. "Damn it, Andrew. You can't face them all."

I turned to glare in his direction, incensed. Claybourne must pay, and I would not allow anyone—even Alexander—to stand in my way. I growled low in my throat before turning to the Novanian commander once more. I was on the brink of losing myself to a dark rage, and it would only be moments before it consumed me. I hoped Alexander would see reason and stay out of my damned way.

Claybourne's pock-marked face leered from beneath his helm. His eyes were cold as he gestured for battle formations, but rather than signal a charge, he turned toward the nearest Novanians. When he spoke, his tone dripped condescension.

"You see, the thing about beasts is they're slow to learn. They don't know when they've already been bested." He spat, then drew his sword from its scabbard as he spun toward me. He paused to aim its tip in my direction. "Show this mongrel what we Novanians are capable of!"

His soldiers hesitated a heartbeat before charging over the earthen wall. I heard our forces approaching rapidly from behind, their noise a mere undercurrent to the deafening rage that flooded my senses. A chorus of roars marked the bears' progress as they lumbered forward to engage our foes. Emmarie sprinted at their heels, sword poised for attack.

Rynn appeared on my other side. She glanced at me briefly, her jaw set with determination, her fists clenched at her sides.

Alexander swore. "Tom said *I* was the reckless one," he muttered furiously. "Holy hell, Andrew, this is madness."

"This ends now," I snarled as the first wave of Novanians clashed with our soldiers.

Alexander released a wordless cry of rage as he engaged a pair of Novanians, his swords a blur too swift for my eyes to follow. He may have been frustrated by my actions, but his attack was indicative of his unspoken support.

I swung my right fist at three others, striking two with a solid backhand that sent them flying into the next wave of their own forces. One collapsed and didn't rise again. The other regained his footing but coughed blood as he did so. No doubt both harbored internal injuries and wouldn't survive the day.

I no longer cared. They'd chosen Claybourne's orders over reason. I'd see them all dead.

I whirled to my left to slash another soldier with my talons, cutting through his armor as though it were made of nothing more substantial than linen. His blood spilled into my palm, warm and sticky, before I tossed him aside.

My gaze locked on Robert Claybourne's. I roared another challenge before swinging my tail to knock another pair of Novanians away from Rynn's position. Both crumpled at the impact, ribs snapped and organs ruptured. They fell and remained still, their life ebbing away.

I turned to face another set of adversaries and bellowed in rage. I tore my claws through them, their armor useless against my onslaught. Gore splashed the soldiers at their rear.

A shout came from somewhere to my right. I recognized Rynn's voice, but I was unable to make out her words. I glanced toward her, noted she was unharmed, and continued my bloody rampage through the Novanian line. I was dimly aware that the area smelled strongly of wintergreen, but I ignored her use of magic in my rage.

So long as Claybourne's threat was ended, I didn't care what methods were used.

More Novanians rushed toward us, seeking to avenge their fallen brethren. Several charged toward Emmarie. She'd become separated from the bears, and fearing for her safety, I bore down on them, slashing through armor to rending flesh as I cut another blood-soaked swath through the melee. As the last of her attackers fell, I paused a moment to make eye contact with her. She was breathing heavily but appeared uninjured, her eyes narrowed in concentration. She nodded to me, an indication she was unharmed.

As I turned away from Emmarie, I noted Claybourne had abandoned the earthen wall and was stalking toward me. All of the Novanians near him were engaged with our people or were lying dead on the field. The grass was slick with blood, much of it spilled by my hands.

Claybourne's eyes locked on mine. Hatred twisted his features into a malicious sneer.

I knew our encounter wouldn't end until one of us was dead. Without his war machines or skilled soldiers to back him up, he stood little chance of defeating me. His blade could not penetrate dragon scale, he was outmatched in both strength and size, and my claws could easily rend the steel plate he wore.

He was thirty paces from my location when Alexander shouted a warning. Another group of Novanians was rapidly approaching from the west, and he'd be surrounded if I didn't intervene. With a growl, I tore my gaze from Claybourne and sprinted toward Alexander's position. I would not abandon my brother to pursue my own revenge.

I reached Alexander moments after the Novanians surrounded him. He was cut off from the other soldiers, myself, and Rynn. He spun in a deadly circle, his movements so rapid they were a blur. He'd attack one foe, slicing with one or both weapons, then would engage another enemy at a different location a heartbeat later. The stench of blood was stronger near his location. Despite his rapid assault, his features were drawn and gray with fatigue.

I must act before Alexander's energy failed him.

I roared as I backhanded a group of soldiers savagely, creating a gap in the Novanians' line. Without hesitation, I struck down another who was already bleeding from a sword wound to his forearm. The force of my blow crushed his armor to his torso. He gasped helplessly as he fell, but his breaths were numbered.

I lashed another pair with my tail, narrowly missing one of our people in the process. The woman leapt back in surprise. She gave me a wary glance and a wide berth as she rushed to Alexander's side.

"You think you're clever, beast?" Claybourne taunted from my right.

As I turned to face him, several things happened at once.

Claybourne leapt from his position paces away from me, his sword aimed directly at my right eye.

Alexander shouted in surprise and alarm, and was abruptly at my side. He vaulted across the remaining distance to block Claybourne's strike.

I jerked my head back in an attempt to avoid Claybourne's weapon and closed my eyes instinctively. His sword could not penetrate my hide, but I had no doubt it would inflict lasting damage to the soft tissue of my eye. I could not move fast enough to avoid the blow, and Claybourne had anticipated my movements precisely.

I bellowed in pain and rage as his blade found its mark. I thrashed blindly. The back of my right hand connected with something, but whether it was Claybourne or someone else, I didn't know.

Blood leaked from my wounded eye to cascade along the side of my jaw. I shook my head in a futile attempt to dislodge the blade, but it remained firmly imbedded.

After several moments, I realized Alexander was calling my name. He said more, but I couldn't make out his words over the surrounding din.

I opened my left eye and was shocked to find Claybourne on his back, his skin turning an unnatural shade of blue-gray. Rynn stood over him, her hands outstretched. A rime of frost was rapidly developing on his steel plate.

Alexander stood in front of me, his face pale beneath his gore-spattered helm. His eyes were wide and his mouth worked, but no words issued from his lips.

"You will not touch him again," Rynn seethed.

Claybourne's breathing was labored. With considerable effort, he lifted his right arm toward her.

Rynn's eyes blazed with righteous indignation. She clenched her jaw as she loomed over him, unrelenting.

Claybourne cried out as visible icicles appeared, encasing his arm up to the shoulder.

"I said, you will not touch him." Her voice was a growl filled with unmitigated rage.

"I won't…be bested by a…filthy…*mage*," Claybourne spat as he attempted to sit upright.

Alexander turned toward the pair, finally tearing his eyes away from mine. He gripped his swords, prepared to strike should Claybourne move from his position. Galewing dove from the sky to land on my brother's shoulder.

Rynn made a sound of disgust as icicles burst from the commander's body, piercing his flesh from every direction. His eyes widened in shock, his sneer disintegrating. He collapsed on his back, unmoving, another corpse to decorate the blood-soaked field.

Alexander gaped at Rynn. "Holy hell," he managed, before turning to face me again. "Andrew…" He shook his head, his expression pained. "Lay still, brother. Let me get that out of you."

I lowered my head and braced myself. I knew instinctively that a burst of unwelcome pain would accompany Alexander's next actions. He grasped the hilt of Claybourne's sword, then drew an unsteady breath. He jerked the blade free in one swift motion.

I grunted in response to the flash of searing pain. Blood continued to pour from the wound and trickled down my face. I tried to blink it away, but could see nothing out of my right eye. I turned my head to look at Alexander with my left.

"Get back to camp, brother," he said shakily. "Lydia needs to tend your eye. I'll speak with you later."

He spun to face the remainder of the Novanian soldiers. Those nearest our location were beginning to lay down their arms in a gesture of surrender now that their ruthless commander was dead.

Ignoring the remnants of battle, I turned to Rynn. Her expression was weary, and her fair skin was ashen. I suspected she had expended a considerable amount of energy during the fight, but I was grateful for her timely intervention. Claybourne would have inflicted further injury if he'd been given the opportunity.

"Thank you," I said.

She shook her head, blinking unshed tears from her eyes. "That bastard had it coming. Andrew, your eye… I wish I'd been faster."

I shrugged, then glanced at Alexander. He gestured for me to go, to return to camp. He had the Novanians' surrender well in hand.

"Let's go," I replied. "I need to see Lydia."

She nodded once before clambering onto my back.

I leapt into the air, flying low over the field. Word of Claybourne's defeat was spreading rapidly through the ranks; evidence of surrender stretched far across the battlefield.

With Claybourne slain, a profound relief washed through me, and I realized I was exhausted. Rage and adrenaline had propelled me through the battle. As both faded, I was left with a hollow sensation, and the pain in my eye intensified. I swiveled my head continuously to survey the field. The vision in my right eye failed to return.

Rynn seemed to understand the reason for my erratic movements. "Do you believe it will heal?" she asked.

I was silent for several moments. I'd never received an injury like this and didn't know if my natural healing was capable of repairing the damage to my eye. And my father had warned me that some injuries could not be overcome.

"Andrew?" she asked, her voice trembling.

"I don't know," I replied truthfully. "At least the damage was minimal, thanks to you."

She shuddered. "When I saw what he planned… I just reacted." She paused to collect her thoughts. When she spoke, her voice was roughened by emotion. "He has caused you so much pain. I could not allow him to inflict any more. I'm glad he's dead."

SEVENTEEN

"Andrew, wake up." Rynn's voice floated to me through the last vestiges of a hazy dream.

I groaned, unwilling to open my eye. It had been three nights since the last battle with Claybourne, and this had been the first in which I'd managed any real measure of sleep. I often had difficulty sleeping after a battle's conclusion, but the continuous ache in my right eye had prevented me from achieving what little I would have managed otherwise.

Lydia had cleaned my wound after we'd returned to camp and performed what healing she could, but it was unlikely my sight would return. My eye was bandaged and a strip of cloth was wound around my head to hold it in place.

I tried to turn over, to face away from Rynn and return to sleep, but she slid around my body to kneel in front of me. She leaned close, and I felt the chill of her skin even though she hadn't touched me.

"It's already midmorning. Alex has been here three times seeking you." Her tone was amused. "I told him you haven't been sleeping well and to leave you be, but he's becoming rather insistent." She paused, and I imagined she smirked. "It seems both impatience and stubbornness run in the Winston family."

I rolled away from her again. "I'd like to sleep. Tell Alex I'll find him when I'm rested."

She grasped my shoulder gently. "You slept the whole night through and then some. I'm grateful you've finally settled enough to rest, but you need to speak with your brother. He wouldn't tell me why he's been so persistent, but I'm certain something has come up."

I released an exasperated sigh and forced my left eye open. "I hope for his sake something has," I replied, surly. I sat up and stretched the stiffness from my back and shoulders.

"Tom has been planning our next move," she replied as she rose to her feet. "Or perhaps Alex merely wants to talk with you. He hasn't been given the chance since the battle." She stooped to pick up the shirt and pair of trousers I'd discarded the previous evening and tossed them in my direction.

I raised my hands in time to catch them, pleased I was beginning to regain some of my depth perception, but I frowned at Rynn in mock displeasure, eliciting a laugh. I tugged the shirt on over my head as the sound of footsteps approached from outside. They stopped just beyond the entrance.

I sighed again while Rynn ducked outside.

"He'll be out in a moment," she stated. Her voice was low, but I heard her words clearly enough.

"It's about time! Holy hell, was he planning to sleep all day?" Alexander asked in an amused tone.

With a groan, I stood to finish dressing.

Outside, Rynn said, "You've told me yourself he often fails to rest for some time after he's been in battle…"

"I have," Alexander conceded, "but I also believe it's true any time he's stressed. It's just how he copes with it. Or fails to cope, as the case may be. But this time…"

I rolled my eyes as I tugged my boots on. "I can hear you," I called, which brought a swift end to their conversation. Emerging from the tent moments later, Rynn offered me a sheepish smile while Alexander smirked.

He crossed his arms. "I said nothing that wasn't true, brother. Besides, if she insists on remaining with you, she'll need to learn your quirks sooner or later."

"And I suppose you've appointed yourself as her informer?" I asked.

Alexander grinned. "Of course."

"I'll leave the two of you to…whatever Alex has planned," Rynn said after a moment. "I'll visit Lydia."

Alexander smiled. "She'd like that."

He said nothing more until she was beyond earshot. "Lydia told me you plan to marry her," he blurted, his face flushing crimson. He shook his head and stared intently at the grass between his boots. "I didn't mean for it to come out quite like that."

I laughed. "I'm surprised it took this long for you to learn of our conversation. I was certain it would be the talk of camp for a while."

"Rynn told her yesterday," Alexander managed, clearly surprised by my words.

I nodded thoughtfully. "I mean to ask her properly, you know. After this business with Colin is over and done."

He studied me for a time. "Tom said he'd asked you to stay in Novania once Colin is ousted. He told me what you said."

I recalled the conversation and shook my head. My position hadn't changed—if anything, it had been strengthened. I'd go where Rynn went, and she didn't plan to linger in Novania. And considering recent events, the kingdom no longer felt like home.

"We aren't planning to stay here, Alex."

"Nor are we. Lydia wants to return to the Citadel. We'll make our home there." He frowned. "I tried to persuade her to choose a location a bit farther from the Oracle, but her mind is set."

"Perhaps when the time comes, we'll travel with you as far as the Citadel," I replied. "I'd like to speak with my father again, but I doubt we'll stay there long."

Alexander nodded. "She misses her family."

"Yes. I've no doubt we'll go to Dwymm, but…" I trailed off, wondering if she'd finally written to her brothers regarding our intentions—and what I was.

Alexander tilted his head, his eyes narrowed. "What is it, brother?"

I laughed uncomfortably. "Her brothers don't know that I'm…not fully human." I ran a hand through my hair. "She was going to write them, but I don't know if she has yet."

"Perhaps you should remind her," Alexander replied with a shrug. "We'll be here for a while longer, and with Claybourne out of the picture, I doubt we'll see any further resistance until we move on the Capitol. This is the perfect time to send a message." He paused to study me once more. "I doubt you have anything to worry over, brother. The people in the Southlands have a high opinion of the dragon-kind. Why would her brothers be any different?"

"She's afraid they'll disapprove. Not of what I am, but of our union." I sighed as I recalled a conversation I'd had with Emmarie, seemingly a lifetime ago. "Not everyone in the Southlands is comfortable around skin-changers. The Merael are a prime example."

Alexander appeared skeptical. "I understand why you're nervous, but I truly believe you have nothing to fear. This is the first time you've been with someone who *knew* what you were from the start, isn't it? I know you never told Claire, and Vera learned after you were married."

I nodded. "I want to do right by her, Alex. For the first time in my life, I have the opportunity to do so, and I'm terrified that I'll ruin it somehow." I gestured toward the bandage obscuring my wounded eye. "And after the battle, I'm not as certain as I once was. I don't know the extent of the damage."

Alexander laughed. "You won't ruin anything. It's plain to everyone who sees you together that you make a fine pair, and I don't believe your eye will deter her. I suspect her brothers know more than she realizes, as well. After all, no one else can safely touch her—and you were together often enough while we were in Dwymm, according to what I've been told."

My face flushed. "Yes. That was before..."

"I know, brother, and I still believe you have nothing to worry over." He clapped me on the shoulder. "We should see what Tom has in store for us today, now that we've spoken."

I gestured to him, indicating he should lead the way. "Rynn said you'd been by three times before she awakened me."

Alexander chuckled and scratched the back of his neck. "When Lydia told me the news, I had to talk to you. I wanted confirmation before word spread." He glanced in my direction, his green eyes sparkling with amusement. "I'm happy for you. She's good for you, whether you see it or not."

I smirked. I suspected I knew the true reason behind Alexander's adamant desire to speak with me. "You wanted to hear it from me before Tom did." When he laughed nervously in response, I said, "At least some things haven't changed."

Two days later, Thomas called a meeting with his advisors. A Corodan I didn't recognize was present—it was another large female, but smaller in stature than Rizzt-tok.

"I am Kresh-tik," she said once everyone was assembled. "I speak for hive while Rizzt-tok recovers."

I glanced at Alexander. It was the first I'd heard of the Corodan warrior's injury. Alexander shrugged and tilted his head toward Thomas, but our younger brother's attention was elsewhere. Thomas had tasked us with interviewing the Novanians who had surrendered since the battle's conclusion, and busy as we'd been, I was unaware of Rizzt-tok's condition. There was also the matter of my own injury to preoccupy my thoughts.

The wound to my eye had nearly healed, but my vision had not returned. It was unlikely that it would. I'd bear the scar of my last battle with Robert Claybourne for the rest of my days, however many that may be. I continued to sport a bandage across my face at Lydia's insistence, and I had not yet gathered the courage to look at my reflection without it in place. I wasn't certain what I'd find when I did so.

"Will Rizzt-tok recover?" Thomas asked when Kresh-tik finished.

Kresh-tik tilted her head, contemplating his words and more than likely discussing the question with the hive. After a moment, she said, "Rizzt-tok will live. Rizzt-tok will not fight again."

Kresh-tik struggled to convey her thoughts as succinctly as Rizzt-tok had, but her implication was clear: Rizzt-tok's injuries were severe enough that her days as a warrior were over.

"A shame," Jonas stated after a moment of silence. "Rizzt-tok is fearsome. She will be missed on the field."

Kresh-tik tilted her triangular head in the other direction. "Rizzt-tok pleased with human's words. Rizzt-tok…plans…to return here when recovered. To lead."

Thomas nodded. "She is always welcome here, Kresh-tik. I assume you will take over her role on the battlefield?"

"Yes." The Corodan's buzzing tone indicated regret.

Alexander shook his head. "The hive has sacrificed so much for our cause. We will always be grateful for its assistance, and to Rizzt-tok for the role she has played."

Kresh-tik swiveled her neck to face him. "Kash-kah commands it. Kash-kah says we must defeat red king."

At the mention of the "red king," the tent fell silent. Everyone present had their own reason for opposing Colin, whether it was his blatant tyranny or more personal matters. I glowered as I considered all he'd done to our family. The hive was right—he must be defeated.

After a moment, Thomas said, "The red king—Colin—is why I have called you all here today. I've received word from our scouts in the Capitol."

I scanned the faces of those assembled, noting Jonas and Everett seemed to have been expecting the announcement. Shyala nodded thoughtfully while Alexander visibly stiffened. Kresh-tik appeared stoic, though it was always difficult to measure emotional reactions from the Corodan.

Thomas studied us in turn, and when his eyes met mine, I nodded. I was curious to learn what the scouts had uncovered during their time in the Capitol and hoped the news would prove useful, if not grant us a small measure of hope.

Thomas drew a breath and steeled himself. "The Capitol is under martial law. Colin has imposed curfews, and the garrison continues to sweep the populace for Marks. There are few within the Capitol willing to harbor anyone bearing the Mark for fear of their own safety. Colin has apprehended people under suspicion of treason if a neighbor accuses them of sympathizing—even if the accusation proves false. Many of those apprehended are never seen again. Our scouts believe they've either been thrown in the dungeons, or sent to the labor camps outside the city. Those slated for execution are dealt with mercilessly. Colin holds the executions in the plaza outside the castle." He paused to look down, a frown creasing his brow. "The inner city has been all but emptied of its residents. Only the king's garrison and those slated for execution reside there now."

"The residents aren't allowed in the inner city," Everett added bitterly. "They are often summoned to bear witness to their neighbors' arrests in the lower city, but if someone is conspicuously absent, they are immediately placed under a cloud of suspicion and often go missing themselves."

"Holy hell," Alexander whispered, shaking his head in disbelief.

I clenched my jaw, appalled at what Colin had become, and furious on behalf of the people I'd once sworn to protect. "If your father had realized how Colin would defile the throne, he would have sought permission from the Council to name a different heir."

Thomas nodded knowingly. "Yes, but none of us could have predicted how twisted Colin would become. With each new report, my conviction to remove him from his post grows." He glanced down for a moment, a slight frown tracing its way across his lips. When he looked up, his gaze was directed at Alexander and me. "Even two months ago, I struggled to accept the role you've thrust me into, but now I understand the necessity. Colin must be stopped for the sake of the people, for the good of Novania. I am…" He sighed and closed his eyes briefly. "I am the last eligible Marsden, and as such, it is my responsibility to undo the wrongs my brother has committed against the kingdom and her people."

I smiled at Thomas, proud of his declaration. In that moment, I knew with a clarity I'd never possessed previously that we'd made the right decision in naming him Colin's successor. Thomas would do right by the people of Novania and would continue to do so once he replaced Colin as king. His path had already been difficult, but he'd finally accepted the mantle of leadership and was determined to correct the mistakes of his predecessors.

"The hive stands behind dragon-brother-new-king," Kresh-tik stated after a moment, her insectile voice carrying through the tent.

"As do the magi," Alexander said with a fierce determination in his green eyes.

"The Merael also wish to see you replace the tyrant who makes a mockery of his throne," Shyala added. "For the good of both our peoples, he must be removed from power."

Thomas' eyes met mine, and I nodded in encouragement. He studied me for a moment, though his blue eyes were unreadable. "And what of the dragon-kind?" he asked pointedly.

I blinked, caught unaware by his question. "Tom, you know I'll always be there should you need me," I replied. "You don't have to ask."

He managed a small smile and nodded. "Perhaps I don't," he countered, "but not everyone present knows your mind as well as your brothers do."

Alexander laughed and nudged me with his elbow. "He has a point, brother."

I shrugged. "I suppose that's fair. You'll have my aid, Tom."

"Good. I'm relieved that everyone still plans to continue this fight, given the recent events and the news we've received from the Capitol." He gestured toward Jonas, indicating the older man should speak.

Jonas' gray eyes swept across those gathered. "With the defeat of Robert Claybourne and the dispersion of much of the king's army, I believe the time to move against the Capitol has come. As many of you know, the Capitol is a veritable fortress. The castle where the king resides lies at the heart of the city, surrounded by a wall with the inner city beyond. The inner city has its own wall, though in the past, it was largely decorative and rarely guarded. Our scouts have reported the occasional guard there. I believe its status remains unchanged. Beyond that wall is the lower city, which includes the marketplace and many businesses, taverns, and warehouses. The lower city is surrounded by another wall, which marks the outer boundaries of the Capitol. This last wall has always been guarded carefully, and the king has increased the garrison's presence over the past months. The scouts entered the city through an old tunnel system—the sewers. They didn't believe it safe to pass directly through the city's gates."

"We'll be in for a lengthy fight," Shyala remarked.

"Potentially, yes," Jonas replied briskly. "I have no doubt we'll be forced to lay siege to the Capitol. It's likely we'll face the most resistance along the outermost wall, but once breached, I believe we can advance rapidly through the city. The second greatest obstacle will be breaching the castle's defenses and locating the king himself."

"Do you believe Colin will name another commander once he learns Claybourne is dead?" I asked.

Everett answered, his dark eyes troubled. "I have no doubt he will, but who he'll name is difficult to judge. That he named Claybourne at all was a mystery. The king's mind has become unfathomable."

"If he names another commander, our scouts will send word," Jonas stated firmly.

"Once we arrive, can we utilize the same tunnel system the scouts did?" I asked. "It may be prudent to leave the scouts at their posts to send word as necessary."

Jonas smiled faintly, amused. "That was my plan, Andrew. The scouts will stay where they are after our arrival. The system leads through the city's sewers, and its paths are narrow. While a small force may work through it and into the city proper, it isn't an ideal means of transporting our people inside. I don't want to draw attention to our use of the tunnels. I believe it best to use them only for urgent communications until we've breached the walls."

I nodded, satisfied with his answer. I was familiar with the tunnels he'd mentioned. Most were only just large enough to accommodate one person at a time, and they were dark, dank, and filthy. I'd inspected several sewer entrances during my time as the former king's commander and knew they'd rarely been guarded—but that may have changed since Colin's ascension.

"We've secured the allegiance of several local farmers," Everett said after a time. "Elias and I have spoken to them on several occasions, and they've agreed to supply food during the siege in exchange for our protection. They don't fear their neighbors, but they fear the king and his soldiers."

"The people have grown weary of Colin's rule," Thomas added. "Each day, more join our cause, hoping to take up arms in opposition of the crown. It is…surprising, and a bit overwhelming."

"Tom—" I began, but was cut off by Alexander, who stepped forward, hands on hips.

"Let's take this fight to him," he stated boldly. "Colin has disgraced our family enough, and I am finished with him. We all stand behind you, brother, and I'll be damned if one day we don't call you king in his stead."

Alexander's declaration was met with nods and further words of encouragement from the others. Thomas reddened slightly, embarrassed by the attention, but he appeared pleased nevertheless.

"I suppose it's settled then," Thomas said. "We'll begin preparations to march on the Capitol."

EIGHTEEN

"You're certain?" Lydia asked, her hands on her hips as a concerned frown etched her pretty features.

We stood outside one of the healers' tents as afternoon began to fade into evening. I crossed my arms but didn't repeat my request.

"*Yes*," Rynn said, exasperated. "Andrew says it feels as though it's healed, but… We both need to see…" She trailed off, struggling with the decision I'd made earlier in the day. I needed to see for myself how much damage Claybourne had inflicted.

Lydia sighed, resigned. "Very well. Let me fetch Claire—she has a mirror." She turned to leave on her errand, then paused mid-stride to face us once more. "Andrew, it isn't as bad as you're imagining. You heal remarkably well. But your eye is clearly blind and there is nothing further I can do to remedy that."

I nodded. "I know."

"Then if you're certain…"

"I am." I turned to Rynn as Lydia departed. Without sight in my right eye, I found I was turning my head more often than I was accustomed to simply to make eye contact with those around me.

Rynn's blue eyes brimmed with compassion. "Andrew…" Her voice was a bare whisper.

"It could have been worse," I reminded her, not for the first time. "You were there when Lydia discussed the injury. If the wound had been any deeper, it would have been fatal. You stopped him in time to save my life, and I will always be grateful."

She shook her head. "I should have acted sooner. I should have—"

I pulled her into my arms. "Hush," I said gently. "What Claybourne did wasn't your fault, and I don't believe any of us could have prevented this. Please don't blame yourself." When she shook her head, I said, "He paid the ultimate price for his crimes while I'm still here, thanks to you."

She reached a hand toward my face, her fingers trembling as she placed them over the bandage. "But your eye. You have such beautiful green eyes…"

I smiled in an attempt to reassure her. "I still have one, you know."

She forced a half-hearted laugh. "I suppose that's something. I'm afraid of what we'll find…"

I held her closer and kissed the top of her head. "You did all you could."

She sighed heavily but made no reply as she leaned her head into my shoulder. We remained that way for several minutes, neither willing to speak nor break away. I wished there were something I could say to her to assuage her guilt. I'd never blame her for the actions of Robert Claybourne, and I hoped my embrace was enough to convey that.

I turned and dropped my arms to my sides as I heard a pair of footsteps approach. Lydia had returned with Claire, who held a small hand mirror. She looked at it pensively as they neared, then her dark eyes met mine. Her expression was troubled, but I realized with a shock that many of her previous injuries were gone. Her jaw was in proper alignment once more, her nose had been straightened… She was once more the beautiful woman who had aspired to be queen.

"Claire, you're—" I began, but she waved one delicate hand dismissively, cutting me off.

"Lydia has mended most of my hurts, but I didn't come to discuss that. It is unimportant. I came for you," she stated evenly. As she spoke, I noted her teeth were no longer broken, though a gap remained on her lower jaw where one was missing.

"If you don't mind kneeling, I'll remove your bandage," Lydia said somberly. She glanced at Rynn. "Would you like to hold the mirror?"

Rynn shook her head. "No, I will stand at his side. We'll face this together."

I smiled and wondered yet again what I'd done to deserve her love. She clasped my left hand in her right as I knelt. Claire walked forward hesitantly until she was at arm's distance. She positioned the mirror to face us, her hands steady though her eyes never left mine. She didn't outwardly show it, but I knew Claire well enough to sense she feared what she'd see once my bandage was removed.

The reflection peering back at me through the silvered glass appeared weary, and other than the bandage, my face appeared unchanged. The same short blond hair that never required trimming, the straight nose, stubble-free cheeks, and that solitary green eye looked back at me, unwavering. Rynn's expression was determined as she looked over my left shoulder into the glass. On my right, Lydia began unraveling the bandage, and I closed my eye.

As the last of the cloth fell away, relief washed through me. The bandage had grown hot and itchy throughout the day, and it was a welcome respite to have it gone. Slowly, I opened my eyes once more.

The wound had healed, but the eye was a milky, colorless orb, occluded by scarring. Even with the bandage gone, I could discern nothing of my surroundings through that eye. The blindness was absolute. I'd be forced to learn how to navigate life with only half my field of vision.

Rynn's grip on my hand intensified, and I glanced at her through the mirror. She offered me an encouraging smile, one meant to reassure. When I looked at Claire, I was surprised to find compassion in her expression, something I'd rarely encountered there before.

"Andrew, are you alright?" Rynn whispered.

I nodded. "Yes. I was expecting worse." I looked at each of the women in turn. "Tell me: Should I continue to cover it up?"

"It's healed," Lydia replied evenly. "The choice to cover it or not is yours alone."

"Perhaps once Thomas has taken the throne, you may wish to cover it for formal occasions," Claire replied. "It wouldn't do for the king's brother to terrify the court… But I suspect the court has been terrified enough of late, and they may not take notice of your eye at all."

I raised my eyebrows. "Am I truly—?"

Claire laughed with a shake of her head. "It was a jest, Andrew. As always, you are far too serious."

"People will notice it, of course," Lydia remarked, "but it doesn't look so bad."

I nodded as I rose to my feet. "Thank you."

Rynn remained silent as the others departed. Once we were alone, she turned to face me directly. "Lydia is right, you know. It isn't so bad."

"You never answered my question," I replied.

She gazed at me for several long moments, her expression unreadable. Finally, she said, "You aren't terrifying to look at, and you need not cover it up. You are the same wonderful, attractive man I fell in love with. You simply have more character now." She reached up to touch the side of my face, her fingers tracing the edge of my right eye. "Does it still hurt?"

I shook my head. "No. There is no pain, only darkness. It's going to take some time to adjust."

She nodded and dropped her hand. "We should return to Thomas' tent."

I chuckled. "Yes, he and Alex will both require a status report before long, even though it's obvious what the prognosis is." I sighed and raked a hand through my hair. "They'll try to keep me from the field. I'm not certain I have it in me to hold back any longer—not when it comes to Colin."

"It's only natural that they worry," she replied. "There have been times when you've acted rashly. You aren't invincible, and some of us fear we'll lose you."

I nodded and stared down at the muddied earth between my boots as my face flushed with shame. "I know. This injury has been a sobering reminder of that." I paused to collect my thoughts, morose and disappointed with myself. "My father tried to warn me that some injuries won't heal. I ignored his advice, confident I'd overcome anything. I've risked myself to protect everyone else because I believed I'd walk away unscathed, just as I've always done. Have I been a fool to think that?"

She took my left hand in her right as we began to walk from the healers' tents toward the center of the camp. "You are no fool, Andrew Caein. I just hope you'll be more careful from now on."

As we strode past the tents and crossed paths with other people, many glanced in my direction, then hurriedly looked elsewhere when our eyes met, ashamed they'd been caught staring. When my eye was hidden behind its bandage, the same people had acted normally. Now that the true extent of my injury was visible, they were unable to stop themselves from gawking. By the time we reached Thomas' command tent, I was frustrated and irritable.

Alexander was speaking with Elias outside, and the pair turned at our approach. Alexander grinned, but it faltered and fled when he studied my face. Elias' expression remained carefully neutral, though I detected a note of concern in his green eyes.

"Ah, hell, it's worse than I'd believed," Alexander said as he stepped forward to peer into my face. "Lydia said the eye would be useless, but I kept telling her you *always* heal. I believed you'd recover." He hung his head, unable to hide his disappointment. "You'll need time to reacquaint yourself with a sword, brother. It's going to be tough if you can't see on one side."

"I'll manage," I replied gruffly, determined to overcome this minor setback. I was alive thanks to his intervention and Rynn's, and I wouldn't allow this injury to sway me from my course. "Is Thomas inside?"

Alexander frowned but nodded. "He's with Jonas and Uncle Ev discussing logistics. They may be a while."

"I'll let them know you'd like a word," Elias offered before ducking inside the tent.

"I'll run drills with you tomorrow," Alexander said. "I know you'll 'manage,' Andrew, but I was trained to use a blade by Rossley, if you recall. When his son returned from campaign minus an eye, it took him months to reorient himself. Rossley tasked me to spar with his son to help him regain his depth perception—and I was no older than ten."

I growled in frustration. I knew he was trying to help, but I wanted to lash out nevertheless. He was undeserving of my anger—he wasn't at fault for my damned injury, nor was he responsible for the gaping bystanders that had landed me in a foul mood—but I didn't want his sympathy. I closed my eyes in an attempt to quell my building rage.

"Alex," I said after a few moments, "I know you're trying to help, but I've been the recipient of countless stares since I left your wife at the healers' tents. I'm in no temper to discuss this right now."

Rynn placed her hand on my arm in an effort to calm me. "Andrew…"

Alexander nodded. "I understand, brother. I think many others believed you'd recover, just as I did. I hope you'll take up my offer when you're ready. We need you on the battlefield despite this setback."

"I will, Alex, but I need more time."

He clapped one hand against my shoulder. "Take care, brother. I need to see how Lydia fares. She's been busier than ever, and in her current condition, she tires easily."

I nodded as he made his farewell to Rynn and departed.

"I hope once the initial shock has passed, people will stop fussing over me," I grumbled. "Holy hell, I'm not helpless."

"Andrew, they care about you," Rynn replied evenly. "And seeing a permanent injury incurred on one of the dragon-kind *is* a bit unsettling. We've all heard tales, and many of us have seen for ourselves how quickly you heal."

I frowned but didn't argue. "Claybourne planned that strike. It was as if he *knew* it was a weak point."

"You said he'd thoroughly researched the dragon-kind," she replied softly. "Between Claybourne's last actions, the war machines, and the treatment you received during your captivity, he knew precisely how to inflict damage." She paused and averted her gaze. "We must be careful. If Claybourne knew these things, the king does as well."

"I know."

The thought had occurred to me numerous times since my captivity. Claybourne had known exactly what to do to keep me subdued, had known how best to inflict pain, had known where to strike in order to inflict lasting injury. He'd boasted of the books he'd read, acquired at Colin's behest, and his desire to ensure he knew every aspect of my physiology. He'd incapacitated me with such ease; I still shuddered when I recalled those moments when I'd been shrouded in the net, unable to break free.

Colin may not have any interest in books or research, but surely Claybourne wasn't the only person he'd enlisted to ensure my demise.

I was continually surprised by Colin's ferocity and his relentless pursuit of me. We'd been rivals for years before he learned he'd assume the throne, but his actions had seemed nothing more than an attempt to outpace his older brother. Something had changed when he learned he'd become king, and I still didn't understand what motivated him to become the damned tyrant he was.

Time and again, he'd gone out of his way to humiliate us, and he'd made attempts on each of our lives as well. He'd been no less cruel to Claire and the late princess, Verena. What would drive a man so far over the brink that he'd see his family dead and knowingly commit infanticide on his own child? Or had he always been a damned monster, and we'd failed to see it?

Movement inside Thomas' tent drew me from my tangled web of thoughts. I turned toward the opening as Thomas and the three former dukes exited. Thomas' eyes widened slightly, but he kept his emotions in check as he studied me.

"Elias told us of your eye," he said after a moment.

He stepped toward me, his curiosity overriding his desire to maintain his carefully crafted composure. He peered at my face as I'd expected he would, and after a moment, he retreated.

"Does it hurt?"

I chuckled, amused his response was focused on my welfare, whereas Alexander's had been bitter disappointment with the injury. "Not any longer. Lydia says it's healed, and I believe her… But the eye itself is useless."

Thomas nodded thoughtfully, a flicker of sorrow in his eyes. "You've risked so much for both of us. For me. We wouldn't be here without you, but this… Colin is going to answer for every drop of blood he has spilled, every scar he has inflicted." He clenched his fists in a momentary display of anger, then shook his head. "You didn't deserve this."

I shrugged. There was nothing we could do to change the past, and I'd learn to cope. "I'll manage, Tom. I always do."

"I think we should speak in the morning," Jonas cut in. "Many of Alexander's plans focus on your actions, your capabilities, and this injury will effect them."

I nodded as understanding washed over me. Alexander's disappointment hadn't been due to my wound, but from the realization he'd be forced to rewrite many of his schemes. "Send for me when you're ready, Jonas."

He nodded and took his leave. Everett followed suit soon after, leaving Tom and I alone with Rynn and Elias.

"I've mentioned to your brothers that it was unlikely your eye would recover," Elias said. "Alex has a tendency toward unabashed optimism, and there was little I could do to dissuade him. The Winstons have long been associated with the dragon-kind, long before your mother came along, and I know enough to understand there are some injuries that can't be overcome."

I nodded. "I know. Alex had to see for himself before he'd believe it. It's his way."

"At the very least, this should prevent Alex from goading you into any more reckless decisions," Thomas replied with a frown. "If he'd remained with the line as he'd been ordered, none of this would have happened."

I lifted my eyebrows. I hadn't been aware Alexander had defied orders and charged headlong toward Claybourne.

Thomas' expression darkened at my reaction. "He didn't tell you?"

"No. We've been busy since the battle, and there was little time to talk."

Thomas crossed his arms. "He's had ample opportunity to speak up. He's been avoiding the issue. Damn him."

"Perhaps he's been avoiding the discussion because he feels guilty?" Elias suggested. "I can't fault him for it, given how close he and Andrew are."

Fuming, Thomas said, "I'll speak with him tomorrow. He needs to stop skirting the conversation and admit he's partially at fault."

I didn't share Thomas' fury, but I was disappointed. I didn't know which was worse. I sighed and ran a hand through my hair.

"If Alex is to blame, then I am as well," Elias replied after a time. "I was with him that day, and I made no move to stop him when he chose to break formation."

I shook my head. "I'm not surprised Alex acted as he did. I had to save his skin countless other times during our war with the Corodan."

Thomas rolled his eyes, his exasperation with the situation finally reaching its limit. "That's exactly my point! Alex has a history of reckless behavior, and every time, you've been there to rescue him. He has never learned from his mistakes, but I think he will this time."

"That's what you were doing when Claybourne charged," Rynn said. "You went to Alex because he was surrounded. Your concern for him overpowered your perception of the battle… Tom makes a valid point."

"As I said, I'll speak with him tomorrow," Thomas replied. "He needs to admit his mistake at the very least, but I'd be thrilled if I can convince him to be more circumspect. I will *not* have you suffering any further harm because Alex can't control his impulses."

"Make certain Alex knows I don't blame him for what happened," I said, concerned it would sow an unwanted rift between us. "And I'd like to speak with him as well, once you're finished."

Thomas studied me for a moment, worry creasing his brow. "Are you certain you're alright, Andrew? You seem…downcast, which is understandable, but it isn't like you."

I forced a tired smile. "I suppose I am. I understood the outcome of this injury almost immediately. Lydia made it very clear. But I'd been holding on to the tenuous hope that maybe she was wrong." I shook my head ruefully. "I should have listened to her. Lydia has never been wrong when it comes to the healing arts."

Rynn clasped my hand in a gesture of reassurance. I smiled at her, glad for her presence. Until Thomas had asked his latest question, I believed I was coping well enough, but I realized my blind right eye was a source of internal anguish—and I'd been suppressing it. Rynn's support meant more than she'd ever know, but I would not allow my internal struggle to become apparent to anyone else.

As I'd told my brothers, I would manage.

Thomas nodded solemnly. "If you need anything, I'll do all I can. And I *will* speak with Alex. He owes you more than you realize."

NINETEEN

Jonas met me near the southern palisade the next morning. Orders had been given to prepare for departure; a few dozen of Everett's people distributed rations nearby, while wagons were loaded with supplies. A contingent of soldiers worked to uproot the palisade with the assistance of several magi, and Jonas spoke to some of them as we walked past. He hoped to have most of the work complete before nightfall, and we'd begin the trek toward the Capitol the following morning.

"Alex wasn't wrong," he said after I relayed our conversation from the previous evening. "I encourage you to accept his offer if you plan to do battle as you currently are."

I suppressed a groan. Jonas was right, but it was difficult to relinquish the role of mentor I'd played with Alexander over the course of our lives. It seemed Claybourne had wounded more than my eye—my pride suffered as well.

"I'll speak with Alex later," I replied. "I don't relish the notion of standing aside while everyone else fights."

I'd spoken with Tomas earlier and he was undoubtedly with Alexander at present. I hoped for their sakes that neither lost their temper. Our family was strained enough by the prospect of facing Colin, and I wasn't certain I possessed the patience to act as mediator between Thomas and Alexander should their discussion devolve into a pointless argument.

"I understand." He paused, contemplative. "I'd also suggest you learn how this affects you as a dragon. I know you flew back to camp at the end of the battle, but it may be useful to experiment with some staged combat situations. I can arrange something for this afternoon if you're amenable."

I nodded absently. My field of vision was narrowed, but I believed I'd manage while human. The notion that the blindness would further affect me as a dragon hadn't occurred to me, but Jonas was right. My eyes were spaced differently when I shifted, and it was likely the blindness would be a greater impediment when I assumed my dragon form.

I tried to recall the brief flight I'd undertaken from the battlefield to the healers' tents, but my memory was hazy. I'd been preoccupied and consumed by pain, but I remembered turning my head more frequently in order to effectively see the world below.

"I think that would be wise," I agreed.

He nodded. "Good. Once I arrange it, I'll send word."

As he left, I heard footsteps rapidly approaching on my right. I turned toward the sound to find Alexander, his jaw set in determination. He was upset, and I knew immediately his talk with Thomas hadn't ended well.

He paused when he reached my position, then said, "Walk with me, brother."

I nodded and followed him toward a stand of trees some distance beyond the palisade. He walked at a brisk pace, and I was forced to lengthen my stride to keep up. He stared at the ground as we traveled and didn't look up until we were beneath the boughs of the trees, where he stopped abruptly. When he looked up, his expression was one of guilt mixed with sorrow.

"I've just been to see Tom," he began haltingly. "I knew he wanted to talk. Some of our plans must change, but…" He sighed heavily and looked down again, defeated.

"Alex, Tom spoke with me last night. I know what this is about."

He risked a glance in my direction, and I was surprised to find him fighting off tears. "Damn it, this is my fault, and I know it's my fault, but I don't know what to do about it. I've spoken to Lydia countless times while I tried—and failed—to find the words to say to you. I don't know what I should tell you other than I've been a colossal ass and I'm sorry." His words had come in a torrent as he struggled with his emotions.

"I don't blame you for what happened. I told Tom as much last night."

He nodded and ran a hand through his hair, pulling several long strands from their binding. "I know, but if I had done as Jonas ordered, you'd still have use of your eye. We were holding our position for a while, and then there was an opening. I could see that cursed bastard, and my only thought was I'd be damned if I let him live a second time. I charged, and the others followed my lead without question. I shouldn't have done that. I should have—"

"Alex," I cut in firmly, "none of that matters. Claybourne is dead, and that's the important thing. What I didn't tell Tom was that I *also* had it in my mind to kill him that day. It's just as likely I'd have suffered the same fate even if you hadn't been involved."

I blinked, surprised by my own admission. I'd told no one of my plan that day, not even Rynn, knowing she would have tried to talk me out of it. It had been a rash idea, but one I'd been unable to ignore once it lodged in my brain. That Thomas had laid the blame solely on Alexander was unfair.

Alexander studied me silently for a time, a glimmer of hope in his eyes. "But I *was* involved, and if I hadn't been surrounded, you would have maintained your focus on Claybourne. Tom is right to be angry with me." His shoulders slumped as he looked away. "I'm just grateful you aren't. I feared you'd resent me, Andrew."

I snorted. "You know me better than that, brother."

He shrugged noncommittally. "I wasn't expecting our youngest brother to lecture me for an hour, either. He accused me of being selfish and hotheaded. Perhaps he's right." He scratched at the nape of his neck but still refused to meet my eye.

"Tom is trying to do what he believes is right," I replied. "His words stem from concern for you, as well as concern for me."

Alexander looked up, but pain lingered in his expression. "I understand. I've acted just as I always have—without thought for how my actions will impact *you*, or anyone else, for that matter. Lydia scolded me last night and said I must be more careful, since it's unlikely you'll be able to protect me as well as you've done previously. She doesn't want to raise our child alone, and I can't fault her. I promised I would not disobey any further orders without good reason."

"I'm glad to see you're finally starting to grow up, Alex." I clapped him on the shoulder.

He chuckled dryly. "That's one way to put it. Receiving a scolding from Tom as though I were a child was a shock… But I needed to hear it." Abruptly, he smirked. "You know, Tom has truly begun to show the sort of leader he'll become. It's odd to look at him and remember that just a year ago, he was the fidgety, book-minded brother that most of the nobility tended to ignore. Now he's primed to take the throne and has learned to command their respect. He's still Tom, but he's now…something more."

I nodded my agreement. "We made the right choice. He reminds me of your father. He'll be a great king so long as we manage to oust Colin."

Alexander laughed grimly. "Mark my words, Andrew: Colin will be overthrown, and he'll be lucky if his own people don't tear him to shreds in the process."

"On that topic, I think I'd like to take you up on that offer of sparring. I… I need your help, as much as I hate to admit it."

He arched an eyebrow in surprise before breaking into a grin. "I knew you'd come around eventually. Let's go."

It didn't take long before I realized just how right Alexander was in his assessment of my new situation. Without half of my vision, I constantly left myself open to counter-attacks as we sparred. Alexander intentionally moved toward my right side in order to test my reflexes and my ability to parry his blows. I'd always been a passable swordsman, but I grew frustrated with my inability to *see* his attacks before they struck.

After a half-hour, I threw down the practice blade with an angry snarl, cursing myself as inept. I'd anticipated some difficulty, but had not accounted for the true magnitude of my problem.

Adding to my irritation, we'd gathered a crowd. Alexander's skills had an almost legendary status amongst our army, and many watched, enraptured, as we sparred. I wanted the audience gone.

"Don't give up, brother," Alexander said, exasperated. "We've only just begun. It will take time. Be patient."

I growled in indignation. Patience wasn't something I had an abundance of even on the best of days, and today was not one such day.

"Alright, don't be patient," he said with a shrug. "But we need to work through this before we reach the Capitol."

I glared at him and retrieved the wooden sword from where it lay in the trampled grass.

"I know that look," he replied. "Remember, I'm trying to *help*. Raging and throwing your brute force into this game will only make matters worse."

"It'll make *me* feel better," I grumbled.

Alexander rolled his eyes heavenward and shook his head. "I'll never understand how Rynn abides your damned temper," he muttered as he prepared to strike again.

He charged forward in a straight line. I parried his first strike and shoved his blade away. He side-stepped, and as I pivoted to face him again, he aimed a blow at my ribs. I moved my blade in time to block it, but I lacked the leverage to shove him back. I was forced to await his next move.

He held the position for several seconds before sliding his blade along mine. He thrust toward me, giving me little opportunity to parry, but I met his sword with mine once more. I glared a challenge, silently daring him to strike again.

He grinned and shoved me back with more force than I'd anticipated. I stumbled, felt my right heel catch on a rock, then fell heavily on my backside, unable to regain my balance.

A moment later, Alexander stood over me, smirking as he extended his hand toward me. Cursing under my breath, I gripped his hand and allowed him to help me to my feet. Our audience broke into excited commentary, and I shot them a glare.

"*That* had nothing to do with your eyesight, brother," he remarked once I was upright. "It was our best series yet until you found that stone." He paused to study me thoughtfully. "Have you considered striking with your left? Perhaps if you wore a shield on your right, you'd be less vulnerable on that side."

I frowned obstinately. I'd never trained with a shield and was reluctant to use one even now. Shields could be cumbersome, and though the weight wouldn't be a burden, I disliked the notion. It simply wasn't my style, and in my frustration, I was unwilling to consider the change.

Alexander returned my frown with one of his own. "Fine, no shield. But at least humor me and try fighting with your left. I want to see if there is any improvement. If there isn't, we'll continue as we were."

Reluctantly, I agreed. I shifted the sword to my left hand and was struck by how unfamiliar the stance was. I'd trained since childhood with a blade in my right. This felt utterly wrong, backwards and awkward. I shook my head and adjusted my grip on the hilt even as Alexander rushed me again.

I parried his strike, realizing that switching hands forced me to concentrate on my movements more than I would have done otherwise. I was acutely aware of what I must do, and it provided a brief opportunity to anticipate his next strike. When he side-stepped to my right, trying to take advantage of my blind side, I pivoted toward him. His sword slashed toward my gut, but I blocked it, then swung my right fist.

His eyes widened in surprise. He ducked, but my fist grazed the top of his skull. He stumbled away with a grin while our growing audience began to clap appreciatively.

"I think we have something to work with," he said with a laugh. "I hadn't considered you might become something of a brawler on the field, but this is good."

My skepticism with his declaration must have been evident in my expression, for he threw his head back and laughed even harder. "With your strength, you'd be formidable fighting in that manner. Not to mention it'll take most people unaware." He grinned and adjusted his stance. "Again, brother."

After two hours of sparring with Alexander, and another two with Jonas' chosen recruits, I was beginning to regain my lost confidence. My effectiveness as a dragon hadn't been diminished as much as when I was human, but it was due more to my natural armor than it was to any difference in my field of vision.

Jonas was pleased with the outcome, which came as a relief. The last thing I wanted was to be relegated to the sidelines as we approached the Capitol. I wanted—*needed*—to be a part of the action.

As we concluded the exercises for the day, Rynn and Alexander left the crowd of onlookers to meet me. Rynn carried my clothing and boots, while Alexander grinned knowingly.

"You seem to be doing well enough as a dragon, brother," Alexander remarked. "That white eye makes you seem a bit more terrifying too. I certainly wouldn't want to be among the king's men assigned to face you."

Rynn shook her head in amusement as I shifted and began to dress. "He won't be alone," she replied firmly. "They'll have to contend with me as well."

Alexander smirked. "And that is equally terrifying, believe me."

Rynn laughed while I arched an eyebrow in my brother's direction. "You're one to talk, Alex. There is no warrior in the whole of Novania who can match your skills when you work your magic. It's like watching a whirlwind with swords."

Alexander blinked, his face flushing crimson. "I, ah…" He shook his head, at a loss for words.

I laughed. It was rare when I left Alexander speechless.

"Tom wanted to speak with you," Rynn said while Alexander continued to flounder. "Alex was to tell you, but it seems he's lost his tongue."

I snickered. "I'll speak with him after I've found something to eat."

We walked toward camp in companionable silence. The sun was nearing the western horizon, painting the clouds in shades of flame. The camp bustled as final preparations were made for our departure, but the atmosphere was hopeful, upbeat, and determined.

A rumble reminiscent of thunder crashed through the clear sky moments later, accompanied by the unmistakable reek of ozone. Every exposed inch of my skin began to tingle, then itch. I stared skyward for several seconds in an attempt to locate the source of the noise or the uncomfortable sensation, but there was nothing marring the twilit expanse save for those few wispy clouds.

But the scent and my discomfort meant only one thing: *Magic.*

"What was that?" Alexander asked, his voice loud as the camp fell eerily silent around us.

Rynn shook her head. "I don't know. Even Siorus' power doesn't rumble through—"

Her words were cut short as a second thunderous wave, louder and more powerful than the first, resounded above and around the camp. My skin prickled and grew warm. I resisted the urge to scratch despite the overwhelming desire to do so. Nothing would ameliorate the itch short of shedding my skin.

If a third wave crashed through our camp, I'd require a measure of protection.

"I'm going to Tom's tent," I said over my shoulder.

I broke into a sprint, heedless of their questions. The magical energy caused significant discomfort, and I was reminded of Lileen's failed experiment in the Stone Grove. I couldn't risk remaining in the open to face this, whatever it was.

Rapid footfalls echoed behind me. I knew without looking that Rynn followed in my wake.

"I'll fetch Lydia!" Alexander called.

Thomas stood at the entrance of his command tent gazing skyward, his expression troubled. Without pausing to explain, I darted past him and into the nearest corner of the tent, hoping the canvas would protect me if another blast of magical energy passed through our camp.

Rynn spoke to Thomas while I took a moment to catch my breath. I rubbed my hands against my forearms futilely, but the fire beneath my skin remained.

Thomas entered with Rynn as a third rumble tore through the air, but this one seemed less potent than the last. I smelled ozone, but the tent shielded me enough that my skin wasn't affected any further. I drew a breath and sighed with relief.

"Andrew?" Rynn asked, concerned.

"It's magic," I replied. "Being inside helps. It blocks some of the effects. What's happening?"

She shook her head, uncertain. "I don't know. I've never experienced anything like this."

Thomas frowned. "If it's magic, then Colin didn't do this."

I nodded. "I know. Colin would never agree to the use of magic, even if it meant victory for his cause. But it *is* magic. Powerful magic. And I don't believe it's the work of *our* magi."

"What could possibly—?"

Thomas' words were cut off by a fourth peal of thunder ringing with the echoes of a thousand panes of glass shattering simultaneously. The ozone scent was nearly overpowering. I made a face as my stomach roiled. Even with the scant protection the tent provided, this final blast of magical energy left me so uncomfortable I wanted to sprint for the nearest river and dive beneath the surface to soothe my skin. I ground my teeth and clenched my fists in a desperate attempt to ignore my discomfort.

"Andrew!" Rynn's voice was laden with concern as she raced across the tent to my side. She touched the side of my face, and the chill of her hand was an instant relief. I leaned into her palm.

"That feels nice."

She placed her other hand on my arm. "Your skin is cherry-red. Whatever this is, it isn't good for *you*."

I nodded. "I hope it stops soon, otherwise, I'm going to make a dash for the river."

Rapid footsteps approached from outside, and Thomas beckoned to someone urgently. It was Everett, followed by Bryson Feige, clasping a message in his hands. Thomas tied the tent's entrance closed after they entered.

"My lord," Bryson said as he handed Thomas the message, "when the first wave passed through, I sent a letter to the Oracle. This is her response. It is…troubling."

Rynn moved her hands to my forearms, running them between wrist and elbow where my skin had been exposed to the air. Her icy touch was a balm to my irritated skin.

Bryson peered at us curiously for a moment while Thomas read, but he made no comment. I had no desire to explain the details of my greatest vulnerability. He could wonder, but I would not confirm his suspicions.

Thomas sighed as he lowered the message and placed it carefully atop the table we'd so often used to plan our strategies. "The Oracle says what we just experienced is the result of the Barrier's collapse."

"Is it finished?" Rynn asked without looking toward him. Her concern for my welfare outweighed the implications of the Oracle's words.

Thomas nodded. "She expected no more than four waves would result from the collapse. The histories she refers to—which, as a Novanian, I am unfamiliar with—claim there were four tiers of magic that emanated from the Barrier when it was created. The same should have occurred with its downfall."

"Yes. There is always symmetry." Bryson glanced toward us, but didn't question Rynn's actions or remark on the state of my flushed skin. "It should be over now. It's fortunate we're so far away. Each wave would have been stronger near the Barrier, and the Citadel sits at the heart of the encircled lands. It was struck from all directions by the blasts." He paused, considering his next words. "The Oracle said there was no lasting damage, but many broken windows resulted. We knew of her prediction, but to learn it has actually happened…" He trailed off, bewildered and overwhelmed.

"If Colin learns what happened, we may be forced to change our plans," I said as Rynn began to massage my hands.

"If we move on the Capitol swiftly, he won't have the opportunity to strike the Southlands," Thomas countered. "Jonas believes we'll reach the Capitol in three days. Let's see if we can't make it two."

TWENTY

Between Thomas' determination and the news that the Barrier had collapsed, our people were willing to press on without further delay. The urgency of the situation was clear, and the sooner we began our assault on the Capitol, the sooner the threat to the Southlands would be removed. Most magi seemed to take the news in stride, but the Merael were visibly shaken. Their ancestral home in the Thornhallow was near the former location of the Mage's Gate and would be the first area attacked if Colin sent his army south.

By the time we'd broken camp, my reaction to the previous evening's magical encounter was gone. My skin had healed during the night—as much from Rynn's assistance than from my natural ability. I was in better spirits than I'd been in for days and was eager to move on.

We left Willever just after dawn and marched in a southeasterly direction at a rapid pace. There were a few grumbles throughout the ranks as we moved, but the majority were willing to advance at speed. Rynn and I walked near the head of the column with Thomas, Alexander, Everett, and Hulda, who had taken it upon herself to bear the crimson and ivory dragon standard. Behind us, Emmarie marched with her uncle, Tylmar, alongside the Roche twins. Jonas, Elias, and their personal guards walked ahead. Lydia had elected to ride in a cart near the end of the procession due to her advancing pregnancy, but had expressed her frustration at her inability to keep pace with Alexander.

We made excellent progress the first day, and moved at first light on the second. It was midmorning when we reached the first of the rumored camps Colin had built in the countryside surrounding the Capitol. Not far from the road, a stout stone wall had been erected, encircling an expanse roughly the size of an average farmstead. Inside the wall, wooden structures could be seen, and the sound of countless hammers resounded from within.

A half dozen men garbed in the armor of the king's garrison stood watch at the entrance. As our column became visible, they continued to lounge against the wall, apparently unconcerned. I wondered if they believed we were part of Claybourne's army, returning home from the field.

I caught glimpses of the poor wretches stationed within the walls. Their ankles were chained to one another as they stood in long lines, toiling in backbreaking labor. Some hammered enormous chunks of stone, while others chiseled the broken pieces into shape. More of the king's garrison wandered amongst them, overseeing their work. When a prisoner appeared to fall behind, the nearest soldier struck them with the hilt of a sword or the back of a gauntleted fist.

"Holy hell, the rumors were true," Thomas whispered, horrified. He stared at the Novanians chained at Colin's behest for a time, then turned to Alexander. "Tell Jonas I want those guards disarmed and the people within freed. I assume this is one of the work camps we've been told of. I will *not* stand for this. Our people deserve better."

Alexander nodded, pausing to glance briefly at me before departing. His expression relayed his thoughts clearly enough; he was disgusted with Colin's methods and wouldn't question Thomas. Our youngest brother was justified in his desire to see this atrocity dismantled.

When Alexander returned a few minutes later, Jonas had called a halt to our march. Alexander grinned knowingly as he approached. "There aren't many soldiers guarding the camp," he said, "and Jonas believes we'll subdue them swiftly, but he wants to put on a display of intimidation. He wants those who elect to run home to their king to tell Colin we're a force to be feared." His grin widened. "He requests the presence of my brother, the Lord Dragon."

I was unable to stifle my laugh. "I assume you'd like me to shift?"

"Yes, brother, that's the idea."

"I'm coming with you," Rynn said in a tone that indicated she would tolerate no argument.

"Of course," Alexander replied before he turned to speak with the twins. "I'd like you to accompany us as well. Jonas has sent word down the line to various others who will join us." To Thomas, he said, "This will be over before midday, Tom. The people have suffered far too long already."

Thomas nodded once. "Good. Colin will answer for this."

"He will," Alexander replied in a low growl, his expression a mask of rage.

"Alex…" I said in a warning tone.

His temper was dangerously close to overriding his sense of reason. I'd have to watch Alexander carefully when we finally confronted Colin. We'd seldom spoken of what we planned to do with our brother once we were face-to-face, but I feared Alexander would act rashly when that time came. I wanted to prevent him from committing a deed he'd come to regret, one he'd rue for the rest of his days, one that would undoubtedly affect Lydia and their unborn son. Alexander wasn't considering the consequences despite his vehement promises to do better.

And whatever Colin had become, he was still our brother, still family. Alexander would feel his death keenly, no matter how furious he was.

Alexander glowered at me before turning to stride toward Jonas. I shook my head and frowned, uncertain how to defuse his temper.

"I'll speak with him later," Thomas said. "I believe I understand his rage better than you do. After all, I was there when Colin threw him in the dungeon."

I nodded. I'd failed to make the connection myself, distanced from the Capitol as I'd been when Colin imprisoned Alexander. While I had spared Alexander from the executioner's blade, his treatment in the dungeon was a topic he refused to speak of. He'd been bruised and beaten when I'd encountered him that day on the tourney field, but he'd never once spoken of how he'd been injured. Had it been the jailers, under orders from Colin? Or had Colin himself perpetrated the crime? He'd certainly never refrained from using his fists against Claire.

"Go, Andrew," Thomas said firmly. "Alex and I will work through this."

A few minutes later, I was in dragon form, staring down several of the king's garrison, Rynn perched between the spines on my back. Jonas and his chosen contingent were arrayed in front of me, weapons drawn, while the king's soldiers glanced nervously between his steely gaze and the looming threat I posed from above.

"I order you to throw down your weapons and surrender, or you'll have a fight on your hands." Jonas' voice held an edge that commanded attention.

The woman in charge of the garrison managed a nod at his words, her dark eyes fixed on me rather than the speaker. A fine sheen of sweat coated her brow and her face was pale. When she made no further movement and none of the soldiers under her command obeyed the order, I rose to a greater height, peering above our forces to growl in their direction. Rynn snickered softly.

"I will not repeat myself," Jonas said, his voice lowering to a threat. "Drop your weapons."

The woman nodded again and motioned for her people to comply. As the garrison began to slowly disarm and lay their weapons on the ground, Jonas signaled Alexander. His eyes narrowed, Alexander charged forward in a flash of motion nearly too rapid to follow. He collected the weapons before the Novanians could react to his presence amongst them.

Jonas motioned to a group of soldiers who proceeded to surround the king's garrison. A young man who looked to be less than twenty managed to voice the question all of the king's people likely had in their minds.

"What do you intend to do with us?" His voice quaked despite his best efforts to swallow his fear.

"Lord Marsden will decide," Jonas replied dismissively as the group was led away. He peered up at me. "I believe you are best suited to demolishing the wall, given your size and strength. As for the rest of you," he said, turning toward the others, "unshackle these poor souls and see that any wounded are taken to the healers. Be on your guard. There may be more of the king's men inside. Deal with them as necessary."

Thomas' decision to dismantle the work camp cost us the better part of the day, but no one complained. We learned the prisoners had been sentenced to hard labor by the king, their crime nothing more than the *suspicion* of harboring those bearing the Mark. Many claimed innocence, and I had no doubt it was true. A few admitted they'd been sheltering a family member or close friend with the hope of sparing them from the executioner's block. All were convinced the king had fallen to madness, and most wanted to see justice served. Some who were healthy enough readily agreed to join forces with Thomas. Many simply planned to return home.

We learned there were three other camps in the lands surrounding the Capitol. Thomas issued orders for a small contingent to march on the other camps and free those held within. Elias volunteered to lead them, and was granted the post. The stone walls surrounding this camp had been erected with haste and were of poor craftsmanship—Elias and his people would have little difficulty toppling the others without my aid.

We planned to remain overnight at the camp, then part ways with Elias in the morning. We'd reach the Capitol by noon on the following day, so long as we maintained our previous pace. The atmosphere throughout the ranks was one of grim determination; everyone had a reason for following Thomas, and many of those decisions had been reinforced by the discovery of the labor camp. Colin must be stopped for the good of the kingdom and the lands beyond.

Our army was large enough to surround the outermost walls of the Capitol, and we possessed the resources to build additional siege towers, trebuchets, and battering rams. Due to Elias' negotiations with the farmers near Willever, we'd have food enough to last the spring and into summer. Trapped within the walls of the city, Colin could not boast the same.

I awakened well before dawn the next day, prepared for the final leg of our march. The morning was cool, the grass along the road soaked with dew as the sun lightened the sky. I noted Thomas was awake, pacing near the head of our column. Hulda and another soldier accompanied him at a distance. I walked toward them, stepping over and around sleeping bodies where they lay, cloak-wrapped, on the ground.

Thomas glanced toward me as I approached, a flicker of a smile crossing his features. He'd trimmed his hair and beard since the previous evening and had donned a cloak bearing the same dragon insignia as his standards. I knew without asking that his appearance was due to the influence of Everett—it was imperative he make a worthy first impression on the people of the Capitol when we arrived. To successfully take the throne, he must look the part of king.

"Nice cloak," I said as I fell in beside him.

He chuckled. "It was Elanor's doing. She insisted I should have a cloak to match the standards, as befits my rank and title. It's likely I have neither at present, if Colin has had any say in the matter."

"Colin's time is nearing its end, Tom," I replied. "We'll see this through."

He studied me carefully for a moment, his head tilted in thought. "Yes, I believe we will. Even three months ago, I would have thought it impossible to gather such a following. It's humbling to realize so many believe in our cause, that so many believe in *me*."

"You'll be a worthy king, brother."

He shrugged. "I hope so. There are times when I still don't know what I should do next or what the best course of action might be."

"Every person in a position of leadership feels that way," I said in an attempt to encourage him. "And as I continue to remind you—"

He laughed and waved a hand. "Yes, I have advisors and the governor's council. But you speak of leadership as though you know from experience."

"I was commander of the king's army, brother. While not as prestigious a title as *king*, I was expected to lead. I understand more than you realize." I shrugged. "Your father once told me he often lost sleep over important decisions, fearing he'd follow the wrong path. You remind me of him."

"You would know better than I," Thomas replied. "You'd talk for days after you returned from campaign. He respected you, Andrew. But with Colin being groomed as heir—though he didn't know it at the time—Alex and I were often left to our own devices. Certainly, we had our own duties to attend to, but we weren't afforded the same time with our father as you were." He managed a smile then. "I will take it as a compliment that you believe I possess some of his traits."

"Your uncle has done well since you left Bridgewaters," I replied as I reminisced on the days we'd shared within the royal castle, seemingly a lifetime ago. "I used to wonder if you'd ever learn to speak a full sentence without fidgeting. Now you're articulate, calm, collected… Your heart has always been in the right place, but now your mannerisms reflect your status." I beamed at him. "Your father would be proud of you, if he were here."

"I believe he'd be proud of all of us," he countered. "If Alex had been revealed while father still lived, he would never have reacted as Colin did. You wouldn't have been forced to flee, to fend off assassins, to fight for your very right to exist. Father would have accepted what the two of you are."

In that moment, he spoke with such conviction that I believed him wholeheartedly. Perhaps I'd been wrong to spend decades in fear of discovery, but we'd never know for certain with Carlton gone.

"You'll make things right again, Tom," I replied. "I believe that, and I believe in you."

It was evening by the time we'd surrounded the outermost walls of the Capitol. The king's garrison closed the gates after our forces were sighted, but it took them more time than it should have. I frowned at their disorganization.

Before Colin had become king, our presence so near his city would have been noted and prepared for days in advance. As it happened, no such preparations had been made—the garrison scrambled to place soldiers atop the walls, to shore up defenses, and prepare for what could very well become a lengthy siege. Colin had either alienated those who would forewarn him of our approach, or he'd dismissed our threat as meaningless.

Jonas had planned our formations weeks ago and swiftly dispatched various groups to specific locations around the city's perimeter. Each unit was comprised of magi, Merael, and Corodan, though the bulk of the hive's warriors remained together, stationed near the main gate leading into the city. Jonas had anticipated most of the king's defenders would be dispatched there, and the Corodan presence would be intimidating. Each contingent of soldiers and magi possessed one of Thomas' dragon standards, making it clear to those now trapped within the city that we were not allies of the king.

Thomas' command tent was erected some distance away from the main road leading into the city. Its location was near enough that he was accessible to the army, but far enough away that he'd be out of harm's way.

Alexander and I stood on each side of Thomas as the army began to stoke campfires in the gathering darkness, while pinpoints of torchlight flickered above on the city's walls. Jonas and Everett were inside the tent, studying maps and laying out plans, but for the first time in many weeks, we three were granted a few moments alone.

"I'll wager Colin appears on the wall before morning." Alexander pointed to a location midway above the main gate with his finger.

Thomas shook his head. "He'll be there before midnight, Alex."

I crossed my arms. "And what will the two of you do when he appears, I wonder?"

Thomas fell silent and Alexander scowled in the direction of the city.

"I haven't decided," Alexander said. "But if the opportunity presents itself, I *will* make him pay for every damned crime he's committed."

"You won't kill him," Thomas stated firmly. "He'll sit in judgment by the governor's council as befits his status."

Alexander laughed grimly. "I never said I'd kill him, Tom, but I can make him wish I had."

Thomas' eyes drifted slowly to meet mine. "What do you plan, Andrew?"

I frowned. Thomas' course of action was the more noble approach, but a part of me wanted to see Colin suffer as I had. As Alexander had.

"I don't know. It will depend on the outcome of our next meeting."

TWENTY-ONE

A messenger arrived less than an hour later. I remained outside the command tent with my brothers, the space illuminated by the flickering light of a nearby campfire.

The woman knelt before Thomas. “My lord, the king’s garrison is preparing for their monarch’s arrival atop the wall.”

I studied Thomas’ reaction. He narrowed his eyes slightly, but gave no other indication of his emotional state. “Where?” he asked.

“Above the main gate, sir,” she replied without looking up.

Thomas nodded, then motioned for us to follow him into the command tent. Our arrival drew the attention of the former dukes, who fell silent as Thomas relayed the news.

“I will speak with him,” he said. “Perhaps he can be reasoned with. I will not engage in hostilities unless he refuses to accept my terms of surrender.”

I believed Thomas wasted his breath. Colin would never yield. His damned pride would never allow it.

Alexander snorted, sharing my sentiment. “He won’t, brother.”

Thomas shrugged. “Nevertheless, he is our brother, and I must try.”

A half dozen advisors were gathered in the intervening minutes, and twice that in soldiers to accompany us to the city’s main gate. In addition to Alexander and myself, Everett, Jonas, the injured Rizzt-tok, and Shyala were chosen to attend what I anticipated would be a brief exchange of words.

Hulda led the soldier escort, holding the dragon standard proudly aloft. Several others carried torches. Everyone was armed.

"I suppose this means you've won our wager, Tom," Alexander said in a somber tone as we approached the designated meeting place.

There was no sign of movement from the city's gate, but I spied a number of soldiers on patrol atop the wall. Torches flickered at intervals amongst them, but Colin hadn't arrived yet.

Thomas glanced at Alexander, his expression grim. "We'll worry about that later. I need you alert and prepared for anything. I don't trust Colin to abide by the terms of conventional parley."

"Don't worry," Alexander replied grimly. "I've prepared for this moment for nearly a year. If Colin orders an attack, he'll regret it."

We stopped at an area beyond the perimeter of our camp, just outside of the walls' archery range. The conversation between my brothers fell abruptly silent as Thomas peered toward the gate.

Protocol dictated that an assessment must be made of any enemy force before the king or his emissary were cleared by the garrison to begin negotiations. As dusk bled into night, the task would become more difficult for the garrison, but I knew they'd note every member of Thomas' entourage was armed.

I didn't know if Alexander or I would be recognized from the wall, but there was a strong possibility. I wasn't certain how those loyal to Colin would react to our presence once it was known.

Alexander grew impatient as time marched on. I prayed for Thomas' sake he'd keep his temper in check and wouldn't resort to anything that might compromise our tenuous situation. We couldn't afford to have Alexander charge ahead, rash and unthinking, into what might be a carefully-devised trap. Even if Colin followed the long-standing rules of parley and kept our meeting civilized, I knew he'd goad us in an attempt to force our hand, further securing his position.

"Alex," I hissed, "now isn't the time."

He frowned in my direction, the torchlight flickering across his ageless countenance. "The right time will be decided by Colin, brother."

I sighed, disappointed. I wanted to say more, to advise against whatever he might be thinking—it was undoubtedly nothing *good* for our cause—but a trumpeter on the wall announced the arrival of the king. I turned away from Alexander in time to see the gate swing open just enough to allow for the passage of Colin and his personal guards. Colin had forgone the presence of advisors or nobility.

"Either he's alienated most of his allies," Jonas said, "or he's simply so arrogant he believes he doesn't require their input."

"Knowing Colin, it's both," Alexander replied, his mouth twisting into a scowl.

"Alex, enough." Thomas' command was whispered, but it rang with authority. To my surprise, Alexander nodded and didn't comment further.

Colin had changed little in the intervening months, though I noted he'd grown stouter around his middle. He was dressed in his usual finery; black and crimson trousers and tunic with a gold chain at his waist. Enormous jeweled rings encircled each of his fingers in a blatant display of wealth. He crossed his arms as his soldiers parted to reveal him in their midst, his blue eyes unreadable in the flickering light.

"If it isn't my two wayward brothers, come home at long last," he sneered, his tone dripping with acid. "And Andrew, the queen's bastard, never one to leave well enough alone." He unfolded his arms and paused to examine the fingernails of his left hand, his expression imperious. "I'll skip the niceties since it's obvious why you've come."

Thomas straightened to his full height and stepped forward to glare at Colin. "You've destroyed everything that our father built, Colin. You are unworthy of his title."

Colin lifted an eyebrow with a smirk. "And you are, little Thomas? Is that why you play at war, marring my very doorstep with your foolish games?"

Alexander tensed, and I reflexively placed one hand on his arm. Our eyes met briefly and he nodded, but his expression was stormy.

The exchange wasn't lost on Colin.

"Ah, Alex. It seems your temper still drives you. A pity." Colin narrowed his eyes as he studied Alexander. "It seems you've changed since our last meeting. You've become the very abomination our people have always feared. A damned *mage*." He spat the final word.

"*You* are the abomination, Colin. We've seen your camps." Alexander's tone was low, threatening, but he didn't move forward. He clenched his fists and glared, but I believed he wouldn't act against Colin—yet.

"Hard labor is the sentence required by law for those guilty of harboring Marks," Colin replied in a carefully controlled tone. "If you had paid attention in your history lessons, you'd know this. Tell me, Alex: If your schemes fail, will Andrew be willing to risk his scaly hide to save your pitiful life a second time? It seems he has already paid dearly for assisting the two of you with your childish games."

Alexander clenched his jaw and I shook my head in warning. Colin was goading him, nothing more, and I sincerely hoped he understood that.

"This is no game, Colin," Thomas broke in evenly, sensing he must intervene before Alexander's temper ruined all of our carefully laid plans. "If you don't surrender, we'll be forced to storm the city. We have the forces to do so, and you're intelligent enough to realize this."

Colin smirked and studied each of us in turn. "You propose a siege, little brother? How very quaint." His eyes drifted to those surrounding us. "I shouldn't be surprised to see you here, Uncle," he said to Everett. "And Jonas. I'm disappointed you've chosen to accompany this rabble."

Jonas crossed his arms and met Colin's gaze with a steely one of his own, but didn't take the king's bait. After a moment, Colin returned his attention to Thomas.

"I suggest you abandon this farce, Thomas," he stated with mock civility. "It has gone on long enough, and I grow weary. You can't win this war you've made."

Thomas' gaze met Colin's unflinchingly. "You began this war with your orders to destroy Vinterry and the reinstatement of the Mark inspections. Our people, the *Novanian* people, have done no harm. Why do you fear them so?"

Colin's carefully composed expression twisted in sudden rage. "I fear no one," he growled through clenched teeth. "I am the king. It's best you remember that, for when this is over and done, I will show you no mercy."

Thomas shook his head sadly. "I would expect nothing less from you. Mercy is something you know nothing of."

Thomas had struck a chord; the king ground his teeth together and glared at our youngest brother with unmitigated hatred.

"You and your army of misfits will come to regret this," he hissed before he wheeled around, gesturing for his guards to accompany him back to the gate.

As they strode away, I released a sigh of relief. No one had fallen for Colin's act, and the tension was beginning to clear. Our first encounter with Colin after many months of exile had gone much smoother than I'd anticipated, and Thomas had proven his mettle.

"You did well," Everett murmured to Thomas.

Thomas nodded briskly. "I didn't expect him to surrender, even when he knows he's outnumbered and outmatched." He turned toward Alexander and offered him a tired smile. "Thank you for keeping your head, Alex. Andrew was right when he said now was not the time."

Alexander shrugged as we began to make our way back to camp. "I'll have my chance," he replied. "Colin will wish he'd taken your offer of surrender, Tom. I'll make certain of it."

I glanced in Alexander's direction, but his ferocious gaze was focused elsewhere. Instead, I shifted my attention to Thomas. "Please tell me this is all a part of your plan."

Thomas smiled wearily. "It is, and we've spoken as I assured you we would. Alex will lead a small group on a special task later this evening. We'll speak more of this once we've arrived at the command tent."

Alexander huffed. "It's always a pleasure to know I've been volunteered for a task I know nothing of."

"As it was Jonas' idea, he'll be the one to present it," Thomas replied evenly, ignoring Alexander's sarcasm. "I'll not speak of it further at present, but I believe you'll be willing to accept the task."

"And when did you have time to speak with Jonas? We were with you—" Alexander began, but Thomas cut him off with a chuckle.

"There was plenty of opportunity during our march here," Thomas replied. "And you weren't at my side every moment. As I recall, you spent several hours with Lydia this morning."

Alexander frowned, but managed a nod. "I still don't like that you've made plans for me without my knowledge."

"You'll have the final say," Thomas countered. "You can always say no."

I didn't know the details of Jonas' plan, but I understood from Thomas' tone that it was both dangerous and imperative—a combination Alexander would find irresistible.

Lydia and Rynn awaited us at the command tent. Thomas motioned for them to join us inside, while Hulda and the other soldiers were dismissed to rejoin their units and go about their evening duties. Everett lit several candles and placed them at intervals around the map spread across the table. It wasn't the same map we'd used at Willever; this one detailed the intricacies of the Capitol's layout. Streets and primary buildings were labeled in precise script and several points had been circled in blue ink.

"Jonas," Thomas said, "please share the plan you've concocted for Alexander."

Jonas stepped forward with a brisk nod, and indicated a point circled on the map with his forefinger. "This is the entrance to the sewer tunnels. I've made contact with our scouts inside the city, and one has agreed to assist us with navigating them."

Alexander scowled. "I'm not certain I like where this is going," he grumbled as he crossed his arms.

"Hear me out," Jonas replied with a frown. When Alexander nodded, he continued. "I would like you to lead a small group through the tunnels. You'll exit here." He moved his finger to a point on the map just inside the city's walls. "The exit is located behind a derelict warehouse and has been the site of our meager operations for some time. It's secure. Our scouts have managed to steal a dozen sets of armor from the king's garrison. You and your charges will disguise yourselves as soldiers of the king, but you must take your own weapons."

"I would have done so regardless," Alexander replied, his tone thoughtful. "Where I go, so do my blades."

Jonas nodded. "Once you're inside and disguised, your group will travel to the outer wall. Do what you must to dispatch the soldiers you encounter, then make for the gates. I've asked Niall Roche to accompany you as well. He'll signal us when the Novanians are no longer in control of the gate. A flare of fire will be visible, no matter the time of day or night."

"I assume you have a timeline, Jonas?" Alexander asked.

"I'd like the gates taken by noon tomorrow," he replied. "Before you depart, I'll speak with Niall regarding the signals he'll use to indicate your status. I don't know how much resistance you'll face, but I believe you'll be successful, given your unique abilities. I'd like to prevent a lengthy siege if I can manage it. The people deserve better than what their king will provide them, trapped in the city as they are."

"No doubt," Alexander replied, his expression unreadable.

"Please be careful," Lydia said quietly. Fear clouded her gaze as she looked up at him.

Alexander turned to smile at her. "I promise I'll return to your side, but Jonas is right. This is the best way to break into the city without this turning into a months-long siege."

She nodded, and her eyes flitted toward me for a moment before settling on Jonas. "Other than Alex and Niall, who will be part of this mission?"

"I'll allow Alex to decide on the rest of the party, but we only have a dozen disguises. The group must remain small to avoid detection."

She sighed. "What of Andrew?"

"I have need of him here, my lady," Jonas replied evenly.

"Alex can handle himself," I said in an attempt to reassure her. "He may be better off without me, truth be told."

"Lydia, I grew up in the Capitol," Alexander added. "If anyone is suited to this task, it's me."

She averted her gaze, unable to hide her disappointment. "Very well. I'll be in the healers' tent if you have need of me." She whirled away and strode into the night.

"I'll speak with her, Andrew. I'll find you when we're finished," Rynn whispered before she departed too.

"Once we have secured the gate and the signal has been sent," Jonas continued after a moment, "I will lead the strike directly into the city. I believe we can take the lower city by the end of the day. Our scouts report the garrison was sorely depleted when Claybourne marched from the city to engage us at Willever. It's likely that many of the soldiers we faced were members of the king's garrison."

"Are you saying that Colin has left himself with nothing more than a token guard?" I asked in disbelief. "His advisors should have warned him—"

"His advisors have all been sent away or executed," Everett cut in. "The king has refused to acknowledge when he's wrong and silences any who disagree with him."

"But this is madness!" I spluttered, unable to fathom why the king would leave himself so vulnerable to attack. "It's good news for *us*, but I don't understand what he's thinking."

Alexander barked a laugh. "I doubt anyone does, brother. We may as well take advantage of the situation before something changes it."

"My thoughts precisely," Jonas agreed. "When I received word from our scouts, I devised this plan based on our intelligence. We can't hesitate. We must act, and soon."

"Lydia will come around," Alexander said, more for his own benefit than ours. "I'll speak with her once we're finished. She'll understand the necessity. I *will* secure the gate, Jonas. You have my word."

"I knew you'd agree to this plan," Jonas replied with a faint smile. "Now, let's discuss who should accompany you…"

I slept fitfully for a few hours after our meeting concluded, but was awakened by Rynn not long after midnight.

"Alex is prepared to leave," she said.

I nodded and reached for my shirt. "I'd like to see him off."

Moments later, I was dressed. We threaded our way through the sea of canvas toward the camp's perimeter. When we reached Alexander, Niall, and the ten chosen to accompany them, my brother was in high spirits. Lydia struggled to contain her tears, and Niall was uncharacteristically subdued.

I had no doubt that Alexander would return; his skills, coupled with his magical abilities, gave him a distinct advantage over the average soldier. I merely hoped he wouldn't get carried away and leave the others behind. I prayed he'd learned his lesson in Willever.

We walked with the group until we reached the entrance to the sewers. Even from a distance, the foul odor wafting from inside was overpowering. I didn't envy those tasked to go forward. One of the scouts who had infiltrated the Capitol previously stood sentry near the entrance.

Alexander paused as the others followed the sentry inside and turned to Lydia. He caressed the side of her face, his expression stoic. "I'll see you tomorrow. Stay safe."

She nodded, grief and fear warring for dominance in her eyes. "You as well."

As he disappeared into the darkened sewer tunnel, Lydia burst into tears, unable to compose herself any longer. Rynn and I walked with her as we returned to our own tents, but we said nothing for several minutes.

Finally, I said, "Alex will return hale and whole. Don't worry."

She waved a hand dismissively. "You don't understand. I *know* what Alex is capable of and I believe in my heart that he'll be fine. I simply can't stop from crying. Belora says it's due to the baby."

Rynn gave me a look that said I should stop speaking, that I wasn't helping the situation. "No one faults you," she replied gently. "Andrew may not understand, but I do. I can chase him off so we can talk privately if you'd like."

Lydia managed a smile. "That won't be necessary, but thank you."

I feigned hurt. "You would chase me away?"

Both women laughed, and Rynn said, "Of course I would."

"I'd much rather watch her chase you as a dragon," Lydia said after a moment. "That scene would be priceless."

I laughed. "It seems I'm outnumbered."

We'd reached the healers' tents, and Lydia paused at the entrance to one. "I meant what I said. I know Alex will be fine. Thank you for the laugh. There has been far too little of that lately."

I nodded, and Rynn said, "Good night, Lydia. Try to rest. If not for your sake, then for the child's."

We walked back to our own tent in the darkness. I knew I wouldn't get any more sleep, not with my brother heading straight into the heart of the enemy's lair. If he were discovered, Colin would execute him on sight, and I wouldn't be granted an opportunity to intervene.

Alexander was on his own.

The sun was just beginning to rise when I walked to Thomas' command tent the next morning. Though it was early, Rizzt-tok was inside with Jonas and Thomas. I'd hoped to find my brother alone, but was disappointed to find him deep in discussion with the others. I loitered near the door, hoping I hadn't interrupted.

"We have built the palisade," Rizzt-tok said. "Kresh-tik leads a group of hive warriors at the wall. They burrow beneath as you've asked."

She shifted, her movements sluggish, as she leaned over the map. Her carapace was deeply scarred, and I suspected she was still recovering from internal wounds.

"Good," Thomas said. "And the garrison?"

"They have done nothing to stop us," Rizzt-tok replied. "The tunnels are almost complete."

"If Alexander takes the gate as we're anticipating," Jonas said, moving his finger across the map, "then we can strike in three places simultaneously. With the Corodan tunnels nearly finished, our forces can break into the lower city at the gate, then here, and here."

Thomas nodded and glanced at me briefly before returning his attention to the map. "Even if Alex can't open the gate by noon, we can still use the tunnels to enter the city."

"Yes," Rizzt-tok replied. "The hive is ready. Kresh-tik will lead the assault when the time comes."

Thomas turned to me. "Andrew, did you—?"

His question was cut off by a commotion outside. Despite the early hour, dozens of voices shouted at once, competing to be heard. Without waiting for Thomas to finish his question, I ducked outside and peered at the city's walls. There was little movement, and the source of the noise came from the opposite direction.

A moment later, Rynn sprinted around the corner of the tent and crashed into my side. She startled, her eyes wide with horror until she realized it was me and no harm had been done.

"Andrew! I'm glad I've found you. I didn't *think* it was you we saw, but I had to make certain."

I shook my head, confused. "What do you mean? I've been here with Tom."

Thomas and Jonas stepped outside. The camp was beginning to quiet, but I couldn't determine the source of the momentary excitement.

"There was a *dragon*," Rynn said. "It flew overhead and disappeared around the curve of the city not long ago."

I frowned. "Are you certain? As I said, I've been here."

She rolled her eyes in exasperation. "I know what a dragon looks like." She was about to say more, but stopped to point behind me, bouncing with excitement. "There! Do you see?"

I followed her finger and was astonished to see a black dragon flying low in our direction. I stepped forward and pulled away from Rynn, unable to tear my gaze from the spectacle. As the dragon drew nearer, his eyes locked on mine and a smile broke across his features.

I recognized his countenance, so like my own. I'd been the last of the dragon-kind not trapped within stone and couldn't fathom how he'd been freed. What had occurred to break my father's curse?

TWENTY-TWO

I sprinted through the camp, leaping over obstacles and narrowly avoiding other people as I raced toward my father's location. I refused to look away from the dark form that had landed just beyond the westernmost tents, even when it resulted in me stumbling. Rynn ran in my wake, struggling to keep pace as I dashed past tents and cartloads of supplies, between soldiers and magi. A number of curious onlookers gathered a short distance from the dragon who had flown unexpectedly into their midst, murmuring amongst themselves.

I pushed and elbowed my way through the crowd. Those who recognized me gaped as they realized the dragon they'd come to see wasn't the dragon they'd anticipated. The tone of their conversations changed from hushed excitement to outright astonishment.

As I broke through the crowd and stepped forward, I stared up at him. "Father?"

He smiled, but deep sadness swelled in his eyes. I noted with a start that his eyes were a dark shade of violet, wholly different from mine. I'd incorrectly assumed they would have been the same hue.

"Andrew, what happened to your eye?" he asked, concerned.

I scratched at the back of my neck, suddenly uncomfortable. "It happened during the last battle. I was—"

Zayneldarion shook his head and glanced behind me. "There will be time enough for stories later. It seems there are others who require introduction."

I gaped at him, unable to comprehend how he was standing in our camp, no longer encased in stone. My father laughed softly and tilted his head toward the crowd, forcing me to focus on our present situation.

I turned to find Thomas and Jonas had emerged from the throng. Rynn stood on one side, arms crossed as she observed our exchange, a knowing smile on her lips.

"You've met Rynn," I said, before gesturing to Thomas. "This is my youngest half-brother, Thomas, and our commander, Jonas Everly." I shook my head, baffled. "Father, what happened? How—?"

"The magic released with the Barrier's collapse was strong enough to break the curse of the Stone Grove. Had we known it was simply a matter of time, perhaps our long years spent trapped wouldn't have seemed such a burden."

"That means Caelmarion and Miranetha—"

He smiled patiently. "Yes, they're free as well. They've chosen to remain near the place where the Mage's Gate once stood, to defend our lands should the Novanian king attempt another strike in the south." He studied me carefully for a moment. "I could not sit by when I knew my son was elsewhere. I stopped for nothing. I've come to assist you. Cael called me a dozen different kinds of fool, but I needed to know you still lived. The shockwaves the Barrier's collapse released could not have been good for you." He glanced at the growing crowd of spectators. "Perhaps it will be best if I assume my false form. I'll draw less unwanted attention."

Without waiting for a response, he changed form to appear human. Unlike my transformations, his was a product of magic and occurred instantly. He was clad in a manner similar to my own, but his hair was raven-dark, the same color as his dragon scale. The face he wore possessed a strong jaw and straight nose, with a hint of dark stubble across his cheeks. Now we looked nothing alike.

He flashed a grin in my direction and strode toward me. A subtle scent akin to vanilla permeated the air around him.

"I have not assumed this face since the day I left your mother," he said. "It always feels strange at first, but it will make conversation easier."

I nodded but didn't know what to say. Learning he'd been freed from the petrification was nothing short of a miracle, but seeing him in this human guise was unsettling. I'd never imagined what he may have looked like when he'd known my mother.

As I turned to face the others once more, I realized with a start that Rynn was kneeling, her head bowed in deference. Thomas appeared uncertain of how to react, and Jonas managed an awkward bow. I shot a questioning glance at my father.

"I require no special treatment," he said with a genial laugh. "I'm here to help your cause as a friend and a father."

"But, my Lord Dragon—" Rynn began.

Zayneldarion arched an eyebrow in her direction. "The members of my clan who would have expected—nay, *demanded*—such deference from other races are long gone, Rynn. I insist you treat me as an equal. This war affects us all, no matter our heritage."

He extended a hand to help her to her feet. She merely stared at it, her blue eyes wide.

"Rynn," I said, amused, "you can't harm him, just as you can't harm me."

She nodded and hesitantly reached up to grasp his hand. Once she was on her feet, Zayneldarion released his grip but paused to study her with his violet eyes.

"I understand why you've become so interested in my son," he said with a faint smile. "Your condition is unusual."

Her face flushed crimson. "There is more between us than that, my lord." Her words were scarcely audible as she averted her gaze.

He smiled. "Please, call me Zayne. There will be time enough to speak of that later, I believe. For now, I'd like to learn your plans and how I may assist."

"Holy hell," Jonas growled under his breath before addressing the soldiers clamoring for our attention outside the command tent. "Yes, a dragon has arrived—and it wasn't Andrew. I'm certain you all have a dozen questions, but they must wait. We strike at noon, and your loitering here will only delay our scheme. I will not be responsible for Prince Alexander's capture if you lot can't follow orders and work as instructed."

Their previous excitement marginally diminished, many of the curious turned to go about their assigned duties. I slipped inside the tent after Thomas and Rynn, while my father paused at the threshold to study the dwindling crowd. When he entered moments later, he appeared amused.

Jonas muttered curses as he entered, but quashed his temper as he strode toward the table. He acquainted Zayneldarion with the planned attack, Alexander's role, and the Corodan tunnels carved beneath the city's walls.

"I don't know how you may help with this matter," he admitted as he finished. "I'm open to suggestions."

Zayneldarion smiled knowingly. "I'm more than a mere dragon, Jonas. I'm a dragon-mage, and disguising myself as human is but one of my abilities." He glanced around the tent, taking a moment to study each of us in turn. "That being said, I cannot use my other abilities while I funnel magic into maintaining this false form. If you'd like me to strike with any real force, I must stop playing at my current charade."

"And what are your abilities?" Rynn asked, breathless. "I can sense your power, and it far exceeds my own."

"Yes." He paused to study his hands in a very human gesture. "The dragon-magi have always been stronger than our human or Merael counterparts, and we aren't restricted to a single attunement as you are. Perhaps it's why we've become so feared." He shook his head, sorrow in his eyes. "To answer your question, my primary ability allows me to create powerful shockwaves through any medium I focus on, whether it be air, water, earth, or stone. I also possess a meager healing talent, though Caelmarion is the true expert in that regard."

"The shockwaves could prove useful," Jonas mused. "I assume they're destructive in nature?"

Zayneldarion nodded, his expression guarded. "I have rarely used my primary ability. I've had little reason to. We were at peace. But do not mistake me: I'm capable of unleashing as much or as little destruction as you require. I've had nearly three hundred years in which to hone my skills."

Jonas nodded, contemplating his words. "We plan to strike at noon, no matter if we have secured the gate. The Corodan have completed the tunnels and can storm the city through them. I'd like you to attack from above. Strike down any of the king's garrison who choose to resist." He shifted his steely gaze to meet mine. "Andrew, I'd like you to accompany him. Take Rynn with you. She can strike from afar. Given the outcome of the last battle, I implore you to remain at a distance."

"I'll go one step further," Thomas stated firmly. "I *order* you to do so, Andrew. Alex and I will need you when we finally confront Colin."

Grudgingly, I nodded. There would be no arguing with them, even though I was perfectly capable of defending myself. The injury to my eye had rattled them, and now that my father had joined us, they believed their overprotection justified. Despite my annoyance with Thomas' order, I couldn't deny that I was thrilled with the prospect of flying alongside my father for the first time, even if it meant I'd be kept from the direct fighting.

Zayneldarion's violet eyes met mine. "It will be an honor to fly alongside my son. It's something I've longed for since the day we met."

An hour later, I was on the outskirts of camp in dragon form, sitting between my father and Rynn. Her pack was slung over one shoulder; its contents included rations for her, my clothing, and boots. Zayneldarion carried nothing but his Mark, but at present, it was obscured beneath his wings.

We'd been granted a short time to converse, and I related the events that had transpired since our last meeting in the Stone Grove. Zayneldarion listened carefully but said little until we'd concluded our tale.

"That man, Claybourne, knew precisely how and where to strike," he said after a time, clearly troubled. "Have you encountered any others with such apparent knowledge of our kind?"

I shook my head, but it was Rynn who answered. "No. Not yet, in any case, but I suspect the king is behind it. He has been seeking Andrew since he learned the truth of what he is."

"Perhaps it's best that Thomas wants us to strike from afar."

He sighed and adjusted his wings, as though the implication caused him physical discomfort. As he moved, I was afforded a brief glimpse of his Mark, an enormous crescent that arced across his left flank. It was a pale blue-gray, contrasting starkly against his black scales, and possessed an iridescent sheen.

"It's strange," he remarked after a moment. "When I was younger, I used to long for battle. I grew up amongst many elder dragons, some of whom were present for the Mage Wars, and I loved hearing their stories. I wanted to be part of those tales—to become a hero of legend, renowned for my valor and bravery. Now that a true battle is imminent, I'm uncertain—and somewhat fearful."

I laughed, though there was no mirth in the sound. "And I have known little else. I long for peace, if only for a short while."

Compassion shone from his eyes, even as sorrow etched his brow. "If I had only known your mother was with child, I would have done everything in my power to ensure your life was far better than what you've known. You deserve to know peace, and I will help you achieve it however I can."

"Then we have to stop Colin."

I'd never be granted the respite I craved until my wicked half-brother was removed from his throne. Colin's hatred had become all-consuming, and he'd stop at nothing to see me dead. It still baffled me, but perhaps before this was over and done, I'd receive a few answers.

"We will," Rynn replied with conviction.

We were silent for a time, then Zayneldarion laughed. "The longer I watch you together, the more it's obvious you've foresworn your previous reservations, Andrew." He grinned. "I believe it's a good thing."

I nodded and opened my mouth to say more when his attention was diverted to the city's walls. I followed his gaze to see a column of fire erupting above the main gate. I grinned as relief flooded my veins; Alexander had accomplished his task.

A flurry of activity accompanied the spectacle as Jonas and Rizzt-tok began to issue rapid orders some distance from our location. I crouched low to allow Rynn to climb up to her customary perch between my wings as we prepared for our own role in the attack.

When I rose to my feet, Zayneldarion nodded and leapt into the air. I followed in his wake, grim and resigned to do my part as we began our assault on the Capitol, the city that had once been my home.

TWENTY-THREE

As we soared high above the Capitol, I peered down at the city I'd been raised in with a new perspective. The cobblestone streets followed a wheel-and-spoke pattern, something I'd been aware of but could only now truly appreciate. The streets of the lower city were largely empty, its residents gone or in hiding as our assault began.

Above the main gate, a number of tabards lay torn and shredded on the wall, the remnants of the disguises worn by Alexander's unit. As the gate was winched open and our soldiers began to pour through the gap, Corodan burst from the ground just inside the wall at two different locations, surging forth from their tunnels.

Few townsfolk risked the streets. Those who ventured outside fled toward the nearest buildings, seeking refuge from the fighting as it advanced through the lower city. A flurry of activity erupted atop the inner walls as the king's garrison fortified the gates. I'd expected the move, but hadn't anticipated the garrison would refuse entry to those attempting to flee; the gates remained shut, even as desperate townspeople swarmed their bases, crying out for entry, for refuge. It was yet another poignant and heartbreaking failure of Colin's reign.

Our orders had been to attack only those who resisted with force and avoid killing innocent folk when possible. We'd also been given instructions against razing or otherwise compromising any of the city's buildings. Thomas hoped to spare the people from as much pain and sorrow as he could, though some damage would be inevitable.

Zayneldarion targeted members of the king's garrison as they raced through the streets, striking with nearly invisible pulses of magic. Each wave created a strange rippling effect in the air as it passed, shimmering at the edges. Those who were struck crumpled where they stood, unable to rise again. If I flew too near my father, I was overwhelmed by a scent akin to black pepper.

It became impossible to avoid sneezing. I paused to hover as the urge overcame me, fearing Rynn would be toppled from her perch if I continued to move forward.

"Damn, I'm sorry," I said over my shoulder.

She laughed. "I'd expect nothing less from you, dragon-man. Don't apologize."

She began to cast her own brand of magic when I dipped lower in the sky, wintergreen momentarily overriding black pepper in the air. My nostrils twitched as I fought off another bout of sneezing.

Despite my role as aerial transportation for Rynn, our forces faced scant resistance in the lower city, and I would have seen little action had I been on the ground. My brothers' concerns regarding my welfare were unfounded, but I wouldn't bring it up when I spoke with them later. Most of the king's forces were centralized in the upper city and around the castle.

It seemed Colin had foresworn the lower city and its residents, preferring to focus on his personal defenses. From a tactical perspective, I understood his motive, but it pained me to realize he thought so little of his people. He'd abandoned them in the face of his enemy, a move I doubted his father would have contemplated unless given no other option.

We continued to circle above the lower city, keeping a safe distance from the inner wall and its defenders. Arrows and spears wouldn't harm the dragon-kind, but I wouldn't risk Rynn's safety. And we had only sparse information regarding Colin's movements in the upper city. It was possible we'd encounter trebuchets nearer to his stronghold, and I didn't relish the notion of becoming trapped a second time—with or without Claybourne alive to torture and torment me.

"There are fewer enemy soldiers than I'd expected," Zayneldarion said after we'd wheeled above the fighting for a time.

"It's good news for us," Rynn replied.

I was less optimistic. "Colin will have something planned," I growled. "Stay vigilant."

She snorted and slapped a hand against my back. "Jonas' strategy today was for the lower city only," she reminded me. "If the king has planned anything, it'll be in the upper city or the castle grounds. We'll have time to prepare."

I frowned but didn't reply. We'd learn soon enough what the king had in store, and if our forces continued to subdue the tattered remnants of the garrison, the lower city would be ours soon enough. Rynn and Zayneldarion continued their attacks, but they gradually became less frequent as more of the garrison surrendered or fell.

By mid-afternoon, we controlled the lower city. There had been few casualties on our side, but only a handful of the king's garrison had chosen to surrender. Most of the meager force Colin had tasked to defend the lower city had been decimated.

By evening, some of the townsfolk began to emerge from hiding, seeking news on the events of the day. Many merchants and innkeepers opened their stores in direct defiance of the king, offering their services and wares to those their sovereign had deemed enemies and traitors. While it confounded some, I understood most of the business owners were simply looking to capitalize on the change in leadership, seeking easy coin.

It was an unexpected turn of events, but one beneficial to all parties involved. The townsfolk bore little love for Colin and fear had become the hallmark of his reign. Once they'd learned Thomas and Alexander led the opposition, many expressed relief, even joy. I wondered what the true extent of the people's suffering had been. Colin had clearly failed the people of Novania, but I knew he'd never see it that way.

We were summoned to Thomas' new command post as the sun set, an inn called The Princess' Rest. It was a well-known establishment, a place where merchants, travelers, soldiers, and nobility were traditionally welcomed as equals.

Alexander had often stopped at the inn after returning from our summer campaigns to regale the patrons with stories of our battles—and he often exaggerated tales featuring my exploits. After I'd learned of his habit, I tried to persuade the regulars his stories held less than a grain of truth, but to no avail. By then, he'd become well-liked by the inn's patrons and owners, and it didn't bother his listeners that his stories were little more than fanciful fabrications.

I smiled at the memories The Princess' Rest held; those had been simpler times. Better times.

"It's been a few years since I last visited The Princess' Rest," I commented as I strode through the outer gate with Rynn and Zayneldarion. My father and I had both adopted our human forms since the conclusion of the battle to make conversation easier.

On the wall above, a dozen armed soldiers were posted to monitor those passing through the gate. One of Thomas' dragon standards hung above, billowing gently in the cool evening breeze.

"And what would the commander of the king's army be doing at a lowly inn?" Rynn inquired, one eyebrow raised incredulously.

"Usually, it was to persuade the regulars that Alexander's tales about me were flights of fancy," I replied with a grin. "It never worked."

"I should think not. I've seen you in battle myself," Rynn replied with a smirk. "Even when he didn't know what you were, I'm certain your skill with a blade was impressive."

"Will your brother regale us with one of his tales tonight?" Zayneldarion asked, amusement twinkling in his eyes.

My face flushed and I shook my head. "I hope not."

Zayneldarion laughed good-naturedly. "I'm certain he has collected a number of astonishing stories since you fled Novania. I understand you dislike the attention, but I'm curious to learn some of what you've experienced from another's perspective."

When I began to protest, he held up one hand and smiled. "You spent hours with me in the Stone Grove when first we met, yes. But the manner in which you tell your story is very straightforward. I don't believe you give yourself enough credit for your achievements, and considering all you've suffered recently, I believe a story—even an embellished one—may well be in order."

I sighed and rolled my eyes.

Rynn laughed and poked a finger into my shoulder. "I suspect the locals who know you will agree with your father. And I didn't know Alex had a following. Who knew he was such an accomplished storyteller?"

I snorted. "I'm not sure 'accomplished' is the right word. He was granted significant latitude because he was a prince, and a round of drinks goes far when capturing the attention of one's audience."

"Nevertheless," she persisted, "I'd like to hear him spin a tale or two."

"As would I," Zayeldarion replied.

I groaned dramatically and shook my head.

I knew if asked, Alexander wouldn't deny them a story. He took far too much enjoyment from the attention to be persuaded otherwise, even if I begged him to remain silent.

The Princess' Rest had changed little during the last year. The windows had been shuttered, but the door was thrown wide in a gesture of welcome by the proprietor. The inn had been one of the cleaner establishments in the lower city, a fact that I assumed led Alexander to frequent it. There had been several other inns and taverns the late king had forbidden all of his sons to patronize, though Colin had defied his wishes and visited all of them.

The wooden sign above the entrance depicted a red-haired woman wearing a golden tiara, her face serene as she reclined on a divan. The painted woman was in a state of undress, her gown pulled low, and her skirt drawn up to reveal what I'd always assumed were supposed to be lacy undergarments.

"Are you certain this was merely an inn, Andrew?" Rynn asked in an amused tone.

I shrugged. "It has always been an inn since I've known it. I can't say what it may have been prior, but I have my suspicions."

Rynn smirked. "I'm sure you do. Somehow, I don't believe any princess would enjoy seeing herself portrayed in that manner."

I shrugged. "I have no sisters, and Everett's wife was dark-haired. If the woman painted on the sign was truly a princess, she's one from long ago."

Zayneldarion laughed. "I know the story behind the sign. When I traveled here in my youth, this establishment was newly built, and there was a very real, very red-haired princess residing in the castle. She wasn't liked by the people. I found her quite vain, myself. She would never have allowed herself to be seen in such a...compromising state, so much of the artist's work is likely imaginative." He chuckled. "At the time, this was a brothel."

I lifted my eyebrows. "How long ago was that?"

He contemplated the question as we ducked inside. "It was one hundred-seventy years ago, more or less. It wasn't long after my fallout with your grandfather, and some years before I met Caelmarion."

The common room was at capacity. Most were locals, but I recognized a fair number of soldiers from our forces mixed in the crowd. The serving staff flitted between tables with food and ale, smiles plastered on their faces, though their eyes remained wary. The innkeeper, a wiry man with white hair and an amused grin, recognized me as we entered and motioned animatedly that we follow him. He led us to a door located behind the bar and ushered us inside.

Near silence descended as the door closed behind us and the clamor of the common room was muted. Thomas and Alexander stood near a fireplace on the opposite end of the room, while Everett and Jonas were seated at a rickety wooden table, deep in discussion as they supped. My brothers looked toward us in unison as we entered, and Alexander flashed a rakish grin. He still wore his dragon scale armor but the helm sat atop the mantle next to an empty mug.

"I'd like to declare this day a success," Alexander stated boldly as we approached. He held up one finger, then began ticking off the others as he continued. "We had few casualties. We've taken the lower city. The townspeople have *welcomed* us, and most want to *help* us. And above all, we remain standing at the end of the day."

I smelled alcohol on Alexander's breath as we neared and shook my head, both amused and concerned. My gaze met Thomas'. "How much ale has he had?"

Thomas rolled his eyes and shrugged. "Enough that I've told the barkeep to stop furnishing him with refills. He started on the ale at least two hours ago while he was 'preparing' my new quarters."

"Oh, come now, Tom," Alexander replied, his words mildly slurred. "It's just a bit of celebratory drink."

"It's premature," Thomas replied evenly as he crossed his arms. "We still have half the city to conquer and Colin to deal with. Or have you forgotten?"

Alexander's grin soured. "Of course not." He frowned in my direction. "Surely you've come for more important matters than monitoring my sobriety level, brother." He glanced longingly at the mug on the mantle. "I've missed this inn. The best ale in all of Novania."

"I disagree with you on that point, brother," I replied.

Alexander snorted a laugh. "You always preferred the swill they serve in Calder's Point at the… I can't recall the name of that shoddy inn. When you requested a cask for the banquet celebrating your first wedding, I thought Mother was going to throw you out of the castle herself."

"It's hardly swill, and it came from The Blue Swan. Mother had…other reasons for her displeasure with me that day. It had nothing to do with my choice of drink."

"Tell me," Alexander continued with a wicked grin, "why was she so angry with you?"

I groaned and shook my head. "Now isn't the time."

His gaze slid to my left, where Zayneldarion stood, his violet eyes conveying unspoken amusement. "I don't think we've met," Alexander said. He stepped forward to offer his hand in greeting and stumbled on the rug.

"He's had entirely too much ale," Thomas said with exasperation as my father stated his name.

"Wait." Alexander paused, holding one hand out to steady himself. He peered at Zayneldarion closely, scrutinizing him. "I knew you were a mage as soon as you walked into the room, and I know your power surpasses mine." He turned to glare in my direction. "When were you going to tell me your *father* was here, Andrew?"

"It's hardly his fault you've drunk yourself into a stupor," Thomas replied with a smirk. "And I believed you'd have guessed he was present, given there were *two* dragons overhead most of the day."

Alexander nodded. "You're right, Tom. Maybe I *should* sit down."

I guided Alexander into a chair at the far end of the table where the former dukes were seated. He sat heavily and shook his head as though trying to clear it.

"I'd hoped to strike the inner wall at dawn," Thomas stated as he took the chair across from Alexander, "but if we do, Alex will need to sit out most of the fight. I won't risk him charging through the inner city in a drunken rage only to get himself killed."

I chuckled. "I don't think you'll need to worry about *that* scenario. Alex is more than likely going to awaken with a headache primed to split his skull."

Alexander glowered between us. "I'll be fine in the morning. I'll have Lydia do something about the hangover…"

"You should allow your wife to focus on the wounded," Zayneldarion replied quietly. "If we must strike in the morning, I can clear your system of alcohol once we're finished here. We'll need you aware, alert, and capable of focusing for more than three seconds at a time."

"You see, Tom?" Alexander asked with a lopsided grin. "It's fine."

Zayneldarion shook his head. "Curing a man rapidly of drink is liable to make him wish he had never asked for it. I doubt he'll thank me afterwards," he said to Thomas.

The door swung open and the innkeeper appeared briefly as he ushered Shyala and Rizzt-tok inside. Thomas nodded a greeting to them and said, "Now we wait for Elias."

"He's returned, then?" I asked.

Thomas nodded. "Yes. He located the three camps we knew of, and another that had been abandoned. The guards gave him little resistance. He arrived late this afternoon with a number of Novanian followers. Our numbers continue to grow even as Colin's dwindle."

The news was uplifting, but I couldn't shake the sense that we were missing something important, that Colin had more planned in his defense of the Capitol than we were aware of. I shrugged off my unease and focused on Thomas.

"What's your plan for the morning?" I asked.

"I'll present it once Elias arrives."

The door opened again, but it was only a pair of servers who'd come to clear away the dishes at the other end of the table. One made her way toward us. "Would you like anything? Our ale is the best—"

"—the best in Novania!" Alexander exclaimed before breaking into a laugh.

"My brother has had his fill," Thomas replied.

"Of course," she replied with a smirk. "And for the rest of you?"

Thomas and Rizzt-tok declined, but Rynn ordered a round for the remainder of the group. As the server left, Alexander climbed unsteadily to his feet. He stumbled around his chair and nearly fell. I rose with an exasperated sigh and went to his side.

"Alex," I whispered, "what are you doing? You're drunk."

He giggled. "I know. I also need the privy."

With a groan, I guided him toward the door and across the common room. Nearly every time Alexander had entered The Princess' Rest, he'd drunk himself into a giddy stupor and tonight was no exception. And the ale wasn't half as good as he claimed.

While Alexander was in the privy, Elias entered the front door. He spotted me before the innkeeper signaled him, then wended his way across the crowded room.

"I was told Thomas was keeping his new command quarters here, but I'd expected somewhere a bit more private," he remarked.

I shrugged. "Tom's in the back room with the others. Alex is—" I gestured toward the door of the privy. "He'll be out in a minute, or so I hope."

Elias raised one eyebrow. "Is there trouble, Andrew?"

"You could say that."

As if on cue, the door banged open and Alexander stumbled out. He managed a grin when he noted Elias' presence. "Cousin. Glad you've made it."

Elias grimaced, then nodded to me. "I understand. Alex, you reek of ale."

"It's the best ale in the kingdom, and I've not had any since…" Alexander trailed off, a frown of confusion twisting his features. "It's been far too long. Ah, I have missed it."

"Clearly," Elias replied drily.

I grasped Alexander by the elbow and led him through the common room once more while Elias followed my lead. When we returned to the command quarters, Thomas met Alexander's grin with a disapproving stare before rising to greet Elias.

When Elias noted my father's presence, his eyebrows rose sharply. "I know you," he said, stunned. "You were Carra's—" He shook his head. "That means you're Andrew's father. How is this possible?"

"We can explain later," Thomas replied briskly. "For now, know that he's here to aid us, and Jonas and I have a new plan to unveil."

Thomas and Jonas took turns detailing their plan for the next morning's attack.

"Now that we've claimed the outer city, we no longer need to rely on tunneling beneath the walls," Jonas said.

"It's fortunate, since the inner wall is more secure than we'd anticipated," Thomas replied. "Colin is safely ensconced within his stronghold."

Jonas appeared troubled, but nodded. "He is. But I have a plan." He rose from his seat and began to pace restlessly along the nearby wall. "Between the magi and the Tree-speakers, I believed we had the power to break through the inner wall with ease, but I'm not certain it will be enough. However, Ev has some news that should help."

Everett forced a smile, but it failed to reach his eyes. "Perhaps. It may be more dire than not."

"Tell us," Alexander said, leaning forward to rest his elbows on the table.

Everett glanced between myself and my father. "Our scouts discovered several partially assembled trebuchets hidden at intervals throughout the lower city. The workmen assigned to their construction have been detained for questioning, but I don't believe they're at fault for their actions. They were merely following orders. I'm grateful none were operational."

I studied my father's reaction as I contemplated Everett's words. His jaw clenched and his eyes narrowed imperceptibly, but his expression remained neutral.

I closed my eyes momentarily, then said, "I'm grateful too."

Rynn grasped my hand beneath the table and gave it a frigid squeeze.

"We're repurposing the trebuchets to aid in breaking the inner wall," Jonas said after several moments of strained silence. "Since the king graciously left them behind, we may as well use them for our own purposes."

Alexander snorted a laugh. "I believe that's the first time I've ever heard Colin and 'gracious' used in the same sentence."

Thomas scowled at him, but Alexander was oblivious.

"We'll strike at several points along the inner wall simultaneously," Jonas continued. "The magi, the Tree-speakers, and the trebuchets will attack until it's breached. The rest of our forces will be split between each location, prepared to storm once the walls topple." He paused to study Thomas and Alexander. "I also suggest you prepare yourselves for another encounter with the king."

Thomas nodded wearily. "I have no doubt Colin will make a nuisance of himself now that he's cornered."

Alexander muttered darkly, glowering at the mention of Colin's name.

"Once we've breached the wall," Thomas said, ignoring him, "I'd like to proceed through the upper city in the same manner that we did with the lower. Fight only those with the king's garrison, and avoid harming the common people, though our reports suggest most of the populace was…relocated. Colin is our true enemy—the people of this city are merely caught in the midst of our feud."

"I'll lead the soldiers stationed on the western side," Jonas stated. "I'd like Elias to lead a group on the eastern side. Rizzt-tok, can the hive take the southern position?"

She tilted her triangular head slightly. "We are willing to do so."

"That leaves the northern front to you, Andrew," he said. "Alexander will accompany you along with our soldiers, given that his ability lends itself to combat rather than breaching walls." He turned to Rynn. "I'd like you to lead the magi. I assume you'll take the northern position. Designate others to lead in each quadrant."

Rynn nodded, and a faint smile crossed her lips. "You're right—I'll take the northern area. I have several others in mind, and I'll speak with them when we're finished. Thank you, Jonas."

He nodded. "When you've decided on the others and have spoken with them, please send word."

"I will."

"As for you, Zayne," Jonas said slowly, "it'll be helpful if you can learn what goes on inside the wall. Attack if you're able, but we sorely need more information regarding what awaits us on the other side."

Zayneldarion nodded. "A scouting mission it is, then. Good."

Thomas rose carefully from his seat and straightened his tunic. "Tomorrow and the coming days may prove some of the most trying in Novania's history. I *will* bring Colin to justice, but should our plans fail, I want you each to know that it has truly been an honor." He closed his eyes briefly, steeling himself, then went on. "I'm aware of the consequences of my decision to defy the present king. I believe we can remove the threat he poses, and I believe in the strength and courage each of you possess. It's my fervent hope that we'll prevail."

I studied Thomas carefully, noting the fragility that lay beneath the surface of his stoic façade. Everett had taught him much during their time together, and to most of those present, he appeared calm and assured. While the others praised his speech and reasserted their convictions to his cause, our eyes met. I offered him a smile and nodded once.

"I'd like a few minutes alone with my brothers," he said as the conversation abated. "There's a final matter to discuss."

"I'll await you outside," Zayneldarion said to me as he rose from his seat. "I'll tend to Alex when you're finished."

Thomas didn't speak again until we were alone. "We must decide what to do regarding Colin's fate." He stared at the ground, much of his previous fire extinguished.

Alexander rolled his eyes and scowled, then reached for a half-empty ale cup one of the others had left behind. "If we're to speak of *him*, I need another drink."

"Alex—" Thomas began, but Alexander cut him off.

"It was thoughts of Colin that started me on the ale earlier," he admitted, glaring into the cup. "I'd like to skewer him like the animal he has become." He downed the contents and grimaced. "Perhaps put his head on a pike and place it atop the wall for the whole kingdom to see."

"Alex, you'll regret doing that," I cut in.

He laughed grimly. "I'm well aware. Unless Colin presses me, I'll allow him to live to face the council of governors once Thomas has taken the throne. I may hate him, but he's my damned brother, like it or not. I don't want to have his tyrant's blood on my hands, though I know he'd never hesitate to kill all of us."

I nodded, relieved. I only hoped he remembered his promise in the morning once the haze of alcohol no longer clouded his thoughts.

"I believe he'll attempt to goad one of you into action when we face him," Thomas continued. "He has learned how to manipulate your tempers far better than he has mine."

Alexander reached for another partial cup of ale, but Thomas stayed his hand. "Alex, enough," he said gently. "See Zayneldarion, then find your wife. Spend your time with her tonight before the muster is called. Take care of yourself foremost, then we can focus on Colin."

Alexander blinked in surprise, but managed a nod. "Of course. I'll do that."

"Let's go," I said as I stood and pulled Alexander along with me. "We'll get through this, one way or another. Colin's time as king is coming to an end."

Alexander leaned heavily on my arm as we walked outside. Zayneldarion awaited us in the road near the inn's stable. He'd assumed his dragon form but appeared decidedly uncomfortable given the narrow street and his current size. Elias was with him, and the two were talking as we approached.

They looked up as Alexander stumbled on the steps leading from the inn's door and laughed loudly at his misstep. I steadied him and cursed myself for positioning him on my blind right side. I'd been unable to see his feet.

"Thomas is finished, then?" Elias asked.

"Yes."

"Good. I'll remain with him through the night. Jonas was to send a few soldiers our way to act as guards." He smiled wryly. "One can't be too careful now that we're in the monster's lair."

Alexander mumbled something unintelligible and began to giggle. I sighed and glanced at my father while Elias shook his head and returned to the inn.

I was genuinely concerned for Alexander. His binge on the eve of battle was out of character. The inevitable confrontation between us and Colin was taking a greater toll on him than I'd realized, but I'd never believed he'd resort to drowning his troubles in ale. Once more,

I wondered what Colin had done to Alexander while he'd been a prisoner in the castle's dungeon.

"Alex, you've got to remember we're in this together," I whispered as we staggered across the cobblestone street.

He grimaced. "I only wanted to forget him for a while."

"I hope you can do something for him," I said to Zayneldarion. "I'll need him alert come morning."

Zayneldarion nodded and peered at Alexander with unconcealed worry in his eyes. "Alexander, look at me." Once he held my brother's attention, he said, "This is going to be unpleasant, but it must be done."

"It's Colin's fault," Alexander muttered, his tone bitter.

Zayneldarion looked around the area, then gestured to a sewer grate not far away. "Lead him there. Then I'll do what I must to clear his system. He'll likely vomit." He followed us to the indicated location. "It's fortunate the streets are relatively empty. Hold him steady, Andrew."

I supported Alexander as best I could while he leaned against me. The familiar herbal scent of healing magic enveloped us, and after a moment, Alexander lurched forward. He fell to his knees and began to empty the contents of his stomach before I could react.

"He'll be well enough in a few minutes," Zayneldarion said.

Several seconds later, Alexander spat and sat back on his heels, his face pale. "Holy hell," he swore with a shake of his head. "Never do that again."

"I should tell you to do the same," I replied with a frown. "The next time you decide to drown your sorrows in an ale cup, I'd prefer if it wasn't the night before a battle."

Alexander groaned. "I'm not certain I'll be able to stomach even the smell of ale for some time. I feel as if I've been trampled and my guts turned inside-out."

"At least you're sober," Zayneldarion remarked evenly. "I tried to warn you that a rapid cure would be unpleasant."

Alexander shrugged. "I suppose it's best this happened tonight rather than in the morning as I'd originally planned. Lydia would have flayed me alive had she seen me in that state." He frowned and stood up shakily. He no longer swayed on his feet and had regained his sense of balance, but his face was ashen.

"Can you walk back to Lydia alone?" I asked.

He barked a laugh. "I can now. I'll see you in the morning, brother. I want nothing more than to sleep and dream of Colin's demise."

TWENTY-FOUR

"I'm worried about Alex." I raked a hand through my hair as I spoke and cast a worried glance at Rynn.

I hadn't slept. My mind refused to relinquish its hold on what could prove a fatal confrontation between brothers. It was now two hours before dawn, and Jonas had called the muster. I walked between Rynn and my father, who had opted to remain in his false form until given the signal to begin his scouting mission. We threaded our way through the night-darkened streets, circling toward the northern sector and our rendezvous point. We'd forgone torches as we moved, hoping to avoid detection by the garrison stationed along the inner wall.

Rynn and I had discussed Alexander briefly after she'd returned from her errands the night before, but she had been exhausted and fallen asleep within minutes. I'd risen silently, unable to shed my doubts and fears, and spent the remainder of the night pacing the room we'd been given on the top floor of The Princess' Rest. It had been weeks since I'd last slept in a proper bed, but I simply could not escape the visions of our final confrontation with Colin and drift into slumber.

"The drunkenness was unusual," Rynn replied, "but I don't blame him for it. What you're planning to do…" She shook her head and shrugged helplessly. "I'm not certain I could face my own brothers as you hope to, even if they were twice as wicked as Colin."

"I worry for you both," Zayneldarion added. "It's plain you didn't rest last night."

I shrugged. "I'll rest when this is over and done."

Rynn rolled her eyes. "I'll believe that when I see it. I've become familiar enough with your habits to know how unlikely that is."

Zayneldarion shot me a meaningful glance. "I hope you learn to take better care of yourself, Andrew."

As we approached our appointed location, I noted with relief that Alexander was already present. He carried a bundle of fabric in his arms and it appeared he'd been awaiting our arrival for some time.

He flashed a sheepish grin when his eyes met my father's. "I, ah, should thank you for what you did last night. When I told Lydia, she was none too pleased with me."

Zayneldarion shrugged. "It was necessary. You must be in possession of your faculties this morning." He glanced at the bundle Alexander held in his arms. "What is that?"

"Claire and Elanor have been busy," he replied. "They've done more than make Thomas a set of standards. Here," he said, handing me a portion of the cloth, "this larger one is yours."

I unrolled the bundle to reveal a cloak sewn with Thomas' colors and the dragon insignia. I smiled as I studied it in the darkness.

"It may be hard to see, but it's Thomas' standard on there," Alexander said, then laughed at his words. "I just delivered cloaks to Jonas, Elias, the twins, and Siorus before coming here. You can see it well enough, can't you, brother?"

"Yes."

I drew the garment around my shoulders and fastened it, pleased at how well it fit. Claire had remembered my sizing.

"They thought all of Tom's commanders should have one," he continued. "Well, those who can wear them, that is. Here," he said, handing another to Rynn. "That should be yours. If it's too large, I've got it mixed up with mine."

When she hesitated, I took the cloth from Alexander and handed it to her. As they donned their cloaks, Zayneldarion nodded appraisingly.

"You make a gallant pair with your dragon scale armor and those cloaks," he remarked. "I'm pleased to see the sacrifices we've made have been put to good use."

I shrugged uncomfortably and looked down. Alexander still resented my decision to supply my scales for his armor, but I maintained the sacrifice had been well worth my pain.

Alexander crossed his arms and frowned in my direction. "I maintain that the gift was too much, but it has served me well."

"The dragon-kind rarely deem humanity worthy," Zayneldarion replied gravely. "If you had refused his gift, it would have been a grave insult—not only to Andrew, but to me as well. The armor my son now wears was meant for another, and he refused to take it. After the pain of my sacrifice, the least he could have done was to accept the armor once it had been crafted. Though he's long dead, I'm still bitter."

Alexander averted his gaze, chastened. "I hadn't considered it that way."

Zayneldarion's expression was unyielding. "Humanity rarely does. Your kind often takes this world and the others who inhabit it for granted. You act without forethought, rarely considering what the long-term consequences might be. It's why my people chose to depart. Most believed we no longer had a place here." He expelled a breath, then his expression softened. "I believed differently, which is why I chose to assist with the gateway. I didn't want to leave this world. I believed, given time and opportunity, that humanity would one day redeem itself. What you have done so far is proof enough that change *can* be wrought. It's why I promised to assist you. If Novania can change for the better, there is hope it can happen elsewhere too." He smiled in my direction. "I was also eager to see my son again."

I looked away as he spoke, decidedly uncomfortable when he mentioned humans and the dragons' perception of them. I was an amalgamation of both worlds, but understood the humans' half of the equation far better than I did the dragons'. Had my father's people truly been so disenchanted by humanity alone that they'd sought refuge on an entirely different world?

I was startled when I felt a hand on my shoulder. I looked up to meet my father's eyes. He smiled, understanding clear in his expression.

"I have no doubt we'll speak more of this later, Andrew. For now, know that I *do* believe in your cause and I'm here to help. It must be difficult to hear me speak of your mother's people in that manner, but sometimes the truth is just that: Difficult."

I managed a nod but said nothing in reply.

"You'll understand our position better one day," he said. "Humanity is short-lived, and they often forget the reasons precluding many important events. Even I am considered young, yet I've outlived several generations of humans already. And an Elder like Caelmarion has seen the passing of millennia. It's difficult to forget the wrongs endured at the hands of other people, even when they cannot remember it themselves."

"But we aren't all like that!" Alexander cried, indignant. "I'm doing my damnedest to make things right. To make things better!" He spun to face me, his expression wounded. "Andrew, you *know* me—you know so many of us. Tell him!"

"You misunderstand," Zayneldarion replied evenly before I could respond. "I wasn't accusing you. As I said previously, I didn't share the same outlook as most of the dragon-kind. I believe we can bring change. I simply wanted you to understand *why* the dragon-kind decided to leave. Most didn't think change was possible, that humanity wouldn't be amenable."

I didn't question his words. We'd spoken previously of Zayneldarion's role as an emissary between the dragon clans and the Oracle, and he held little animosity toward humans—at least those from the Southlands. He'd mentioned that he'd loved my mother, and I believed he'd been sincere. I had no reason to doubt him, but I also understood Alexander's frustration.

"This war may have begun with our desire to oust Colin," I said evenly, "but it has grown into something more, Alex. Thomas has promised to repeal the laws which would have seen us both needlessly killed. And for what? Because we exist. At first, I thought Tom made that promise to protect us, but that isn't true. Tom has *always* striven to do what he believes is *right*—and I'm convinced he understands what is truly at stake. It isn't merely *our* lives any more, but the lives of so many others. Every mage who followed you here, the Corodan, the Merael…my father. They knew the risks when they chose our side over Colin's. Even the Novanians who have defected have placed their lives on the line because they know it's the right thing to do. Colin may be the source of the recent atrocities, but what we fight for goes far beyond his reach. He must be removed from power in order for Tom to bring that promised change—a change I believe will bring hope to every person in Novania and those beyond her borders. Don't you see? It's no longer just a family matter, a quarrel between brothers. We're destroying an institution of oppression, borne of irrational fear. The dragon-kind may not have believed it possible, but *I* believe we can prove them wrong."

As I finished, a cheer erupted around us. I hadn't realized we'd gathered an audience, nor had I realized so many had stopped what they were doing to listen. I spun around, taking in the crowd with a measure of astonishment.

"*That* was the reason my father named you his commander," Alexander said after a moment. "You're skilled enough with a blade and you know strategy, but few people possess the gift of inspiration."

Zayneldarion wore a proud smile. "I wish my own father could have been here to listen to your speech. Perhaps it would have given him hope and changed his perspective on humanity."

As dawn broke golden across the eastern sky, we received word that Colin had made an appearance at the southern gate of the inner city. Thomas' message was brief, but it instructed us to begin the assault without delay. Colin had refused the offer of surrender a second time, as we'd anticipated. And while Thomas didn't explicitly state it, I understood his patience with our brother had nearly evaporated.

Zayneldarion departed soon after. He remained high enough above the city that if Colin possessed any more trebuchets, he was well beyond their range.

As Rynn prepared to leave, she said, "Take care of yourself, Andrew. I…" She looked down and shook her head as she struggled with a rush of emotion.

I drew her into my arms and planted a kiss atop her head full of curls. "I'll find you when this is over."

She nodded, then stared fiercely at Alexander. "Keep him safe, Alex."

After she was gone, Alexander laughed. "When did I become your keeper, brother?"

"When you decided to take it upon yourself to rescue me from Claybourne," I replied. "I don't believe she'll ever forgive me for being captured, but I would never have forgiven myself if I'd allowed her to fall that day."

"I'm glad you've found her," he said, his tone meaningful. "Tom and I spoke some time ago, and he said he felt Rynn is a better match for you than Vera was. Perhaps you don't agree, but I do."

I shrugged. "I loved Vera, but it was different. I love Rynn too. I don't know what else to say." With our attack about to begin, I hoped he'd drop the subject; we had more important matters to focus on than my history with women.

Alexander nodded, a knowing smile on his lips. "You don't have to say anything, brother. And it's time." He gestured to the wall, looming a short distance ahead.

Moments later, the magi began their assault. The air thrummed with energy and countless scents permeated the still morning air. Gusts of wind buffeted the wall, accompanied by shards of ice. The earth beneath our boots rumbled as magi began channeling energy through the very foundations of the city. A bolt of lighting cracked overhead from an otherwise clear sky.

Near the eastern gate where Elias' group was staged, two of the trebuchets we'd reappropriated hurled blocks of stone and other debris at the wall. I could just make out the tops of the war machines from our location and suppressed a shudder.

I would *never* be captured in that manner again.

Alexander smiled grimly as I attempted to stave off a bout of sneezing. My eyes began to water, and to my surprise, even the right one was affected despite its blindness. As the magical assault continued, I sneezed several times in succession, unable to resist the urge any longer. I shook my head, noting my skin had begun to itch.

"I hope we breach this damned wall soon," I growled.

Alexander laughed. "We will, brother. If not here, then elsewhere. It won't be long." He pointed toward the top of the wall, where a handful of the king's garrison huddled together, clearly terrified by what occurred beneath them. "Those poor bastards weren't expecting mages. When a breach finally occurs, they'll be too stunned to fight back." He shook his head. "It's almost a pity. I was rather looking forward to a challenge today."

He peered skyward. As I followed his gaze, I spied Galewing soaring above the city. The gray eagle floated effortlessly, taking in the view spread out beneath him. In the eastern sky beyond, the dark shape of Zayneldarion paused for a moment as he cast a wave of magic through the air.

"Your father isn't the only scout we have up there," Alexander said with a smirk. "Galewing says we'll find little resistance on the other side of the wall. Colin has recalled most of his soldiers to the castle's grounds."

"I still find it puzzling." I crossed my arms and frowned in thought. "While I've gone over the numbers with Jonas several times, and it seems Claybourne took the majority of the garrison with him during his multiple defeats, I believed Colin would keep more than a token guard inside the Capitol itself."

Alexander shrugged. "Colin didn't believe we'd make it this far, brother. That seems clear enough to me."

"Even so, it doesn't make sense." I shook my head. "I can't dismiss the feeling that he still has a few surprises in store. Colin isn't stupid, and leaving himself unprotected and vulnerable seems like a feint. What is he truly plotting?" I turned away as another bout of sneezing overcame me. "Holy hell, that needs to stop."

"I don't believe Colin is plotting anything. He's lost too many soldiers, and he drove away or executed most of the nobility who might have allied with him. He was left with Claybourne, and that other man, who seemed none too eager to return here after his defeat at Willever. Claybourne is now dead." Alexander scowled. "And good riddance."

Another rumble vibrated through the ground. This time, I felt the earth quake beneath my feet as the wave of magic passed directly beneath us. Moments later, there was a deafening crack as the inner wall began to split apart, a vertical crevice snaking up its side. It would topple within seconds.

I drew my sword and raised it above my head, preparing to signal the soldiers. It still felt strange to hold it in my left hand, but Alexander's theory had proven right on more than one occasion, and I'd worked to become effective at wielding the weapon in my left hand.

Rynn's voice rose above the clamor, calling for further strikes on the wall now that it was visibly damaged. The king's soldiers disappeared from the ramparts. I assumed they'd departed for solid ground and expected a fight once we broke through.

"The soldiers are fleeing toward the castle," Alexander said after a moment. "I've asked Galewing to follow their progress." He glanced at me. "The streets are completely empty. It's strange. I expected to see more of Colin's lackeys."

I nodded warily as cold fingers of dread snaked along my spine. "I did as well. Where are they?"

Before he could respond, a deafening crash resounded ahead. I turned toward the noise to find the wall crumbling. Enormous blocks of cut stone tumbled to the ground and spilled across the nearby street. Dust plumed in the air, and the magical attacks abruptly halted.

My gaze met Alexander's as I dropped my sword arm, signaling the soldiers to press forward. "It's time."

He nodded solemnly and kept pace with me as we strode forward. A pair of magi cleared the debris from the breach, while others slowly widened the gap in the stone. As we passed, I caught a glimpse of Rynn; her back was to us and she didn't see our passage. I prayed that I'd see her again at the end of the day.

"I'll keep to your right, brother," Alexander said, his voice grim.

We strode through the gap and entered the inner city, stepping over chunks of crumbled stone as the magi continued to clear the space around us. The street was eerily still and would have been silent aside from the noise of the assault drifting through the air from our other points of attack. I glanced skyward as a shadow passed over us, and noted my father was circling above.

I scanned the empty road, the abandoned buildings that loomed on either side. There was no sign of life within the dwellings; the windows had not been shuttered and many doors hung open to reveal interiors left in disarray. Furniture was overturned, food and dishes were left on tables, toys were scattered on the floors. It was as if the people had vanished in the midst of their daily routines.

"I don't like this," Alexander said uneasily. He scanned our surroundings and pulled his swords from their scabbards. Galewing descended to perch on the roof of the nearest dwelling, his keen golden eyes fixed on Alexander. "What has Colin done?"

TWENTY-FIVE

I dispatched messengers to Jonas, Elias, and Rizzt-tok to inform them we'd breached the inner city, then turned to face the soldiers under my command.

I gestured to a man I recognized as one of Jonathan Horace's former lieutenants, though I couldn't recall his name. "Take a dozen trusted people and move ahead. Follow this street to the plaza outside the castle's main gate, but stay back. I don't want anyone taken out by archers if it can be helped."

"Yes, sir. What do you need us to do once there?"

"Observe. Listen. I want to know what Colin plans, what defenses you can see from the plaza… Anything that will help us formulate a strategy for the next attack."

He saluted. "Consider it done. I'll send reports as soon as I have information to share."

I nodded as he turned to gather his unit to depart. It was a mile-long trek to the plaza, and I doubted we'd receive word for at least an hour once they arrived.

The streets surrounding our breach remained eerily silent, the nearby houses still and empty. It was damned unnerving, and I wondered again where the people had gone. Was Alexander right, and Colin had done something unforgivable?

I shrugged off my unease and focused on another group of soldiers. "Investigate the nearest houses and businesses. Report anything unusual you find within."

As they left, Alexander shook his head. "I don't like this," he said again. "Holy hell, something about this city feels *wrong*, and I'm certain Colin's the cause."

I nodded as I watched the retreating forms of the second unit disappear through a nearby doorway. "Has Galewing seen anything?"

Alexander pointed to the roof where the eagle was perched. "I asked him to keep his distance from the castle. I won't risk his welfare if Colin has archers waiting."

A few minutes later, our soldiers exited the first dwelling they'd entered, their expressions grim.

"No sign of anyone inside," one reported with a shake of her head. "There's a good bit of blood on the floor in one room. But it's *old.* Been there for some time."

"Thank you," I said as my unease continued to deepen.

We'd witnessed Colin's cruelty first-hand when we'd discovered the labor camp, and rumors had abounded of the executions he was said to have ordered. I didn't know what had transpired to reduce the inner city to this state of abandonment, but I had no doubt Colin was responsible. What I didn't understand was why he'd turned on his people at all—they were innocent and even those bearing the Mark were harmless until trained. What had spurred him onto this path of wanton destruction?

"Bloodstains—even old ones—don't bode well for the people who lived in that house," Alexander said, his voice hushed. "I don't like this, brother."

"Nor do I."

I scanned the area uneasily and hoped we'd learn something from the unit dispatched to the plaza. The silence and inexplicable abandonment of the inner city left me on edge. I wanted to do more than merely wait, but Jonas' orders had been clear. We were not to engage with the king's forces until the other groups had breached the walls.

I clenched and unclenched my right fist in an attempt to ward off my disquiet. The pervading stillness was fundamentally *wrong*, and the longer I waited, the more restless I became.

A messenger arrived from the Corodan before we received word from elsewhere. Rizzt-tok had sent a smaller, subservient female as her liaison due to her inherent speed. Rynn followed her as she skittered toward us, her expression pensive.

"The hive and magi will breach the wall by midday," the Corodan said. "The magi leader is very powerful. The hive knows earth, he knows earth magic. The wall will crumble."

Rynn flashed a grin in my direction. "I thought Siorus would prove useful to the hive."

I nodded, recalling how he'd split the ground in front of him only to close it again, swallowing countless enemy soldiers during the last battle at Willever. He disliked using his power in that manner, but working alongside the hive, his magic would bolster the Corodans' efficiency at moving earth and rock. It had been a sound decision to select Siorus for the task.

I glanced skyward to note the sun was still low in the eastern sky. It was several hours before noon, which meant we'd be waiting for some time yet. I suppressed a sigh and refocused my attention on the Corodan. "Will you return to the southern wall, or will you remain here with us?"

The Corodan tilted her head slightly as she conferred with the hive. "Rizz-tok says I must remain. We can speak faster this way."

"Good."

I was pleased Rizzt-tok had sent this warrior to our location. She wasn't overly powerful or large—she was neither—but she was more fluent in our tongue than most of her people. Communication would be imperative during the next few hours.

"And your name?" Alexander asked.

"Shrii-kezt."

Rapid footfalls approached from behind. I turned as one of the soldiers I'd sent to the plaza returned from her task. Her face was ashen and slicked with a sheen of sweat, but it appeared she had not engaged in combat during her errand. I recalled her name was Wylla; she'd defected to Thomas' side after the battle at the keep. She stopped before me and swiftly removed her helm. Thin strands of blond hair were plastered across her brow, damp with perspiration.

"What have you found?" I asked, ignoring Shrii-kezt for a time.

She shook her head, blue eyes wide. "Lord Dragon, it's…" She drew a breath to steady herself and shook her head. "The plaza is a scene from nightmare, my lord. I don't know what occurred there, but the number of bodies is nothing short of staggering. It's as though all of these people," she gestured toward the empty homes around us, "were herded into the plaza and killed like sheep for the slaughter." She swallowed and squeezed her eyes shut. "Most of the dead were shackled or bound in some manner. I knew the king was capable of cruelty, but this…" She shook her head again, allowing her words to fade into silence.

I turned to Alexander, my mouth dry. His jaw was clenched in rage and determination, his green eyes fierce and unyielding. "If this is truly Colin's handiwork, he *will* pay for what he has done. Damn him to the farthest reaches of the deepest hell."

I didn't have to ask what Alexander was thinking, and I suppressed a groan. He would break his promise and take matters into his own hands if given the opportunity. I'd have to watch him carefully to ensure he didn't commit regicide. I couldn't allow Alexander to ruin his life, to destroy his future with Lydia and their unborn son—no matter how badly Colin deserved death.

To Wylla, I said, "We'll make certain the bodies are tended to. Did you see any movement on the castle walls?"

She nodded. "Yes, the garrison is holed up inside. Word of your wall breach was received, and the king placed the castle on lockdown. The gates are closed and archers stand on the ramparts. Our people will keep their distance until reinforcements arrive."

"Good. It may be a while before the others join us." I glanced at Rynn. "How long until the breach is cleared of rubble?"

She shrugged. "It won't be much longer. With Gwerin here, clearing the path is simple."

"We'll leave some of our people here once the breach is clear," I told Wylla. "The rest will march to join your group soon. Stay clear of the archers, and send word immediately if the king makes an appearance. My brother and I have many questions for him."

"Of course, my lord." She bowed deeply before departing.

Rynn appeared amused as I turned to face them once more, her blue eyes sparkling. "I believe this is the first time I've truly seen you in your element, Andrew. It's fascinating to watch."

Before I could form a reply, she turned away with an enigmatic smile and walked back toward the sundered wall. I wasn't certain what I would have said in response; I didn't fully understand the meaning behind her words, and there were more important items that required my attention.

"Your father is on his way here," Alexander said after a moment.

I followed his gaze; Zayneldarion's course would take him directly to our location. Even from a distance, I could see his attention was fixed on us.

"Perhaps he has spoken with Jonas."

"The hive has entered the city," Shrii-kezt said a moment later. "The mage found a weakness in the earth. We exploited it."

I nodded in acknowledgement, but didn't reply. I shielded my eye from the sun's glare while marking Zayneldarion's progress. He descended rapidly as he neared our location, landing gracefully some distance away in the center of the cobblestone street. Without waiting for Alexander, I strode toward him and hoped he brought good news.

He nodded as I approached, his expression grim. "When the magi breached the wall, every member of the king's garrison fled inside the castle grounds. They have barricaded themselves within. They number less than one hundred strong, but that isn't what troubles me." He paused to study me carefully. "From above, I can clearly see the horrors that have been wrought in this city, Andrew. I doubt there is a soul left alive amongst those who once dwelt here. I pray Jonas' earlier reports are correct, and most were relocated, but the devastation to the populace is clear."

A chill colder than a winter's snow skittered along my spine. I needed to know what had transpired, but I feared learning the truth. Alexander joined us in time to hear my father's words, and a stream of curses spilled from his lips.

"What has he done?" I asked, unable to stop myself. "We've heard of what awaits us in the plaza—"

Zayneldarion nodded. "Yes, and that is but one location where bodies have been piled high. To my eye, they were city folk. Merchants, shopkeepers, servants, and the like. Based on their attire, I suspect some were nobility as well. The inner city is utterly devoid of life, save for our soldiers and magi. There must be hundreds of dead, perhaps thousands." He closed his eyes and hung his head, sorrow etched across his scaly countenance. "This man who calls himself king, who defiles Carra's memory with such atrocities, such *horrors*… He must be stopped."

"He will rue the day he began the damned Mark inspections," Alexander replied through clenched teeth. "If I have to kill him myself, I will."

"No, Alex, you won't." My words were an order, and I received a reproving glare from him in response. "We will subdue Colin, but his fate will rest with Tom and the governor's council. Think of Lydia. Of your child."

He scowled, but managed a nod. "As you say, *Commander*."

I bristled at his use of the title, but events could not play out any other way if Alexander hoped to avoid a trial for his hand in Colin's demise. His anger and frustration with me would disappear given time.

I turned back to Zayneldarion. "We saw you fly in from the east. Did you speak with Jonas?"

He laughed grimly. "I suppose you could say that. When the garrison retreated, I took it upon myself to stop at each gate once they weren't guarded. It was simple enough to open them from within. Our people are on their way to the plaza you mentioned."

I nodded before turning to address the soldiers awaiting my orders some distance away. "We march on the plaza. Tell the magi to join us once they've finished their task."

We were still a quarter-mile away from the plaza when the true horror of what lay ahead became apparent. What had once been a pleasant stone-paved walkway encircling a green space lined with trees was nearly unrecognizable.

The trees had been cut down and the grass was withered and dead where it hadn't been trampled into bare earth. In the center of what had once been the green space, gallows had been erected, flanked on each side by a pair of executioner's blocks. Every inch of the scene was spattered with gore and congealing blood, shards of bone, and clumps of hair. Scores of bodies were piled in the streets, blocking access to the street beyond.

The dead had been discarded haphazardly. Servants were thrown alongside nobility, craftsmen amidst merchants. As Wylla had indicated, most were shackled at ankle and wrist, some with chains, others with rope. The bodies nearest the gallows were in the earliest stages of decomposition, perhaps only a few days dead. Others were far older, bloated and split from exposure to the elements, while some were little more than skeletons garbed in the clothing that marked their previous lots in life. The arcing crescent of the Mage's Mark was visible on only a few. Flies swarmed the scene, flitting between corpses as they gorged themselves on rotting flesh. The stench was unbearable.

I'd witnessed plenty of gore and grievous injuries during my years as the former king's commander, but nothing compared to this. Nothing would *ever* compare to this.

The soldiers I'd sent ahead kept well away from the plaza, daring to draw near only when required to do so. Most held their cloaks over their faces to block the odor wafting from the scene.

The sight was appalling. I studied the macabre display from a distance, unable to escape the nightmare vision even when I closed my eyes. Colin had committed murder on an unprecedented scale.

I resisted the urge to vomit, but many of the others succumbed. I didn't fault them. I couldn't. This was nothing short of horrific.

Once the Roche twins arrived, I'd order a pyre built and the remains dealt with expediently. We'd need the way cleared in order to maneuver, and the dead deserved to be tended properly. The other locations my father had mentioned would follow suit.

Alexander gagged and hastily covered his mouth with a gauntleted hand, horror evident in his green eyes. Zayneldarion's expression was grim. He'd assumed his false human form, but the vanilla scent of his magic did little to mask the odor of decay.

"Monstrous." Zayneldarion's tone was laden with disgust. "I have seen much in my time, but *nothing* like this. Even Cael would find this sight difficult to stomach."

"Why would he do this?" Alexander asked, his tone pleading. "I know I've said Colin has fallen to madness, but I was only speaking generally. *This*...This is truly madness. Holy hell." He shook his head, his eyes haunted. "I never imagined anyone could be capable of something like this, not even Colin."

"I mean to ask him why, Alex," I replied with a growl, rage replacing my initial shock and disgust. "This is fucking barbaric."

Alexander nodded, unable to tear his eyes from the scene. "I can't imagine what those last poor souls endured. To be led here, seeing this… Holy hell. Holy *fucking* hell."

A quarter-hour passed before Elias and his unit approached the site. Alexander and I met them a short distance away to warn them of what they'd find in the plaza. Nevin Roche was the mage leading his group, and he followed Alexander toward the scene as I continued to speak with Elias. Alexander's desire to ensure the space was cleared and the dead put to rest overrode his relief at seeing our cousin alive and well. My brother was shaken to his core, though he'd never admit it openly.

Elias' expression alternated between a scowl and a grimace as we spoke. "The rumors surrounding the king have been foul for months, and after seeing the labor camps, I believed I'd witnessed the extent of his depravity. It seems I've underestimated your brother's capacity for evil."

"As have I," I replied gruffly, but his words gave me pause to reflect. "I think I may know why he was compelled to do this, but it makes the crime no less appalling."

Elias arched an eyebrow. "What are your thoughts?"

"If Colin feared we'd storm the Capitol, he'd have wanted to make a statement. A display meant to demoralize our people when they finally arrived," I replied slowly, thinking over my words. "He would have known how the sight would affect Alex and Tom. He's trying to stoke their anger, to force them into a rash decision. He gave no thought to the people themselves—they were nothing more than tools used to threaten and intimidate his subjects, and to disparage us." I shook my head. "If he hoped to stoke Alex's rage with this display, he's done so."

Elias tilted his head as he scrutinized me. "And what of you? Colin's animosity toward you is unparalleled when compared with your brothers."

I shrugged, unwilling to speak of the smoldering anger in my heart. "Colin doesn't know me as well as he believes, cousin. I won't be drawn into his game of murder."

Elias' expression was skeptical, but he didn't contradict my words. Instead, he turned to issue orders to his people while we awaited Rizzt-tok and Jonas. Several were given instructions to assist Alexander and Nevin with their grisly task.

By noon, Jonas established a new command base in a vacant inn on the edge of the plaza. Pyres had been built in the center of the street some distance south, where the wind would carry the stench of burning corpses away from our location. Several dozen soldiers and as many Corodan had been tasked to transport the dead; at intervals, one could peer through the grimy windows of the inn to watch them moving their macabre burdens along the street. Uniformed members of the king's garrison were glimpsed periodically atop the castle's wall, though they seemed interested in merely observing our movements. Colin had not been sighted since early in the day.

It was fortunate he'd remained hidden within his stone fortress. I wasn't certain I could prevent Alexander from killing him if the two spied one another.

Jonas summoned those wearing the dragon standard cloaks, but Nevin insisted he remain to tend the pyre's flame. I arrived with Niall, Siorus, and Rynn. Soon after, Alexander, Elias, Rizzt-tok, Thomas, Everett, and Zayneldarion filtered inside.

Jonas spread a map of the Capitol across an oaken table in the common room, his expression stern as he studied it. Thomas, clearly agitated by the state of the plaza, paced the length of the room, his arms crossed as a tight frown creased his face. Siorus appeared stoic, but I'd rarely seen a flicker of emotion in the man's features since meeting him. Everett was pale as his gaze darted between Thomas and the activities beyond the windows, worry lining his forehead. Elias stood with Alexander alongside the map table, the two wearing nearly identical expressions of grim determination, their familial resemblance unmistakable. Rizzt-tok stood across from them, peering down at the map; what her thoughts were regarding our gruesome discovery were unfathomable. Niall and Jonas were visibly troubled by the day's events and spoke softly to one another. Zayneldarion remained near the windows, an expression of sheer hatred twisting his features as he observed the movements beyond the glass. He folded his arms as his glare shifted to the guards striding atop the castle's walls.

Rynn was at my side, the fingers of her left hand twining through my right, her icy grip fierce. She'd said little since her arrival at the inn, but her blue-eyed gaze was haunted, her face drawn and pale. She focused on the map and those around her, averting her gaze each time her eyes strayed too near the windows.

She'd shown strength time and again, but the horrendous scene beyond the glass was more than she could endure. I gently extracted my hand from hers and slid my arm around her waist, hoping to provide comfort with my presence alone. She leaned into me, and as I looked down, silent tears froze to her cheeks—but she said not a word to express her anguish. I drew her closer, wishing for all the world that I could have spared her from witnessing the horrors my brother had left in his wake.

"There is only one entrance into the castle," Jonas said somberly after a time. His gray eyes held less steel than usual, and his expression was strained. He indicated a point on the map with his forefinger, the location of the gate across the plaza.

"Once the plaza has been cleared, we'll break the gate." Thomas paused his pacing long enough to speak. "The magi can focus their full might there, and—"

"No," Zayneldarion stated, his voice like stone as he turned from the window. "The magi will need to save their strength for the fight within. Andrew and I are more than capable of demolishing the gate."

Thomas gaped at him, and Alexander shook his head. "No, we had an agreement," Alexander said. "Andrew stays with us. Once the gate is open, there will be no time for him to change and don his armor. I will not have a repeat of our last battle."

Zayneldarion's violet-eyed gaze was unyielding. "Nor will I, Alexander. Your brother—*my son*—will be safe enough at my side." He frowned around the room, challenging the others to contradict him. "We will break the gate. It will be the fastest way to end this fight, and I doubt those ill-trained guards the king employs will know how to deal with a pair of dragons."

His declaration was met with silence. Finally, Jonas said, "Then it's settled."

I understood from a tactical position that my father's plan was sound. Even if the guards rained arrows on us, they weren't capable of penetrating our scales. With our combined strength, the ornate wooden gate would not withstand the assault.

I nodded my affirmation and received a tight smile from Zayneldarion in return.

Rynn huddled closer. When I looked down, she stared into my eyes, her expression sorrowful. "I know I can't accompany you this time," she whispered before turning her face away.

Jonas detailed the remainder of his plan while Thomas stressed the necessity of taking Colin prisoner, but I scarcely heard their words. My part in the coming battle had been decided, and I wanted nothing more than a few moments alone with Rynn before it began. There was so much I needed to say that I hadn't yet shared, and if our plan failed, my time on this world would be at an end.

"It will be hours before the plaza is clear," Everett said wearily after a time. "We can't strike until the dead have been properly tended to, and the king has killed so damned many…"

"We will strike at first light," Thomas stated firmly. "I will not give Colin any more time to prepare his defenses. He has troubled this kingdom too long already."

Rations were brought up from the lower city as the afternoon faded into evening. I shared a brief meal with my brothers and Rynn, but the atmosphere was subdued. We all knew the next day would decide the fate of Novania's future, one way or another. After a time, I rose and nodded to my brothers as Rynn scrambled to follow my lead.

We ascended the wooden steps from the inn's common room and made our way to the chamber on the third floor we'd taken for our own. We didn't speak. As I pushed the door open, she hesitated in the hall, collecting her thoughts before she followed me inside. I closed and barred the door behind her. I wanted no interruptions during what could be our final evening together.

"Promise me you'll take care of yourself." Her voice was a bare whisper, her gaze fixed on the bare wooden floor.

I touched the side of her face gently. "I will, Rynn. And when this is over, I—"

She shook her head adamantly. "No, don't speak of it yet. Whatever your plans, save them for after your brother has been dealt with." She looked up then, her expression fierce. "We don't know what will happen tomorrow… Let me have this night with you. I want *this* to remember you by should the unthinkable occur."

I nodded and didn't resist her advances further, drawing her into my arms as her icy lips met mine. I wanted her as much as she needed me.

I'd give her the night she asked for. I prayed it would not be our last.

TWENTY-SIX

A series of rapid knocks sounded on our door, waking me from a deep sleep. I sat up with a grimace, taking a moment to note the sky was still ink-black beyond the tiny window our room sported. Rynn stirred and mumbled a complaint about the noise as she rubbed sleep from her eyes. I rose and crossed the small room, locating my trousers in the process. I was in the midst of tugging them on when the knock repeated.

I growled wordlessly and stalked toward the door to unbar it. As it swung open, I was unsurprised to find Alexander standing in the hall; he looked as if he'd only just been awakened himself. I heard movement in the room behind me as Rynn rose from the bed, and I positioned myself in the doorway to block my brother's view of the interior.

"Tom wanted to speak with us before the others arrive," Alexander said, stifling a yawn with the back of his hand. "I don't believe he slept last night."

"I'll be down in a few moments," I replied quietly.

Alexander managed a tired smirk and nodded. "Yes, I suppose you'd like to finish dressing first. I'll tell him you won't be long."

I closed the door and turned to study Rynn as she searched the darkened room for her discarded clothing. She glanced in my direction briefly, questions clear in her blue eyes. I walked toward her, picking up the items she sought as I did so, then offered them to her.

She smiled ruefully. "Even with one eye, you still see far better in the dark than I do."

I chuckled. "That's why I decided to help, though I must admit, watching you flounder a bit can be interesting."

She snorted. "A fine time you've chosen to become a tease, Andrew." She sighed, then her expression dissolved into concern. "You'd best return after this is over and done. If you don't, I'll… I'm not certain what I'll do, but I imagine it won't be pleasant." She pulled her tunic over her head, then sat down heavily on the end of the bed, her gaze riveted on the floor.

"Rynn—"

"It's the truth." Her words were deflated, hollow. "Since I met you, my life has been utterly changed, and I can't imagine carrying on without you at my side. We can make all the promises in the world today, but none of them matter." Finally, she looked up, her expression pained. "I will always love you, Andrew, no matter what transpires."

I kissed her passionately before stepping away to don my shirt. She sighed and leaned back, gazing at me longingly.

"I wish this was over," she said softly.

I managed a smile. "As do I. It will be done soon, one way or another." I reached for my boots and pulled them on before pausing to study her. "I'd best go."

She nodded reluctantly. "I know. Luck be with you, Andrew."

"Stay safe," I replied. "Luck be with you as well."

Leaving the tiny room and Rynn behind was one of the most difficult things I'd ever forced myself to do. Saying goodbye was never easy, and I'd become accustomed to it as a soldier. But it had never been this hard to leave someone behind. The stakes were higher than ever before, and if we failed to defeat Colin in this final push to end his tyranny, I wouldn't see tomorrow. Thomas and Alexander would share that dire fate, leaving Novania in the hands of a madman and our loved ones mourning our losses.

It wasn't the future I'd envisioned for Rynn. She deserved better… And I'd do my damnedest to see us reunited after Colin's demise.

I shook my head in an attempt to clear the dark thoughts from my mind, then made my way downstairs to the common room. A fire blazed in the hearth, and Thomas paced before it, his expression dour in the flickering light. Alexander stood a few steps away, donning his black dragon scale armor while he awaited my arrival.

Jonas stood near the windows, gazing at the night-darkened plaza, but he paid me no heed as I strode past. His gray eyes remained fixed on the site of Colin's bloody atrocity. I glanced through the smudged panes to find the plaza had been cleared, the remainder of the bodies taken to the pyres during the night.

Thomas nodded as I stopped alongside Alexander, who paused in his task only long enough to acknowledge my presence. His helm, gauntlets, cloak, and sword belt lay across the nearby table while he adjusted the straps of his shoulder guards. His swords were sheathed and lay next to the remaining armor. I frowned uneasily as I spied the carved hilt and curved outline of his cursed blade.

A plate of hard biscuits occupied the far side of the table, leftover from the previous evening's meal. My stomach was sour due to my previous bleak thoughts and didn't seem capable of handling a meal, even a meager one. I turned away from Alexander and the stale bread to focus on Thomas.

"I wanted to speak with you before the assault begins," Thomas said, his tone somber. "During the night, I thought of a thousand different things I wanted to say, but now that we're gathered, I don't know how to begin."

"We'll get through this, Tom," Alexander stated with a confidence I wished I shared. He reached for his cloak and pulled it around his shoulders, the dragon standard prominently displayed across his back. "Only we can stop Colin properly, and we'll do so."

Thomas sighed, and in that moment, he appeared a decade older than his twenty-five years; the strain of the past months had wrought fine lines across his forehead, and dark circles pooled beneath his blue eyes. "You're right. I don't believe anyone else can put a stop to Colin's madness—it must be us."

"Are you prepared for what you must do, Tom?" I asked.

He'd make a fine ruler, but restoring Novania after the destruction Colin had wrought would require a monumental effort. He'd grown into his role with grace under Everett's watchful eye, but he was still young and the war had taken its toll on all of us—but Thomas most of all.

Thomas paused to stare into the fire, then said, "I know what must happen, and I'm as ready as I can be. I will make things right… So long as we survive the day."

"We will." Alexander flashed a grin in Thomas' direction as he reached for his sword belt. "Jonas' plan is sound. We'll break the gate, and Andrew will return here to shift and put on his armor. You and I will be waiting. We'll face Colin together, once our army has cleared the way." He shot me a sidelong glance. "It would be best if your armor is here in the common room before you leave, brother. It'll make things faster."

"I'll fetch my trunk once we're finished here," I replied.

Thomas stopped pacing but continued to stare into the hearth's flames. His expression was solemn. "I struggle to understand why Colin murdered so many. Less than a third of them were Marked! They were innocent. Why?"

"It's a question we'd all like an answer to," I replied with a frown.

Thomas shuddered involuntarily. "I'll never erase the sight of so many dead, left to rot in the plaza, from my memory. Perhaps the Corodan knew more than we realized when they began calling him the red king." His shoulders slumped as he hung his head in despair.

"None of us anticipated Colin would do that," Alexander said uneasily. "At first, I was horrified and angry, then I was disgusted. I want to make him pay." He clenched his fists, his face twisted in a wordless snarl. "The countless dead deserve justice. We'll avenge them."

Thomas looked at him sharply, his blue eyes unyielding as stone. "We made an agreement, Alex. You'll leave his fate to the council, no matter what he might say or do. Do you understand me?"

Alexander blinked, stunned by our youngest brother's sudden ferocity. "I gave you my word, Tom," he stammered after a moment. "Besides, I know what the penalty is if I *don't* allow the council of governors to rule on Colin's fate, and I won't do that to Lydia or our son."

Thomas' expression softened and he nodded slowly. "Good. Remember that, Alex. If for nothing else, remember it for the sake of your family."

The penalty for slaying any member of the royal family—even one so vile as Colin—was death by the headsman's axe. Colin must be brought before the governor's council alive, and it would be their job to decide his ultimate fate. But the difficulty was in locating Colin before one of our soldiers did, then ensuring his safety after his capture. Colin had more enemies than he realized, and we'd need to keep close watch over him until his sentence was carried out. I had no doubt the governors would call for his execution, but there was a possibility he'd be granted exile instead. I doubted they'd be so lenient, but stranger things had transpired over the course of Novania's long history.

Alexander pulled on his gauntlets and flexed his fingers several times. "It's beginning to lighten outside," he remarked before he abruptly turned to draw me into a rough one-armed embrace. "I hope you and your father know what you're doing, Andrew. We need you there when we face Colin."

I nodded. "I'll be there, Alex."

"Be safe, Andrew," Thomas added. "We'll be waiting for you."

I returned to the tiny room Rynn and I had shared during the night to collect the trunk containing my armor, sword, and other belongings, then went back to the common room. Rynn had gone while I'd been speaking with my brothers, and I didn't see her again that morning. I left the trunk near the hearth with Thomas, and Alexander promised he'd have my armor ready and waiting upon my return. We didn't say goodbye; those words would remain unspoken, but we each felt the parting keenly.

Alexander followed me outside and across the plaza to the place where my father paced in his human guise. His violet eyes were fixed on the shadowy figures of the garrison as they marched atop the castle's walls, torches in hand. He peered over his shoulder at our approach, but didn't speak for some time.

"They've been patrolling the wall for the entirety of the night," he said. "Most carry crossbows, though a few have standard long bows. The arrows and bolts won't be a problem." He turned to face us, arms crossed. "I've counted the number of men on that wall, and our forces outnumber them ten to one. Certainly, there should be more inside that we can't see, but even so, our numbers are superior. It seems this man who defiles the throne has been left with very few allies."

Alexander snorted derisively but made no reply.

"Colin never excelled at keeping friends," I said. "The few he possessed often feared him, long before he became king. His violent temper was well-known in the castle."

Overhead, the shrill cry of a bird pierced the air. I didn't have to look skyward to know Galewing soared above, undoubtedly scouting what lay beyond the castle's wall at Alexander's behest.

A faint smile crinkled the corners of Zayneldarion's eyes. "What does the eagle tell you, Alex?"

Alexander closed his eyes, then shrugged. "Movement on the walls, but little else. The barracks appear empty. If Colin has an army laying in wait, they're inside the castle itself."

It was possible Colin was keeping his remaining soldiers beyond our sight with a plan to surprise us with the only trick he had remaining. We wouldn't know until the gate was breached and the garrison—what remained of it—called to arms.

Orders were issued in the road behind us, drifting on the still morning air. I could hear Elias' voice clearly, while Siorus' deeper tones spoke to the magi. Moments later, Jonas reminded the men and women, Corodan and Merael, of our objectives and our plan.

I glanced at my father, who merely nodded. It was time to make our presence as dragon-kind known to the garrison. It was time to breach the gate.

I undressed and handed my garments to Alexander, then strode a short distance away across the defiled plaza. Though the bodies were gone, the ground was sticky beneath my bare feet, and I had no doubt I'd stepped through congealed blood. A wave of revulsion pulsed through me, but I shoved it away. I required space to accommodate my transformation and I could bathe later—if I survived to see the end of the day.

Once I was certain I had enough space to shift, I did so, ignoring the flood of power that filled my senses as rage and determination honed my focus like a blade. Across the plaza, my father dropped his guise and instantly appeared in his true form. Our eyes met and he nodded once, the flicker of a smile alighting on his dark-scaled features.

"Luck be with you, brother," Alexander said before he returned to the inn, my clothing bundled in his arms.

I was glad he'd be with Thomas during the initial phases of the assault; he could protect Thomas if necessary, and I suspected the time together would benefit them both.

"Do you truly believe we can break the gate faster than the magi?" I asked Zayneldarion once we were alone.

He smirked. "I'm certain of it. Humans build to keep out other humans—they rarely consider an attack by a species with superior strength or magical power. The Novanians are particularly notorious for such oversights, and to my eye, the walls of this city have not improved since my last sojourn here."

I nodded, though I remained unconvinced. I'd grown up in that castle, had practiced countless hours in the training yard, lived nearly half of my adult life within the barracks, spent scores of nights upon the walls on watch duty. I knew the workings of the castle, its defenses and shortfalls, and I'd always believed the stout wooden gate solidly barred before us would withstand even our combined assault. Perhaps it was a notion borne of my life of security within those walls, or perhaps it had come from the former king or my mother, but until I witnessed the gate fall, I'd remain skeptical of the apparent weakness my father perceived.

"When Jonas signals, I will strike at the soldiers above," he continued. "One blast of magic should clear most of them. After that, we'll charge as one. It may require a few strikes, but our combined power is greater than any battering ram Jonas could have constructed." He gazed at me levelly. "Do not hold back, Andrew. The soldiers behind us are counting on a swift breach."

I frowned, certain he'd spoken with Alexander. There was no other explanation for his present concern, and I wondered briefly what else my brother had told him.

Jonas approached, grimacing as he strode across the plaza. In the gray pre-dawn light, the smears of blood spattered across the cobblestones were visible, remnants of the butchery Colin had orchestrated. The area that had once been the green space was cleaner, but the ground was muddied. He shook his head, disgust creasing his angular features, before he pushed his discomfort aside and looked at us in turn.

"The sun will rise within the hour, but I'd like to begin the assault sooner," he said, his voice like steel. "If you're ready, I'll signal the others to prepare for the breach. The garrison won't be ready; it's tradition to strike at sunrise, not before. And I made certain they overheard me last evening when I said our attack would begin at dawn." He allowed himself a brief, satisfied smile. "I hope we finish this, and I hope the damned tyrant is toppled from his throne by day's end."

Zayneldarion glanced at me, then nodded to Jonas, but I could read nothing from his expression. "We're ready. We'll move on your signal."

"Consider this your signal," he replied before turning to stride toward the ranks of soldiers awaiting his next command.

Zayneldarion waited mere seconds before striking at the soldiers atop the wall. It required every scrap of willpower I possessed not to succumb to a bout of sneezing as the black pepper scent of his magic enveloped us. A shimmering column of energy shot from his location toward the wall. Over a dozen soldiers were hit; they tumbled backward through the air to fall from the stonework to the courtyard beyond our line of sight. The few who remained swiftly abandoned their posts, gaping at what they'd just witnessed. Above, Galewing released a piercing cry as he observed the scene from the air.

"Don't hold back," Zayneldarion said again. With those words, he motioned toward the gate, the signal we should make our first charge.

I sprinted across the plaza toward the gate with as much speed as I could muster, matching my father stride for stride. At the last moment, I turned my head so my right shoulder would take the brunt of the impact. I threw my considerable weight into the strike and was rewarded with a resounding crack as wood splintered beneath my scales. Shouts of alarm erupted beyond the wall, accompanied by shouted orders, screams, and curses. We backed up to prepare for a second charge while a handful of arrows fell harmlessly around us.

"Once more should be sufficient," Zayneldarion said as we prepared for our next assault. "Prepare yourself. When the gate is breached, we'll have a fight on our hands."

"I know."

He motioned for the next charge. As I hurled myself into the gate, it abruptly gave way. I staggered while I regained my balance, but the garrison milled about beyond the gate, eyes wide beneath their helms as they gaped in stunned silence.

I glanced across the ranks of Colin's soldiers. Less than one hundred stood inside the castle's courtyard, and most had weapons drawn in preparation for a fight. A heartbeat later, they recovered and a bellowed command prompted them to rush forward. I braced myself for the onslaught while my father did the same.

I backhanded the first trio and sent them flailing backward, then plowed forward through the gate.

My father was only steps behind. He swatted several others away as though they were mere insects; when comparing size differences, perhaps they were. Behind us, Jonas signaled to the first wave of our soldiers above the roar of the enemy, and Siorus' deep tones indicated the magi were entering the fray as well. I continued to strike at the king's garrison, rending armor with my claws, lashing forcefully with my tail, batting others away with the extension of my wings.

By the time the first of our soldiers entered the courtyard, the king's garrison had been reduced by nearly a third. A group of Corodan darted toward my location, and with their appearance, the Novanians began calling for a retreat into the castle itself. The Corodan pushed the Novanians back savagely, clearing an area around my location.

Krish-tek paused at my side as the other hive warriors charged forward. "The dragon-man's brother seeks your return. Go to the inn now."

I nodded. It was still a bitter disappointment to be called away from the battle when it had only just begun, but I'd promised my brothers I'd return. I glanced toward my father where he battled alongside a number of human and Merael soldiers, but his gaze was focused elsewhere and he didn't see.

"I'll return to Thomas. Luck be with you and the hive, Krish-tek."

She tilted her head before charging forward to regroup with her people.

The gate was choked by our soldiers as they streamed through to join in the fight. I could not exit in that direction without causing disarray and distraction within their ranks. I leapt skyward and beat my wings several times in order to clear the wall, then landed in the street beyond some distance from the inn.

Rank upon rank, our people marched through the plaza toward the courtyard, weapons drawn and expressions grim. I considered shifting where I'd landed, but rather than risk a lengthy dash down the street without protection, I opted to wait for a break in the ranks. A handful of the king's garrison remained on the wall, and I didn't relish the notion of dodging their arrows without my scales to deflect them.

Alexander must have witnessed my landing, or perhaps Galewing had and relayed my movements to him, for he bounded through the doors of the inn moments later. He stopped two paces out from the door, unwilling to disrupt the soldiers and magi as they filed past him, and stared in my direction for a time.

The sound of steel striking steel issued from beyond the wall, shouts and screams filled the air as soldiers fought and died, and the occasional roar that could have only come from my father swelled above the cacophony. When the magi began to attack, dozens of scents filled the air. Even from a distance, the combination irritated my nostrils and I began to sneeze. The guards on the wall above turned their attention to the events unfolding inside the courtyard and paid me no heed.

Finally, the last of our soldiers marched across the courtyard, and I raced to Alexander. He smirked, mischief in his green eyes.

"You made short work of that gate. Even Siorus was impressed."

I shrugged. "My father was right."

"Hmm. I suppose he'd know better than anyone the strength dragons truly possess, and that includes yours." Alexander arched an eyebrow. "Tom is expecting us inside. I hope you don't plan to stand there looming over the inn for the rest of the day, brother."

I forced a laugh and glanced once more toward the wall. We were well beyond the range of the archers, who were rapidly dwindling in number now that the magi had engaged them. I shifted forms and followed Alexander inside. True to his word, my armor was laid out and my sword was in its scabbard alongside. I began to dress and strap on my armor before Thomas crossed the empty common room.

"Alex says there were less than a hundred soldiers in the courtyard," Thomas said as he stopped near the table where my armor rested. "If father had been alive, the castle would never have held less than three hundred. Do you believe there were others inside, beyond Galewing's sight?"

I paused in my work to study Thomas for a moment. His blue eyes betrayed fear and concern, but outrage as well.

"I don't know, Tom. I was called away before the doors to the castle were opened, but I suspect those in the courtyard weren't all Colin has at his disposal. It's difficult to know for certain. I can't imagine many wanted to remain loyal after the atrocities we discovered in the plaza and elsewhere."

"Even so, Jonas is leading the charge into the castle himself, and our uncle and Elias are with him," Thomas replied. "I tried to dissuade them from it, but they don't trust the soldiers to obey orders if faced with the king alone. There are scores of our people who'd rather see him dead than imprisoned, consequences be damned." He sighed and looked down, the strain of the past months abruptly bubbling through to the surface.

"We're in this together," I said evenly. "Whatever happens, you won't be forced to face it alone."

He forced a smile. "And I thank you for that. Both of you."

TWENTY-SEVEN

Noon came and went without further word from the castle. Alexander kept us apprised of what Galewing could observe, but once our people had cleared the courtyard, the eagle was of little help. Rizzt-tok joined us in the common room as the afternoon progressed to share what she knew of the hive's activities when she wasn't preoccupied with issuing commands.

Colin had kept a sizeable force within the castle, where it had remained hidden until our people charged inside. Some of the king's garrison dropped their weapons in surrender when they realized the true scope of our army, but most continued to fight, loyalty or fear of their tyrant king driving them on. The casualties were steep, though Colin's forces fared worse, outnumbered as they were.

Thomas insisted that we eat, despite my protests and Alexander's repeated refusals. With each new report from Rizzt-tok, I became more numb; I pushed my hunger aside, a thing to be dealt with at a later time. The death toll was staggering, and I loathed that we'd been relegated to the inn, safely away from the bloodshed. I should have been there to fight alongside the people who had given up so much simply to bring us here.

A meal seemed an affront to their sacrifices, but Thomas persisted. Finally, I picked at a stale biscuit from the previous evening simply to appease him. Alexander scowled, but after a moment, he followed my lead.

At two hours past noon, Rizzt-tok informed us that a group of our soldiers were leaving the castle. She indicated there were severe injuries amongst them, and a pair of her fastest runners had been dispatched to the lower city to notify Lydia, Belora, and their numerous assistants.

"Your cousin-duke is with them," she said, "but he is better than most. He will live." She tilted her head, and for a moment, a dark shadow passed through the many lenses of her compound eyes. "The commander is near death. I understand the urgency of your uncle-duke's command to the healers."

I swore and shook my head. Without Jonas, who would continue leading the assault? He had been one of the greatest assets to Thomas' campaign since joining us at the keep, particularly after the loss of Jonathan Horace.

"If he's alive when they reach the healers, Lydia can mend him," Alexander stated confidently. "But who leads our people within?"

"Your uncle-duke leads now." She tilted her head in the other direction and studied us for a time. "The red king is alone, barricaded inside the chamber of the large chair."

Alexander's face twisted with confusion, and it took me a moment to puzzle out the meaning of her words. It was Thomas who spoke next; he'd understood immediately.

"The throne room."

"Yes," Rizzt-tok confirmed. "Your uncle-duke believes the time is right. You will face the red king."

I exchanged a glance with my brothers. As one, we moved toward the door. Thomas paused at the threshold to thank Rizzt-tok for relaying the message and for her continued support of our cause. She responded with a series of clicks, their meaning a mystery.

I positioned myself on Thomas' left, while Alexander stood on his right. We donned our helms, and I loosened my sword in its scabbard. Thomas was dressed in what remained of his finest garments; he'd never learned the art of combat and didn't possess armor. It would be up to me and Alexander to ensure his safety as we traversed the castle to the throne room and Colin.

"I feel so vulnerable," Thomas remarked as we passed through the plaza toward the sundered gates.

"We'll protect you," Alexander replied, "though I doubt Uncle Ev would have summoned us if there was any resistance left."

I nodded my assent. "But if there is resistance, stay behind us. I won't let you come to harm after everything we've overcome to get here."

Thomas' eyes widened as we entered the castle's courtyard. He studied the broken panels of the gate briefly before shifting his gaze to the yard itself. Several groups of wounded were stationed throughout the space, tended to by other soldiers. I spied my father near the more distant barracks, bent over a young Merael woman with bloodstains on her leather armor. My heart sank as I realized he tended Emmarie.

"Shit." I shook my head and gestured toward them. "Alex, it's Emma."

"Your father can heal," Alexander replied, but I detected a slight waver in his tone. "If she's with him, she'll be fine, won't she?"

I sighed, furious that I'd allowed her to become involved. I wished I'd persuaded her to remain behind, that I'd impressed upon her the magnitude of the danger she'd face by traveling north with Alexander. Her wounds were my fault, my failure to bear.

"I certainly hope so."

A number of Corodan and human soldiers guarded the main doors of the castle. We passed them in silence, but several nodded to Thomas or bowed deferentially. He acknowledged them with a nod, his features drawn.

The great hall lay just within the doors, its tables converted into makeshift pallets to tend the wounded. Soldiers from both sides were being treated by our people, and those wearing the traditional Marsden colors appeared grateful for the assistance, even though they were kept under guard. Some sported minor injuries, while others were more severe. I noted with despair that several groups were removing dead bodies from the room, taking them outside through a servants' entrance. The Roche twins, if they were well, would be busy with funeral pyres for days.

Thomas sighed, the sound the embodiment of sorrow. "So much needless death. Why did Colin persist in this madness?"

Alexander shrugged, and I shook my head. We didn't have answers.

To see the castle in this state of disarray, its walls and floors bloodied, its people wounded and dying, was something I'd never imagined possible. Novania had been relatively peaceful, the Capitol and the castle at its heart a place of safety. That illusion had been shattered, first by Colin's tyranny, then by our attacks. The current state of the kingdom was as much our doing as it was his, but *someone* had to put a stop to his wicked ways. There had been no choice but to draw him into battle after battle while the people of the land suffered for it.

We reached the far end of the great hall and began to ascend the broad staircase that led to the landing outside the throne room. More of our people lined the stairs, many with blood smeared across their armor, but most appeared unhurt themselves. Each knelt as we passed.

The stair was wide enough to accommodate six walking abreast, allowing us to maintain our formation. At the top of the stairs, we met Everett, a mage named Iva, and another two dozen human soldiers. They stood at attention and saluted Thomas as we neared.

Everett offered a strained smile. His leather armor was spattered with gore, and a gash marred his forehead, but he was otherwise unharmed. One hand gripped the haft of an axe, which he held loosely at his side.

"How is Jonas?" Thomas asked before Everett could speak.

He shook his head. "Not well. Krish-tek took it upon herself to deliver him to the healers. The hive's warriors can move far faster than we can. I didn't argue with her. I've seen the Corodan in action enough to know what they're capable of." He closed his eyes momentarily. "He took a sword wound to the chest. It came from the side, and I don't believe he saw his assailant until it was too late. He was engaged with another, his arms raised to parry, and the sword caught him just there," he said, pointing at a space below his left arm where even the best-fitted armor often left a gap.

I looked down, my heart heavy. Jonas and I had come to an understanding, and perhaps even a tentative friendship after years spent despising one another. I respected the former duke and hoped he'd survive.

The wound Everett described was often fatal. If the blade had pierced his heart, even Lydia's magic would be hard-pressed to mend the damage.

"And Elias?" Alexander asked.

Everett nodded, a guilty smile twisting his lips. "I'm not the swordsman I used to be. Elias was wounded when he blocked a blow that would have likely ended my life. His arm was laid open, but even without a mage's touch, he will heal in time." He shook his head. "The damned rascal was laughing at his own injury as they escorted him away as if it was nothing. He insisted that he would accompany Jonas."

Thomas drew a breath and steadied himself. "And Colin is within?" He gestured toward the closed doors of the throne room.

"Yes, but he has barred the door." Everett shrugged. "I'm not certain we can open them—"

"Allow me," I interrupted. "I may appear only human now, but I still possess the strength of a dragon."

"If anyone can break through the doors, it's you, brother," Alexander said with a weary grin. "And if the door proves too much, I can assist." He fingered the hilt of the cursed blade where it hung in its scabbard.

"I don't think that will be necessary." After the morning's work with the castle's gate, I was confident in my ability to break down this door, even if it was barred from within.

Alexander arched an eyebrow, but I ignored the unspoken jibe. As I strode toward the door, he whispered something to Thomas, but I was focused on my next objective and didn't hear what was said.

I glanced over my shoulder as I stopped in front of the door. "Be ready for anything."

As they moved toward me, I charged the door, throwing every ounce of my might into the blow. Wood cracked and snapped as my shoulder made contact, and the door reluctantly gave way. The bar clattered to the tiled floor on the other side as the brackets holding it in place were wrenched from the wall by the force of my blow. The door's hinges squealed in protest and wrenched free.

I stepped inside and unsheathed my sword, holding it in my left hand. Colin was perched on the throne, his face haggard, though his blue eyes remained defiant. He scowled and rose to his feet. I remained at the threshold until Thomas and Alexander joined me, meeting Colin's glare with one of my own.

"It seems I can't be rid of the three of you." Colin's voice dripped with contempt. "I suppose you think you've won this fight."

"Surrender, Colin," Thomas said, his voice like iron.

Colin arched one eyebrow in haughty disdain. "You think to command me, little Thomas? You should be kneeling. Pay homage to your king."

Alexander snorted and began to retort, but Thomas held up his hand. Alexander fell silent.

"You are no one's king, Colin." Thomas appeared unruffled by Colin's words. "Your army has been defeated, your castle stormed, and your own people have defected in order to fight against you at every turn. The people no longer believe you are fit to rule."

Colin threw back his head and laughed derisively. "What do the people know, Thomas? For that matter, what do the three of you know? I received word only yesterday that the rest of my army will be mustering beyond the gates of the Capitol this very evening. Robert Claybourne has unfinished business with at least one of you." He smirked in my direction.

I glanced at Alexander in question, receiving a look of confusion in return. Colin believed Claybourne was returning with his army, but Claybourne was weeks dead. Rynn had made certain of that.

"There is no army coming to save you," Thomas stated. "Your army is gone."

Colin sniffed, but a flicker of uncertainty flashed through his eyes. He reached inside a pocket and withdrew a slip of parchment. "I received this missive yesterday. Claybourne is on his way here, even as we speak."

I shook my head. "Robert Claybourne is dead, Colin. I watched him fall myself."

"I'll not be tricked by your filthy lies, brute," he growled.

"I think you've already been tricked, but not by us," Thomas mused.

He moved a few steps toward Colin while Alexander and I kept pace with him. I heard the soldiers from the hall filing into the room behind us, prepared to apprehend the disgraced monarch who continued to spew defiance, refusing to acknowledge his reign's end.

"If my soldiers were here, you would have been thrown in the dungeons by now. I'd have your heads," Colin seethed. "I am not without resources, even now."

He moved swiftly, but Alexander was faster. In one abrupt movement, Colin pulled a dagger from his belt and sent it hurtling at Thomas. The scent of blood filled the room, and in a blur, Alexander moved to deflect the weapon. He knocked it from the air with a gauntleted fist. It clattered to the tile, spinning toward the wall.

Colin blinked, unable to mask his surprise as he gaped at Alexander.

"I am no mere mage, Colin," Alexander said, his eyes narrowed into slits. "I am a mage-warrior. If I had a mind, you'd be dead before drawing your next breath." He pulled his swords from their scabbards, but held them at his sides.

Once he'd recovered, Colin sneered. "You defile these walls with your presence. Had I known what Andrew was capable of, you'd have been dead almost a year now, and Novania would be better for it."

I ground my teeth and moved several steps toward Colin before I realized it. As was his way, Colin had found a sore spot and begun prodding, trying to goad me into action. It had almost worked.

He stood two steps away, a cold smirk twisting his features. I forced myself to relax the grip on my sword. I would not allow Colin to anger me further.

"Novania would be a happier place without half-bred mongrels as well," he continued, never taking his eyes from mine. "The dragons were supposed to be gone, and yet here you are. A disgusting, unnatural creature that should never have been allowed to draw his first breath."

I forced myself to breathe evenly, to relinquish my rage. I would not ruin all we'd worked toward by striking him down. I must remain calm.

With an effort of will, I sheathed my sword. Colin was alone, and I would not have need of it.

"Your silence indicates that I'm not wrong," Colin said with a note of triumph in his voice.

"Before you became king, people bearing Marks—people like Alexander, our brother—were left largely alone," Thomas cut in before Colin could press my temper further. "There is no evidence any of them caused harm. None! And the dragon-kind were once our allies in ages past. Andrew served this kingdom for many years, loyally defending the people during the war with the Corodan. In fact, he brought us *peace*, something we didn't believe would ever come." Thomas shook his head, disappointment and outrage in his expression. "And what have you done, Colin? You have ruined this kingdom, murdered its people and its former king, our father."

Colin narrowed his eyes. "You have no proof, little Thomas. Father named me his heir, and I ascended the throne as tradition dictated." He crossed his arms, assuming an air of haughty indifference. "Had you and Alexander been here, rather than visiting the countryside like fools, perhaps Father would still be alive. Perhaps one of you may have protected him from his fate. Or perhaps not, seeing as he died in his sleep without a mark on him."

Alexander glanced at Thomas, who nodded. "We found the vial, Colin," Alexander said.

I frowned in confusion before I realized he was bluffing. If they'd found anything to tie Colin to their father's death, they would have informed me of it. They were attempting to draw out a confession while Everett and several dozen soldiers were present to bear witness.

Colin laughed. "A vial, you say? That's fascinating, coming from a mage. How can we be certain *you* did not manufacture this item to lay false blame at my feet?"

Alexander clenched his jaw, his eyes flashing in anger. "Magic doesn't work that way. An ignorant bastard like you would never understand."

Alexander had touched a nerve. Colin's face burned crimson and a dangerous light entered his eyes. "Do not compare me to *that*—" he flung one finger in my direction, "—for I will not tolerate it. You are both abominations! Why you weren't dealt with at birth, I'll never know. Mother must have been sympathetic, a traitor to this kingdom, to have let you both live!"

"Do not bring our mother into this!" Alexander bellowed, incensed.

The scent of blood enveloped the room. In that instant, I knew what Alexander planned, and I was the only one who could stop him.

He began to move, a blur of rapid motion, and I only had time enough to step across his path before he reached Colin. I wished I had not sheathed my sword, but there was no time to concern myself with it at present. Alexander's steel blade struck my abdomen with such force the wind was knocked from my lungs and I grunted in pain.

I gasped for air and doubled over, shocked at the strength he could muster when he chose to.

Alexander staggered backward, horror etched across his features as his cheeks drained of color. He dropped both swords, stripped of his remaining stamina, leaving them to clatter to the tiled floor. He fell to his knees, his eyes wide with shock.

I wanted to tell him the sword had failed to penetrate the dragon scale armor, that I'd recover in moments, but I struggled to regain my breath and was unable to speak.

"No, no, no," he whispered. "I can't have… No…" He hung his head and continued to moan and mutter, unaware that I was relatively unscathed.

After a moment, I managed to stand upright, gasping as air returned to my lungs. I'd have a nasty bruise for a few hours, but I'd live. Thomas strode toward me and placed a hand on my arm.

"I'm fine, Tom," I said between gasps.

He nodded before turning his furious gaze on Colin. "This is your last opportunity to surrender," he said as I walked to where Alexander knelt, anguished, on the floor. "If not for Andrew, you'd be dead right now, but a swift death is too good a fate for you." Thomas paused, and I imagined he gestured toward the soldiers gathered on the far end of the room. "Take him to the dungeons. Shackle him. He will remain there until the governor's council meets to determine his fate."

I knelt beside Alexander. "Alex," I said, "I'm fine."

He shook his head miserably, and it was clear he hadn't heard my words. "Not Andrew. I couldn't have just killed my brother. Not Andrew. No…"

"Alex," I said more forcefully, placing one hand on his shoulder. "Alex, look at me."

He rolled his eyes toward me, then blinked several times in confusion. He swiveled his head to look at Colin, surrounded by our soldiers as his hands were bound behind him by Everett, then turned to me once more.

"Andrew? I thought I'd—" Relief flooded his expression, then he burst into tears.

"You've left me with an ugly bruise, but otherwise, I'm fine." I dragged him into a rough embrace. It had been years since I'd seen Alexander reduced to weeping.

After several moments, he pushed away with a shaky laugh. "It was the dragon scale. Holy hell, I'd forgotten it was dragon scale. I need to thank your father when this is over and done."

"I'm sure you'll find plenty of time to speak with him, Alex."

I rose and offered him a hand. He took it and pulled himself upright, then bent to collect his swords.

"You're right. It will be weeks before some of the governors can attend a council," he replied, watching as Colin was led away in disgrace. "We'll have plenty of time to talk and plan the future."

TWENTY-EIGHT

"How are you feeling, Emma?" I asked.

We walked a circuitous route through the castle's inner courtyard, our shadows stretched long as the sun prepared to disappear for the evening behind the stonework surrounding us. The day had been warm, and much of the pleasant Spring weather still lingered even as night prepared to descend.

"Better than the last time you visited," Emmarie replied with a faint smile. "Your father's magic repaired the worst of my injury, you know. I haven't seen him since that day…" She paused to scan the courtyard, as though willing Zayneldarion to appear.

"He has been busy between helping the healers and attending councils with Tom," I said.

"What's it like now, knowing he's near? That he's free?" she asked abruptly.

I laughed uneasily. "Honestly? It's strange. I grew up believing he was gone, then when I visited the Stone Grove, I understood what had truly happened. He's my father, and I'm grateful he's been released from that hell, but we're still learning about one another. Sometimes, it's awkward."

She nodded. "Do you think it'll be the same for me?"

"Are you planning to track down your father?" I asked, genuinely surprised. Emmarie hadn't mentioned seeking him since our conversations in the Southlands, seemingly a lifetime ago.

"I am. With my uncle gone, I…" Her voice cracked, but she shook her head and clenched her jaw, refusing to shed more tears. "My father is the only family I have left, and my uncle can no longer forbid my visit to the Green. I've spoken to Shyala, and she's agreed to let me undertake the journey. She says I've proven myself capable."

"Andrew!" I spun to find Alexander jogging toward us. "There you are. I've been looking for you—for both of you." He paused to grin at Emmarie. "I heard you're planning to leave with the rest of your people in the morning. I'm not about to let you go without a proper goodbye."

"I was going to find you next," Emmarie replied. "But Andrew was first."

"Ah, the perks of being the eldest," Alexander teased.

"No," Emmarie countered with a smirk, "I just like him better."

I smiled as I watched them banter. It felt as if years had passed since I'd last seen Alexander so relaxed, or Emmarie truly smile. In truth, it had only been three weeks since Colin's arrest, but the Capitol had been in an uproar for most of it as the citizens came to terms with the shift in leadership.

Changes had abounded. New standards had been sewn bearing Thomas' black dragon on its crimson and ivory backdrop and hung above each gate in the city. Matching banners were created and erected above the guard towers and the entrance to the castle. People were hired to replace the cooks, maids, tailors, smiths, and the myriad others who had been killed or maimed during Colin's Scourge, as it came to be called, and the castle was thoroughly cleaned and wrangled into a state of residence fit for its new king.

A small carnival had appeared on the plaza outside the shattered gates of the castle after the first week. Thomas had ordered it disbanded. He'd wanted no celebrations until the dark business with Colin was concluded.

Funeral pyres lit the night sky for a week after Colin's capture. Nearly every resident and every soldier had a relative or friend who had been killed for one reason or another by the deposed monarch. The loss of nearly half the city's populace to Colin's Scourge had left a gaping void, one that would take years to overcome. Colin had refused to speak of his motives, and I began to doubt he had any at all, beyond sheer depravity.

Jonas Everly was among the dead, his wound so severe that he had not reached the healers before drawing his last breath. Emmarie's uncle, Tylmar, had likewise been killed, leaving her without any blood relatives other than her distant father. They were but two of many. The kingdom would be in mourning for months, if not years. There had been so much death during Colin's reign, so much senseless heartache…

But not every snippet of news I'd received was so dire.

Elias had recovered, though his arm would remain scarred for the remainder of his life. He still had use of it, though it often pained him. Lydia wasn't certain if his discomfort would ever completely fade.

As the Capitol had begun to rebuild, many of the people who had journeyed north with Alexander began a return trek to the Southlands. A handful of magi elected to remain until Alexander departed, hoping to bear witness when Thomas officially changed the laws regarding those born with the Mark.

Most of the Corodan also departed, though Rizzt-tok remained with ten warriors to act as her personal guard as she oversaw the conclusion of events for the hive.

And now, the Merael were preparing to leave as well. I blinked stinging tears from my eyes and refocused on the conversation.

"Shyala plans to leave before dawn," Emmarie said. "I'll travel with the rest of my people back to the Thornhallow, then I'll prepare for the longer journey to the Green. I only hope my father will recognize me. I was a child when he last visited the north."

"He will," I replied, certain that if my father had known me on sight in the Stone Grove, then Emmarie's father would likewise remember her.

"I hope so, Andrew." She turned to throw her arms around my waist and bury her face against my chest. "I'm going to miss you. Alex too, but you more than anyone else here. You'll write to me, won't you?"

"As often as I can," I promised, returning her embrace. "And if you ever need a dragon's aid on your future adventures, all you need do is ask."

She hugged me tighter, then broke away to grin triumphantly at Alexander. "And that's why I like Andrew best. You're no dragon."

Damn it, I was going to miss her.

Another month passed before the governors from each district had assembled in the Capitol after a summons was sent. Several were shocked until they learned Thomas had sent the messages, rather than Colin. Wasting little time, they convened a mere hour after the last member arrived. It wasn't long before Thomas sent for others to join them within the council chamber. Rynn and I were sent for, as was Alexander, Elias, Rizzt-tok, Claire, and Everett.

"I don't know why I was invited," Rynn said as we walked through the castle. "I hope I don't make a terrible impression on these governors. I hardly know the proper way to act around the nobility and—"

"Rynn," I said with a laugh, "none of that matters. The governors sent for those they believe will give a truthful account of Colin's alleged crimes."

She snorted. "Alleged? After everything we've seen—"

"I know, I know," I replied wearily. "It's the lay of the law in Novania. The governors will deliberate after we're questioned, then they'll determine if Colin is guilty of the crimes he is accused of. Based on how quickly we were summoned, I doubt they'll take long to make a decision."

As we approached the door to the council chamber, a woman I vaguely recognized rushed toward us carrying an armful of colorful silks. "Mistress Rynn?" she asked uncertainly. When Rynn nodded, she said, "Lady Claire asked me to assist you with a fitting. She said you required a proper gown for next week's ceremonies, but it seems you're busy at present."

Rynn turned to me, her eyes wide and her expression bewildered. I laughed; I'd played no part in Claire's apparent scheme.

"We've been summoned to the governor's council," I said after a moment. "When we're finished, I'm certain Rynn and I can accommodate you."

The woman smiled and bowed. "Of course. Lady Claire said I'd likely require your assistance with the task, though I can hardly understand why, my lord."

"You may await us in our room if you'd like," I replied. "I don't believe this will take long."

She bowed again before scurrying away.

"What is this about a gown?" Rynn demanded, one hand on her hip.

"This is the first I've heard of it," I replied, "but Claire is right. You'll need something for Tom's coronation ceremony, and I must admit, I'm rather intrigued by the prospect of seeing you in a formal dress."

She rolled her eyes, exasperated. "I've not worn a skirt in *years*, Andrew. I'll hardly know how to walk in one." She sighed as we arrived outside the door and the pair of stoic guardsmen stationed there pushed it open silently.

The eight men and women who made up the governor's council sat behind a horseshoe-shaped table at the far end of the room, with Thomas seated at the base of the U. Thomas looked well, despite the bustle and constant demands for his attention that had plagued him since Colin's capture. The dark circles that had ringed his eyes during our months of exile and the subsequent battle were gone, and the hint of a smile was present on his lips.

Most of the others who had been summoned had already arrived, though Elias was conspicuously absent. Thomas had named him as one of his advisors a week ago; I assumed he was busy with another task and would arrive presently. We took our place near one end of the horseshoe, allowing the others to stand across the opening until they were called forward. Moments later, Elias arrived, striding forward to join us as we awaited the council's words.

Thomas rose from his seat. "I have gathered the governors to hear for themselves the crimes for which the king, Colin Marsden, has been accused. As the next in line for succession, the council has tasked me with the oversight of this hearing."

The words had been rehearsed, but Thomas made them sound natural. I smiled, recalling a time not so long ago when he'd been nervously fidgeting outside this same chamber while we awaited entry, unable to maintain even a pretense of calm. Now, Thomas was in control of his emotions, cool, collected, seemingly prepared for any event that might transpire.

On Thomas' left, Lon Calder stood and introduced himself. He'd seldom made the long journey from his home in the far north to attend council meetings, but he'd always come when the reason was of great import. It had been more than two years since I'd last spoken to him, and though he was no more than five years older than me, he now looked aged. His hair was completely white, and he appeared shrunken, a shadow of his former self. If he hadn't made the introduction, I would have failed to recognize him.

"Lord Marsden has asked me to question each of you on behalf of the council," he said in a tone laced with sorrow. I wondered what he must have endured for such change to have been wrought in his features.

Lon plucked a sheaf of papers from the tabletop. "We'll begin with Everett Crossley."

As the questions were asked, it became clear the council already knew much of what Colin had done during his reign and they merely sought confirmation. Everett spoke of his exile from Bridgewaters, stripped of his ancestral title and lands for the crime of offering shelter to Thomas when Colin had driven him from the Capitol. He spoke of their time in the Gloaming Highlands and of his role as advisor to Thomas as we marched across Novania toward the Capitol.

Elias was called next. He detailed the Mark inspections that had taken place on numerous occasions in Dresdin's Forge. He spoke at length of what he'd discovered in the labor camps after Thomas and Jonas had tasked him with disbanding them and freeing the prisoners within. His description of the conditions he'd uncovered left the council gaping, appalled their king had sentenced so many of his subjects to hard labor and squalid quarters for crimes that could never be verified, and likely had never occurred.

Rizzt-tok was questioned after Elias. She described how the Corodan had become involved in the war and explained my agreement with the Hive-queen. She explained that the Corodan desired peace, but knew the red king would not abide by the terms of the truce the dragon-man had achieved. The council appeared amused by her term for me, but uneasy regarding her name for Colin.

When Claire was called forward, I was startled to see just how much the child within her had grown in the intervening weeks. I'd scarcely seen her around the castle, and when I had, she'd been seated. There was no doubt she'd deliver the child within days; I simply could not imagine her body swelling any more than it had already. She stood before the council with an air of calm, her hands resting atop her belly.

She began with what she deemed her greatest mistake—her decision to nullify her marriage to me in order to secure her place as Novania's future queen. She spoke of the abuse Colin had inflicted time and again and of her long confinement in the tower. She told the council of her handmaiden, Leta, and the plot Colin had hatched with her to assassinate Thomas. When the council asked her about the status of Princess Verena, Claire was unable to maintain her composure and began to weep. In broken tones, she recalled what occurred on the fateful night when Colin tossed the child from the tower's window in a drunken rage.

Most of those gathered were shocked by her words. Everett and I had revealed her tale to no one after she'd shared it with us. She had been through enough pain and humiliation at Colin's hands, and I believed there was no reason to add to her hardship. Claire had suffered enough.

"And the child you now carry?" Tyrus Walsh asked.

Claire stared at him evenly. "This child will be mine alone," she replied. "Colin may have fathered it, but I'll not list his name on the birth record. Not after what he did to Verena." She drew a breath and steadied herself. "It would also be in the child's best interest if it never learns who its father is. Colin's name carries much stigma, and I will not force that upon an innocent."

Lon Calder nodded. "Thank you, Lady Claire. I believe that will be all."

They called Alexander forward next. Though much of his story was common knowledge, they pressed him for details regarding the events leading up to his imprisonment and scheduled execution. Alexander appeared decidedly uncomfortable, but he spoke with a clear, unwavering voice.

"Thomas and I believed that Colin was responsible for our father's death," he began. "We had been attempting to gather evidence to support that, but Colin learned of our activities. He became overbearing, and I'm certain he was having us followed. Around that time, he began the Mark inspections. I had good reason to oppose his policies and I protested his decision at every turn." He smiled ruefully. "He didn't like that."

He paused for a moment to gather his thoughts. "I'm not certain what made him snap that day. The topic of the Mark inspections came up, as it always seemed to do, and I pleaded with him to stop them. *Again.* The people were innocent. They'd done nothing wrong! Thomas voiced his opinion to Colin that morning as well, and it mirrored my own. Perhaps seeing us united, Colin lost his temper. Regardless, he called for the nearby guards. He ordered us to be inspected immediately. I... I knew what they'd find and I tried to resist. With three guards on me, I was eventually forced to comply."

"May we have a look at the Mark in question?" Lon asked as the others around the table murmured their assent.

Alexander seemed to shrink in on himself and his face grew pale, while his eyes darted between the faces scrutinizing his every movement. After several tense seconds, Thomas said, "Alex, if you don't want to do this, I won't force you. The question was merely asked out of curiosity. I promise no harm will come to you."

Alexander swallowed and turned his head to look at me. Fear shone in his eyes.

"I'm here for you, brother," I said quietly. The decision would be his, and I'd support him no matter what he chose to do.

Finally, he nodded and began to unbutton his shirt with visibly shaking hands. The Mark, once revealed, arced across his torso from above his heart to its second point near his left hip. The flesh inside the Mark was mottled gray and white and the outer edges were raised, reminiscent of scar tissue.

The council murmured their surprise. Few Novanians had ever looked upon a true Mage's Mark. As Alexander began to button his shirt again, Lon said, "Thank you, Alexander."

"It's the Mark of a mage-warrior," he said after he'd finished with his buttons. "I didn't know what its colors meant at the time of my imprisonment—I learned that much later. I will never forget the look on Colin's face when my Mark was revealed. Satisfaction, and something akin to sadistic glee, I suppose. It made my skin crawl. I was taken to the dungeons to await execution. Execution for the simple fact that I exist." He shook his head and looked down at the tiled floor, sorrow in his eyes. "Colin visited me daily, sometimes more than once. He was always accompanied by a cruel man whom I didn't know at the time. That man was skilled at various forms of water-torture, and…" He trailed off, tears in his eyes.

"Take your time," Thomas said gently.

Alexander swallowed hard and when he looked up once more, his expression was wounded. "Water-torture rarely leaves visible marks on the victim, but it is no less painful, no less horrific than other varieties. Colin demanded that I tell him what my supposed powers were, and he pressed me for details regarding Andrew. Andrew isn't Marked, but Colin believed he was. He wanted a reason to attack our eldest brother, and promised that if I told him what he wanted to hear, he'd stop the torture." He shook his head, and glanced briefly in my direction. "Andrew is not Marked, and I refused to give Colin the affirmation he sought. I endured the torture hoping Colin would leave Andrew and Vera alone. They had done nothing wrong."

"Alex…" I said, shocked and appalled by his tale. He'd never spoken in detail of his imprisonment with me and now I understood why. He'd tried to protect *me* from Colin at the cost of his own life.

He forced a laugh, but the sound was strained. "You were the last of the dragon-kind, Andrew. I couldn't let Colin kill you."

I nodded and my throat tightened with emotion. Rynn took my hand in hers, offering her unspoken support.

"When Thomas arrived to tell me Colin had scheduled my execution, I asked him to send a message to Vinterry. I didn't believe Andrew would rescue me—it was a fool's notion if ever there was one—but I needed him to know what Colin had done." Alexander paused for a moment, then nodded to himself. "After Tom left on his errand, Colin believed I had something to do with his disappearance. I suppose I had, but it wasn't what Colin believed. The torture became more frequent and more…difficult. I was beaten numerous times. It wasn't until months later that I learned the man who accompanied Colin to the dungeons was Robert Claybourne."

I stared at Alexander, stunned and unable to hide my reaction. I understood why he'd been compelled to charge forward that day near Willever. It hadn't been revenge for Claybourne's treatment of me that had driven Alexander as I'd suspected—it had been an act of vengeance for himself after enduring days of torture at the man's hands. So many of Alexander's actions were now clear, when previously I'd only speculated on his motives.

Alexander continued for some time, speaking briefly of our time in the Southlands, then at length when he came to the battle near the Mage's Gate. He told the council of the journey to Willever and how he'd discovered my whereabouts through the Corodan scout and Galewing's keen eyes.

"When I learned Claybourne was responsible for Andrew's capture, and when I saw for myself the extent of his injuries, I wanted to kill Claybourne then and there," Alexander said fiercely. "I should have, but I let him go. I wanted to believe I was better than Colin, that I could show mercy to a man who had tortured me and had very nearly killed my brother. Had I ended it then, Andrew wouldn't have that scar, and perhaps we would have avoided at least one major battle and the deaths that resulted from it."

When Alexander was finished, I was called forward. Lon Calder asked that I start my tale at the beginning, so I did. I spoke for what seemed an hour, covering everything from the day I'd met with the king regarding his succession, to my decision to rescue Alexander and the consequences that stemmed from it. I spoke of the assassins that trailed us through the Southlands, of my search for Thomas in the north, the agreement I'd made with the Hive-queen to secure the Corodans' aid, and of the battle at the keep, where I'd been captured by Robert Claybourne. I told them of the torture I'd endured, of my rescue by Alexander and the magi, of the battles we fought at Willever, and the storming of the Capitol. The room fell silent after I finished speaking and returned to stand beside Rynn.

"I would very much like to have your stories recorded by the scribes," Thomas said after a moment. "Yours, Andrew, and also Alexander's. The history of how we came to this junction in time should be preserved."

"We plan to leave after the ceremony, Tom," Alexander replied. "But if you'll allow us some free time between now and then, I believe we can meet with the scribes."

Thomas smiled. "I'll make certain you're given the time. Novania needs your stories. This kingdom will be better for it."

Each council member nodded in agreement, and Lon said, "Then it's settled. We thank you for speaking with us and answering our questions today. We will now convene to determine what must be done with the deposed king."

Dismissed, we were free to leave the council chamber. Alexander made his way toward Rynn and I once we were in the hall. "I know what the council will decide. A part of me is glad to have this over with, but I wish it had been *anyone* but our damned brother who was on trial. This has been…damned difficult, to say the least."

"I won't argue with you on that point," I replied. We began walking toward our room while Alexander continued to follow.

"I'm looking forward to leaving this behind," he said. "It was home once, but now I feel as though I'm a stranger here. Even with Tom's decree that magi aren't a threat, I still receive strange looks, and some people avoid me altogether." He sighed. "Novania is no place to raise a child who will likely bear the Mark just as his parents do."

"Things will get better, given time," I assured him.

"Lydia has two months yet, doesn't she?" Rynn asked.

Alexander nodded. "Yes, and we plan to have a home purchased and be settled in before then. She insists we live in the Citadel. I suppose it could be worse, but I plan to avoid the tower as much as I'm able."

"We'll accompany you as far as the Citadel," I replied. Rynn, my father, and I had discussed our travel plans the night before. "From there, we'll go to Dwymm. And—"

I stopped myself before I went any further. I planned to ask Rynn for her hand in marriage before we departed the Capitol, perhaps during the celebration following Thomas' coronation. When we arrived in Dwymm, I would marry her, and hoped her family would attend. I had told no one but my father of my plans, and he had agreed to go as far as Dwymm with us. He wanted to be present as well.

"And?" Rynn asked, a knowing gleam in her eyes.

"And we'll see where our path takes us from there," I replied evasively.

We'd reached the door to our room, and Alexander smirked. "I believe I may know what you have in mind, brother. I'll speak to Lydia." Before I could respond, he whirled away and was gone.

"You have something planned," she said as she pulled the door open.

"And you have a date with the tailor," I replied as I followed her into the room.

The woman we'd spoken with earlier was inside, an array of colored silks and satins lined up on a table she'd pushed to the center of the room. She smiled in greeting.

Rynn groaned. "I can't believe—"

A tap sounded on the door, and I turned to open it. Claire was in the hall and offered me a smile. "I've come to assist Rynn with her fitting. I'll make certain her gown is perfect." She brushed past me and swept into the room, the very essence of a woman who was in her element and would not be dissuaded from her chosen path.

She selected a sapphire blue silk, and lifted it toward Rynn. "Yes, this will do nicely. It brings out your eyes. Now, then…"

TWENTY-NINE

I followed a sprightly older man into the castle's library the next morning; he was a scribe and had been tasked to record my tale. I recalled the last time I'd been inside the library, seemingly a lifetime ago. Claire had demanded my presence on that long-ago day, and had ordered me to sign the annulment to our marriage. It had been one of the first of many humiliations I'd faced at her hands, but I was glad we'd reconciled since that time. We'd both matured significantly during the intervening years.

We walked to a secluded table nestled in a corner between a window and several bookshelves. A pair of cushioned chairs sat on either side, and a collection of writing implements were arrayed across the table, along with a thick stack of blank parchment.

The scribe gestured to the nearest chair with a grandfatherly smile. "I assume this will take many hours. Please sit, and we'll begin when you're ready."

I took the offered chair, and as he seated himself across the table and placed the first sheet of blank parchment from the pile, I began to speak. We remained in the library for most of the day; I told my tale while he diligently recorded my words, pausing only to ask for more details on occasion.

Thomas had chosen the scribe well. The man worked tirelessly and didn't once complain of cramps in his hand or ink stains on his bony fingers.

It was well into the afternoon when a messenger arrived. The scribe paused in his work as I turned to peer over my shoulder at the teenaged boy hovering nervously several steps away.

"I've a message, Lord Dragon," he said as he withdrew a slightly crumpled missive from his pocket.

I nodded and accepted the letter as he disappeared behind the bookshelves once more. My throat was parched and my voice was gravelly as I croaked a belated thank you. I hoped the note was from Thomas—I could use a break from speaking. I unfolded the letter to find it wasn't in my brother's hand, though I was certain it had come at his command.

Your presence is requested in the council chambers without delay.

I glanced at the scribe. "It seems I'm needed elsewhere. I'll return in the morning."

He offered me a smile. "Very good. I'll be awaiting you."

I departed the library and crossed the distance to the council chamber swiftly, though the journey still took several minutes. Alexander paced outside the closed chamber door, while Everett and Claire stood near a wall.

Alexander stopped midstride as I approached, met my eyes, then scratched the nape of his neck. "The council has reached a decision. Tom just went inside, but they'll send for us soon."

We didn't wait long.

When the door opened, a soldier garbed in Thomas' colors and insignia appeared to usher us inside. We were made to stand at one end of the horseshoe-shaped table, while Claire and Everett stood on the other. Lon Calder rose slowly from his seat to address us.

"We have reached a decision regarding the events of the past two and one-half years, and will make our final statement once the king is brought forth. As is customary, he will be offered the opportunity to explain the reasons guiding his actions." Lon's face twisted into a momentary frown of displeasure before he continued. "A summons was sent to the dungeons. Colin James Marsden will appear before us—and before you—to answer for his perceived crimes."

Alexander groaned. "I'd hoped to avoid seeing him again," he whispered.

"As did I," I replied. "At least it's nearly finished."

The doors swung open as he nodded in agreement. A pair of guards strode inside flanking Colin. His hands were bound behind him and he appeared weary, but was otherwise unharmed. Dark stubble covered his cheeks and his hair was slightly mussed. He wore the same clothing he'd been apprehended in; the black and crimson fabric was rumpled and soiled, but he managed to maintain an air of nobility nevertheless. His blue eyes were focused on the table ahead. He pointedly ignored us as he was led forward to stand before Thomas and the governor's council.

Lon Calder cleared his throat, then began to address the room. "Colin James Marsden, heir of Carlton James Marsden, you have been brought forth to hear the charges laid against you by the people of Novania. What say you?"

Colin lifted his chin in an expression of defiance. "I maintain my innocence in all matters. The crimes I'm accused of have been largely fabricated."

It was clear that Colin had prepared himself for this moment while he'd been locked in the dungeon. I was unsurprised by his claim of innocence; it was unlike Colin to admit his own wrong-doings, no matter how heinous the act.

Lon frowned. "The council has convened to investigate your alleged crimes. We have no reason to believe the reports were 'fabricated,' to use your own words." He gestured toward one end of the table where the governor of the Eastern Plains perched quietly in her chair.

She rose. "I find him guilty."

The next in line stood. "Guilty."

And so it continued with each governor along the table. Not one entered a verdict of innocence on Colin's behalf, nor did any abstain. By the time the last governor had spoken, Colin had closed his eyes and hung his head; he knew his fight was at an end.

Lon paused to allow Colin time to absorb the verdict. "The vote is unanimous. Colin James Marsden, you have been deemed guilty of the crimes of murder, false imprisonment, torture, and a staggering list of atrocities against the people of Novania that for the purposes of this council we will refer to as 'tyrannical abuse of power.' The penalty for your crimes is death."

Though I'd known it was coming, it was still a shock to hear the words spoken aloud. Colin, my half-brother, would be executed. At one time I believed I would rejoice at hearing the news, but the sentence left me cold and deeply saddened. Despite all he'd done, he was still my younger brother. Still family.

Thomas stood, his face a mask of poorly-concealed grief. "I ask that the sentence be carried out at dawn in the private courtyard beneath the king's chambers. The people of Novania have borne witness to enough death. They don't need to see yet another." He chewed his lower lip and looked down, grappling with his emotions. "It's the best I can do for you, Colin. I'm truly sorry it has come to this."

Colin merely nodded, but didn't look up to meet Thomas' gaze. Finally, he said, "You were right. Claybourne didn't return and I am without allies."

"Robert Claybourne was killed during the last battle at Willever," Lon replied.

"I know that now," he snapped, then turned to shoot a heated glare at Claire. "I wasn't wrong when I said I'd been tricked, and you spoke the truth when you claimed it was not of your doing, Tom."

I studied Claire carefully for a moment as I understood what must have occurred. Claire was a master of intrigue and knew the workings of the castle and its people intimately. She must have written to Colin after Claybourne's death, pretending to be the late commander. She'd provided false information to Colin, and he'd believed the army was on its way to the Capitol to defend against our assault. Only after Claybourne failed to arrive as planned did Colin begin to suspect he'd been duped.

Claire's expression was carefully composed and she made no reply to Colin's implied accusation. Her dark eyes were unreadable as she continued to observe the proceedings.

"I have one further question," Thomas said after a moment. "I must know why you massacred so damned many people at the plaza. What foul notion took hold of you that you believed such an atrocity was necessary?"

Colin's gaze was baleful, remorseless. "Many were Marked. Those who weren't planned to rally against me. I was their king. I would not stand for it." He sneered at each council member in turn. "I suppose the bodies of those traitorous fools served a purpose. They slowed you lot down for a time. A pity they could do no more."

Thomas closed his eyes briefly, disappointment and rage flitting across his features. "I always believed you better than this." With a sigh, he gestured to Lon Calder, signaling for an end to the proceedings.

Lon nodded. "Let it be known that Colin James Marsden, forty-seventh king of the Marsden line, has been stripped of his lands and title, his life forfeit due to the severity of the crimes he has committed." He motioned to the guardsmen flanking Colin. "Please lead the condemned back to his cell. The execution will be carried out at dawn according to the prescribed terms."

At Thomas' behest, I attended the execution along with Alexander and the governor's council. I didn't want to be present, but I understood the necessity. Thomas couldn't face our brother's execution alone, and it was prescribed by law that witnesses must be present.

The governor's council arrived in the courtyard as dawn broke across the eastern sky and formed an arcing line facing a huge stone block. We gathered above on the king's private balcony—Thomas' balcony now.

Colin was led into the courtyard by several guards, to the stone block where the execution would take place. A hulking man dressed in a black hood strode toward the block as Colin was made to kneel. He hefted a two-handed axe with a curved blade in his hands and paused to brace himself.

I turned my back on the scene, unwilling to watch my half-brother's death despite the suffering he'd put us and the kingdom through. I heard the axe strike as it was brought down, heard Lon Calder's pronouncement moments later that Colin was dead, heard the call for the guards to take the body away. Only then did I turn around once more.

Silent tears spilled from my eyes. Alexander and Thomas had reacted in a similar fashion. Despite everything he'd done, Colin was still our brother, our kin. His death, however deserving, still elicited grief. I wiped at my eyes and stared at the courtyard below.

The council had begun to depart while Colin's lifeless body was carried away by the executioner and a pair of castle guards. A spray of dark blood marred the stone.

"Well," Alexander said hollowly after a time, "I suppose it's good this business is done. I hope we never have to attend an event like this again."

Thomas nodded solemnly. "The criers will inform the city of his death. I wish we could have reasoned with him. Perhaps none of this would have happened."

I shrugged. "Perhaps, perhaps not. Colin is—was—never one to negotiate."

Alexander nodded. "If nothing else, some good has come of this dark business. You can change things, Tom. Repeal the laws regarding the Marks and the dragon-kind. You have an opportunity to make Novania a better place for everyone."

"And I will." Thomas forced a strained smile. "I've written the documents for both items. It's a matter of waiting now—the coronation is in five days, and I plan to sign them immediately after the ceremony. I expect you'll both to be present?"

"We'll be there," I promised while Alexander broke into a tremulous grin.

I spent the next four days with the scribe in the castle library, dictating the remainder of my lengthy tale. I doubted anyone other than Thomas would bother to read it once it had been bound in leather and cataloged, but at least the tale was recorded for future generations of Novanians to discover.

"Your tale will become legend," the scribe said during the final day of our work.

I didn't argue, but I was skeptical. Legends were the stories of heroes, and I didn't feel particularly heroic, not after witnessing so much death and suffering.

We were thrilled when the task was complete. I'd never spoken so much or so long in my life, and I was certain it would be days before my voice regained its normal timbre. When I returned to our room after the final pages had been penned, Rynn teased me relentlessly. She claimed I sounded little better than a bullfrog.

The following morning, the castle was in a frenzy as the staff prepared for the coronation ceremony. Servants began their tasks before daybreak as they transformed the great hall for the festivities. The kitchen staff had begun baking bread and pastries shortly after midnight and worked tirelessly through the day to prepare the grandest feast I suspected I'd ever attend. Flowers were procured to decorate the walls and tables, more of the dragon standards appeared, replacing the former Marsden boar, and every inch of every surface was cleaned and polished to a shine.

Claire sent a maidservant to assist Rynn with her new gown when we returned from breakfast, but the woman could do little more than supervise given Rynn's unusual condition. When I attempted to help, I was chased from the room, but the woman ordered me to return within the hour. She was also responsible for my wardrobe, and we only had a short time in which to prepare.

I sought Alexander and located him roaming the hall outside his own quarters with an amused smile on his face.

"Did Lydia send you away as well?" I asked as I approached.

He laughed. "Of course she did. Claire sent a maid to assist her, and as soon as the woman arrived, I was told to occupy myself elsewhere. Lydia has become rather self-conscious of her looks lately, though she has nothing to worry over. She's beautiful, just as she's always been." He shook his head, seemingly mystified. "In another two months, our child will arrive and then perhaps she'll stop berating herself. Holy hell, two months! I'm thrilled but terrified, particularly when I recall what the Oracle said."

"You'll make a fine father, Alex," I replied. "And who better to raise a mage-warrior than another mage-warrior?"

He rolled his eyes. "It doesn't make the prospect any less terrifying."

"Every father feels the same way," Zayneldarion said from behind us. I startled; I hadn't heard him approach.

Alexander laughed nervously as we turned to face him. "I've no doubt you're right. I keep telling myself I shouldn't be afraid. And yet I am."

"How long have you been standing there?" I asked.

He'd altered his human appearance slightly; the clothing was more formal than what I'd become accustomed to seeing on his person.

"Not long." He smiled. "I went to your room, but the maid said they'd sent you away. It seems Rynn hopes to keep her new gown a surprise for as long as she can."

I rolled my eyes. "I'll need to return at some point before the ceremony starts. I need to change into something more formal myself."

He nodded, then turned his attention on Alexander. "Have you spoken to Lydia regarding your plans for travel?"

His eyes flicked toward me for a brief moment before returning to Zayneldarion. "Yes, and she has agreed to travel to Dwymm first."

"Good. I've sent word to Caelmarion and Miranetha as well. They should be there well before we arrive." He fixed me with a smile. "Now to the real question: Have you asked her yet?"

I flushed and shook my head. "I mean to do it tonight, after the ceremony, as I've told you both more than once."

Zayneldarion flashed a grin. "Excellent. I've always enjoyed weddings, but this will be the first that has any true meaning for me. The ceremonies and vows are a thoughtful touch. It always makes me wish my people had a similar custom."

Alexander's eyebrows rose. "You mean dragons don't marry?"

Zayneldarion chuckled. "No, and it's unusual for a skin-changer to marry as well. Some dragons take life mates, but those pairings would seem unusual to you, Alexander. There were always far fewer female dragons than males, and it is the females who choose their mates when their cycle is at the right stage. For some, each child had a different father. Others, like Mira, would cycle between a few select males. Many males were never selected, and I was among that number. The life mates I speak of were always two male partners, and many were childless." He shrugged. "Fortunately, I possess the ability to go about in this disguise, which allowed me to become a father by other means."

Alexander appeared bewildered. "The more I learn of the dragon-kind, the stranger they seem." He shifted his gaze in my direction. "Particularly a certain skin-changer." He grinned even as I playfully swatted him away.

The door to Alexander's room opened, and the maid peered out at us. "Lord Marsden, your wife awaits you." She fixed me with a scowl. "No doubt your lady is awaiting you as well, and has been for some time, if I know Cerise's handiwork."

Taking that as my cue to depart, I waved at Alexander with the promise I'd see him after the ceremony. Zayneldarion followed me as I returned to my room.

"Did you know Thomas asked to speak with me this morning?" he asked after a time.

I shook my head. "Tom never mentioned it, but that's hardly surprising. He's been busier than ever."

"It seems you told him something about my former role as emissary to the Oracle." He paused to offer me a smile. "He has asked me to perform a similar function between Novania and the dragon clans, such as they are. I have accepted."

I smiled. "That's great news. For us and for Tom."

He nodded. "Progress has taken a long and circuitous path, but it has been well worth the wait and the many trials that came with it. Thomas will make a fine king."

"He will," I agreed.

We reached my door, which remained closed. When I hesitated uncertainly, Zayneldarion laughed and rapped his knuckles against its surface.

"I'll leave you to your preparations, Andrew. We'll speak again tonight."

When the door opened, Cerise fixed me with a glare that could have boiled water. "Where have you been, Lord Dragon?" she demanded. "The ceremony will begin in less than an hour, and I must ensure you're dressed as well as she is." She shook her head in consternation as she turned inside. "Men! Sometimes I'm not certain you lot are worth the trouble, and from what I've been told, you're more trouble than most."

Rynn's laughter echoed from within and I followed Cerise inside. She stood near the window, her back toward me. The gown she wore had a full skirt and long sleeves, sewn of the same sapphire blue silk Claire had selected the previous week. When she heard the door close, Rynn turned, smiling uncertainly.

Claire had been right; the blue fabric made Rynn's eyes even more captivating, more alluring, and I could scarcely pull my own away. Her hair was pulled back, though a few blond curls framed her face. Sapphires were strung through her hair and a matching pendant hung from her neck.

I was standing in front of her before I realized I'd moved across the room. I took her hands in my own. "Rynn, you're more beautiful than ever."

She blushed prettily. "It was mostly Claire's doing. And Cerise's, of course."

"Of course she's beautiful," Cerise replied, exasperated. "Lady Claire didn't employ me for nothing, Lord Dragon."

"No, I suppose not." Reluctantly, I turned around.

Cerise placed her hands on her hips and fixed me with an imperious gaze. "As for you, we'd best get started. You mustn't be late."

THIRTY

We were ushered into the throne room an hour later. I noted with wry amusement that the doors had been replaced since my last visit and the damage I'd caused to the frame was no longer visible. Chairs were set up in rows facing the throne that Colin had so recently occupied, their backs adorned with late spring blooms. A crimson strip of carpet ran from the entrance to the throne, contrasting sharply with the ivory tile. One of Thomas' dragon standards had been placed behind the throne, where it hung above the proceedings. We were led to our designated seats in the front row, with Alexander and Lydia on one side, and Elias and his wife on the other. Most of the seats were filled; we were among the last to arrive.

Rynn sat down carefully and moved her chair slightly toward mine to create more space between herself and Elias. He understood her reason and didn't remark on it.

Alexander leaned across Lydia to whisper loudly, "I was beginning to fear you'd miss this, brother." He studied me for a moment. "The eyepatch is a nice touch."

"I wouldn't miss this for the world," I replied, ignoring the last half of his statement. Cerise had insisted I wear the patch due to the formality of the occasion, but I felt it drew unnecessary attention to my scar.

He flashed a grin while Lydia complimented Rynn on her gown. A blush rose in Rynn's cheeks and she mumbled a thank you before returning the favor. Lydia's gown was pale gold and was cut to make her pregnancy appear less pronounced than it truly was. Her lengthy tresses were swept into an elaborate bun and pale gems were strung through her hair; topaz, I assumed.

"Alexander, will you sit still?" Lydia hissed, though her tone was more amused than annoyed. "You're going to drive me mad, husband."

Alexander mumbled an apology even as he twisted in his seat to peer toward the door, which elicited an exasperated sigh from Lydia.

"I certainly hope your brother learns to calm himself before this child comes into the world," she grumbled. "It's going to be trial enough to raise one child. I don't know if I can manage two of them."

I chuckled. "He's excited, Lydia."

She said something in reply, but her words were lost to the blare of trumpets in the hall outside. We stood as two pairs of soldiers marched inside the room, dressed in brilliantly silvered ceremonial armor and livery matching the dragon standard. They carried spears tipped in gold and stood at attention flanking the empty throne. Another brassy fanfare was played, and Tyrus Walsh strode inside seconds later, bearing the golden circlet the king traditionally wore during special occasions, nestled on a pillow of ivory satin. Behind him, Lon Calder entered holding several sheets of parchment, a stoppered ink pot, and a fine goose-feather quill. The two men moved to the front of the room and knelt before the throne.

A final series of notes issued from the trumpeters outside. As the sound faded into nothingness, Thomas entered the room, regal in black, with a crimson and ivory cloak bearing the dragon sigil thrown across his shoulders. He appeared composed and certain of himself, but I noted his hands were clenched at his sides in an effort to contain his nerves. He nodded to us as he made his way to the front of the room, where he knelt before the throne between the governors.

Lon Calder rose and began to read from the parchment. "On this, the twenty-fourth day of the month of May, we gather to crown Novania's next king. Honored guests, please be seated. Thomas Winston Marsden, please rise."

As Thomas regained his feet, Alexander leaned across Lydia with a mischievous gleam in his eye. "It's your name day, brother," he whispered so quietly that I had to strain to hear his words. With a frown, Lydia pushed him back into his seat.

I smiled faintly as I listened to the governors recite the traditional words of the coronation ceremony, and wondered if Thomas had planned to hold this ceremony on my name day intentionally. Based on Alexander's reaction, I suspected he had, perhaps with Alexander's encouragement.

Tyrus Walsh stood as Lon Calder said, "By the authority of the governor's council, Thomas Winston Marsden is crowned the forty-eighth king of the Marsden line, to rule over Novania as a fair and just sovereign, and to serve the best interests of the people."

The circlet was placed upon Thomas' head, and the governors turned him to face those gathered to witness the ceremony. "May your reign be prosperous, and your rule be just," Lon added as he and Tyrus knelt once more.

"I thank all of you for taking the time to bear witness today," Thomas said, his voice unwavering. "Please join us for a feast and dancing in the great hall at your earliest convenience. All are welcome." His gaze searched the crowd of faces before settling on mine. "I should like a few moments with my brothers. We will join you in the great hall presently."

We remained seated while the room emptied, all save the two governors and Thomas' honor guard. When Rynn began to rise, I reached out and took her hand. "You should be present for this. Tom won't mind."

She nodded uncertainly, but seemed to relax as she noted Lydia had remained behind as well. As the last of the attendees exited the room, Zayneldarion entered, and Thomas nodded to him, his late entrance clearly arranged.

"There are three important matters I must complete before we can enjoy the festivities," Thomas began. "The first is the nullification of the Mark inspections and corresponding laws. From this day forward, the magi will be welcome within Novania's borders and shall be treated as equals and friends."

Lon produced a sheet of parchment and the quill, which Thomas took from him. He signed his name to the document with a flourish while Alexander beamed and Lydia stammered an emotional thank you. I glanced at Rynn to find hope sparkling in her eyes as she gazed at my youngest brother.

"The second, and equally important matter," Thomas said, "is the nullification of the law prohibiting the dragon-kind from entering Novania's borders. The dragon-kind have proven time and again to be allies and must be treated as such." Another sheet was produced, which Thomas dutifully signed as well.

When he finished, he said, "Tyrus, Lon, I'd like to introduce you to Zayneldarion Caein. I have named him liaison between Novania and the dragon clans. As you may not be aware, he is Andrew's father."

The two governors were surprised by the revelation, but greeted my father warmly. They knew of his involvement during the final days of the war, but had not yet been introduced.

"There is one final item I'd like to attend to," Thomas said quietly. "Andrew, please come forward."

I glanced uncertainly at Rynn, then Alexander, as I rose to my feet. We had discussed only two items previously; what more did Thomas have planned?

Lon produced a third sheet, one I immediately recognized. When I'd last seen this document, it had been placed on the table in the council chamber as evidence that I could not be named Carlton's heir. It was my official birth record.

"Thomas, I don't understand."

He smiled. "Mother was afraid to list your father's name on this record. Now that the laws have been changed, I wanted to give you the opportunity to have it amended."

I stared at him for several seconds, then turned to gaze at my father. I was stunned yet thrilled, and I managed a nod. "Yes. I'd like that."

Thomas smiled. "I thought you would."

He bent down to make the changes to the record himself, using the seat of the throne as a writing table. I laughed, unable to help myself; it was so like Thomas to use the first available surface—no matter what it happened to be—as a writing table, even now that he was king. The words "man unknown" were carefully lined out, and my father's name was written on the document instead.

"From this day forward, you will be known as Andrew Caein in the official records of the kingdom," Thomas said with a smile. "Happy name day, brother."

As soon as we were seated at our places along the head table in the great hall, Rynn rounded on me. "You didn't tell me it was your name day, Andrew!"

I shrugged. "Until the date was read during the ceremony, it had slipped my mind."

"Thomas planned that weeks ago, you know," Alexander said with a grin from across the table where he was seated with Lydia. "He told me what he hoped to do, but he wasn't certain you'd agree to the change." He shrugged. "I told Tom to stop overthinking it. I knew you'd be pleased."

"This must be your thirty-ninth name day," Zayneldarion mused from the other side of Rynn. Thomas had made certain her seat lay between ours so she could enjoy the evening without fear of accidentally harming someone sitting next to her.

"It is." I leaned to one side as a servant placed bowls of soup before us, the first course in what would ultimately be a lengthy feast.

Rynn studied me carefully for a few moments. "I've known for some time that you're older than you appear, but I didn't realize your true age."

Startled, I turned to face her. "What do you mean?"

A sudden, irrational fear gripped my heart; the woman who I loved more than any other was primed to shatter my hopes for our future together. I knew I was several years older than her, but it had never been an issue between us. It simply was. And now, on the night I'd planned to propose, she was unexpectedly concerned about my age.

She smiled. "There have been so many times when you and Alex are talking with one another, laughing, jesting, that I failed to remember he's a full decade younger than you are. What I'm trying to say is that you often fail to *act* your age."

Alexander threw his head back in a gale of laughter, while Lydia merely nodded her agreement. I flushed and raked a hand through my hair, but I was immensely relieved by her words.

Rynn leaned closer and whispered, "I rather like that about you. Please don't change."

I grinned. "I don't plan to."

I managed to sit through the first four courses of the feast before I could wait no longer. My appetite had been sated, the conversation at our end of the table had begun to flag, and Alexander had taken Lydia to the dance floor for a time. I'd never been one for dancing, but if Rynn asked it of me, I'd dance with her and hope I didn't stumble, making a fool of myself in the process. It was warm in the great hall, crowded, and noisy. I wanted to go somewhere quieter to ask the question that had been nagging me for weeks.

I stood and offered Rynn my arm. "Will you walk with me for a time?"

She took my arm and rose with a silent nod. As we passed my father, he smiled knowingly and winked once Rynn wasn't looking.

I led her to the north end of the room and up a staircase to a landing that overlooked the great hall. On the other side of the landing were a series of doors that fed into a wide balcony above the rose garden where I'd spent so much time strolling with Vera in another lifetime. The doors were propped open to allow the warm spring air into the castle. I led Rynn onto the balcony and was surprised to find we were alone. The sun was beginning to set and the sky was awash with color. I smiled despite my nerves; the moment had coalesced more perfectly than I'd hoped.

We walked to the rail. I noted with a pang of sorrow that the rose garden was no longer there. In its place was a practice green for jousting, complete with straw-filled targets and stalls for horses on either end.

My disappointment must have shown on my face, for Rynn said, "Andrew, what's wrong?"

"The rose garden used to be there." I shrugged and turned to face her. "I didn't bring you here to take in the view, however."

She gave me one of her enigmatic smiles and shook her head in amusement. "Why did you pull me away from Tom's lovely feast then, if not for the view?"

My face reddened under her scrutiny. "I wanted to speak with you."

"And you are," she replied with a laugh. "Andrew, why are you so anxious? I don't believe I've ever seen you like this."

"I, ah…"

I released a breath and shook my head. It was a mystery why I could face countless enemies on the battlefield without a second thought, but when it came to a matter of the heart, I was flustered and unable to form a coherent sentence. I averted my gaze, fumbling at the words I'd rehearsed countless times.

When I looked up, she was smiling. I drew a breath, steeled myself, and took her hands in mine.

"Rynn," I said, my insides writhing and roiling into knots, "I know I haven't been very forthcoming about my feelings, but I hope you know that I love you. I always will."

She laughed. "I know that. And I love you, but I still don't understand why you're acting so strange tonight."

I managed a nervous laugh. My throat was tight, but I was determined to say what I'd planned before someone else arrived on the balcony to ruin our moment alone.

"I promised I'd ask you properly when the time came, and I've only managed to make a fool of myself." I shook my head, but when I met her eyes once more, she was beaming. Her smile granted me the courage I'd been lacking. "Will you marry me?"

She threw her arms around me to wrap me in a fierce, icy hug. "Yes, Andrew. Yes, I will." She stepped back and took my arm, a dazzling smile on her lips. "I should have mentioned this sooner, but given all that's happened, it slipped my mind. I sent a message to Syllas some time ago, and my brothers are thrilled that you'll be part of the family. Let's return to the feast. I *must* tell Lydia."

I laughed and led her back to the great hall and to our appointed seats. Alexander and Lydia had returned, but my father was absent. I noted with some amusement he was dancing with Elanor Horace. Thomas had taken his empty seat and was talking animatedly with Alexander until our arrival made them fall silent. Alexander flashed a grin, and Thomas waited with an air of expectancy.

Lydia seemed to understand what they were waiting for and looked pointedly at Rynn. "Did he finally ask you?"

Rynn laughed as a blush crept into her cheeks. "Yes. We are going to marry." She looked at each of them in turn. "I didn't realize it was common knowledge that Andrew planned to ask me *tonight*."

"Well," Lydia replied, "arrangements had to be made. We're leaving the Capitol tomorrow after all, and I made certain that Claire was compensated for your gown. You'll have need of it again."

Rynn blinked. "Lydia, I can—"

Lydia waved her hand in dismissal. "It's been taken care of. It was the least I could do for a friend like you. Besides, Alex and I will accompany you to Dwymm. We'd like to be present for the ceremony."

Rynn stared at her, uncomprehending, then turned to face me. "You've planned it all, haven't you? I knew we'd be returning to Dwymm, but—"

I grinned, but felt my face flush. "I didn't plan this alone, Rynn. My father has—"

She shook her head, amused. "Of course, your father has a hand in it! I should have known." She laughed and threw her arms around me once more, unconcerned about the stares she received from several of the nobles at the far end of the table.

"I had a gift of sorts sent to your room," Thomas said after a moment. "Since I cannot attend your wedding, I wanted to ensure you had it before you departed."

"Thank you," I replied. "I wish you could be there, but I'm certain we'll return to visit you on occasion."

"I expect you to." He leaned back in his chair with a smile. "I expect *all* of you to."

At midmorning the following day, we prepared to leave from the castle's courtyard. I'd assumed my dragon form, as had my father. A small crowd was gathered to see us off, most notable amongst them Thomas, Elias, Everett, and Claire.

Rynn elected to fly with my father for the first day. I suspected she had a dozen questions and more for him. Alexander helped Lydia climb up to a safe perch between my wings, but it took her several moments to find a comfortable position.

"I can scarcely fit between your spines any longer," she complained. "This baby had best not grow too much more before we reach Dwymm, or I'll become lodged here and unable to move."

Alexander laughed softly. "You're hardly that big. Besides, you and the baby are healthy, and that's what truly matters."

He settled into a space behind her and patted my side twice, indicating they were ready to fly. I looked down at the others, standing a short distance away, but my gaze was fixed on Thomas.

"Take care, Tom," I said. "I'll return when I can."

He nodded. "I'll be waiting, Andrew. And yours, Alex. This castle already feels too empty, and you haven't even left its grounds."

I wished for all the world that I could draw him into an embrace one final time, but it wasn't feasible given my current form. I would have been just as likely to crush him. Instead, I nodded.

"We'll be back before you know it, brother!" Alexander called.

With that, I leapt into the sky. I circled the castle twice before banking south, and soon I was enjoying the cool morning air as it washed over my scales. Zayneldarion matched my pace and flew a short distance away on my right side, a decision I understood was his means of protecting my blind spot. Clouds were building in the west, and I wondered briefly if we'd encounter storms later in the day. The sun was shining at present, however, and the morning was pleasant. Galewing called shrilly somewhere above, and I heard Alexander laugh in response.

It had been difficult to say goodbye to Thomas, but he'd excel in his new role as king. Novania required a ruler of his caliber, someone unafraid to change the ancestral laws and prepared to do what was necessary to make the kingdom a better place for *all* of its residents. I hoped he'd find happiness, and realized I was already anticipating our next meeting.

The days passed smoothly and without incident, our journey unremarkable. It took a week to reach Dwymm, and when the vast lake finally came into view, sparkling in the sunlight, we were grateful for the sight. We were still some distance away when a pair of dragons leapt into the sky and began to fly toward us. The larger had crimson scales and a fading scar along his flank—Caelmarion Zorai. The other was perhaps half his size, with pale, almost white scales that held a pearlescent gleam. Though I'd never spoken with her, I knew she was Miranetha Fohn.

Alexander was perched on Zayneldarion's back, and he released a whoop of delight as he spied the other dragons flying toward us. Rynn leaned forward on my back so that I could hear her words over the wind.

"You didn't tell me they were coming, Andrew!"

I laughed. "You didn't ask."

They circled us once before matching our pace to fly alongside. I was between my father and Caelmarion as we banked toward the southern lakeshore and the pair of fishermen's cottages that stood not far from the water's edge.

We landed on the beach near the cottages. A pair of blond boys burst from within one to charge in our direction. Rynn slid to the ground immediately, laughing as her nephews approached. Moments later, her brothers and Petyr's wife appeared as well.

"Andrew," Caelmarion stated in a gravelly voice, "before you shift forms, there is a matter I'd like to discuss."

I frowned uncertainly, but nodded. He motioned for me to follow him toward the water.

I glanced at Rynn; she was speaking with her family and paid me no heed. Zayneldarion was with Alexander, but my brother's eyes were focused on me. I didn't know what Caelmarion wanted to discuss with me—we'd spoken only a handful of times in the Stone Grove, and I knew very little of him.

"Has your father told you what sort of mage I am?" he asked after we were far enough away from the others that they could not overhear.

I considered his question, then said, "He mentioned you were a healer."

He nodded. "Yes, one of the best our kind had to offer. I'd like to attempt mending your eye."

"Lydia did what she could," I said with a shake of my head. "But my father mentioned—"

He smiled, amused. "Lydia is a fine healer, but she is only human. She lacks the power of a dragon-mage. Allow me to try. If nothing comes of it, then I will leave you be."

I nodded uncertainly. "Very well."

He reached up to place one hand over my blind eye. As he did so, a powerful, green scent enveloped us, and a searing heat penetrated deep within my eye socket. It was an effort not to flinch away from his touch, but gradually, the heat began to recede, fading to a gentle warmth. Several minutes passed before he dropped his hand.

I stared at him, but the vision had not returned to my right eye.

Disappointment clouded his features, and he shook his head. "I had to try."

"I… Thank you," I managed after a time. "My father said some injuries can't be overcome. I think I knew the instant it happened."

His smile was strained. "I'd hoped it would work, given all you have done for our kind, Andrew. What you and your brothers accomplished in Novania was a feat the dragon-kind had long since given up on." He shook his head wistfully. "Your father was right. We should not have lost hope. We should have persisted."

I glanced longingly toward the others, and Caelmarion laughed. "Yes, we should return. No doubt your father has explained what I hoped to do. Knowing what little I do of your brother, the anticipation will be eating away at him by now."

I laughed. As we approached, Alexander broke away from the others and sprinted toward us. He stopped to peer at my face intently, but his smile faltered, replaced by disappointment as he continued to stare.

"I'd hoped it would work," he said. "I'm sorry it didn't. So damned sorry."

"Alex, we've been over this," I replied. "I've learned to manage the blindness."

Caelmarion cleared his throat. "Why don't you make yourself useful and untie that chest from your brother's back? I'm certain he'd rather speak with the others in his human form."

Alexander blinked. "Of course."

As Caelmarion trundled away, Alexander climbed up to complete his task, muttering under his breath.

"Alex, if you untie it, I can—"

He slid down my side before I could finish, the trunk cradled in his arms. "I've got it, brother. Let me find your clothing."

Once Alexander had dug a set from within the trunk, I shifted and dressed quickly. As I finished, Rynn walked toward me. Without a word, she lifted her hand to touch the right side of my face, her fingers brushing at the corner of my eye.

"He tried to mend it," I said.

She nodded and offered me a smile. "I'm sorry it didn't work, but I still maintain the scar gives you a bit of character. And there's always the eyepatch Claire had made, should you wish to hide it, but I don't believe it's necessary." She smiled, then paused to glance at her brothers, who were in conversation with Alexander. "Pete and Syllas have given their blessing, and the boys are beyond thrilled at the prospect of having a dragon for an uncle. I told them of Thomas' gift. We can build our cottage near theirs and furnish it easily enough with that much coin. Syllas said we may stay with him until our home is ready." Her eyes sparkled with sudden mischief. "I don't want to wait any longer, Andrew, and everyone is here. Marry me today, here on the lakeshore, while the sun is still shining. It won't take long to put on that gown."

I grinned. "Let's not keep them waiting. May I call you Lady Caein when the ceremony is over and done?"

EPILOGUE

"Andrew, I received word from Alex and Lydia," Rynn called from the steps leading up to Syllas' home.

I glanced over my shoulder to find her striding toward where I worked alongside Petyr. We'd been thatching the roof of the newly constructed home on the lakeshore, one of the final steps needed before Rynn and I could move our meager belongings inside. Rynn had made a point to speak with several woodworkers from Dwymm and had plans for furnishing the place. I'd leave her to the task; I was happy with the mere prospect of sharing the home with her, and furniture was of little consequence.

She stopped several paces away from the home and gazed up to where I stood on the slanted rooftop. She waved a sheet of parchment in one hand, an impatient expression upon her face.

I glanced at Petyr on the other side of the roof. "I'll be back soon," I said.

He laughed and shook his head in amusement. "Yes, it's best not to keep my sister waiting. I'll continue while you see what she needs."

I dropped to the ground as Rynn waved the parchment again. "It's from Alex," she repeated. "I thought you'd like to read it."

I nodded, unable to suppress a smile as I took the sheet from her icy fingers. Alexander and Lydia had gone to the Citadel after their brief stay in Dwymm. Several weeks had passed since I'd last received word from Alexander, and I was eager to hear from him.

Andrew and Rynn,

I wanted to share the greatest news I've ever received with the two of you. Lydia has borne a son. We've named him Jonas Everett.

True to the Oracle's word, he has a Mark similar to mine. His birth brings me great joy, but his Mark fills me with dread. I know what he'll one day endure should he choose to undertake the pilgrimage of the magi. Lydia says I worry too much, but he's my first born. I can't help it.

I've also heard from Tom. Since Bryson Feige returned to the Citadel, it's easiest for me to pass his messages to you, so I hope you don't mind this coming second-hand. Tom is handling affairs in Novania well enough, and from the tone of his message, he's enjoying his new role. After all his misgivings, I find it a bit surprising.

Additionally, he is now betrothed to the young Duchess Kessler from Three Points, and the wedding is planned for the week following the harvest. He expects us both to attend. I suppose he has given us ample time for travel, though I'm uncertain how Jonas will fare during the trip. Perhaps you'd be willing to accommodate us, brother?

I hope you are well in Dwymm.

–Alex

I flashed a grin and looked up to find Rynn watching me expectantly. "We'll be returning to Novania sooner than we anticipated."

She nodded. "Yes, but this time, it's different. We're flying north for a joyous occasion, and we have no fear of being hunted. I wouldn't miss Tom's wedding for all the gold in the world. Besides, it would be good for both you and Alex to see him again, even though it's only been two months." She frowned pointedly. "It has also been nearly that long since you last went flying, and I know you miss *that*."

I laughed. "I do, but my wife does not."

She rolled her eyes skyward and shook her head, though a faint smile crossed her lips. "I'll send a reply to Alex while you and Pete finish up."

I nodded as she turned away and paused to look across the lake for a moment, watching the sunlight glint on the ripples traveling across its surface. In the distance beyond the far shore, the snow-capped peaks of the Southern Pinnacles stretched across the northern horizon.

It would take a few days to reach the Citadel, and another five or six before we arrived in the Capitol.

After spending so much time traveling during the last year, I'd grown to appreciate the quiet routine of life on the lakeshore in Dwymm. While I didn't relish the idea of leaving again so soon, I would make the trip for Thomas—and Rynn was right. I looked forward to seeing my half-brothers again. Despite the vast distance separating us, I knew we'd remain close.

For all of his vicious scheming, Colin had united the rest of our family in a way that could not have been achieved otherwise.

As I prepared to climb onto the roof once more, Petyr appeared along its peak. "I've finished, Andrew," he called. "And not too soon, it seems. There's a storm coming."

I glanced briefly at the western horizon and nodded, taking note of the dark thunderclouds building in the distance. "I'm glad we're done. I owe you and Sy a great deal."

He grinned as he made his way to the ledge and climbed down. "You owe us nothing, Andrew. You've done so much for our sister, and it's a wondrous thing to see her happy."

The door to his home burst open, and his sons raced outside, bounding toward us in a cascade of laughter.

He chuckled. "Darynn told me he wants to learn how to use a sword from you. He has it in his head that he'll be Altynn's guardian one day, as you were for your brother."

I smiled, watching the pair as they continued to run in our direction. "I'd be happy to teach him," I replied. "Since I'll never have a child of my own, I'd be honored to pass that part of my legacy to your son."

THANK YOU FOR READING LEGEND!

If you enjoyed reading this book, please consider leaving a review.

Information about new books and their release dates will be posted on my website (www.ajcalvin.net), as well as shared via my newsletter. If interested, you can subscribe by visiting my website and clicking on the "Newsletter" tab.

ABOUT THE AUTHOR

A.J. Calvin is a science fiction/fantasy novelist hailing from Loveland, Colorado known best for The Caein Legacy and The Relics of War series. A former microbiologist, she lives with her husband, a turtle, a bearded dragon, and a salt water aquarium.

When she is not working or writing, she enjoys scuba diving, hiking, and playing video games.

For more information on the author and news about her writing, please visit her website at www.ajcalvin.net.

www.ingramcontent.com/pod-product-compliance
Lightning Source LLC
Chambersburg PA
CBHW020258030826
48979CB00026B/1383/J

* 9 7 9 8 9 9 0 8 1 6 9 0 9 *